D0913199

Wait Till The
Sun Shines, Nellie

Wait Till The Sun Shines, Nellie

RITA NELLIE HUNTER

Hamish Hamilton: London

First published in Great Britain 1986
by Hamish Hamilton Ltd
Garden House, 57–59 Long Acre, London WC2E 9JZ

Copyright © 1986 by Rita Nellie Hunter

British Library Cataloguing in Publication Data

Hunter, Rita Nellie
    Wait till the sun shines, Nellie
    1. Hunter, Rita Nellie   2. Opera –
    Biography   3. Singers – Biography
    I. Title
    782.1′092′4   ML420.H9/

    ISBN 0-241-11873-5

Typeset by Rowland Phototypesetting Ltd
Bury St Edmunds, Suffolk
Printed and bound in Great Britain by
Billing & Sons Ltd, Worcester

Contents

This book is dedicated to: My parents, who gave me life, love and devotion. My husband, who gave me joy, as well as love, and who also taught me the meaning of sacrifice. And my beloved daughter, Mairwyn, whose birth was my greatest achievement, and with whom I learned the most satisfying of all my roles, that of her mother.

R.H.

List of Illustrations

With my daughter, Mairwyn, born November 30th, 1967. *(Jerry Munson)*

My first Leonora in *Il Trovatore*. With the Basilica Opera Company, March 1968. *(Bob Johnson)*

Brunnhilde in the Sadler's Wells *Valkyrie*. *(Anthony Crickmay)*

The '24 carat' Leonora in *Il Trovatore*. *(Anthony Crickmay)*

My first Donna Anna in *Don Giovanni*. *(Donald Southern)*

Between pages 134 and 135

Santuzza in *Cavalleria Rusticana*. *(English National Opera)*

At the Metropolitan Opera, New York: my first *Walkure* Brunnhilde and my first *Gotterdammerung* Brunnhilde. *(Louis Melançon)*

Norma in San Francisco. I loved this. *(Ron Scherl)*

Norma in New York. This was a nightmare. *(J. Heffernan)*

Elisabeta in *Don Carlos* for Sadler's Wells. *(John Carner)*

Abigaille in *Nabucco* for New Orleans. *(New Orleans Opera)*

Turandot for Welsh National Opera. *(Welsh National Opera)*

Brunnhilde for the Pacific Northwest Festival, Seattle. *(Chris Bension)*

In recital, with Hazel Vivienne at the piano. *(Francis Loney)*

Macbeth, with Robert Allman, Australian Opera. *(Branco Gaica)*

On the Michael Parkinson Show in Australia. *(Channel 10 Television)*

Commander of the Most Excellent Order of the British Empire. At Buckingham Palace with Mairwyn and John. *(The Press Association)*

The sun shines on Rita Nellie Hunter. Diva and daughter, Australia, 1981.

Acknowledgements

Thanks to Mr Ken Groves at Qantas Airways London and to Qantas themselves for arranging for the transportation and delivery of the manuscripts from Sydney, Australia, to London.

Thanks also to Rosemarie Cave at the English National Opera and Lord Harewood for their help in research into dates and places of performances.

Last but not least the biggest thank you of all to my many loyal and devoted fans around this world of ours . . . your applause and cheers have always kept up my spirits and made all of this very worthwhile. God bless and thank you all.

R.H.

CHAPTER ONE

The Birth of a Mistake

I am proud of my Merseyside heritage, we breed them tough and determined up there. You have to be tough to survive and you have to be determined if you want to spread your wings and fly away. The family circle is a tight one, and family ties are strong; it is hard to go out into the outside world.

I am not a Scouse, who I understand are exclusive to Liverpool. I was born in Wallasey, the other side of the river. A Cheshire Cat maybe, a Merseysider certainly – but not a Scouse.

My parents were born in Birkenhead and later moved to Wallasey and, although they were not poor, times were often very hard. My father had served in the Cammell Laird shipyards as a boilermaker. When they first moved to Wallasey he was out of work but got a job on the river ferry boats as a stoker, and when I was born he got a job in the Wallasey Electric Works, and eventually a permanent job in the Wallasey Gas Works, where he remained for the rest of his working life. In his last year at the gas works, his top wages were £9 a week.

The tales told me by my parents about their own childhood would make a book on its own. They both came from large families. My mother's father was a John Parkinson. I have never been able to discover what happened to him; maybe he just went off to sea and never came back, or perhaps he died an uninteresting death. In any case Grandma Margaret married again, this time a George Davis, and my mother and her brother Jack were brought up by their stepfather.

My mother and grandmother were sometimes thrown out into the dark winter street, even when it was snowing, to bring George Davis 'a jug of ale'. My grandmother worked in the laundry that was in the cellar of the house they lived in. It was owned by a Mrs Townly, who eventually sold the laundry to my grandmother for the sum of £25, at the rate of five shillings a week. I still have the deed of sale. Everyone who was old enough had to help out, and my mother and Auntie Nellie had the job of ironing the starched collars.

There were seven children: my mother, Nellie, William, Arthur, Henry, Ruth and Doris. There was one other child, Margaret, who died in infancy. And of course Jack who went off to Canada. I don't think he got on with the stepfather.

They all seemed to have hobbies. Mother had her mandolin and her two cats, Sailor and Benny. Grandma Margaret kept hens in the backyard which were always being chased by the cats; the cats also used the eggs as footballs.

Uncle Arthur was mad about all animals, and once brought a goat home and hid it in the cellar overnight. The next morning the goat had chewed all the newly-starched collars of the local gentry. He also rescued a pony that was destined for the glue factory, and tried to keep that in the cellar as well.

Grandfather George seemed to be out of work more than he was in. To help the income from the laundry, my grandmother used to clean house for a family who entertained the D'Oyly Carte family when they came to Liverpool. Grandmother had a lovely voice, and a prized stack of opera records, the most cherished of which were by Galli-Curci. One day while hearing my grandmother sing as she went about her cleaning, and on being told of my mother's ability with the mandolin, the D'Oyly Cartes gave them two tickets for a concert at the Picton Hall, Liverpool, to hear the great diva in person. My mother said she did not sound a bit like the records and grandma was so disgusted that the records were never played again. Poor Galli-Curci must have had an off night.

Father's background was not quite so colourful, but I do remember his mother, six foot if she was an inch, with a great booming voice. A domineering and opinionated woman, feared by her brood of five boys, John, Albert, Fred, Tommy and Charles, my father. She would have had twin girls if she had not miscarried on a trip to the Isle of Man. She scared the wits out of all her sons and, while they respected her, I doubt if any of them loved her. When my father and Albert were courting my mother and my Auntie Nellie, they were allowed to woo their lady loves only in Grandma Pauline's sitting room, and she kept the four of them occupied by insisting that they cleaned her collection of brass. This was quite a considerable collection, as Grandpa Hunter made most of it himself.

Eventually my father left home and went to live with my

mother's family. They were by now married, but my poor father ended up fending for all the children (there was a fourteen-year gap between my mother and the next child, Nellie). Grandma Pauline was convinced that my mother was 'in trouble' and had her followed to see whether any offspring was expected. She had a long wait.

My parents were quiet, God-fearing people who went to church twice on Sundays, said prayers in the kitchen morning and evening, and said grace before all meals. They asked little of life, and were content with each other.

I was a mistake. After twenty years of married life my mother became prone to travel sickness, and went with my father to the doctor for pills to combat it. He examined her and then said, 'You're expecting!'

'When?' gasped my mother.

'In about six weeks,' he replied.

They staggered out of the surgery thunderstruck. To recover before going home to break the news to the family, they went to the local cinema. The film was *Rio Rita*.

'If it's a girl we'll call it Rita,' said my mother.

'Aye, and if it's a lad we'll call it John,' said father.

*

Six weeks later on August 15, 1933, in a thunderstorm, I arrived. My mother had struggled for several days to give me life.

My father was told by the doctor, 'I can't save them both.'

'Save my wife,' was my father's reply. And he sat down on the stairs to wait.

My mother lost a great deal of blood, and hovered on the point of death, but eventually I was born, black as ink and apparently dead. I was laid on a sheet in the corner of the bedroom while the doctor and midwife fought for my mother's life. When they had won this battle the midwife began to clean up the room, turning to the limp black bundle on the floor and beginning to wrap it up in the sheet.

The doctor took it from her.

'This baby's got to live.'

'But it's not possible, doctor.'

'After twenty years, it *must* live.'

He then began his second battle for life that day; he slapped me, massaged my tiny chest, but no sound came, no movement.

'It's no use, doctor,' said the midwife.

'Maybe not. But I can try a new idea I've not used before.'

He took a deep breath, and blew his own breath into my

3

mouth. I squeaked, and he blew again, but this time up my nose, and out of my mouth came a cloud of white dust. I squeaked even louder and he slapped my bottom. I yelled indignantly. After several more slaps, he rushed downstairs holding me, into the kitchen, passing my dazed father on the way. Auntie Nellie was waiting in the kitchen with some neighbours. He thrust me into her arms. 'It's a girl,' he said. 'For God's sake keep her crying.'

The neighbours were awestricken by this child, born dead but now very much alive. They hung over me in wonder – my first audience. I must have sensed it because I stopped crying and gazed up at the light, looked all around at each one and gave a big smile.

'She's sent for a purpose,' they said, and a future Brünnhilde made her debut.

*

In the months and years that followed it must often have seemed that the purpose for which I was sent was to drive them crazy with worry at my endless crying and my frequent illnesses. After my birth my mother was too ill to nurse me so my Auntie Nellie cared for me for about three months. Mother had to have liver injections to make up for the large amount of blood she had lost. On one visit to the doctor he asked if I was well. 'Yes, but she cries a lot,' mother told him. He replied that children born late in life were either very bright or very dull.

Mother felt he was trying to tell her that I might be mentally retarded. 'I don't care how she turns out,' she said. 'We'll still love her and care for her.'

*

My Auntie Nellie was still looking after me for a good part of each day in November 1933, when they were holding the local Council elections, and she announced that she would take me in my pram when she went up to vote that evening. The radio had forecast fog, which worried my father, but Nellie said, 'Oh she'll be all right, I'll have her back before dark.'

'Well, I wish you would wait until the sun was shining before you take her out,' said father.

This was to be my first outing since my birth in August, so Nellie said, 'If you wait for the sun in this country, Charlie, she'll never see the outside world!'

Father, and the radio, were proved right and the fog descended while Nellie was in the school voting, and young Rita Nellie Hunter caught a magnificent cold that quickly turned to pneumonia. Even then I didn't do things by halves. I lay for three days and nights in a coma, and mother kept me alive by brushing my lips with a feather dipped in brandy.

I was always ill with something. I had all the usual children's ailments, well interspersed with regular doses of tonsillitis and bronchitis. I cried all night and most of the day too, and eventually the doctor told my mother that no matter how much I cried at night she was not to pick me up, so they put me to sleep in the bathroom and let me scream my head off. God was obviously preparing my Wagnerian lungs early in life.

When I was about three years old I was taken to the doctor who told them they fussed about me too much (no doubt I was carted off to his office every time I burped). But this time they were really scared. I lay around the house all day long, my skin pale and bloated, so they decided to try another doctor – this was Doctor Bell, whose daughter grew up to be Ann Bell, the actress. Doctor Bell told them I had chronic anaemia and after being treated for this I began to improve and put on weight. By the age of eight I weighed eight stone. Back to Doctor Bell for more tests. This time a severe thyroid deficiency was diagnosed, and I was put on a strict diet until the age of sixteen. For all those years I was put on whatever new pills came on the market. I think the worst thing was the raw iodine, four drops on a half teaspoon of sugar four times a day. It was vile and I still can't look at seaweed without my tummy churning. Whenever someone gives my husband Welsh lava bread, I could throw up just to see it lying in the fridge.

I was never allowed sweets so when they were rationed during the war it meant nothing to me. What you never had you never miss. My sweet ration cards were given to my cousins. I remember the eldest, Albert, at the end of the war taking me to buy a big bar of chocolate and a bag of sweets which we munched all the way home. When I got indoors, I was sick but I didn't dare tell my parents why I was sick as I was still on a diet.

At the age of five I went into hospital to have my adenoids out, and though the operation was successful I contracted scarlet fever. 'It never rains but it pours,' observed my father.

My earliest memory goes back to the age of four, sitting on my Grandfather George's lap. He was now living with Nellie and family next door and he used to call every afternoon to sit in our kitchen by the fire and chat to my mother. We had a large black leather chair stuffed with horse hair and edged with brass buttons. One day as I sat on his knee I coloured all the buttons with a different coloured chalk.

'Look, Grandad, those are the footlights.'

He turned to my mother. 'In the name of God, Lucy, who gave her all those ideas?'

'I don't know,' replied mother and carried on pouring the tea, unaware that I had said anything out of the ordinary, But Grandad might well have asked, for who *had* given me the idea?

Although my parents were musical they had no connections with the theatre. Dad played the harmonium and the bugle. He had played the bugle at Caernarfon for the investiture of the last Prince of Wales, and that bugle still hangs over our fireplace. Mother played the mandolin brilliantly and sang to me in her high clear soprano. They were both keen on the music hall, but neither of them had ever been on the stage. Yet from somewhere a still small voice whispered to me of footlights.

We had a rosewood piano in our parlour and when mother was cleaning out that room she used to put me up on the stool to keep me out of mischief. My childish bangings on it gave way over the years to the songs I had heard my mother sing to me with her mandolin. In time I began to sing and accompany myself.

I was sent for piano lessons to the lady who lived on the opposite corner of our block, and although I learned to read music I was always happier playing by ear, to the despair of my teacher. When she was in the room I would stumble painfully through 'The White Swan's Waltz' but when she had left I would play it with great flourishes by ear. In my innocence I thought that she did not know what I was up to. But of course she must have known and gradually the lessons fizzled out and I think she must have told my parents that they were wasting their shilling per hour.

Rest in peace, Mrs Denham, you taught me to read music, so all was not lost. My first and only piano teacher.

CHAPTER TWO

My First Audition

We sat on little green mats on my first day at school. I don't remember if I cried or not, but my mother said I clung to her like a limpet, although I made no fuss otherwise.

For many years we went for a week's holiday to North Wales, though how they ever managed it on their small income I will never know. We stayed in a bungalow attached to a small farm house, and my mother did all the cooking. We had to collect wood every day from the woods to burn on the old-fashioned stove.

One year I got sunstroke from working too long in the fields at haymaking time, and often we would get up very early to collect mushrooms for breakfast. We had a black spaniel called Tony, which I would push for miles in my pram, despite the fact that I could only just walk myself. One day while out I ran away from a friendly cow and fell flat on my face in a heap of cow-dung. While mother was desperately trying to get the mess out of my long hair, father, ever the eternal optimist, said, 'Never mind, Lucy, where there's muck there's brass.' But I stank for days – and even the dog kept away from me.

Over the years I lost a lot of schooling through constant illnesses, then the war came and a German land mine obliterated my school. That morning I stood shivering in the kitchen as the air raid the night before had blown all our windows out. Dad had left for work and as mother was pulling on my liberty bodice he came back and called through the open window, 'You can stop getting her ready for school, there's no school to go to, the Jerries have blown it away!'

I was delighted. I had grown to hate school. For a start I was not good at lessons, but worst of all the other children made fun of my size and called me names – the favourite was 'Barrage

Balloon' – that great cigar-shaped object suspended in the sky. (I suppose today's overweight children are called 'Goodyear Blimp' – poor souls.)

Sometimes they would lie in wait for me and then jump on me and while I lay pinned on the ground crying they would jump up and down shouting, 'Bet we will bounce if we jump on her,' or sometimes 'If we stick a pin in her she'll burst.' I was always coming home from school with cut knees and torn stockings. At last my dad said, 'She can't be *that* awkward, Lucy, I'm going to get off work early and see what happens. He hid across the road and saw the attack and gave those involved a good thumping – and that was when they took me to Doctor Bell and he put me on the diet.

Father joined the Home Guard, where one of the other officers was the chairman of the local pantomime society. They were hoping to put on a production of Cinderella that Christmas but couldn't get hold of a glass coach, so Dad, the handy man, said he would make it for them. He built it in our back bedroom out of plasterboard, painted it white and then sprinkled it with Christmas Tree frosting to make it glisten, then he illuminated the window frames with the fairy lights from my Christmas Tree.

All the local kids wanted to see it, so I obliged by showing them upstairs, but only after they had bought a ticket for the show. Thus we filled the St Luke's Church Hall for a week. I had spent long hours in the bedroom 'helping' Dad to make the coach.

'Can I sit in it, Dad?'

'Aye, go inside it and hand me out the nails.'

I dreamed of being Cinderella. 'Will Cinders have long hair, Dad?'

'Yes, chuck, I suppose so.'

'Will it be black?'

'What? Oh, I don't know, lass.'

The day they took the coach away to the hall for the dress rehearsal, I cried. 'You can't take it, it's mine.'

'Hush, love,' my Mum said.

'But it's got *my* fairy lights on it.'

'Hush, chuck,' said Mum, cuddling me. 'He'll get it back when the pantomime is over.'

He did get it back but I never bothered with it again. Someone else had had the glory of sitting in it. It wasn't mine any longer.

On Saturday afternoons I went along with Dad to the Church Hall and watched the man who was painting the scenery. The canvases spread out on the floor seemed vast to me as I picked my way through the drying paint. But how small those same backcloths would appear today if hung on the stage at the Sydney Opera House.

Even then I was entranced by the theatre and Dad made me a model theatre, and painted the sets while I made endless sets of dolls to play the characters. Then the family had to sit round the kitchen table with the lights out while I entertained them – I did all the female voices, and Dad all the male voices.

I have had a special affection, in recent years, for the exploits of 'Dad's Army' on television, since it brings back so many memories. Surely only those who had members of the family serving in the Home Guard can truly understand its humour, especially if one's father was the definitive 'Captain Mainwaring'. My father, who never did anything by halves, flung himself into the Home Guard as he did with everything he got involved in. I recall one weekend being told that my Saturday afternoon and evening in Central Park was off. (I used to go fishing, and we always kept bowls of jacksharps and newts in our backyard.)

When I indignantly enquired why there was this change in our routine, Dad told me that there were to be Home Guard exercises in the park that day. It was Wallasey Division against the Birkenhead Division, which meant that Uncle Fred would be on the opposing side to Dad. I asked if I could go and watch.

'The public are invited to see the final battle in the evening and applaud the winners.'

What fun, I thought, and waited eagerly for the big night.

Mother, Auntie Nellie and I turned up at the park at six o'clock and observed that there seemed to be a lot of spectators and not many 'army'. However, we wandered around and then saw the troops of men lying in the long grass – Dad's troop facing Uncle Fred's troop. They had real guns, but someone had forgotten to order the blanks to fire, so they had all been instructed 'When you see the enemy, kneel up and shout "Bang"'! So there they were, all these grown up men lying in the grass, and from time to time they would jump and shout 'Bang!' and then one man would go off the battleground – dead. . . .

The big showdown at the OK Corral came when my Dad stood up and shouted 'Bang!' as he pointed his gun at Uncle Fred. Fred refused to 'die'. He was grinning all over his face. Dad stood up and shouted 'Bang!' again. Still Fred, who was a dreadful tease, didn't die, so father shouted, 'Fred, will you bugger off to the first aid tent, I've just shot your leg off.' Fred winked at me and stood up and said, 'Bang, you're dead, Charlie.' Dad stood there like an enraged seagull, then crossed the line into the enemy camp and hauled Fred by the collar out of the grass onto the path right by the spectators and marched him in the direction of the first aid tent. The last I heard was Fred saying, 'Well you got the message at last, now we can both bugger off home.'

The family had stood silent through all this, but when they had gone my Mum said, 'Oh, Nellie, the language.' Nellie sniffed and said, 'I'm not worried about the language, Lucy, but you know with those silly buggers looking after us against Hitler, we've got no bloody chance.'

Mum took my hand and said, 'Come on, chuck, let's go and see if we can get any jacksharps.'

The following year the pantomime society, called, by the way, 'The Merrymakers', decided to stage 'Babes in the Wood'. By this time my father was the stage manager-cum-props-man-cum electrician and was also asked to sit in on the audition committee to help choose the children for the dancing troupe, and for some solo acts who were to do a speciality act in front of the front-cloth while they changed the sets. He took mother and me along for an evening out, telling Mum that 'It would be just like a concert.' However, I soon became bored with the endless line of 'Boy and Girl Wonders' so I crept away and made for the table where the committee were sitting. 'Can I have a go, too?' I asked. Dad refused, but the chairman said, 'Yes, have you brought your music?'

'No,' I said, but added quickly, 'The lady at the piano will know it.'

Dad was certain that it would all end in floods of tears, but I skipped along to the platform, asked the pianist if she knew 'Silver Bell', a Gertie Gitana song. Yes, she knew it, and so I asked her to play a chorus, a verse and another chorus to end with.

Dad sat looking at his feet, worried sick, and Mum, who had not even missed me from her side, nearly passed out when she discovered that the next little horror was her own. But she told me that I sang the song without batting an eyelid, no mistakes, used my arms, walked about and even had the gall to do a little dance. I was given not only a place in the junior dance troupe but a two-minute solo spot at the end of the show.

That was my first public appearance, and I had never had a lesson in my life.

I was the apple of my parents' eyes and, as for me, well I had at last found a way of stopping people laughing at my figure. I made them clap instead. My own daughter has that same determination; at the age of three she could sing Brünnhilde's battle cry and at the age of four any part of *Cavalleria Rusticana* you care to choose.

And so my first performance was in the St Luke's Church Hall in Poulton when I sang 'China Town My China Town'. It was part of a pageant ending with 'Rose of England' sung by a girl dressed as Britannia. I really fancied myself as Britannia, but I didn't have a chance; I wasn't even her understudy.

I don't have any photographs of me as Susie Wong as they were all taken on the last night, and I didn't get any flowers as I was not in the line-up on the last night. My understudy took my place and my flowers, as Rita Nellie Hunter had taken to her bed with measles.

*

The following year the company did 'Dick Whittington', and I had a speciality act again, this time a solo in front of the cloth. Mum and I spent hours sewing sequins onto my costume and, as cloth was hard to come by, the dress and cloak were made of flour sacks washed and dyed and trimmed. And so, dressed as a pirate I sang, 'On the Good Ship Yakkie Hiky Do Da'.

The producer of all these shows was a Mr Flowerday who owned the local greengrocers and flower shop. We were told by the mothers of several of the children that if we bought all our things from his shop, I would be certain to get a good part the next year. I don't know if there was any truth in these rumours, as my mother never availed herself of these offers. She purchased her things either from the Co-op or from Bertha Teggins' shop at the end of our road.

I suppose that with his position in the company Dad could have done a lot to push me, but he never did. Mum often asked him to, but he would say, 'If she gets anywhere she'll get there on her own merit.'

He paid for all the clothes and the lessons, the make-up and the shoes, to further my budding career, but never once put my name forward when a suitable part came. I had to fight hard and long for the position, but, bless him, he was right, and my word, he did teach me a lot.

*

It might seem that the war years went by without incident for us, but we lived in the same hell as everyone else. We had the same hardships and did our best to survive. Like so many children, I was evacuated, but because of my poor health Mum came along too, leaving Dad to life on bomb-torn Merseyside.

The farm we went to was perched on a hill in North Wales overlooking the River Dee, and at night Mum and I could see the flashes of the guns and the flares of the fires. It was agony knowing that Dad was in the midst of it all, but the doctor had advised my evacuation because of a severe nerve condition. Whenever we heard the siren we would rush into the shelter that Dad had built under the stairs in our house; everyone else I knew either had shelters in their gardens or went to the communal shelter down the street. But it seems I was too delicate to go out in the dead of night and so we had the shelter under the stairs. Anyway as soon as I heard the siren I would be doubled up with stomach pains and spend the duration of the air-raid on a bucket, suffering with diarrhoea.

On most of these occasions, Dad would be prompted to try and brighten up the situation with his usual 'Where there's muck there's money', but I remember one time when Mum retorted sharply, 'Buggered where I can see the sense in that remark, Charlie.'

Well, it couldn't have been much fun cooped up under the stairs night after night with a kid on a bucket!

The problem with my innards gradually eased, but on my return home to the air raids another form of nerves took over. I began to go bald. My lovely hair, my mother's pride and joy, jet black and falling to my waist, began to fall out. I spent each air raid sitting in front of my mother while she rubbed all the bald patches with sulphur ointment until my head hurt. But after many months we were rewarded by the appearance of soft down on one of the bald patches. Now she rubbed with renewed vigour and slowly each patch grew a covering of fine down and finally my hair began to grow again.

*

While Mum and I were in Wales, we missed Dad and worried about him. The family were prissy, although we got along well with the farmer. I loved messing around the cow-sheds and helping with the hay, but his wife was a fuss-pot; all day long she would be saying 'Don't, Rita,' about something or other. They had a daughter called Vera, who was having piano lessons, and would thump out, all day long, Chopin or Debussy. But I was not allowed to touch the precious instrument, though I longed to play it. Then one day the farmer's wife and Vera were both out, and the farmer invited me to play it. So I gave him my full repertoire, 'Rose O'Day', 'Silver Bell', 'Lily of Laguna', but while

I was deep in song, with both my Mum and the farmer lapping it up, Mrs Jones and Vera walked in. They had been to Vera's music lesson in Hollywell and caught an early bus home. There was hell to pay. Mr Jones was sent to milk the cows without his tea and we were banished to our room. After that the piano was kept locked. Vera became more and more nasty towards me and so, when Dad came to visit us, it was decided we would all take our chances together at home, and with sighs of relief all round the exile ended.

We returned to the new menace of the whistling bombs and daylight raids. Then the Germans topped up with the follow-up night raids and we would spend long hours in the shelter, only popping out in the lulls to rush to make a cup of tea. I remember that Mum suffered with lumbago and would crawl around in pain for days. One night it was getting very hot in the shelter when a passing ARP man yelled that the Germans had hit the water works. Dad went to find out why it was so hot, and discovered that halfway up the stairs there was a large incendiary bomb burning its way through the steps. There was no water in the taps so Dad raced up the stairs, jumped over the flaming bomb and made for the bathroom where we kept the bath full of water, but there was nothing to decant the water. Dad, undaunted, found a potty under one of the beds and with this he put out the fire. A call at the back door from another ARP man told us that the back shed was also on fire. Mum began leaping about to help and never suffered with lumbago again.

Living next door were Mum's sisters and their husbands and children. Their backyard was separated from ours by the garden well. On their side of the wall they kept a row of buckets containing water and sand, and this my Uncle Albert began to throw over the wall to help put out the fire in our shed. Unfortunately one of the buckets contained coal and this all fell on the head of a fireman who was kneeling in our garden trying to put out the fire. I cannot repeat his words in this book, as it would be scorched at the edges.

Mum's three sisters next door were Nellie, married to Dad's brother Albert, and so she was Mrs Hunter too, Doris who was not married, and Ruth. Ruth was married to Uncle Johnny and there were their three children, Albert, Alex and Margaret.

As a young girl Ruth had toured the country in a dancing troupe called 'Madam Clark's 12 Parisienne Maids'. It was Ruth who took me to Liscard to buy me my first stage make-up, a stick each of 5 and 9 and an eyebrow pencil. It was she who showed me how to use it and also how to apply 'Hot Black' – this was a wax which you melted over a candle flame onto a match, and applied to your eyelashes.

We had a family routine at Christmas. Christmas morning we always spent next door with mince pies and port wine – my wine always well diluted with lemonade (until I got older and Uncle Albert used to wink at me as he handed it to me and I would know that it was neat and felt most grown up). On Boxing Day they all came round to our house for a slap-up tea. Then we would cut into the Christmas cake that Mum had made and to this day I can still remember the taste of Mum's huge trifle. On New Year's Eve we would all go next door and Dad always let in the New Year and, when we got home after, we would go round our house and hang up the new calendars. Dad would give Mum and me a new shilling for our pockets.

On November 5 we went to Nellie's, as the street bonfire could be seen through her kitchen window. Nellie would make a huge plum pudding to give to all the children when the fires were put out. I would spend the evening indoors watching the fire through the window. My Dad still worried about my health and his stock remarks were still the night air wasn't good for me and wait until it's a sunny day – and so I had to watch all the fun from behind lace curtains.

On VE night, when all the streets were alight with bonfires, I slipped out of the house before my parents realized what was happening. Of course I was ill for a long time afterwards with bronchitis.

Mum was a great cook; she was always making jams and pickles, lemon curd and chutneys. I remember cutting up the red cabbage for pickling – this is a great complement to a plate of 'scouse'. Our huge kitchen table was made of white scrubbed wood, and I would sit under it crying happily as I peeled the onions ready for pickling. I didn't dare show my face in case the sight of my streaming eyes prompted my mother to stop me peeling. I have tried over the years to remember all Mum taught me about cooking and, although now when I am working or rehearsing, my husband or my daughter cooks, I still love to cook when I have no work on. I have managed to make something that was never a success for Mum – and that is marmalade.

14

CHAPTER THREE

Hunters' Modern Minstrels

I was never allowed in the street to play with other children, except in the heat of summer, and then I would only stand on our door step being refused admission to the game of rounders. 'She's too fat to run, we don't want her.' I never had to be called in at bedtime. Fed up with standing alone or with my Auntie Doris, I would come in of my own accord. I was much happier playing the piano or helping Dad to mend the punctures on his bicycle.

It was a great day for me when I got my own bike, a bone-shaker that Dad paid three pounds for, and Dad and I would ride miles round the Wirral countryside on warm summer evenings, leaving the other kids on the dusty streets. Sometimes Dad would take his water colours with him and look for a nice cottage to make a picture of.

My first singing lessons were from Madame Olive Lloyd, the conductor of the Pantomime Society orchestra. I don't remember much about the lessons, apart from learning to hold my breath for a long, long time. I can see that would have been quite a good thing for a future Wagnerian singer, except that I don't think Madame Lloyd had heard of Wagner. Certainly none of our family had.

I really think that my parents decided on a stage career before I did. I was not much good at school and didn't mix well with the other kids, for the reasons already mentioned. I went to a Miss Carol Gatley for dancing lessons and passed all the possible exams for tap and ballet. I was also sent to Miss Hilda Bromley for elocution. Both these ladies had their own concert parties and used to vie for who should be top dog in amateur productions in Wallasey and Merseyside. Some kids went to both ladies and would stay to see which teacher gave them the best roles.

My Dad wouldn't let me do that; for one thing he couldn't afford two sets of fees and he didn't think it was right to go to both. I went to Miss Bromley because she taught drama and elocution, but I still felt a bit of a traitor to the Gatley school.

Once I was entered in the Liverpool Festival, and had to recite a poem called 'The Blackbird'. On this rare occasion my mother came with me. She sat next to a woman who had a bottle of gin in her handbag and took quick nips. By the time I got up to say my poem she was well and truly sloshed. As I said: 'The Blackbird – he comes on chosen evenings, and sings over the gardens of . . .' I was cut short by this woman who stood up waving her gin bottle and shouting: 'You'll get no sodding blackbird here, love, only stinking bloody pigeons.' She then sat down and said to my Mum, 'I can't stand these bloody posh-talking kids from West Derby.' My mother was now shocked to the core by this gin-swigging woman and, meek and mild though she normally was, turned on her and said loudly, 'That's my child you've stopped and I'll have you know that *we* are from Wallasey.' The woman took another slug of gin and replied, 'Oh Christ, chuck, that's even worse, you've got them bloody awful yeller busses over there.'

I had by now cleared my throat and began again. 'The black-bird . . .' At this the woman staggered to her feet and pushed past my mother saying: 'Oh Christ, she's at it again with her bloody blackbird, I'm off,' and away she went.

I didn't get a prize at the festival.

When we got home that day a family council was called. After the men had been given their tea, Mum and Ruth and Nellie, Dad and myself, all sat round the kitchen table. Mum had already told Dad of the 'drunken orgies' at the Liverpool festival, and asked my two aunts if 'that sort of thing had been going on when she had *not* been there'. Ruth and Nellie said quite truthfully that there had never been anything like that when *they* were with me. Dad, always more free-and-easy than sober-sides Mum, grinned and said: 'There you are, Lucy, just one of those things.' Ruth giggled and said: 'Poor Lucy, you always seem to bring the worst out in folk.' Mum flushed with temper, sniffed and waited for Dad to reprimand Ruth, and when she was disappointed stood up and marched off to the back kitchen with the teapot and began to bang around with the dishes. Dad raised his eyes to heaven and said: 'Eeh, Ruth, why couldn't you have left well alone, now she'll have me up all night with her worrying.'

I made my sole contribution to the conference. 'She won't stop me going, will she, Dad?' He said: 'If I were you, lass, I'd get myself to bed.' Nellie then said: 'Charlie, I always told you that too much church-going would make you all narrow minded.'

Mum shouted from the kitchen: 'I heard that remark, our Nellie,' and Nellie, also now flushed with temper, said as she went out of the door: 'Charlie, tell your Lucy that she'll be giving you all bad guts with her stewed tea,' and she swept out of the house before Mum had time to retaliate.

The two families always had long chats over the garden wall, it was better than going round the corner, but it was several days before Mum and Nellie resumed their gossiping. Ruth and I would meet over the wall and talk in hushed voices. But it didn't last long and we were soon all in cahoots again. I was always going across the river to attend some lesson or other, or to take part in a concert, and Nellie was soon in demand to chaperone the budding star to a place where mother didn't want to be seen, in case the vicar got to hear of it.

*

When I was eleven or twelve the Tower Theatre in New Brighton began to hold talent contests. Auntie Ruth, who had heard about them from a woman in the butcher's queue, came to tell me. I didn't think that Mum would let me enter, and so Ruth and Nellie and I got together and it was decided that one of the women who did the flowers in church should tell Mum and of course since it had the approval of one of the 'Mothers' Union' then yes, it was all right for her little star to enter the Tower competition.

I won the first heat and was given ten shillings. Then at the second heat, I won again. My goodness, I was famous, my name in the *Wallasey News* twice. When the third heat came round I was ill and by the time I recovered the contest had finished.

Soon after this the Ritz Cinema in Birkenhead held a similar contest, but I was not even placed. My Mum sniffed and said, 'Well what do you expect, they are all deaf over there.'

I continued to sing in church halls and social centres around Merseyside. One of my big hits at this time was 'Ragtime Cowboy Joe'. Another was 'All the Nice Girls Love a Sailor' to which I danced a hornpipe after the song, taught me by my Auntie Ruth. But it was my Mum who chose most of my songs – and she had a never-ending supply from the days when she and Dad used to attend the music hall.

When I needed a new song, my Mum seemed to spend an

unusually long time in our outside toilet. When I would ask her if she was all right, she would say, 'Yes, love, I have just had a great idea for a new song for you' – (it seems she always got her best inspirations in there).

Then he would have to scour the music shops for the song in sheet music form.

Every Sunday evening we went to church and in the afternoon I went to Sunday school, which I didn't like much as most of the kids were from my day school, and still tormented me. One time they tore my brown hat from my head and threw it from the window which was several storeys from the street below. 'Let's see if Fatty can get down to it before the bus runs over it.' I did get to it and still remember the girl who said it and threw it down. She had ginger hair and freckles, and cooked up a new vile trick to play on me every week. How I hated her! The more I enjoyed the concerts, the more I hated school. It seemed to me a great waste of time and taught me nothing of value, as I thought, for my career. I would tell myself, 'What does a music hall star need with arithmetic and spelling?' I didn't even try to pass the 11-plus as I didn't want to be tied to a long period at a grammar school until I was 18. I just wanted to leave as soon as possible and begin 'my career'. (I was a horrid, spoiled, opinionated little devil.)

So Rita Nellie Hunter went to the local secondary school, Manor Road, changed later on to Liscard Secondary Modern, but to us it was always Manor Road.

We still had the same old problems with my health. The doctor advised the removal of my tonsils. Mum and Dad were worried about the effect the operation would have on my voice. They were reassured and the offending organs were removed, and put on display in the Victoria Central Hospital as the biggest and most diseased pair of tonsils ever seen.

I had fought under the anaesthetic and when my parents came to see me in the evening both my top and bottom lips were badly cut and four of my front teeth were broken. Two days after coming home I woke to discover my pillow covered in blood. Mum rushed me up Mill Lane to the hospital and I was admitted again, shoved into bed and given a bowl to spit into. But a nurse came up and took the bowl away saying, 'I'm fed up with emptying this, young lady, you should try and swallow it.' I tried hard to swallow the thick muck, but around evening it began to stop and a few days later I was restored to the bosom of my family again.

That year was a poor summer. The doctor had prescribed lots

of trips to the seaside to bring back the roses to my cheeks. We seemed to spend a lot of time waiting for Dad's 'sunny day'.

Then back to the dancing school, and now Miss Gatley had decided to use all her pupils in a production of *Snow White and the Seven Dwarfs*. With my long jet black curls everyone (including me!) thought that I would be given the part of Snow White, but despite her golden curls, as head of the dancing school Miss Gatley was entitled to claim the title role for herself. I didn't mind too much as the Prince's songs were nice and my solo, 'One Song, I have But One Song', brought the house down.

Dad was the producer and made all the props including the seven little beds, and seven little chairs, and once again we were busy with the plaster board in the back bedroom. He also devised the make-up and transformed the seven little girls into seven old men. Looking back, I can see that they were nearly all type-cast; he had taken great care in choosing them. Bashful was the most painfully shy child you could ever wish to meet, Happy was the one who could never concentrate and always had the class in stitches, while Sneezy was played by my cousin Margaret, who to the best of my knowledge has hay fever to this day.

The Secondary school had one bright spot. They had real music lessons. I lived for them and the art classes. There was a school choir too, and these sessions were the highlight of the week. I did well in art and was put down to enter for a scholarship to the Wallasey School of Art. I was terrified that I might win – all I wanted to do was sing. Anyway I drew the most vile looking flowers and my portrait would have done Picasso proud, and so I threw the exam.

The headmistress was livid; she didn't like me anyway, and when my Dad joined the PTA she complained to him that I was heading for hell and damnation.

'Mr Hunter, can't you keep Rita quiet, she makes such a noise in school.'

'Where does she make all this noise, Miss Russell?'

'In the playground.'

'Well,' laughed Dad. 'That's the place for noise as long as she's quiet in class.'

But my guardian angels were Miss Watson, my music mistress, Miss Coombs the art teacher and Miss Manahan, my form mistress. They were on my side and I knew it and worked very hard for them. My form mistress wrote on my school leaving certificate, 'She has an honest and sincere disposition and a keen sense of humour.' As for that sense of humour, I had learned early to make a joke about myself before anyone else could. I still do it, although my husband chides me for it.

*

At the PTA Dad met Mr Alf Roddick, a brilliant banjo player, who was to become his life-long friend. He also had a great bass-baritone voice. His friend Bert Price also played the banjo, and Dad could play the mouth organ and the spoons and sing tenor. Mr Roddick's two daughters, Rita and Maureen, attended the Hilda Bromley dance school. So with Ruth's dancing and Mum's high soprano voice and mandolin, together with yours truly, who quickly learned to play the ukelele in addition to my twinkle toes and voice, we soon realised we had an 'act'. Hunters' Modern Minstrels were born.

The troupe rehearsed in our kitchen several nights a week – this was the best place for dancing as we had red quarry tiles. We had hundreds of leaflets printed saying 'The Hunters Are Coming', and spent hours traipsing the Wallasey streets pushing these damn things through letter boxes. We let the public think over this offer for a few weeks, then did the rounds again, this time with leaflets announcing the time and place. We hit them in the eyes with a half-hour concert in St Luke's Church hall. The Dads had devised an act that did not stop for applause; every number ran swiftly into the next, and we all remained on stage for the whole of the act. Dad had made stools for us with the letters H.M. on in blue and yellow.

When the curtain rose the only one on stage was Mum, in the centre, dressed as a 'Mammy', with Arthur Gregson at the piano, and as each one of us came on and did our turns so we sat down, then the next one, or pair, came on until the numbers were complete.

The first show was a huge hit and we soon had dates all over Merseyside; we must have worked in every club and social centre in the area. We were not paid much, and a great many of the shows were for charity, so we were short on funds. Our costumes, yellow with red frills, and our red tap shoes, were purchased out of our own pockets. There were also new strings and maintenance of the instruments. To save on clothing coupons, which were needed for more important things, the women in those days used leg make-up, so we paid a visit to our local chemist, and gave him a stick of the make-up we used on our faces, and asked him to make up huge bottles of leg make-up to match. We got through gallons of this as the four girls had to make up their arms as well as their legs. The residue left on our bodies made a bit of a mess of the bed-clothes.

And whether we were paid or not, we still had to pay the pianist, Arthur Gregson, and he also had to have his free beer. All evening he would have a pint on the piano, and there was always someone there to fill it when it became empty – when it was a long night he was sometimes the worse for wear.

The fares for the troupe to some of the more distant places were a big worry so Dad negotiated with a friend who had a coal lorry. We all helped to clean it on a Saturday morning and then we put a canvas cover on the top (it looked a bit like a covered wagon) and then on Saturdays and Sundays off we would go, all bundled up. The troupe was 'on tour'!

One Boxing Day the Minstrels went to entertain at an Old Folks party outside Liverpool. Auntie Ruth asked Dad if we were to get any food and, on being told no, she and Mum planned what they would take to eat. Mum said she would make butties with the stuffing from the Christmas chicken. Auntie Ruth said that she'd think of something. When we got to the hall, which was a converted church, the back half was partitioned off with wood panels – we were to dress in the back half and the party was in the front half. In our half we had the remains of the choir stalls and the altar and organ loft.

In the interval Mum got out her stuffing butties and Ruth produced a bag that contained the giblets from her chicken and she began to eat them. When she began chewing on the neck, I began to feel a bit queasy, mother turned green and Ruth grinned, 'What's up, Lucy?'

Dad came up to get his stuffing buttie, took one look at Ruth and said, 'For God's sake, Ruth, take your bloody giblets into the organ loft.' She went up there giggling, and after I had eaten my butties I went up to see her. There she was, still laughing. I said, 'You've upset me Dad, and me Mam feels sicks after looking at you.'

'Rubbish,' she said. 'It's the stuffing butties that's upset her, you know how she is with onions, she will have wind all the way home.' She was right!

When performing at the Ellesmere Port Iron Works Ruth and I were in a corner helping each other to put on the leg make-up, and she was moaning, 'It's all right for your Dad insisting that we wear this muck, he wears long sleeves and trousers, he gets on my nerves with this bloody nigger make-up.' Dad heard her and bent down and said, 'Coon, Ruth, coon, not nigger.' 'Coon' was every bit as insulting. Poor Dad went to no end of trouble to

21

be 'in character' – trouble was, we all had to suffer along with him.

Arthur Gregson, the pianist, and his beer was a subject which always upset Mum. Dad had long since realised that Arthur would not play without it. Mum tried to stipulate a certain number of pints an hour and Dad came to an arrangement with Mr Price to bring along 'another banjo'. Actually the banjo case contained not another banjo, but bottles of beer. Then my Mum would say, 'There you are, Charlie, he's worse than ever tonight and he's getting *less* booze, He's an alcoholic.' Dad would shake his head, 'Aye, Lucy, I'm buggered if I know what to think.'

Then one awful day Bert Price tripped up getting on the Liverpool ferry boat and the banjo case fell open and all the beer fell out. Mum sulked all the way to the concert, and on the way home all hell broke loose. The captain of the ferry boat said he'd never heard the like even when there was a football match. It turned out that Arthur had been getting not only his legitimate supply, and the one in Bert Price's banjo case, but Mr Roddick had been bringing him beer as well in *his* music case.

As Mr Roddick said, Arthur *was* good, and it would take ages to get someone to learn the music for the act. However, as a result of the showdown, Arthur was back to his original ration.

The Minstrel act thrived for about three years. Then several things happened. Bert Price wanted us to rehearse in his house and in Mr Roddick's house, not just ours. We tried this but the floors in the other houses were wood and hollow and we felt as if we were going to fall through and Mrs Roddick suffered from migraine and often a planned rehearsal was called off because she was ill.

The other reason we began to fall apart was also Bert Price. He wanted to show off his young daughter, Lorna, who was also learning to dance. I don't know if she was good or not, but apparently she didn't come up to the standard desired, so Hunters' Modern Minstrels drifted off into history.

CHAPTER FOUR

Little Buttercup meets Siegfried

When I was 13, Mr Harry Burgon, the music teacher from the boys' school next door, decided to join his choir with the girls' choir and put on a performance of *HMS Pinafore*. I was summoned to the headmistress's office, along with two other girls, June Groves and Ann Noble, and we were told that we were to be allowed into the boys' school and that Mr Burgon wanted to see us. She made it quite plain that she did not approve of us going into the boys' school – well me anyway, for wasn't it clear I would corrupt all the boys in one fell swoop?

Mr Burgon gave the role of Josephine to June, and the role of Cousin Hebe to Ann, and I was to be Little Buttercup. I was overjoyed, though I might not have been quite so elated had I known this was to be the first of many mezzo roles that were to annoy and disappoint me so much in the years to come.

We began to rehearse in our music lessons, much hampered by the headmistress, Miss Russell – or as we used to call her 'Old Russell of Spring'. She did everything she could to make things difficult for us: extra lessons of anything to prevent us going to music lessons on time, then she refused to let us go into the boys' school to work, and eventually refused to let us work on *Pinafore* in school hours. So we had to stay behind after school, while she would sit in the room to watch our every move, sniffing with disapproval.

Finally the principal singers used to go on a Saturday to Mr Burgon's home in West Derby to work. We all figured that old Russell of Spring would blow a gasket if she saw the love duet being rehearsed.

Mr Burgon was a well known baritone in the Liverpool area. He had just sung Amanasro in *Aida* with the Liverpool Grand Opera Company; his teacher was Edwin Francis.

My father designed the sets of *Pinafore*, and would go up to the boys' school where the sets were being built in their woodwork lessons.

On the first night I received an ovation for my performance of Buttercup. I loved it, and decided that this was the best week I had ever spent in school. The only thing I hated was when the Captain of Pinafore sang to me 'A plump and pleasing person' – said with far too much relish for my liking!

I smiled in triumph towards the head mistress after one of my curtain calls. But she had her revenge. Her response was a frosty and cutting, 'They are doing *Magic Flute* next year, but *you* will have left by then.'

Well, they do say who laughs last laughs longest, and I had a little of my own back. I was asked to return to school for a prize giving. My form mistress had put me down for a music prize but the request had been denied by old Russell of Spring, and she had only been able to get me a geography prize on the grounds that my art work on the maps was so good. When I went up to receive my book from the Lady Mayoress, Miss Russell was sitting next to her with a look that suggested she had been eating too many stewed prunes.

The Mayoress said, 'What are you going to do now you have left school, my dear?' I replied, 'I am going into pantomime as the principal boy.'

'Well,' she said, 'I'm not at all surprised, you were just splendid in *Pinafore*.'

'Move along Hunter, next please,' said old Russell. She hated me to the last. She was certain I would be a trollop by the New Year – I gave her a gushing smile and swept off the stage.

Some years later I received a request to subscribe to a retirement gift for her. I wrote back, 'After making my life a hell, you must be joking.' I gave it to my Dad to post, but looking back, I don't think he did. I don't mind, but if she was at least told about the letter, she could have begun her retirement secure in the knowledge that she had been right about 'that dreadful Rita Hunter'.

*

Some months before I left school, it was thought I should go to Auntie Ruth's old dancing teacher Bess Clark, to perfect my dancing. Ruth said, 'Bess has contacts in the theatre.' Bess was now getting on in years and lived in Walton, Liverpool. Her daughter Edith played the piano and did most of the teaching.

The kids were mostly from the tough dockland area of Liverpool. Bess used to supervise. Her room reeked of cats – she fed all the stray cats in the area. She would sit in state surrounded by the cats, and as I danced my feet off she would yell, 'EEEEEEdith! You're wasting your time with her, she's a singer, not a bloody hoofer.' Edith would shout back, 'Sherrup Ma! She's gorra getter figger in shape,' and then Edith would follow up that remark by teaching me more acrobatics, and would explain to me, 'Y'see kid, if yis going on the clubs the fellers like ter see de judys flinging der legs around and showing der drawers.' (I never told Mum about that!) Bess would come in and see me with my legs all tangled up, and she would poke my bum with her long cane and say, 'Girrup from there and warble. Edith I tell you she's a singer, look at her high cheek bones.' Edith would go pink with temper and say, 'Mind your own business Ma!' and Bess would stomp out back to her cats and Edith would sit on my shoulders to make me do the splits. (Dear Edith – I could still do them right up to the time I had my gallstone operation: I haven't dared to try since.)

Despite the infighting between Bess and Edith, I became a member of Bess Clark's concert party. We did all the tough clubs in Liverpool until the time came to take on the toughest of them all, Tagus Hall – if they didn't like you they threw the empty bottles at you. Ruth was deputised to take me; Mum said, 'If it's going to be a boozy do, I'm not going.'

This was when I had my first taste of nerves. To keep Bess quiet I was to sing a straight song. 'My God,' I thought, 'what a place to sing a straight song.' Not something bright and breezy – oh no, she'd gone the whole hog – 'Ave Maria' of all things. 'They'll lynch me, how can you fling your legs around in *that* song!' After sleepless nights, I put my fears to Bess. 'Oh, yer'll be orlright – they're Catholics and they gits even more religious when they're drunk.'

I didn't want to argue with the oracle, but I didn't have much faith in her predictions. But wonder of wonders, she was right! They loved it, they cheered and waved their beer bottles and, when I did not appear for an encore (only Edith's *top* artistes did that), they began to shout. 'Warra voice,' 'Give us the judy with the lovely voice.' Edith was cross that old Bess had been proved right. She said, 'Go home, yis mother wouldn't like yis in a place like this.'

Ruth and I giggled all the way home, and burst into the kitchen still laughing. Mum began to have the vapours, certain that I'd been corrupted. Dad stood up, his chest heaving like a mad rooster, and smelt our breath. It took several pots of Mum's stewed tea to convince them we were completely sober.

The kids in Bess Clark's concert party were tough and full of ambition, and I often wonder what became of them all. At first they were wary of me, I was an outsider from Wallasey.

'Hey girl, where's yis from?'

I told them.

'Oh we fort so, see yis a posh talker.'

'Hey, yis clothes is posh, is your old man rich?'

One girl shouted to my interrogator, 'Hey Cecilia, who's the new judy?' Cecilia replied, 'Oh, she's from Wallasey.' From then on I was simply called 'Wallasey' by everyone in the dancing school, except Bess and Edith.

Since my parents had declined the opportunity to see me in Tagus Hall they said they would go to my next concert, having first found out that it was to be in a Masonic hall in Bromborough, so it was bound to be respectable.

Ruth was also dancing on that night, so all four of us turned up at the appointed hour at Woodside bus depot. We waited in the queue and presently the rest of the party arrived off the Liverpool ferry boat. They all had small cases or bags and their tap shoes dangling on the laces from their shoulders. They were chattering like magpies and almost all of them had runny noses. I sensed my mother freeze at the sight of them, and Ruth began to giggle. My Mum said, 'We'll go on the next bus, this lot will show us up.' I said, 'We can't Mum, I don't know where the hall is, we have to go with them or we'll get lost.'

By now the 'Ziegfeld Follies' had begun to board the bus; one small girl turned round as she stood on the platform, and shouted to me, 'Hey Wallasey, isn't yous lot goin' on this yer bus?'

My Mum was horrified – after all her daughter had taken elocution lessons. Anyhow, we did get on the same bus but Mum insisted that we went downstairs the 'Follies' had gone upstairs. They made a dreadful din, and everyone on the bus knew who they were and where they were going. Dad and Ruth were laughing quietly, but poor shy Mum sank deeper and deeper into her shell. We heard Cecilia say, 'Oh yis, an that big judy with black hair and the posh relations is gonna sing somfink from H'Opery and somfink Holy. The 'H'Opery' was the laughing song from *Fledermaus* and the somfink Holy was 'Ave Maria'.

*

When I left school, I remember coming out into the sunshine with my leaving certificate, and feeling that I had been let out of prison. I jumped onto my bike and went the long way home, feeling the wind blowing in my hair. I was *free*, free of conforming, free from those awful and embarrassing sports lessons, free from the humiliation of being sent down to the C class for arithmetic, and free from the dreaded Russell of Spring.

I was still bubbling over at tea time and Dad took me for a long ride round Bidston Hill and Frankby and back through Birkenhead Park. The next day, as I had a puncture in my bike and no patches to mend it with, I went to my Uncle Arthur and 'borrowed' his little dog, Nell, and went for a long walk in the direction of the old Wallasey village and then across The Moss to Bidston Village and back through Birkenhead and over the Penny Bridge home. I was so thrilled by all this new freedom I had not noticed that I had walked until the dog's pads had bled. I was mortified and cried myself to sleep.

At my next lesson Bess said, 'It's time yis was earning yer own living.' I nodded frantically in agreement. She had organised an audition for me in Manchester with a firm called 'Jack Gillam Productions'. The job was a pantomime. She took me into her sanctuary of stinking cats. 'Now listen, remember yis is seventeen, if they know yer only fifteen they won't take yis, and take *no* notice of Edie, don't do any dancing, sing. If they want a dancer, they ask yis, and then you can show them.'

I said, 'Yes, yes,' I would do all she said. I felt my heart thumping.

'You'll only get chorus mind, but it's a start and whatever yer gets in the way of money yis have ter give me ten per cent.'

I did all I was told, and Bess, Edith and I were shaken rigid when I came home with a contract for principal boy, at a salary of ten pounds a week! I was beside myself with joy. I would be rich, my name in lights. What a tour! We played the towns of Bolton, Halifax, Huddersfield, Salford, Scunthorpe, Rotherham and Stockton-on-Tees. Some of the working men's clubs in Liverpool had offered better facilities. But I thought that it could not have been better playing Broadway itself. My Mum came with me on the tour – she wasn't going to let her fifteen-year-old pride and joy out into the world alone. This meant of course that my ten pounds a week went nowhere. In fact we ended up paying out on top of this in order to survive.

When I had read the script I had discovered that I had to have a sword fight with the villain. I told Dad I didn't know how to do this, so he cut one of Mum's brooms in half, and taught me to fence. Every night after tea we would move the chairs and table out of the way and we had our fencing lessons in the kitchen. By the time I had to face the villain, I was pretty good, so good in fact that the villain was terrified of me. After the first night he ran to my mother, blood pouring off his hands. 'Mrs Hunter, for God's sake tell her that it's just *pretend*.'

Mum bound his wounds with elastoplast and gave me a lecture. 'But Mum, it's got to look real.' Charlie Hunter wasn't the only one who didn't do things by halves.

We were told by some of the regular principals that after the pantomime finished you often got signed up for a summer show, or sometimes a West End show, and if you were lucky that would take you well on to the Autumn, and then one would be signed up for the pantomime again.

Although I had not been signed up for anything when I returned from the pantomime tour, one thing was clear in my mind. The smell of the grease paint and the roar of the crowd were well and truly in my blood, and there was no going back.

*

Home-life became boring after the ten weeks' tour. I did the rounds of the agents' offices in Liverpool but all they seemed to want was 'Show Girls', which could mean anything from fan dancing to nude shows. Then I got permission from my parents to go and see Jack Gillam in Manchester, provided my cousin Albert came with me. Jack was curt and abrupt, his usual manner, and said, 'Show me your legs.' I opened my coat, and he said, 'Um, well, they're still okay, but I've got a new girl this year to play principal boy.' He stomped off out of the room and there was nothing left but to go home.

On the train my cousin said, 'You'd better not tell your Mam about showing your legs, she won't like it.'

I said, 'I wish I knew what clever sod he's got for next year, I hate her.' Thirty-five years later, at a party in Footscray, a suburb of Melbourne in Australia, I found this principal boy. She was in the chorus of the Australian opera. Olga and I spent a good day chatting over the old days. She told me that Jack Gillam had died in a home for old actors. Olga had to show her legs too – so we came to the conclusion that hers must have been better than mine.

One day a letter came asking me to sing in a charity concert at the Floral Pavilion in New Brighton; it was to be a benefit for the comedian, Tommy Handley. I don't remember what I sang or anyone else on the bill, except for one man, Jimmy Wilde, the boxer. He let me hold the magnificent Lonsdale Belt. While I was admiring it he said to my mother, 'That girl of yours has got something, she ought to have a good singing teacher, get over the water to Liverpool and find one.'

My Mum thanked him profusely, and he said, 'I mean it, Mrs Hunter. Believe me she'll have the world at her feet one day with that voice of hers.'

We came home on air. We discussed his words for days, and were highly honoured that such a great man thought so much of me. I don't think we believed for a moment that it would come about, but nevertheless I now spent all my time learning all the straight songs I could get my hands on. I hung up my dancing shoes for ever.

Another letter came asking me to sing – no dancing, just singing. I was convinced that this would be the turn of events I had been waiting for. I spent all day singing and learning songs in the parlour, coming out only for meals. I was determined that my debut as a straight singer would be a sensation. It was. We turned up at the Adelphi Hotel in Liverpool and were ushered into an ante room and told that I was to sing after the big dinner party. We waited and waited and my Mum began to worry in case we missed the last ferry home. At 11 p.m. a man came in and told us we could go home – the guests were too drunk to listen. My Mum seethed on the ferry boat – 'That's it, I don't care what your father says, you are *not* going to sing any more boozy dos.'

My father laughed and all he said was 'Did you get the three quid?'

Dad would never let any job pass by and a few weeks later he got me an engagement on the river cruise boat *The Royal Daffodil*. This was on November 5th, bonfire night, and I was to sing with a band, solo. This was really going up in the world, solo with a band!

Dad came with me, and I sang 'Far Away Places' and 'The Longest Mile', as we pulled into the Seacombe ferry at the end of the night. I got my fee. Ten shillings and a bag of stale chips.

I began to get several jobs in the clubs as a solo singer. I was at the mercy of the club pianists, and there was many a raised eyebrow as I showed them the operatic arias they had to play. Often they would play in an easier key for them, and I would find myself having to sing top D instead of top A. However, being young and full of my own ability to cope with whatever that was thrown at me, I didn't bat an eyelid.

Once when trying to get to the bus stop after singing in the

Ellesmere Port Iron Works club, Nellie and I fell over some railway lines in the dark into a pool of oily mud. We spent far more than the two pounds fee mending and cleaning our clothes afterwards.

I was asked to sing in the Rialto ballroom in Liverpool with a dance band, and Auntie Nellie came along. When we arrived she came to an abrupt halt on the pavement outside the ballroom looking in horror at the poster. They had billed me as 'Merseyside's Own Sophie Tucker'. Nellie was in such a rage. 'If you were my child I'd not allow it.'

We went into the ballroom and I had a short rehearsal with the orchestra, and Nellie mentioned her displeasure about the billing to the manager. He didn't think that he'd done anything really wrong. I sang 'The Wren' and 'Ave Maria' and the audience shouted 'Warra bout giving us yer Red Hot Momma?' Nellie's cheeks were aflame and, as I sat and quietly did my knitting, waiting for the second half of the programme, she went to the manager and demanded my fee of two pounds ten shillings, and in the interval she pulled my coat on and gathered up our things and we swept out leaving the customers still shouting for the Red Hot Momma.

We got lost on the way home. It was too late for the trams and we had to walk, so we followed the tram lines. I had said, 'They are bound to lead to the pier-head.' They didn't. We ended up in the tram sheds up in Toxteth. A cheerful night cleaner pointed us in the right direction, and we eventually got to the river. We waited ages for a boat, as after midnight they only sailed every hour, so we missed the last bus on the other side and had to walk all the way home from the Seacombe Ferry to Poulton. I may not have been a Red Hot Momma, but my feet were red hot all right.

*

After this episode the Hunters had a council of war. We thought much about the words of Jimmy Wilde, and so it was decided to get in touch with the music teacher from school, Mr Burgon. If I was to branch out as a classical singer then we needed the right guidance, as the family's experience had only been the music hall and variety. Dad called at the school to see him, and as luck would have it he was about to get in touch with me, as he was by now the conductor of the Wallasey Children's Choir, and he wanted to put on a performance of *Faust* – a concert perform- ance, that is. He had two Marguerites and wanted a third, said that he would not contemplate asking any girl of fifteen or sixteen to sing the whole of the role. It turned out that while I had been busy with the Pantomime and clubs, June Groves had been going to him all the time for lessons. Mum was none too pleased about this and began to wish we had taken Jimmy Wilde's advice sooner. Dad said, 'It's no use crying over spilt milk.' Nellie didn't like that attitude, and said to them both, 'You're going to make the poor kid feel that this last year has been a waste of time, and that's not fair.'

I went to the first rehearsal of the choir and discovered that my part in the *Faust* performance was to be the Holy Angels Trio at the end.

The following Saturday I went to Mr Burgon's to begin to learn the trio, then for the first time realised how wasted my voice had been on all those songs, songs that by today's standards were little more than pop songs, apart from the few times when I had sung a light operatic aria.

Then I went to Mr Burgon for lessons, not just to learn the *Faust* trio, but to develop the voice. I went sometimes three evenings a week and Saturday mornings. This meant we had to have another family council, as the fares for all these trips had to be found. I said, 'Let me sign on the dole.' My father was emphatic. 'It's degrading, we have kept you for fifteen years, we'll keep you for another fifteen if we have to.'

One day my father came home from work in a rage. He had seen Nellie in a heated conversation with a neighbour who had said to Nellie, 'What are the Hunters going to do with that fat lazy kid of theirs now she's left school?' Nellie resented not only the 'fat' but also the 'lazy'; she knew better than most how hard I worked at home, and all the trailing round Merseyside to earn a couple of pounds to pay for my lessons. This woman had said, 'Work? You don't call that work, do you?' At this point Dad had shown up, 'Look here, Missus, have I asked you to keep her?' 'No,' said the woman. 'Then mind your own bloody business, and what's more don't come to me for free seats when she's a star.'

Mum was so shocked that Dad had been in a 'street fight' as she put it, that she wouldn't show her face in the Co-op for a week.

I continued to sing in the clubs at week-ends to pay for my fares and lessons and Mr Burgon began teaching me the Act Three duet from *Traviata* and the *Rigoletto* duet. I already knew Gilda's aria and the first aria from *Traviata*, and so Mr Burgon began to get us some dates singing all of these. He would also sing the *Rigoletto* aria and the elder Germont's aria. This potted version of those two operas went down very well, and of course we had a more highbrow class of audience. At this time I was also singing 'One fine day' and Mimì's aria and 'Ritorna vincitor'.

When I was about sixteen-and-a-half, Mr Burgon said, 'Well dear, I've taught you all I know. I think you ought to go to my own teacher, Edwin Francis.' This of course caused my parents more worry about the cost of these lessons 'from a real teacher'. I pointed out that maybe he wouldn't *want* to teach me.

Nevertheless I took great care when I went to meet Edwin for the first time. I spent ages with my make-up and changed my dress several times.

Edwin Francis at that time was teaching over a sheet music shop opposite Owen Owens in Liverpool. He seemed quite impressed by my rendering of 'Caro nome' and said to Harry Burgon, 'She's a young Eva Turner, Harry!' As I sifted through my music for the next aria, I hadn't a clue who Edwin Francis was talking about. I then sang the aria in Act 4 of *Trovatore*. This time Edwin said, 'This young lady will be a great Leonora one day,' and he agreed to teach me. Harry took me for a cup of tea in a café near Central Station. He said that I was well and truly on the right path now and that eventually I would obtain a job in an opera company.

I could have flown over the Mersey. The buses and boats all seemed to go at a snail's pace, I couldn't get home fast enough to tell the family the good news. There were many pots of tea brewed that night and, stewed or not, Nellie swigged them all down as fast as everyone else.

Of course after the night of euphoria, came the cold light of dawn, and we all realised that the lessons from Edwin Francis would be far more expensive than anything we had come up against before. Nine pounds for ten lessons. I gathered several jobs to help, such as cleaning Auntie Nellie's bedroom every week, for two shillings and sixpence; I washed and set Auntie Gladys's hair, for three shillings. She also asked me to help her with her shopping bags and in return for this she would buy me sheet music and records. I kept every penny I earned in this way in a box of soap in my bedroom. One night when I was in bed, I heard Auntie Nellie and my parents talking downstairs. Nellie said, 'You know, Lucy, it's not healthy the way Rita coops herself up with her music and records. She should get out and have a bit of fun, she'll be old before she's young.' And Dad said, 'Well, you know she saves all her money for her fares and lessons.'

'Yes,' said Nellie, 'but she could go to the pictures if you'd let her.'

And from then on I went at least once a week to the cinema. Ruth used to take me to the musicals and Uncle Arthur took me to the Westerns. I knew that none of them was well off and they had their own families to bring up, and I will be forever grateful for the support and devotion of my aunts and uncles.

But there came a day when all the men were on short time, and neither my parents nor I had the cash for my fare to Liverpool. So I went round to see Auntie Nellie. 'I thought you were going to Mr Francis today, chuck?'

I said, 'I can't, Nellie, we've no money left this week.'

She stood up with a smile and a little sigh and went to the dresser, and behind the radio was a little tin money box in the shape of a post box. 'You know, chuck,' she said, 'I keep putting all the odd coppers in this to pay the dog licence, see how much you can get out of it.' I went to work on it with a knife and managed to extract 8 pence for the return fare on the bus to the ferry, and 1/6d for the return fare on the boat. 'Sorry, chuck, but you'll have to walk from the pier-head to the studio and back.' I said, 'I don't mind, Nellie, as it's not raining,' and Ruth said, 'No, you won't have to walk, chuck, I found a sixpence in the gutter outside the bread shop.'

I did walk, however, and I have kept the sixpence to this day. Edwin Francis proceeded to teach me the *bel canto* method of singing. He said if the notes were placed right they should sound like pearls dropping on glass and that, when I was older and my voice matured, it would sound like red ruby wine. He taught me all the soprano arias and some mezzo ones, from 'Una voce poco fa' through 'Vissi d'arte' to 'In questa reggia' – you name it, I sang it. I still have a couple of privately made 78 rpm's of my efforts in those days. I was certainly versatile, but the audacity to tackle so many different arias! Much has been written about the cheeky Cockney Sparrow, but you will have to go a long way to out-cheek a Merseysider.

Mr Francis was a kind man and he knew of our struggles to pay not only the lessons but the fares too, and he gave me a lot of extra lessons free. He would say, 'If you go downstairs and wait in the foyer for an hour, I will have a half hour free and we can do some more work.'

And I would go downstairs to Crains music shop and sit on the little round green velvet sofa.

One historic day Mr Francis said, 'Don't rush off after your lesson, go and have a cup of tea and then come back up in half an hour. I have a new tenor I want you to sing a duet with.' So off I went for tea, and when I got back upstairs there was the most fantastic sound coming from Edwin's studio. Up to this point I had been besotted with the voice of Mario Lanza, and had wild dreams of maybe singing with him one day. I tapped on the door and went in, and was introduced to a tall round-faced boy of sixteen with twinkling eyes and a cheeky grin. We sang together. Edwin was right. He *was* good and I knew then he would have a great career. For a start he was the first person I'd sung with that my voice had not drowned. Edwin preened himself as our voices blended together perfectly. His name was Alberto Remedios. Proud as Edwin was, I am sure that even he did not realise that evening that a future Brünnhilde and Siegfried had been born. The Brünnhilde was eighteen and the Siegfried was sixteen, the ages that Wagner says they are. We had to wait twenty years for it to come to fruition. Alberto and I often smile at each other over the heads of the fans in the dressing rooms, a smile that says, 'Well, *we* knew we could do it even if no one else did.'

As I write this I have just heard of Alberto's CBE. One and a half years after I received mine. He used to tease me about getting mine before he got one, and I would tell him that the reason was just 'age before beauty'.

Still it would have been nice for us to have gone to the Palace together. Never mind, I still think we have done Edwin Francis proud.

CHAPTER FIVE

Opportunity Knocks

About this time I joined the Wallasay Operatic Society which was going to perform *The Bartered Bride*, to be produced by my Dad. I had been asked to sing Ludmilla. There was a tiny old lady in the chorus who always stood as near to the front as she could, and got in everyone's way. My Dad was in despair; 'I've got to move her,' he told the conductor. The conductor was horrified. 'You can't do that, Charlie, she brings the milk for the tea at the rehearsals!' Dad said, 'You mean to tell me that you let her stand there just on account of the milk – well, leave it to me.'

Now Dad may have been a perfectionist, but he was also a gentleman and wouldn't hurt anyone's feelings for the world. He took the old lady to one side and told her that he was giving her an important role, she was to be a gypsy fortune teller and all the members of the chorus were to go to her camp-fire and have their fortunes told. He ensured that the fire was at the back of the stage, and when she wasn't hidden by flames and smoke she was surrounded by singers. However, she was overjoyed, and from then on she not only brought the milk but the tea, and the buns, and my Dad always got a free cup.

Looking through my diaries for this period, it seems I did little apart from going to lessons and learning arias. My aunt acquired a treadle sewing machine and I used to sit in her front window and sew patchwork quilts. One day I noticed a tall dark-haired young chap passing the house on the other side of the road. I quickly bent my head in case he thought I was too bold, looking at him; although I was seventeen I had never had a date with a boy. The next day he came by again, this time on our side of the road, and smiled at me. I didn't dare to return the smile, and bent my head, but saw through the corner of my eye that he had stopped to speak to my Auntie Ruth, and she came in all breathless to tell me that he had said he thought I was 'smashing' and asked if I would come out the next day and talk to him instead of sewing in the window. The next day he stood on the corner waiting and Ruth came in the front room to tell me he was there. I said, 'I know he is, but if Mum sees me she'll play hell.' So Ruth went to chat to Mum over the garden wall, keeping her occupied at the back of the house.

We did not chat for long. He told me that he worked at the Oil Works down the road in the office, and he was on his lunch break. Ruth had told him quite a bit about me, and he asked if I would like to go to the Tivoli Theatre on Saturday night, first house, so I would not be out late. I rashly said yes, and when I told Ruth she exclaimed, 'Oh bloody hell, Rita, how are you going to wangle it?' I really didn't know, and for a couple of days I actually thought I would 'come clean' and ask if I could go, but in the end I got Ruth to tell my parents *she* was taking me to the Tivoli. It was planned that she would wait for me by the bus stop and we would then come home together, and while I was in the theatre she would go and visit her mates.

On Saturday I washed my hair and got myself all dolled up for my first date. I met Malcolm outside the theatre and he gave me a box of chocolates and paid for our seats in the dress circle. I felt like royalty, he was as nice as you could wish, didn't make any passes or even try to hold my hand. After the show we walked to the bus stop, and he bought me an ice cream, and we stood and waited for the bus. We got back to Poulton at 8.45, and I was surprised to see that Ruth was not at the bus stop as arranged. But here she was running up the road to meet us. Her cheeks were white and she could hardly tell us the bad news. Dad had gone for a walk and seen Ruth sitting at the bus stop without me, and he had given her the third degree until she had told him the truth.

My heart fell to my boots. Malcolm said, 'Don't worry, Mrs Reid, I have only kept Rita out about three hours, her Dad won't mind.' I admired his confidence but I knew that disaster was but a couple of streets away. As we turned the bend in Limekiln Lane, there was Dad standing on our front step. I was so scared I was about to throw up. Dad stepped off the doorstep and spoke to Ruth. 'You've done enough for one day, go home.' Ruth fled, then he said to me, 'And you get indoors, miss.' As I went in I was mortified to hear him say to Malcolm, 'You've got a bloody cheek, bugger off and don't let me see you around here again.' Malcolm tried to say he had done nothing out of the way, but Dad swept up the steps and slammed the front door shut.

I felt so ashamed, I admitted I should have asked them first, but between my tears and Mum's sniffles, it seems it wasn't that I hadn't asked them, even if I had there was no way they would have let me go. Dad insisted there was 'my career to consider'. I went to bed and cried myself to sleep. On the Monday I stayed in and pretended to be cleaning my room and stayed upstairs. I peeped through my mother's bedroom window and saw Ruth speaking to Malcolm, and whatever it was she said to him, he never passed by our house again.

Some months later Dad and I were working in the front garden, and as I stood to carry my handful of weeds to the heap, I saw a tall blond chap coming along the road. He stopped at our house and said, 'Afternoon, Charlie,' and smiled at me. I gave him a tiny smile in return, and off he went. I stayed bent down in the flowers and as casually as I could, said, 'Who's that, Dad?' Dad said, 'Oh, he works in the wages office in the gas works'.

Afterwards we went in to tea and Dad washed and changed and went to watch the cricket in Central Park. When he came back he mentioned to Mum that 'young Phil out of the office had been at the cricket'. I took no notice, but the following Saturday, I made sure that I was out in the garden again (minus Dad). I was very busy 'planting seeds', and along came Adonis. 'Hello, Miss Hunter.' I said a very breathless 'Hello' and he asked, 'Why don't you come and sit in the park and watch the cricket, the air is better in the park.' I said I would have to ask my Dad first, and as he had already gone to the park I couldn't this week, thank you all the same. Phil said, 'Well, come on up, I always sit by him, I'll ask him when we get there.' But I made the excuse that I had to help Mum – I was determined not to get into hot water again.

When Dad came home I asked him if I could go to the cricket next Saturday and sit with him and Phil. Dad said, 'I'm not having you sitting on damp grass.' I was shocked at such a feeble excuse and didn't say a word in the hope that the weather would be hot and that Dad could have no objections. It was a very hot week indeed and so with high hopes I got myself ready after lunch and sat in the sitting room to wait. Eventually Phil came along. Dad was waiting outside and before I could gather up my bag and cardigan I heard Dad say, 'Well, that's how she is, Phil, she's full of her singing, and she's not at all interested in young men and dates.'

I could hardly believe my ears and didn't wait to hear Phil's reply. I fled to my room and by Sunday morning I had cried myself into a storming cold which went to my chest and I had to stay in bed for about ten days. It gave me plenty of time to consider my plight. It seemed to me that my father was being unreasonable. I had kept on with my studies, I had not shirked in any way. I was still set on a singing career, but what harm could there be in a little relaxation?

I was ill for some time and not able to go for my lessons. One afternoon when I was lying on my bed looking at some music I heard Mum and Nellie talking over the wall. Nellie had been told the whole saga and she was telling my Mum that she thought they were tying me to their apron strings too much and that when I *did* get a job on the stage she'd have to let me go alone, that they couldn't watch over me for ever, and that when I did branch out, as she put it, not to be surprised if I went off the rails after being so sheltered and spoiled all these years.

Mum was livid and there was silence over the wall for some time. There were high voices at supper and Dad said Nellie had no right to interfere, she had no children of her own and did not understand. I made a vow that men were out from now on for me, but somewhere at the back of my mind I knew that one day I *would* bring home a young man and that nothing on earth would make me give him up, and that I would have to stick to my guns and fight for my love whoever he might be. Otherwise I'd end up an old maid.

*

These two romantic interludes were soon swept under the carpet, so to speak. I call them romantic for want of a better word, but they were so innocent. But as I lay in my bed coughing, it was the first and only time that my determination to go on the stage wavered. I felt that if I pursued my ambition, it would make me its prisoner. I felt badly done by – there I was, going on eighteen, and never had my hand held by a boy, let alone been kissed by one, and yet I felt like a Jezebel.

My diaries at this time tell me that I had developed a nasty habit of shattering light bulbs while singing in the bath. Dad told all and sundry about this and it eventually got into the *Wallasey News* and the *Daily Mail* and then we had a letter from the photographer of the *Weekend Mail* asking me to go to his studio outside Liverpool for a picture to be taken while I was 'shattering' the light bulb.

Auntie Nellie came along. I did my best to shatter the bulb but when nothing happened I casually remarked that it only seemed to happen when I was in the bath. I've never seen a chap run so fast. In no time at all he had filled up his bath tub and frothed it up with Lux soap flakes. Nellie said loudly, 'Come on, chuck, get your coat.' I was dragged off out of the house and on the tram she said, 'We have enough trouble with your mother worrying about the boozy dos you sing at, God help us if you end up on the sex page of the *News of the World*.'

Soon after this Mr Francis got me an audition with a friend of his who ran a touring operetta company, and to my joy I was accepted as a chorister in a touring version of *The Chocolate Soldier* and to understudy the lead. The wages were to be £19 a week. The tour was only for four months but I thought I should be able to save a few pounds, and that when I came home again I would be able to pay for my lessons without singing at the clubs. Out of the blue my mother said she would be touring with me.

I was dismayed and pointed out, 'But I won't be able to save any money.' Dad said, 'Never mind, we want to make sure you stay on the straight and narrow.' My heart sank again, but I could say nothing. I felt a fool at rehearsals, the only one to take her mother along; also I felt the management didn't like it with Mum sitting in on all the rehearsals.

Over the two weeks we rehearsed in the Marquis of Granby Hotel in London, I saw my wages dwindle away with two to feed and two lots of fares to pay every day. In desperation I wrote to Edwin Francis and explained my plight. He wrote to my Dad and explained that having mother there all the time would hinder my chances of advancing my career as the management felt I was of an age when I was well able to look after myself. A few days later Mum went home, 'as it wasn't right to leave Dad to fend for himself for so long'!

I breathed a sigh of relief, and my savings in the Post Office grew swiftly. At the end of the four months I had saved two hundred pounds and, contrary to what my parents might have thought, I did not 'go off the rails'. In fact, boys and romance couldn't have been further from my mind. I was too busy learning all I could about my chosen profession.

*

All the digs on the tour had been booked by my mother with the result that most of the time I was on my own; the other girls were in places they had been to many times and what's more were cheaper than mine. However, there were advantages to being on my own as I had plenty of time to learn new music and to keep the letters home going. One week we were playing the Winter Gardens Theatre in Blackpool, and my digs were so far along the promenade I was almost in Lytham St Anne's. I used to go early to the theatre every day. For one thing I was afraid of being late, and also I would have the chance to do my washing if I was first there.

One Saturday I went in early in the morning to wash a few panties before the matinee knowing they would be dry enough to pack that night. My parents had suddenly decided they wanted to see me, and they turned up at my digs only to be told by the landlady that I had gone to the theatre. Then they turned up quite unexpected at the dressing room door to find their pride and joy quite alone. I was sitting knitting, and the thought occurred to me that they may have tried to catch me out doing something dreadful, but now I would prefer to think that they just couldn't go another week without seeing me.

*

After the tour was over I went home and resumed my lessons with Mr Francis, and again met Alberto, who was getting ready to go into the army. This seemed to me such a waste of his wonderful voice and the two years seemed a lifetime. He said he would get home every leave to see Mr Francis.

I was now able to have my lessons without having to work the clubs as I had some cash saved, and it was bliss to be free of this burden.

Covent Garden came to town and I saw the great Flagstad in *Tristan*. To my regret, I can't remember what she sounded like, just that she looked so wonderful, and although I longed to get into an opera company I never for a moment imagined that *I* would sing Wagner. I hoped to sing Gilda and Butterfly, but something like Isolde was for the goddesses of the profession.

Mr Francis had organised an audition with Covent Garden. I went to him beforehand for a lesson, and then I went and sang 'Ritorna vincitor', and 'D'amor sul alle rose' from *Trovatore*. Afterwards a toffee-nosed young man came up to me and said, 'You really are not what we are looking for, you would be better off in operetta.' I wonder where he was on the nights I sang Senta and Leonora in Covent Garden!

Not long after this, Mr Francis told me that the *Chocolate Soldier* company was going on the road again, this time with *Gay Rosalinda*. Now this time I *did* have a boy friend – well, hardly a boy, he was sixteen years older than me. But he had two things in his favour as far as I was concerned. He had been in the Carl Rosa Opera Company, so I could pick his brains, and, far more imporantly, he played the piano, so I was able to learn many new arias, so of course he was acceptable to my parents.

40

Strangely enough, his age didn't seem to upset them in the least. Perhaps they thought that because of the age difference I would never think of him romantically.

We toured for six months, and I was able to save more 'lesson' money. When the tour was over I went to London to audition for the Glyndebourne Opera. Mother came too – she didn't trust London.

The studio was in Baker Street, and the piece I had chosen was 'One fine day'. Yet another toffee-nosed young man was there (I wonder where opera companies get them from, perhaps they are specially bred to unnerve young singers). He looked at me over the top of his spectacles and when I had finished said, 'And what sort of roles had you in mind, young lady?' I could smell defeat and threw caution to the winds. 'Principal ones,' I said. He smirked. 'Oh, I see.' I fled from the room, and outside I became very cross. I said to Mum, 'I know they don't want me, but by God I will make that bloke rue the day he patronised me – I will blast his ears off one day.'

A few years later this same young man walked into my dressing room in Australia. He was charming, and I don't suppose for a moment he remembered smirking at an aspiring diva in his distant past. I too was charming, but confess that I had a private smirk recalling that I may have 'blasted his ears off' that night with some of my top notes from my enraged Abigaille.

The following spring the Italian Opera company was to come to Liverpool and I had asked Mr Francis to write to them for an audition for me, but for some reason he had not done this, and the financial outlook was becoming bleak. So in between the matinée and the evening performance I followed the maestro to his hotel, and called him up on the house phone, and before he could say a word I sang 'Ritorna vincitor' down the phone at him. It occurred to me that he might have hung up before I got to the end but, as I came out of the box, a rather superior Italian asked, in poor English, 'if the signorina would care to come up to the maestro's room?' The signorina would. I was in the lift before he was.

When I got to the room a charming man greeted me, and I said, 'Thank you for letting me come to see you.'

'Is OK,' (he sounded like Manuel in *Fawlty Towers*) – 'Is better we have the mad lady up in the room than zee foyer.'

I felt my blood beginning to boil again. Why was it that every one who heard me say I wanted to sing in opera, greeted me with smirks, wry smiles, and even sometimes a loud Ha Ha? Didn't they know that the one thing that would make me even more determined was their 'you haven't a chance' attitude? Even today when I hear 'it won't work,' I think straight away, 'We'll see about that!'

But the maestro took me back to the theatre right away and put me on the stage to sing an audition. I sang 'Ritorna vincitor' again and then 'Caro nome'. By this time most of the company seemed to be in the stalls, listening. Then he asked me if I would go to Manchester the following week to sing again. Of course I said 'Yes' – and flew home on wings to tell the clan my news.

*

Most of the week was spent making pots of tea and going to Liverpool to get a new dress and coat for my great adventure. I even went to have my hair set instead of doing it myself. On the train to Manchester, I had visions of being asked to sing with them every time they came to Liverpool and Manchester, and so, full of hope, I walked through the stage door of the Opera House.

A tall man with a quiet manner met me and took me to the diva's dressing room. Her name was Virginia Zeanni. She was not only a beautiful woman, she was kindness itself and insisted I be given a seat in the wings so that I could see the opera. It was *Traviata*. When the performance was over, she asked me if I needed any of her make-up to repair mine, for my audition.

After the audience had left a piano was pushed on the stage and I began to sing. I must have sung about ten or fifteen arias. The pianist, who was also the man who had met me at the stage door, and had also conducted *Traviata* that night, began to smile after the sixth aria. At first I thought, 'Hello, another unbeliever,' but I soon realised that he was on my side. He told me what it was that excited Italians were all on about; they were very interested in the coloratura arias, but the pianist/conductor said to me in one of the pauses, 'Do you know "In questa reggia"? You're a dramatic soprano really.' Well, I didn't know I was a dramatic anything, all I was certain of was that I was a soprano, and anything that had been composed for a soprano I was happy to sing.

The man at the piano, who told me his name was Edward Renton, broke the news to me that the Italians wanted me to go to Italy with them. But I would have to pay my own fare. However once there they would arrange for accommodation. I was stunned. Italy! It seemed like the other side of the world. Why couldn't I sing with them whenever they came to England? Mr Renton gave a gentle smile and shrugged his shoulders. He

42

said that what seemed simple to us was not even considered by the Italians.

I explained a bit about my financial position, and said there was no way we could find enough for the fare to Milan. He told me to go home and tell my parents about it, also to stress to them how well I had done, and in the meantime he would see what he could do about getting the Italians to offer me a role when they came to London next year.

I walked up to Manchester Central Station, half elated that at last someone didn't think I was a fool to want to sing in opera, and half despondent, feeling it was too much to expect that Mr Renton could get them to change their minds. I managed to get the last train to Liverpool and had to walk to the pier head. I waited an hour for a boat and then walked from Seacombe to Poulton. As I was dead tired when I got to the house I didn't want to tell my parents then about finding the fare to Milan. I didn't think they would let me go anyway, and they had done so much for me already. Although I was full of enthusiasm for the way the Italians had treated me, and passed on Mr Renton's message, I saw their faces fall. I knew there was nothing but to wait and see what Mr Renton could do.

After several weeks I received a letter from him. He had not been able to get the Italians to offer me anything unless I went to Italy, but he thought it would be a greaty pity to give up the idea of a career in opera as he said I had great potential. He suggested I ask my parents if they would let me go to his home in London and in turn for looking after his two children and some house-work, he would give me lessons and teach me the roles that he thought I should know. After he had taught me two or three roles, he would see what he could do about getting me an audition with an English opera company.

I was thrilled, but the question again was, would my parents let me go? I was now twenty but they had kept me sheltered, and they might not like the idea of my going to live in someone else's house doing housework. But I also knew that I would *never* get to sing in grand opera if I stayed shut up in Wallasey, I just had to get away. This was the chance I had been waiting for.

I showed my letter from Mr Renton to Mum, and she read it without comment. She then sat looking into the fire, and I started to explain how I felt. We ended up having a long and tearful discussion. I pointed out that even the youngest of my cousins had been earning their own living now for some years, and I was the odd man out. I felt that opportunity was knocking at the door, and, while we were both sniffling, somebody knocked at the front door, and in the silence that followed the knock she said, 'What would you do if we didn't give our consent?' I answered, 'I would go without it.' She sighed, blew her nose, and then said, 'Then we will back you all the way,' and went to answer the door. She looked up and down the street; there was nobody in sight. I felt that indeed opportunity *had* knocked and had gone away satisfied with my answer.

*

They did indeed back me all the way. There must have been many a hungry mealtime while I was away in order that they could send me a pound or two to keep me looking tidy and, whatever decision I made in the years that followed, they stood by me whether it was right or not. No one could have had more loyal support. They came to all my first nights and my father defied the doctors and came after a severe heart attack to the Empire Theatre, Liverpool, to hear me sing Senta. When my Mum had broken her hip, she insisted on being pushed in a wheelchair to the new Liverpool Cathedral to hear me sing in Verdi's *Requiem*. Stuart Burrows, the tenor, stayed with us to actually helped her into the wheelchair, and also helped us to sneak her back into the hospital afterwards.

While I was singing the Immolation in *Götterdämmerung* many years later, she turned to her companion and, with great pride and not a little amazement, said, 'My God, did I really give birth to that!'

CHAPTER SIX

Sadler's Wells

I travelled alone to London, and at Paddington got a taxi to the Rentons' house in Holland Park. I read over the letter Mrs Renton had sent me; she had told me where to find the key if no one met me.

I let myself into the basement – after our little house this seemed like a great mansion; basement, ground floor, first and second floors. No one was home, and Mrs Renton had left a note to say that Mr Renton had gone to Iceland to conduct, and I was to make myself at home till she returned. (I couldn't think what there could be to conduct in Iceland, except perhaps polar bears.)

So here I was, alone in this huge house, not knowing what to expect. By five o'clock I began to panic and think that it was all a huge joke, and then at 5.30 the front door bell rang. 'Good,' I thought. But it was a young man in his early twenties with a Welsh accent, asking for Mr Renton. I told him who I was and showed him Mrs Renton's note. He sat down beside me on the sofa and told me he was a tenor and studying with Mr Renton.

I asked him if he had a girlfriend back home in Wales, and he replied, 'Oh no, Mr Renton has told me to keep away from the women!' We both laughed, and then he said that he would go home and I was left alone again in that big house. I was also getting rather hungry. Mum's breakfast seemed a long way away. It was getting dark, and I was beginning to be a little scared. About 6.30 the phone rang. It was Mrs Renton. She had been delayed but the housekeeper, Mrs Saunders, would be home soon, by eight o'clock at the latest. So I plucked up courage and put one or two lights on. The phone rang again. This time a woman's voice asked for Mrs Renton. I explained that she was

45

out and asked if I could take a message. 'Yes, tell her that Lady Harewood phoned, and ask her to phone me.' I was stunned. Me, talking to Lady Harewood – my legs were like jelly. I thought, 'Just who are these folk to know such people?' I thought, 'My God, what will I do if I meet her – a boilermaker's daughter talking to a relation of the Queen.' I little thought that one day Lord Harewood would become my boss, and that I would also one day sleep at Harewood in the bed used by Queen Mary.

Then I heard someone come in the front door. It was Mrs Saunders, a dour Scot, small, full of energy, and a sharp tongue. She was horrified that I had been left to let myself in. As she made her way down to the basement kitchen, with me following her, I could hear her muttering, 'Nuts, typical, nuts, the lot of them.' She turned on me. 'I warn you, lass, ye'll starve in this mad house if you don't fend for yourself.' She put the kettle on and buttered some scones – I could tell they were home-made – then she said, 'Aye, you'll get used to it, lass, they come and go in this house like a load of gypsies, you never know who you're going to find in the guest room in the morning.' I said that I wouldn't mind at all, but I hoped my parents didn't find out about this sort of Bohemian life, or I would be whipped off back to Wallasey.

Mrs Saunders had a heart of gold and soon became my ally. She made me laugh when she would greet me at breakfast with, 'Well, lass, the gypsies are off again, now *she's* gone away, and so it's you and me feeding the boss.'

On one occasion Mr Renton had brought mackerel for lunch, and Mrs Saunders rounded on him saying, 'And just what am I supposed to do with these withered things?' He grinned at me and said, 'Nothing, I will cook the lunch.' Mrs Saunders raised her hands in horror. 'God bless us and save us, we'll be poisoned.' We were not, of course, but he did make an awful mess in the kitchen, fish scales all over the walls. We watched him attack the fish with a large knife. 'God almighty,' said Mrs Saunders, 'he looks like Sweeney Todd.' I couldn't help laughing. 'You'll no laugh when you've got the belly ache tonight,' she warned.

Mr Renton returned from Iceland the day after I got to London, and I began my lessons. He had married Viscount Lascelles' daughter, Lavinia, which accounted for the phone call from Lady Harewood. Mrs Saunders was right about fending for myself; as regards food, there seemed to be either feast or famine. It soon became clear that these two kind open-hearted people, who had invited me to stay with them, were in some ways no better off than my own parents.

Once when Mrs Renton was going off to Germany to study, Mrs Saunders asked her, 'And what are we supposed to be living on while you're flying your kite in Germany?' Mrs Renton produced a large bunch of green bananas that she had been given and Mrs Saunders threw up her hands. 'Well, thank you very much, my lady. Ye realise that we'll all be swinging from the lamps like monkeys by the time you return!' When we investigated the larder we found a huge box of porridge oats, and Mrs Saunders said, 'Aye, well, that's it, take your pick, lass, it's either the runs or constipation.'

It was a crazy sort of life, but I was happy in it. I don't think I was once homesick, there wasn't time. I worked hard. I learned Mimì in *La Bohème* and the Countess in *Figaro*. I asked Mr Renton if they were dramatic soprano roles, and he laughed and said, 'Someone wants to run before she can walk!' I also learned big chunks of *Ernani* and *Manon* and *Masked Ball*. I did my chores around the house, made the beds, did the ironing and went down the road to the laundrette. The two boys were at school and we only met at half term.

Mr Renton had other pupils beside myself, and the Welsh boy, Trevor. Apart from Trevor, they all seemed wealthy overbearing ladies to my young eyes. I had the feeling that they had nothing better to do, and were just playing at being singers. I remember one lady coming in very early one morning before Mr Renton was up. I told her he was on the phone upstairs and that I would tell him she was here. I rushed up to his bedroom. 'Get up quick, Miss X is here.' He opened a bleary eye and said, 'Oh God, has she got that stinking dog with her?' I told him yes she had, and he told me to buzz off while he got dressed.

The dog was a pest. Mrs Saunders and I would have to 'dog-sit' with it in the kitchen while 'Old Nose-in-the-air' had her lesson. It was Mrs Saunders who gave her the name. Every time its mistress hit a top note, the dog would piddle all over the kitchen floor and Mrs Saunders would spend the lesson hour dashing about the kitchen with a mop and Jeyes' fluid. When Mr Renton came down for coffee after the lesson, Mrs Saunders would say, 'Och, can ye no tell the woman she's a contralto?' Mr Renton asked, 'Why, Mrs S?' 'Och, well, it's only the top notes that upset the creature's water works'. Mr Renton would wink at me and say solemnly, 'Well, Mrs S, if it piddles on the top notes can you imagine what it would do on the bottom ones!' Mrs S would turn to me for the umpteenth time and say, 'I told you, lass, nuts the lots of them!'

In due course, Mrs Renton went to Munich to study (she was also a soprano), and I thought there would only be Mrs Saunders and 'the boss' at home, but Mrs Renton's cousin, Dawn, came to stay. She was Lord Chelmsford's daughter, and had a job in the Palladium pantomime. We became firm friends – she arrived during the banana and porridge era. I often went to her home near Godalming in Surrey for weekends, and had a splendid time. The whole family were very much into show business and seemed always to be putting on some show or other. They were rather like an upper class version of the Hunters, and there were the dogs and the horses, and so I looked forward to these weekends with delight.

Eventually Mr Renton took me to Covent Garden to see *Rigoletto*. This was my first visit and I was enchanted, first by the House itself and then by the singing. We went backstage afterwards to meet the soloists. Gilda was Mattiwilda Dobbs, but I can't remember who the others were. A few weeks later Mr Renton took me to dinner at Lady Sanderson's and I was asked to sing. One of the guests was Norman Tucker, the director of Sadler's Wells, but I didn't know this until after I had sung. He seemed quite pleased and some days later I was asked to go for a stage audition at Sadler's Wells Theatre. I sang 'Porgi amor' from Figaro and 'They call me Mimi'. I thought I had done quite well and Mr Renton was delighted, and so I was content.

About a week later when I was on my knees scrubbing the stove the phone rang. Mr Renton was at the table drinking coffee and Mrs Saunders shouted from upstairs, 'Mr R, Sadler's Wells for you.' When he left the kitchen I remained on the floor with a can of Vim in my hand, and began to pray. Mrs Saunders burst in, 'Och, I don't know why you're praying to get into the theatre, you'll end up nuts like the rest of them.'

When Mr Renton returned he said, 'You have a chorus contract with the Wells starting August 15th.' I could hardly speak for joy. In the background Mrs Saunders was muttering, 'Nuts, she'll be nuts.' I was so happy that I rushed round to her and lifted her up in the air, her little legs were dangling, and she was terrified. 'Put me down, och yer nuts already.' Mr Renton roared with laughter, and to Mrs Saunders' disgust asked me to repeat the display for Mrs Renton when she returned from Munich.

*

I went home for a holiday and to buy some new clothes. My first day with the Wells went without a hitch, although I had not been able to sleep the night before. I was convinced that I would be late, and as a result was far too early and had to go and sit in the little park opposite the theatre.

I met the chorus master and he introduced me to the other new girl, Joan Clarkson, and then showed us round the theatre, took us down to the library to get our scores. 'I hope you are strong girls,' he said. I soon saw the reason for this as I watched the librarian piling up the scores. Marcus Dodds, the chorus master, said that we had two weeks to learn the repertoire. 'Don't worry,' he said. 'There are only twenty-one operas this season!' Joan gave me a kick under the table, and when he was out of earshot said, 'God help us, Hunter.'

I don't know how we did it, but we did learn them all in time. The first one we did was *Tosca*, and the cast was Victoria Elliot, Rowland Jones, Frederick Sharp, Harold Blackburn and John Probyn. Mum came down for the first night and got so excited she ended up with shingles.

*

Then the Renton boys were home from school and so I reluctantly had to find digs. I moved into a boarding house in Wood Green – I was not popular with the landlady, who was highly temperamental and had more than a touch of the Russell of Spring about her. It was a great joy when Dawn moved in with me in time for her stint at the Palladium again; we shared a double room.

I went home for Christmas but my return was delayed as I caught 'flu. But I wrote to the landlady to tell her what train I would catch to London on New Year's Day and when I would get to her house. Unfortunately the train was late, and I got to Wood Green at 5.30 and was greeted frostily. 'Where have *you* been since 1.30?' The landlady didn't believe the train had been held up, and I suggested she phone the station to confirm my story. She went to her room and sulked.

At the end of the following week she got nasty when I offered only to pay her for my share of the room while I was away and not for food. (Dawn had paid for her share of the room and her food.) I maintained that I ought not to have to pay for food I had not eaten; she had not even had to buy any extra food as my father had given her fair warning that I was ill.

The landlady told Equity, and they told her that she had no right to ask me to pay for more than my share of the room. She even told the Wells company manager, and he told her the same as Equity. She was livid, and became even more nasty. Dawn's pantomime finished earlier than some of the operas, so she would wait for me outside the Wood Green Tube station and we would brave the old battle-axe together.

Before the panto season ended the landlady gave us notice to quit, but as luck would have it one of the boys in the chorus was moving to a new flat and so Dawn and I moved into the one he was vacating. It was only a bed-sitter, really, but it was a haven for us. This was in Pembridge Crescent, Notting Hill Gate. What a relief, no more nagging at night, and as Dawn said, 'No more boiled yellow fish with poached eggs slopping around on the top.'

When the pantomime ended in March, Dawn went home and I was left alone for a while, and paid all the rent myself. I had spent too many years as a lonely child to mind. I didn't like the tube journey home late at night, though, especially after one night on the Central Line. I was alone in a compartment after the train left the station at Marble Arch when I was joined by this rather grubby-looking man. He sat across from me and he looked a bit drunk. At the next stop he opened his coat. *Not* a pretty sight! I averted my eyes swiftly. At the next stop, being mine, I got out. I was disturbed when I realised he had also got out. I was petrified when I then realised that he was following me all the way down the road. I did my best not to walk faster and managed to get my keys out of my bag as I was walking. I shot up the steps and, thank God, the key went into the lock without a hitch, as the vile pig followed me up the steps and I literally shut the door in his face. From then on I would always move into another compartment if the one I was in began to empty.

Eventually a new girl joined the chorus; she was from North Wales, and as she had no place to stay I invited her to share the bedsitter with me. It was not a happy period, and I am aware that even today I drive my family mad with my fussy ways and my desire to have the house tidy at all times. But she would have tried the patience of a saint. She would not wash a dish, and would grill her bacon by dangling it in front of the gas fire on a fork to save putting a penny in the gas meter. The result was a greasy hearth. I wouldn't have minded if she'd cleaned it. When I asked her for her share of the rent she was always sixpence or a shilling short, and when she eventually got it all together, she would throw it across the room on to my bed. She seemed to imply that I was cheating her with the rent, so I suggested that on Sundays she should go down for the clean sheets and pay the rent herself. After the first week she resented me having the extra few moments lie-in, so she would 'forget' to bring the clean sheets, so that I would have to go and get them. In the end I asked the landlord to split the rent and give us two rent books, and we would go down on our own. The paying time for the rent was 10 to 12 – and she was always the last to pay every week.

*

In those days the Wells only toured about six weeks a year, and the tour was always at the end of the season. We would do two weeks in Bristol, two in Southsea and two in Bournemouth. There were never any rehearsals those weeks so (with just the operas at night) we would spend all day long on the beach, weather permitting. It was fantastic and I was free of my flat mate into the bargain.

I was with the Wells for two seasons. At the end of the second one, to the dismay of all, we played two weeks in Stockton-on-Tees. No disrespect intended, but Stockton's no substitute for two weeks on the beach at Bournemouth.

I got a letter from Mr Renton, who was now conducting for the Carl Rosa Opera Company, asking if I would go and audition for them. He felt that I was beginning to stagnate in the chorus. The only chance I had been given to show off my voice was as one of the two bridesmaids in *Figaro* (Joan Clarkson was the other). I think that I was the loudest bridesmaid ever, and I also think that Mozart must have turned over in his grave at the sound of an embryonic Brünnhilde singing his delicate music.

I had also been asked to sing the part of 'The Damma' in the second act finale of *Macbeth*. It was performed at a Welfare concert with David Ward, Elizabeth Fretwell and William McAlpine. I shook everyone with my top C at the end, but it had not moved the management into giving me anything further. And so I made the trip, by bus from Stockton-on-Tees, to Newcastle, to audition for the Carl Rosa Opera Company.

CHAPTER SEVEN

Carl Rosa

Mr Renton met me at the stage door of the Theatre Royal, Newcastle-upon-Tyne, and before the audition he said that he felt I would have a better chance in a smaller company, and also that he could resume his coaching and teach me some more roles. We went along to a hall near the Theatre at 3 p.m., and there I met Mrs Phillips and Arthur Hammond, and also the company tenor, Eduardo Asquiz.

I don't remember what I sang and didn't record the items in my diary, but Mrs Phillips and Mr Hammond were enthusiastic. (I learned later that Mrs Phillips was always at auditions.) She promised me the earth, so I handed in my resignation at the Wells, and later discovered that she had sent me a contract for the *chorus*. What a mess I was in – a smaller company and less wages than the Wells and with digs to pay for every week of the tour. After just one week I told myself I had made a grave mistake. Quite apart from the financial aspect, it had all been so civilised at the Wells, with someone to dress you and put on your shoes. Here in the Rosa, if you wanted dressing you did it yourself, and if you were not able to lace up your dress you stood in line and did each other's dresses up. If you needed shoes on stage, you bought them yourself, and the same applied to flowers or jewelry. The only thing the company provided were the costumes.

When I went for my first fitting I was horrified when I was told that the bundles of dirty rags in the corner on the floor were my peasant costumes for *Trovatore*, *Bohème*, *Carmen*, *Cavalleria Rusticana*, *Pagliacci*, etc. They also used some of them when we played the 'tarts' in *Manon*. They stank of BO and could not be washed or cleaned, as they were so old. Every time I wore them I would be haunted by the thought of some long-dead or long-retired chorister leaving behind her body odours for me. (It was this that drove me to my life-long vice of buying endless bottles of perfume.)

The so-called Court costumes for *Manon* and *Tannhäuser* were no better. Also they never fitted. They were all laced up the back or pinned – and woe betide anyone who turned her back on the audience – revealing a wide expanse of knickers and bra.

Some of the theatres we played in were so small that the chorus had to dress in the corridors, taking turns to sit at the one mirror held by another person, and with the wardrobe mistress keeping away peeping Toms by holding up one of the tatty old shawls we had to wear. We had no stage rehearsal before the first night in Ipswich and, as we had been told to 'run on full of enthusiasm', we did so – only to find that the theatre was also used as a cinema and that all the opera sets had been set up in front of the huge screen. We skidded to an abrupt halt to avoid falling into the pit.

The tours were planned in a very awkward way. Dundee one week, then Norwich, and then back up to Aberdeen, then down to Plymouth. The train calls on Sunday were endless. We rehearsed every day as well as the show at night and a matinée on a Saturday. I was convinced I had been mad to listen to Mr Renton and leave the Wells.

I was unable to get digs when playing Stockton-on-Tees and had to stay with friends of my cousin Margaret out in Marton, outside Middlesbrough. I asked to be excused the final off-stage chorus in *Tannhäuser*, so that I could get the last bus from Stockton to Middlesbrough (the last bus went five minutes before the end of the show). They refused, so I had to walk not just from Stockton to Middlesbrough but also from there to Marton. I walked in the pouring rain all the way and got to my friends' house at about 3 a.m. They were worried sick wondering what had happened to me. Next day I had 'flu and was not able to go to the 10.30 rehearsal. The day after I was told to go and see Mrs Phillips and Mr Hammond. Coughing and sneezing, I explained why I had missed one rehearsal and one performance.

'But why did you get digs so far away?'

I told them that all the Stockton digs were full.

'Then you should have got yourself a hotel for the week.'

It was futile to tell them that the wages did not run to hotels or taxis.

We played Liverpool after this and I came home on the Saturday night to find that Mr Renton had been to see my parents and told them that he thought I had lost interest and wasn't trying to get on. They were upset, and I was livid, and when I saw him the following week in Southsea, I told him so. I also said that no one who wasn't dedicated to their art would tolerate such poor working conditions and poor pay. I did however admit that I *had* lost interest in going every week to ask Mrs Phillips for parts; she would smile sweetly and say, 'Oh yes, you can sing so-and-so next tour.' Eventually I realised she was saying the same thing to all the young singers and offering them all the same roles. She would let someone do a small role for a few performances and then take it off them, saying they were no good at it, and then give it to some new singer. If you eventually made friends with the new singer you would find that she had agreed to a fee for the role that was perhaps two shillings less than you had been doing it for.

*

My outburst at Mr Renton may have made him think, for on the next tour I was asked to sing Inez in *Trovatore*, and I was given five shillings a week extra. I still had to buy my own handkerchief to weep into and my own jewelry. My first Leonora was a darling. Her name was Ruth Packer. Waiting to go into the first rehearsal in Nottingham she said, 'There are one or two things you should know, dear. Whatever you do, don't let Mr Hammond intimidate you.' I assured her I wouldn't and she replied, 'Don't be too sure, he'll try it on, and if I think he's wrong I'll stick up for you.'

Ruth Packer was right. He was a real dragon, and all the choristers avoided him. Soon after the start of the rehearsal he tried it on and I found tears prickling the back of my eyes and, as we went to the other side of the room to do the scene again, Ruth said between clenched teeth, 'If you cry in front of him, I shall disown you.'

After the rehearsal she took me for a cup of coffee and said, 'You're a generous artiste to work with, you take care not to upstage me.' I told her that I didn't know what she meant. She was surprised, and said, 'Oh my darling, not all your leading ladies will be so kind,' and she went on to explain the meaning of upstaging. It seemed that when you were singing a line to anyone else on the stage, most of the time you would place yourself downstage of the other singer, so that he or she could sing facing the front. However, if you wanted to make the other singer's voice inaudible, you would deliberately stand upstage on him so the other singer would have to sing his line to you with his back to the audience. Ruth said, 'With your voice, my dear, you'll find a great many of your fellow singers trying to do this to you, so beware . . .' This was one of many lessons she taught me. She did not sing all the *Trovatores*; she came out of them eventually, so she could do *Tannhäuser*. And indeed her successor *did* try to upstage me but, thanks to Ruth she did not succeed.

I was then asked to sing Frasquita in *Carmen*. I loved that role, all those top Cs. My first Inez was at the Alhambra Theatre in Bradford and the first Frasquita in the De Montfort Hall in Leicester. Other sopranos came in and out of the company and were given my two small but precious roles to do; then they would make the mistake of asking either for another role or more cash, and I would get my roles back again.

*

There were long periods of 'resting' between tours when I would wait at home for Mrs Phillips to write and say that a new tour had been arranged. Mr Renton still thought I had lost interest, since I now had a boyfriend. Little did he know that it was only the boyfriend's good sense that kept me in the Rosa – every time I swore that I was leaving, John would say, 'Oh no, Rita, don't, Mr Renton can teach you so much if you stay.

John Darnley-Thomas had joined the company on the same day as I had, along with three others, Norma Kubel and Antonina Child, both sopranos, and a Welsh baritone, Adamo Paccini. New people always stick together and we used to sit in coffee bars talking of our hopes and plans for the future.

It wasn't love at first sight with John and me, not by any means. In fact John's first impression of me was that I was so sure of myself that I must have been married and perhaps divorced. It also annoyed him that, whenever he mentioned a certain aria or a way of singing it, I would say, 'Oh, I know that,' and, 'I can sing it.' He said point blank that it was not possible for any *one* voice to be able to sing so many different roles. I was becoming fed up with this know-all Welshman and more or less challenged him to a sort of 'duel of voices' – to the delight of Norma, Nina and Adamo. Nina said that she would play the piano for us, and so we booked a hall for the afternoon.

'Right,' said John, 'I've just sung the Turiddu in North Wales, and even *you* can't kid me about that opera. Let's sing the duet.' I said, 'No, let me first sing that aria and the duet with the baritone and then we'll sing the duet.' John's eyes narrowed and he frowned (in a way I now recognise as a danger signal!) He was furious at my cheek. Before he could say a word I plonked the music of 'In questa reggia' on the piano and I launched into it with all the abandon of youth. His face went white and he picked up his music and left the room without a word, and didn't speak to me for days.

My first reaction was, Well, you asked for it, sulk if you want to. I did not know then how passionate was his love of opera and voices. I know now that he spurned all the advances of the girls in Wales, saying to them and his family that if and when he got married, it would be to the finest soprano in the world. He also said that if he didn't find one to his standards, he would stay single. Why didn't I realise that I would have trouble with this know-all Welshman one day?

It was many years before I found out from John just how he really felt on that day and the week that followed, and so the next few paragraphs are really John's story.

Adamo Paccini, the baritone who had sung the Alfio duet with me, was sharing a room with John. After he had sung the duet he had left the hall, and so had not heard John and me sing together, nor had he heard me sing the *Turandot* aria. Adamo and John had both been taught by the same man, Redvers Llewellyn.

After the 'duel of voices' John went home to his digs, and lay down on his bed, not even getting up when Adamo came in.

'What's up with you, boyo?'

'Oh, just thinking,' said John.

Half an hour passed and then Adamo said, 'Something must be wrong, not like you to be so quiet, boy.'

John sat up and said, 'I've just heard the best soprano voice ever.'

Adamo said, 'Don't be so daft, man.'

John replied, 'True, Adamo, but she should never be in the chorus, it's criminal.' Adamo was quiet for a moment and then said, 'You sure, boy?' John said, 'Not sure, boy, I'm bloody certain.'

Adamo replied, 'Well if you think that, John boy, it's good enough for me.'

John said, 'Well there's only one man to teach her and that's Redvers.' Adamo asked John what he was going to do and John said, 'Nothing, what can I do, she knows it all, or so she thinks.'

John also told me that his first reaction that I could be the finest in the world was quickly followed by the thought that he wasn't sure if he liked me enough as a person to marry me. But he knew I needed someone to back me up when I made my future assaults on the operatic mountains and someone to stop me burning myself up too soon, in an attempt to make up for the time I thought I had lost. Lost time indeed! I was only twenty-two. Thank God I didn't know that my career wouldn't really take off till I was thirty-six, or I would have packed it in there and then. And if John had known that he might not have been so interested either.

Also in his mind was the thought that *if* we married and I was the great voice of his dreams, then there would only be room in our lives for one career, and if he made the sacrifice would I ever come off my high horse to take his advice and guidance over the years? Poor John, there was I thinking he was sulking, and in truth he was making the most important decision of his life and mine.

My next reaction was 'How dare he ignore me?' Then I became desperate for his opinion of my voice, and somewhere in the back of my mind must have been the thought that he knew what he was talking about. This was confirmed when one morning I had coffee with a pal of his, Bill McGovern. I poured out my troubles to him and he said, 'Well, it would do you no harm to listen to him.' I replied that I would not now mind listening to him, but the Welshman was not now talking to me. Bill laughed and said, 'Oh, the Welsh are all the same, love, give him time to lick his wounds and he'll come round.'

I gave him two days and then I began to hang around the stage door to see if I could get him to walk me home at night, but he would come out of the stage door, and give me a curt nod and say, 'I'm going for a pint,' and leave me with my mouth open. Norma came past one night and said, 'What are you hanging around for? Lord Darnley's gone.'

'I know,' I said, seething with frustration.

'Well, what are you waiting for? I'm going in there for a shandy, why don't you come?'

I was horrified. I'd never been in a pub. But in desperation I threw caution to the winds.

John looked none too pleased when I walked into the bar, but after I had bought him two pints he became less frosty.

We talked about the company, his love of golf. How were his digs? 'Fine.' We got on to the subject of voices *very* slowly, and he agreed, albeit grudgingly, that I had in some ways proved my point. I was able to sing *Turandot* and *Ernani*'s soprano arias with equal aplomb, and throw in the soprano *Ballo* aria and 'Una voce poco fa' for good measure. But he felt that I needed to apply a bit more finesse and less brute force. This infuriated me, but I held my tongue, and got him to make a date for coffee the next day.

Over the top of his head I saw Bill McGovern give me the thumbs-up sign.

Next day we met at the stage door and walked down to the coffee shop. He began making conditions at once. 'I will meet you for coffee tomorrow, but you'll have to learn the *Otello* love duet by next week.' I thought to myself, 'Bloody Welshman,' but gave him an angelic smile, and asked if I could borrow his score.

The coffee dates increased. It was always me who paid. I casually mentioned this one morning and he said, 'Not good for me, coffee. Rather have a beer.' We adjourned to the pub. (Not just a bloody Welshman but a crafty one into the bargain.) He eventually began to walk me home at night, and we went to the studios every afternoon where we would sing and argue about singing. Everyone in the company at this point was certain we were having a wild affair, since we were together so much. What a laugh. He never even helped me off a bus, or carried my case, or held my arm, and when I told him he should walk on the outside, he said, 'No fear, if your legs get splashed, you only have to wash the nylons, but I would have to get my trousers cleaned.' So much for romance.

After two months, he still hadn't kissed me and I realised that I liked this bloody Welshman a lot, and that I wanted him to kiss me. I became depressed, and my pals in the company began to make sly remarks about 'hot-blooded Welshmen'. After a day of nods and knowing looks, I blurted out to John's pal, Dave, that they could stop winking and nudging as John had not yet even kissed me!

Dave was surprised. 'Well, I bet he kisses you tonight,' he said.

'He never will.'

Dave said, 'I bet you half-a-crown he will.'

'Right, you're on.'

After the opera John walked me home as usual. At the gate of my digs we stood as usual to chat, and we heard a giggle from over the road, and then a snort of laugher. John coughed, and shyly touched my arm, sighed deeply, and said in a resigned voice, 'Oh well, here goes.' He then grabbed me by the shoulders and kissed me on the lips, accompanied by cheers from Dave and a friend who had been hiding in a shop doorway.

John, highly embarrassed, said, 'So long,' and fled. I staggered into the digs in a daze, heart thumping, legs like jelly. I was in love . . . and do you know, dear readers, I love that bloody Welshman just as much if not more twenty-eight years later.

The next morning Dave was waiting for me at the door of the rehearsal rooms holding his hand out for half-a-crown. I paid him. And who should come next through the door, and also pay Dave half-a-crown. That's right. The crafty Dave had bet John that I would not let him kiss me. Knowing John as I do now, there was no way he was going to pass up a chance of winning 2/6d, even if it did signal the end of his bachelorhood.

John lost the bet, and so did I, but we won each other. We courted for six years (he *was* making sure, wasn't he!). He showed no inclination to wed, and we were with the Rosa for five of those years. We spent more time on the dole than on the tour, but we remained loyal to the Rosa until it folded in 1958.

*

One Christmas I was to sing in St Luke's Hall for the Poulton Old Age Pensioners' party, of which my Dad was the secretary. John was 'resting', and he wrote to say he would come up to Wallasey and bring his tape recorder to make a recording of the concert. The time I had dreaded for years had arrived – I was bringing what I hoped was my future husband to meet my parents, and I feared the opposition.

When I told them he would be with us in three days, the balloon went up. They gave an emphatic no. And when I told them I couldn't stop him now as there was no time, they countered with 'Whatever has to be done for him during his stay, you do it yourself, we are having nothing to do with it.'

So I cleaned out the back bedroom and made up his bed. I bought food which I thought he would like out of my own pocket. His train was due at Birkenhead at 6 a.m. and, as I had no alarm clock I lay awake all night, as I did not want him knocking at the front door and waking my parents. I needed to prepare him for his frosty reception.

At 5.30 a.m. I sat myself in the front room to wait. It was freezing cold. At 7 a.m. I saw him staggering up the street under the weight of an enormous tape recorder. He had had to walk all the way from Birkenhead with it.

While I made him tea and toast, I told him about the cold war. John wasn't in the least bit worried. We talked in whispers for about an hour and then downstairs came Dad, clearly wanting to treat John in a kindly way, but having been brainwashed by Mum. Dad made their tea and toast and then my mother came into the kitchen. She sat down at the table with her back to John and me, and despite our repeated attempts, she would not talk to John at all. When I went upstairs to dress, John went into the street to have a cigarette. We then went for a bus ride.

When we returned, my mother was in the back garden talking over the wall to Nellie. John opened the tape recorder and began to play a few things and to show me how he would use it that night at the concert. I told him to ask Dad the best place to put it for sound, and so when my Mum came in John asked her where Dad was, and she said, 'In the lavatory,' and sat down to knit. Dad came in and soon he and John were deep in conversation. John recorded Dad's voice and Mum pricked up her ears. 'That's you, Charlie,' she said. John said, 'Yes, it is, Mrs Hunter, and tonight I'm going to make a recording of Rita singing at the concert.'

That did it. 'Is that what you've come for, son?'

'Yes, from now on I am going to record her every time she sings, she's the greatest.'

Mum flew to the kitchen and put the kettle on for a cup of tea, dashed into the yard to tell Nellie all about it. I was up in my room changing and I heard her say to Nellie, 'Well at least he thinks she's great and he's not talking of bloody wedding bells.'

I smiled to myself and thought, Well he might not be talking of wedding bells, Lucy Hunter, but they are very much on your daughter's mind.

And from then on John could do no wrong in my parents' eyes. And the tape recorder, that turned the tide, I have kept to this day.

*

That evening, after the concert, we were having our usual family gathering round a pot of tea and one of Mum's ham pies. I sat there watching Mum fuss round John with the tea, and Dad sat listening to the tape, with Nellie and Ruth adoring my Welshman.

I suddenly felt at peace with the world. No more fearing to get into hot water for bringing a man home. The storm tossed-ship had at last found a quiet harbour.

I got up from the table and surveyed the scene. I was getting parts at last, small ones to be sure, but they were solo parts, and with Mum and Dad behind me and John at my side to guide me, I felt all was right with the world. There were many months, indeed years, ahead of slogging on tour, but I didn't know this then, and the following day down by the seashore, John actually told me he loved me. I felt I had got one of his toes on the road up the aisle. My cup of joy was running over.

CHAPTER EIGHT

Rejoicing, Not Very Greatly!

That Christmas John and I began our 'love-letter period'. Neither of us had phones, and we wrote to each other twice a day, some of them fifteen and twenty pages long. (I had a little peep at them when we were home in England last and, believe me, they would scorch the paint off the wall!)

He got his mother to make my Christmas present: a most beautiful royal blue brocade dressing gown, with a black velvet collar – right out of a Hollywood movie. I felt like the cats' whiskers.

It was now 1958 and we sat in our respective homes and waited for the letter telling us that another tour had been planned for the Carl Rosa company. It would also mean that we would be together again. Instead we were told that the Carl Rosa was no more.

*

We were beside ourselves with worry – not just for where the next pay packet was coming from, but how were we to get together again. In the spring we heard that the Carl Rosa would go out again, but under new management, and with the name of 'Touring Opera 58'. We didn't care what the company was called, all that mattered was that we had a job, and would be together. The director of the new company was Humphrey Procter-Gregg. The first part of the season was more or less routine, but before the end of the first tour Mr Procter-Gregg called me in to see him – we were in Brighton and it was Friday the 13th – and told me they were taking me out of the chorus. I was to be made a junior principal. I was twenty-five.

John was waiting outside the theatre for me; we had been afraid that they might have taken away my small roles or worse, the sack. We were overjoyed and the first thing we did was send a telegram to my parents telling them the news. It was then we discovered the date was the 13th, so from then on we called it our lucky number.

The roles I was to do were much the same as before, the only real difference being that I did not have to work in the chorus on the other nights of the week.

By this time our financial state was desperate; the price of digs was going up but the wages never seemed to. And so the few extra pounds I got as a junior principal made us feel that we were 'in God's pocket'.

But our joy was short-lived. Touring Opera 58 did not last much longer than the year it was named after. Again we went home to wait for the postman to bring us news of more work. That summer I went to stay at John's home in South Wales, and we spent the time going for long walks, sometimes to his sister's for the evening. On one occasion we went for a walk around the Aberdare golf course. There didn't seem any place to sit down for a cuddle and, as it was getting a bit windy, we went down into a bunker by the eighteenth hole. It takes more than damp sand to put a Welshman off. But we had not been there more than two minutes when we were rudely disturbed by an inquisitive sheep, who popped its head over the bunker and gave a loud Baaah. I burst out laughing. We stood up and John said, 'Even the sheep are not the same as they used to be' – and that was the end of romance at the eighteenth hole.

After the holiday we were loath to part, and John came on the train from Aberdare as far as Pontypool Road station, where I had to change trains. I wrote to him as soon as I got to bed that night. A few days later I received a letter from London to say that the Carl Rosa company were more or less being taken in by the Sadler's Wells Opera. Rather like orphans of the storm. I thought that in my case it would be a sort of 'Ritorna vincitor', since I had reached the status of junior principal with Touring Opera 58 and I assumed that I would automatically be hired as a junior principal with the Wells.

But my assumptions were wrong. I was put on a study grant – the princely sum of four pounds a week to live on. I had rented a room over a baker's shop, owned by a friend of one of the chorus, and the cost of the room was £3.10s a week. On top of this I had to feed shillings in the gas and electric meters. I was having lessons from Clive Carey who lived in West London. So by the time I had paid my fares from Islington, there wasn't much cash left for food. I went to see Stephen Arlen and explained my situation, and from then on he gave me five pounds a week.

There were now two companies, 'S' company which stayed in London, and 'T' company which spent the whole time on tour. Needless to say John was in the company which toured all the time.

After a few months I was sent to audition in Mayfair, and won a £1,000 grant from The Countess of Munster Trust. I thought that all my troubles were over, but I never saw a penny of the cash. Before the cheque came, I was told to choose a teacher to study with. I was fed up. I didn't want a teacher, I wanted a chance to sing a really good role to show what I could do, but even my little roles were now all given to other singers who were working in the two companies.

John scrounged a lift from a pal and came to London for the weekend so that we could discuss this new turn of events. After he had paid his share of the petrol he couldn't afford a hotel, so we shared the bed-sitter. At John's suggestion I phoned Redvers Llewellyn and he said to try Eva Turner. This suited me, as Edwin Francis had talked a great deal about her and had drummed the Eva Turner legend into my young head. I had a couple of her recordings, and also had pictures of her as Turandot stuck up in my room.

And so I was taken by Edward Renton and Norman Tucker to sing for the great lady. Edward played the piano, and Miss Turner sat in the hall outside with Mr Tucker, so we were not able to see her reactions to my singing. When I had finished, I heard her say grandly, 'Norman dear, this girl I *will* teach'.

Miss Turner duly got the thousand pounds and I got my lessons.

*

The Wells company manager called me one day and said they needed a cover for Sheila Rex in *Figaro*, for the role of Marcellina to be exact. I wasn't too pleased about it: it was mostly ensemble singing, and low to boot. There was the aria in the last act of course, but it wasn't till Sir Charles Mackerras conducted it some years later that I actually got to do that, and then he wrote in a high 'D' to make it more interesting for me.

Sheila, unlike most of the ladies I had covered, actually got sick one night; although I knew the role musically I had not seen this production and so I was given a swift lesson in how to play old ladies, by the producer John Donaldson. Susanna was Marian Studholme, and for our first act duet my production instructions consisted of 'Go *roond* the chair' (John was a Scot). 'That's it, dearie, keep going rooond the chair.' This went on for two hours and then I was packed off on the afternoon train to Liverpool, where I was to sing Marcellina that night. When I got to the theatre, my heart sank as I saw the costume. It was black, and padded all over, and padded really well on the behind, something I felt that I could well do without. The wig was grey, and I had to line my face, and the more lines I put on the more depressed I became. I was even stupid enough to do it well. My reviews were fantastic . . . the following year when the opera came back into repertoire I realised to my endless dismay that the hateful role was mine for ever. But I had to admit that whenever I sang it the extra ten pounds in my pay packet were very welcome – beggars can't be choosers.

The company then added insult to injury by giving me a role I had sung with the Rosa, Berta in *The Barber of Seville*. However, this was a new production and at least I didn't have to wear smelly old costumes. It was with these two roles that I began my years of dissatisfaction, singing things that were either mezzo or so low that they might have been mezzo anyway. Even Inez in *Trovatore* can be sung by a soprano or a mezzo and, after standing respectfully behind a long line of Leonoras trying to sing the role, I seethed inwardly knowing full well that I could sing it better.

I suppose that the years spent singing these low roles preserved the top of my voice, although at the time I could not see it that way.

They asked me to understudy Musetta in *La Bohème*. There seemed to be thousands of performances and, fit though Elizabeth Vaughan seemed to be, I hoped that at some point on that fourteen-week tour she might go down with something or other. The company promised that they would let me do it half-way through the tour. That point came, and with it another Musetta – but not me.

Tom Hammond taught me the role of Musetta; he was a great coach and also a champion of mine. He always called me 'the diva'. 'And how is the diva today?' he would say when we met. This got up a lot of folk's noses as, up to that point, I had not sung a major role, but from our first meeting to the day he died I was always 'the diva' with Tom.

I also worked on Musetta with Eva Turner. Then one day out of the blue the Wells said I could sing the last Musetta of the season. It was my first major role. It was a 'Youth and Music' performance, so there were no critics at my debut.

John Matheson conducted and Marcel was the Australian baritone Neil Easton. As he hugged his Musetta at the end of the Waltz Song, we were both delighted to have a long and enthusiastic reception from the public. They even cheered. John was thrilled for me, and indeed we both thought that now at last something would happen.

The next morning was pay day so I had to go to the theatre to get my five pounds, plus the extra for Musetta. I saw Tom Hammond who had been out of town the night before and had therefore not been at the opera.

'Well, how did the diva get on last night?'

I told him of my success. He threw his arms in the air and said, 'Of course you were a success. I told them you would be, but no one takes any notice of me anyway. The fools are all deaf in this company.' And off he stormed.

I was amazed by this outburst from this usually quiet man. It was then I realized for the first time how much opposition there was for me to overcome. It wasn't just *me* against the management but management against management.

I always loved working with Tom, he gave me confidence. It was all well and good John saying I was marvellous – he loved me, and maybe love is blind – but Tom was management. I remember Tom saying to me at a coaching for *Götterdämmerung*. 'For goodness' sake, girl, sing it, don't tickle it!' After I made my debut as Brünnhilde, he always greeted me with a shout across the street of 'Ho yo to ho'. There must have been more than one person in St Martin's Lane alarmed by this dapper man calling the battle-cry over the traffic, not to mention the full-throated reply from me! Darling Tom, how I miss you. Even though I am thirteen thousand miles away, I would have loved to have worked on Abigaille and Lady Macbeth and Norma with you.

The afternoon after the evening I had sung Musetta for the first time I went to Eva for my lesson. I must have sung the dreaded 'Rejoice' from *Messiah* well, as she allowed me to sing Musetta's Waltz Song. When I had finished, she closed the lid of the piano and said, 'My dear, you have no idea of this role, you'll never be able to do it justice.' I did not dare to tell her that I had sung it the night before and that the audience had actually cheered.

*

John had gone off on a fourteen-week tour with the Wells, and I was finding it difficult to manage on my five pounds a week, even with the odd extra Berta and Marcellina fee to help out. The fares to Eva Turner cost quite a bit: often I had to walk part of the way there and, unless it was wet, I nearly always walked home. Eva knew nothing of this and I was hurt when she asked me why I always wore the same red dress. I told her the truth, that it was my best dress and the only one I had bought from a shop (the others I had made myself). She went on about how divas should dress, so I explained that it had been impossible to get a good wardrobe together from the poor pay in the Rosa (often inter-rupted by long periods on the dole). I could see that my story, true though it was, was not impressing her. I still wore the red dress to some lessons and although she looked at it frostily she never commented on it again. She did, however, rebuke me for walking to my lessons. 'If you can't afford the fare all the way, then please walk home, that way you will at least have the energy needed to sing.' I had to agree with her on that point, and I began to wish that I could find some clubs to sing in, as in days gone by. I even contemplated going to Merseyside at weekends to do the clubs, but anything I earned would be eaten up in fares.

The owner of the flat I was living in knew how pushed I was for cash and at the end of the day she would leave a little bag of reject cakes on the stairs for me.

This came to my mind years later when I gave an interview to the *Evening Standard*. I asked John to go and buy bread for sandwiches and, as there was no bread in the shop, he brought home some cream cakes, which John and our daughter, Mair-wyn, and the interviewer, Sydney Edwards, ate. I had none as they were busy taking photographs, but to my fury the headline of the article read 'The Cream Bun Diva', quoting Mr Edwards saying that I used to eat them by the dozen to keep up my weight for singing. If he had only known, it was years before I could face a cake after all those rejects of Lottie's. I protested to the Wells' press office about this article and when Sydney Edwards asked if he could interview me again in New York, I especially asked John not to offer him anything, least of all a drink, or I would surely be described as an alcoholic.

*

John and I often went to lunch on Sundays with Dave (the one who had organised our first kiss). His wife, Kath, was a marvel-lous cook. She and Dave called one night to see me in my little attic over the bakers' shop, and as their visit was unexpected and it was the day before payday I had nothing to offer them. I had also run out of coins for the gas and electricity. I was sitting in the dark and Dave's language, as he stood at the top of the stairs, was colourful. 'Christ, Hunter, even . . . Mimì had a bloody candle!'

Kath produced coins for the meter and Dave went out to get fish and chips. Kath said, 'Why didn't you tell us?'

'Oh hell,' I said, 'I'm okay, anyway they say you have to suffer for your art.'

Dave exploded again. 'Bugger that, you can't sing on empty guts.' Every Friday from then on either Dave or Kath called to see me with a little box of groceries, with the addition of perhaps a lipstick or a box of powder or nail varnish from Kath who worked in a chemist's. These little gifts were a godsend and – though I thanked them profusely at the time – I take this opportunity to say a second heartfelt thank you.

I told John about this, and my other anxieties about Eva, when he came home one weekend. He did not often get angry, but when he did he was the archetypal Welsh minister, foaming fire and brimstone. This time he was furious. 'That's it,' he said, 'that's what God put me on the earth for, I knew it would come to this.'

For one glorious moment I thought he was going to propose. He sat down eventually, tired out by his outburst. I did not really understand what he was getting at, until a few days later when his next love letter came with thirty shillings enclosed to pay half of the rent. When the tour came to an end three weeks later he moved in with me, and paid all the rent. The next thing he did was to send me to buy a new dress so that I would not offend Eva any more with the eternal red dress.

It was a long time before my parents knew that we were living together, but the company knew, and John and I didn't care. We were in love and to hell with convention. When my parents did find out they didn't say a word; perhaps they knew it was John's way of helping me to succeed, for if it hadn't been for his intervention at this point, I would have had to give up and go home. I dare say that when my parents did discover that we were living together there were many pots of tea brewed, and heated conversations over the garden wall.

One day while I was cleaning I noticed a brownish-black insect on the draining board and, though squeamish, I plucked up courage to kill it. I have always detested creepy-crawlies (it's the only thing I have against Australia). The smell was repulsive and I mentioned it to John when he came home. His face fell.

'I thought so,' he said. 'Bugs.'

I laughed and said, 'Well of course, all insects are bugs.'

'No, Rit, bach – bed-bugs!'

I didn't know what he was talking about, but then we went into the bedroom and he moved aside one of the pictures on the wall. The creatures ran all over the place, thousands of them, or so it seemed.

I said right away, 'We'll move.' It took several months to find another flat; it had to be somewhere where I didn't have to produce a marriage certificate. Eventually I found a place over an engravers' shop in Arlington Way, a stone's throw from the bakery. I hoped that the walk would be too far for the ever-growing army of bed-bugs.

John was again on tour, so one Saturday I phoned for a taxi, and put all our things into it, and moved us round the corner.

*

My lessons with Eva were becoming a nightmare. She somehow had the effect of making me feel less than the dust, and I had to fight back the tears – it's not easy to sing with a lump in your throat. I discovered that most of her pupils had to learn to sing the dreaded 'Rejoice' no matter what sex or what voice. I hated the wretched aria. One day Eva said to me, 'Don't rush off, dear, I have someone I want you to hear.' I was surprised that she should be interested in my opinion. A young girl of no more than sixteen or seventeen came in and when Eva introduced her to me, she said, 'Oh, Miss Hunter, I'm a fan of yours. I heard you sing the other evening, and you were smashing.'

Eva then told the girl to sing the inevitable 'Rejoice' – she had a sweet voice, not much body, but she was still very young. At the end of the aria, Eva turned to me and said, 'There you are, dear, that's how you should sing it.'

I tried to ignore the fact that Eva might be trying to take me down a peg or two; I also understood that maybe the lighter voice was more suited to that aria. But I was sorry for the girl, she was so embarrassed. As Eva bustled past us to unlock the door, the girl whispered to me, 'Oh, Miss Hunter, I'm so sorry. I had no idea she would say that.'

I wanted to stop going for my lessons. Eva had much to impart to some singers, but I felt she was doing nothing for me. Sometimes I felt I was going to choke when she would make me sing a scale of up to top B and C on the vowel of EEEEh. And there was certainly a clash of personalities! Edwin Francis had brought me up on the *bel canto* method. I don't know if Eva had told him she was also teaching that method, but it bore no resemblance to it that I could see, yet she and Edwin were old friends. So I wasn't able to explain my disappointment to Edwin, who had taught me to believe that singing was a joyous thing, but my lesson days were full of foreboding and I failed to see how I could learn anything when I was so unhappy.

Although I wanted to discontinue my lessons, I was trapped. I had won the £1,000 which had to be spent on lessons and would be paid only so long as I went to Eva, as would the £5 grant from the Wells.

John was by now in London for a time, and had to put up with my moans and groans about Eva. He began to come with me to my lessons, but he was not allowed in the house so he used to stand in the street.

CHAPTER NINE

Wedding Bells

John begged me to go to his teacher, Redvers Llewellyn. I hesitated. I had admired Eva Turner so much that I felt like a traitor even to think that her teaching wasn't right for me. She had been a great help to Amy Shuard. I wouldn't agree to leave her but I did allow John to take me to see Redvers at his home in Port Talbot, South Wales.

When I had sung for him he said, 'Very nice bach, but no feeling, try it this way.' After about ten minutes, I knew that this was what I had been looking for, that this way my voice would expand and get rounder. A letter was waiting for me in London from the Trust offering me a further £1,000 for lessons. I asked Stephen Arlen if I could use it for lessons with Redvers Llewellyn, and explained my reasons. Redvers taught at the Aberystwyth college but his wife said I could stay with them, so I could work with him every Saturday and Sunday. Stephen shook his head and said it was not possible but gave no further reason.

So I gritted my teeth and refused the further grant.

I shall always remember Eva's last words to me. 'My dear, you will never make a singer, you will have to scrub floors for a living.'

And the funny thing is that I *was* scrubbing the floor when my contract from the Metropolitan Opera New York came through the letter box. After I had received my CBE from the Queen a reporter asked me, 'Has it made any difference to your life being a Commander of the British Empire, Miss Hunter?' I told him, 'No, dear, they still let me scrub the floors.'

*

John said he would pay my fares to Wales every weekend, and I could use my five pounds from the Wells to pay Redvers for the lessons. We put this to Redvers and he was kind enough to teach me for the whole weekend for just five pounds.

In those days Elizabeth Fretwell, the Australian soprano, was the leading star of Sadler's Wells and the company had scheduled *Dutchman* and *Ariadne*, both of which she was to sing. However, when the point in the season came when she would have to sing two Sentas and two Ariadnes in a week, even the formidable Elizabeth said, 'No thank you', so I was asked to sing the two *Dutchmans* each week.

I fled to Wales to tell Redvers the news, and to work on the role with him. I had a problem on one note in Act Two and Redvers said, 'Aye, aye, bach, don't panic, I will just write a little thing above the note in faint pencil so no one will ever know what it means except you and me.' I bent over the piano and saw that he had put a very small 'D.J.'. I asked him what it meant. He laughed and said, 'Drop your bloody jaw.' It seemed too easy, but I tried it and the note came out like a shot from a gun. I was delighted, and Redvers said, 'Well now you see, Rita bach, if you remember that little tip all the time you are singing that's all there is to it really.' He was right, and I have based my technique on those two little initials.

I travelled to Wales every Friday afternoon and Redvers would meet me at the station, with the words, 'Well bach, what have those buggers at the Wells been doing to you this week?' We worked all day Saturday and Sunday and then I would travel back overnight. What journeys they were, the train seemed to stop at every telegraph pole. Every penny for the extra performances went on fares and lessons. But what dividends it has paid me!

My Senta went well. My Dutchman was my darling David Ward, and Erich was Alberto Remedios (our first opera together). I had lots of lovely notices, and was so happy to be singing a real soprano role at last, though I still had to sing mezzo roles on the other nights of the week. My first Sentas were the first time I had any real press coverage. I would rush out to buy the newspapers, and the Welsh tenor Robert Thomas said to John, 'Take my advice, John boy, don't let her keep reading the press, they can give you such a complex.'

I kept on reading them and kept all of them, good or bad. But one of them upset me a great deal. 'If Miss Hunter persists in singing her top notes with such abandon she won't have a voice at all in two years.' I am glad that I made a point of keeping that one. Thirty years later I still have my voice, and the review had a place of honour on my toilet wall.

*

I discovered I would be on the next tour full time, singing Senta, Marcellina in *Figaro*, and Berta in *The Barber of Seville*. John's half of the company was also on the tour and he suddenly became prudish and would not let me book a double-room. I pointed out that everyone knew we were living together and we would be laughed at taking two rooms, but he refused to change his mind. That weekend when he telephoned I said, 'You know that two rooms are more expensive than one?' He groaned. (There is only one person meaner than a Scotsman and that's a Welshman.)

'Will you be home the weekend of the 9th December?' I asked.
'Why?'
'We're getting married, that's why!'

There was a short silence, then I heard him sigh, 'Oh well, might as well I suppose.'

I was over the moon. How easy it had been. I had expected him to protest, and I could have kicked myself for not asking him sooner.

I had three and a half weeks, just enough time for the banns to be read. I asked Harry Blackburn where I could get the rings – he always seemed to know men with things that had fallen off the back of lorries. He sent me to a little house at the back of Leather Lane market. A strange little man opened the door, and I said, 'Harry sent me.' He showed me into the front room, and brought out a box full of all sizes of wedding rings; they looked like brass to me. I chose two rings – yes, my bloody Welshman had even said he would also wear one. The man went off to the back room and after a short while returned with the now sparkling rings, and I could see that they were what I had asked for, 22 carat for me and 18 carat for John. I walked home on air clutching my treasure.

I had told John that I would not be married in white, but on the quiet I scoured Oxford Street for the dress and eventually got the London Co-op to make one to measure. I also bought a little hat, but even my boldness would not let a non-virgin wear a veil. I had intended to go home to Wallasey for the ceremony but John's mother wanted the wedding to be in Wales. I demurred as I had always understood the girl should be married in her home church, but his mother wrote again to say what a wonderful wedding she would give us. I didn't doubt this, and began to weaken, but then my parents got upset, so to save any further family feuds I booked the wedding at the Finsbury Town Hall, just down the road from Sadler's Wells, on December 9th 1960 at 11 a.m. I informed both lots of parents that they would have to travel to London. Mum and Dad were to stay the night in our flat, and I booked John's parents into a hotel near Kings Cross. The family in Wales were not happy about any of this, and his two sisters were hurt that they could not be there. However, when the list of performances came out it was clear that we could not have gone to Wales *or* Wallasey, as I had to sing Inez in *Trovatore* the night before the wedding and we were both required to work on the Monday following. In fact they had given me a rehearsal on the morning of the wedding. So I went to ask the company manager, Jack Wright, if I could have the day off. He said, 'Well, it's a Sitzprobe of *Figaro* starting at 10 a.m. You could do the first act duet and then slip down the road to the town hall and be back in time for the second act finale!'

I looked at him to see if he was having me on. He wasn't. He meant it. I said, 'Jack, have you no romance in your soul?'

He replied, 'Oh all right, but don't you dare ask any of the cast or the chorus to the wedding.'

I didn't, but, as we lived just a few yards from the stage door and the reception was in the flat, when they had the morning coffee break, they all popped in for a drink – and I am afraid they stayed. The principals, too, began to leave the rehearsal at noon and the rehearsal was abandoned. Dear Jack Wright – I doubt if he ever forgave me.

After my parents had left to get the overnight bus back to Liverpool, John took his father for a drink, and I sat in my wedding dress chatting to his mother. The last train to Wales went at midnight and, when there was no sign of them leaving at 11 p.m., I began to get a bit worried. Finally John sent for a taxi for them and they left the flat at 11.35. As soon as they had gone John leapt into bed, but I wouldn't even get undressed until I was certain not only that the last train had gone but that I had given them time enough to miss it and return to the flat. Eventually I took off my wedding dress, and put on my new baby-doll nightie and stood in the middle of the room waiting for Romeo to tell me how sexy I looked. But true to form he said, 'Bloody hell, Rit, get into bed, you'll get your death of cold standing there in that bloody thing!' Well, it was December.

The morning after the wedding the blushing bride had to face the frightful mess from the reception, not only in the flat itself but all down the stairs and in the hall below. The people we rented the flat from thought we were married already so I spent

73

the whole day on my knees scrubbing the place from top to bottom and removing every trace of confetti. Then it was back to work – Sadlers Wells didn't believe in honeymoons.

Soon after the wedding I realised there were a lot of hard looks at my waistline and it dawned on me that since it had been a hastily arranged marriage, they drew the obvious conclusions. John and I had a quiet laugh about this. In fact it was seven years before our daughter was born. Years later, my mother told me that they had thought the same thing, hence the lack of protest at the haste, and my father's remark at the reception, 'I don't want to be a grandfather.' Poor Dad, he never was. Mairwyn arrived eighteen months after he died. They would have been good pals, and she told me once that after hearing me talk about him so much she felt that she really knew him.

*

I was asked by the BBC to sing Frasquita in a film of *Carmen*, for a fee of £300. All went well except for the scene containing the card trio, which was left until the last session. We were to climb up the mountain behind live donkeys and into the cave, place our shawls on the ground, then sit on them and sing. The wretched donkeys would not go up the hill, and recording time was running out, Bill Reid, the staff conductor, helped them along with prods in the backside, and at long last they set off, and we all climbed up after them. The donkeys walked through the cave and off into the sunset. But as we followed we realised that they had left large calling cards all over the cave. We hesitated for a fraction of a second and then heard Bill shout, 'Sit on it, sit on it, but for Christ's sake don't stop!' We spread our shawls over the mess, and sat on it, and sang. The donkey dung began to ooze through the silk, but we sang on – and the donkeys and their dung went down in the history of the BBC. Carmen, an American named Rosalind Elias, said, 'Jesus, this is the shittiest show I've ever been in.'

One of the new flats over the road became empty and I applied for it. When John was away on tour I used the fee from *Carmen* to put a deposit on a bedroom suite, a cooker, a table and two heaters. I bought two chairs from one of the girls in the chorus and a carpet for eight pounds. The furniture was delivered, and I put all the rest in myself. I made many trips across the road, picking my way through the snow, and left behind only the kettle and teapot for our morning tea. John had got a lift in someone's car, so I sat down to wait for him to come home. He was amazed that I had done it all myself but I told him I did not want him to spend his short weekend moving house. Then he said, 'OK, I'm fed up with this place, let's move tonight.' So we wrapped up the tea things and, in our night attire and at 3.30 a.m. like a couple of thieves, moved over the road to our new home.

It was wonderful. There wasn't much in the way of furniture, but it was warm and clean and blessedly bug-free. And so much room – lounge, kitchen, bathroom, two bedrooms and small entrance hall. It seemed like Buckingham Palace to us. After all the years of digs and furnished rooms, I was really missing my piano, and when the BBC repeated the 'dung-doomed' *Carmen*, I bought a mini piano with the fee.

I was now earning £19 a week and John's wages had gone up to £22.10s. I was still doing some Sentas but my repertoire was mainly the never-ending Marcellina in both *Figaro* and *Barber*. There were also some performances as Inez in *Trovatore* and Hata in *The Bartered Bride*. Then came a new production of *The Cunning Little Vixen* with the lovely June Bronhill as the Vixen and Kevin Miller as the Fox – both Australians. The forester was Neil Easton, another Australian, and I was the forester's wife. I was also the owl with a classy costume composed of feathers and knickers. I hated that role, it gave me permanent housemaid's knee. I spent the whole of one act kneeling down and hooting. In the first act I had to stand, while the Vixen ran round me and got her lead tangled round my legs, and at the same time I had to count fourteen beats and then sing, 'You devil, you.' One evening June did her bit and brought me to my knees and all the time I kept on counting. I began to realise something was wrong when I got to nineteen, and the prompter whispered, 'You can stop counting, Hunter, you've missed it.' What a fool I felt.

The role I think I hated most of all was Fata Morgana in *The Love of Three Oranges*, especially the bit where I had to fall on my back on the floor, throw my legs in the air and show my knickers (very classy ones, of course). But I hated doing this, as it seemed a far cry from the sort of opera I had learned to love and longed to be a part of. On one occasion, when I threw myself down, the wood and wire mask slipped and the fangs pierced my cheek, and I completed the song with blood dripping from my face. Then there was the other *tour de force*, *Hansel and Gretel*. I have never been one to swing the lead, but I am sure that the sheer misery of those days made me ill and I longed to be sick so that I could miss a performance. As Hansel was on every Christmas, it meant I could never go up home for the festive season, as there was always the children's matinée on Boxing Day. I had a never-ending stream of new children to rehearse. And, whereas the kids seemed to change every month or so, I was always the damn mother.

In the midst of all these hated roles, my darling Tom Hammond sent for me. He had been asked to do a new translation for Verdi's *Attila*, and to my delight I was being invited to do some performances. Rae Woodland, who was to sing it first, had been asked to go to Russia with the English Opera Group, and they needed someone to sing Odabella while she was away, not in London but during the winter season at Stratford-on-Avon. I loved the role. Tom and I spent hours working on it and thinking up all sorts of cadenzas. Critics and management were so pleased by my performance that I plucked up courage to ask for a rise in pay, and got it. Ten shillings. My pay went up every year after that by a pound. After some fuss with the management and Equity, all the contracts were revised and for my last season at the Wells I had the lordly sum of £35 a week.

CHAPTER TEN

Camping

We eventually acquired our first car. I say acquired because we had no way of getting a deposit together, so we rented one. A mug's game, I know, but it did mean we were now mobile and, most important, it meant that when John went on those endless tours he could get home for the weekend without always having to beg a lift. Then in the summer, after we had saved hard, we could go away for the whole of the four weeks holiday to the west country. Each night we booked bed and breakfast, and during the days we drove down the south coast to Cornwall exploring every cove and bay that we came to, stopping in lay-bys to make tea on our primus stove, keeping as close as possible to the sea and cliffs that we both loved.

The further we got from London and the more we paid, the smaller the rooms became. We passed many camp sites and I began to be drawn to the idea of camping. John was not so sure, not about himself, but because he knew that I liked comfort and he was worried that I might catch cold. But after an uncomfortable and expensive night in Mousehole he decided we would give it a try, and we drove into Penzance and bought a tent, two sleeping bags, a bed for me and a lilo for John. The man in the shop tried to sell us a groundsheet but we told him we had a foam-backed carpet in the boot of the car. He clearly thought we were mad. My mother had bought it for our bedroom and we had picked it up from her before the holiday began.

We set up our first camp at Lizard Point, and I was enchanted by this first taste of the great outdoors. But that night, when I went to get ready to go to the local pub with John for a beer and a Cornish pasty, I tried to pull on my Playtex corsets. The tent was not the sort you stand up in. I sat on the floor and pulled and managed to get them past my knees, then knelt up and tried to

77

get them up the rest of the way. They just wouldn't go over my rump. John handed me a tin of talcum powder, then went and leaned on the car, laughing. I was near to tears, and sweating.

'You Welsh pig, don't you dare laugh at me.'

'Dew Rita bach, you should see the tent sides heaving, looks like there's a wild hippo in there.'

We sat in the pub in stony silence.

The next night it rained. I was not sure what to expect, so when it began to come in and spray my face I did not complain at first. But it got worse, and I woke John.

'It's raining.'

'Go to sleep.'

'It's raining inside.'

'Don't worry.'

'*On my face.*'

'Put your face inside the bloody bag.'

'If you think I'm going to lie here and drown . . .'

'Your idea to camp, bach.'

'I shall go and sit in the car.'

'Good, I'll have your bed.'

I crawled out of the tent with as much dignity as I could master and promptly fell over one of the tent pegs and lay and wallowed in the mud, feeling quite a lot like the hippo I had been compared with. I sat in the car and shivered, watched the dawn come up over the Lizard Point, and the colder I got the more I hated John. I would divorce him. How could I spend the rest of my life with such an unfeeling brute, and how could he sleep when I was so cold and miserable?

The rain eased off a bit. I decided to creep back into the tent and get another jumper. Then damn me if I didn't fall over the same bloody tent peg. By now my rage at my own stupidity had reached boiling point and I could have slit his throat. His monumental snores greeted me.

'I won't divorce him,' I thought venomously, 'I'll stay with him and make him suffer for every shiver.' As I stepped over his snoring form I accidentally-on-purpose tripped over him and woke him.

He moved back his sleeping bag and said, 'Bloody hell, it's wet!'

'I know, you twit, that's what I've been on about all night.'

'Oh hell,' he said. 'This is no good. It ought not to leak like this.'

Men!

We spent till 11 a.m. drying off the tent and our clothes, then drove the forty miles back to the shop in Penzance. It was a very damp and irate diva who swept into the camping shop. (I must remember how I did it when I sing *Tosca*.)

They were shocked at our plight but said they could not exchange it as they didn't have another the same size. John said, 'Let's get our money back.'

'No fear,' said the diva. 'I want another tent.'

I sat down in a deck chair and my language sent John out of the shop, as he didn't wish to know me.

In the end they gave us a larger tent. 'No charge, sir, just get that mad woman out of here.'

We drove back to the camp site. We were amazed at the size of the tent – it could sleep at least six and you could have had a barn dance in it.

The next camp site was at Mevagissey on a cliff overlooking the sea. It was heavenly and hot and we were glad of the fly sheet to keep us cool. We both became tanned, and ate and washed in the open. I even wore my new swim suit.

The days flew by and at last the time came when we would have to return to London. We sat in a lay-by having our last cup of primus tea, and I had a quiet little cry as I was loath to give up this gypsy life.

'We could stay another day, Rit bach.'

'You know we only have enough cash for the petrol home.'

'Well, Rit, my dad always told me to keep a fiver for emergency.' And he pulled from his pocket lining a five pound note kept in place with a safety pin.

'Oh, you crafty Welsh sod, I love you.'

So we stayed one more day, and paid £2.10s for the camp site. I shall remember that lovely summer as long as I live.

I was fired with enthusiasm and we spent the winter planning the next year's holiday. We saved Green Shield stamps and got another deck chair, another bed and a ground sheet. Next year we would be more adventurous and drive to Tintagel in North Cornwall and from there to Land's End, changing camp sites only three times. I thought I was sending John mad with my maps and books all that winter but he tells me now that he looked forward to it as much as I did. He says we will one day go home to England and 'do' the south coast again. I wonder.

*

A couple of years before my father died, I had a sudden urge to paint. He had always been a good water colourist and over the years had sold a great many paintings to supplement the family income, especially at Christmas when lots were sold in the local stationer's shop. And now I wanted to try my hand. I tried water colours but couldn't manage them, so my father said, 'Try oils, chuck, most of the same rules apply, so try them.' I bought the materials I needed from an art shop in Camden Passage in London.

Dad died a few months later in the Royal Free hospital in London, and I did a great deal of painting to drown my sorrow in the seascapes I loved. He died in the spring and that summer John took me to Cornwall, where I painted a great deal. One day he took me to the cliffs overlooking Kynance Cove and, while he sat and sunbathed, I painted. I got the sky to my satisfaction and then the weather changed and a gust of wind flung the canvas in my face. I exploded in a prima donna tantrum, blamed the weather on my long-suffering husband, and flung down my brush. He sat there pale and silent with rage while I told him, 'Pack it all up, and take it to the car. I shall never paint again.'

And without waiting I stormed back over the cliffs to the car park. On the way I realised that a lot of people were looking at me and laughing. I was livid, and turned to one giggling pair and said grandly, 'You won't laugh when you have to pay hundreds for my paintings.' (I blush even in retrospect at that silly girl.)

I sat in the car, spluttering. When John arrived he took one look at me and burst out laughing. I screamed, 'Whatever is the matter with you all? You just don't understand an artist!'

He laughed again, and I decided to ignore him, and began to put sun oil on my face. Then I looked in the car mirror.

The painting had blown in my face and I had blue Cornish sky all over it. I almost crawled under the seat with shame.

These days I find that painting, not music, soothes the savage breast and, like Nero fiddling, I paint while all hell is let loose around me. Not all my paintings are finished, so maybe a 'finished Hunter' will fetch a few bob one day.

*

My diary for 28 April reads, 'Dad died today', and underneath in smaller letters, 'The Wells sacked me today.'

What bare statements for two such monumental happenings, especially for someone who usually wrote reams every night.

The months before his death had been quite frightening and yet I knew that when he had the first heart attack it was the beginning of the end. We kept up a façade for the sake of Mother. We learned later that she had been keeping it from *us*, and what we thought was his first attack was, in fact, his third.

I was to sing Senta at the Liverpool Empire on the Wells tour. He was determined not to miss it, and he was not going to worry me when I was at last singing the roles I had so long waited for. So, against the doctor's advice, he got out of bed and went in a hired car to the opera. It was the last time he heard me sing.

We asked Mother to give up the house in Wallasey and come and live with us, but she said, 'No, I'll come and stay for long visits, but I won't give up the house.' She had her sisters next door but I could never understand how she could live alone after she and Dad had been so close. She outlived him by seven years. They never missed one of my first nights, and I know if they were alive today they would be in the queue for the Qantas flight to Sydney.

*

Some weeks after Dad's death I had a phone call from John Hargreaves, then company manager of Sadler's Wells.

After asking me how I was, he said they had some roles for me to sing. I asked if they were putting me back on contract. 'Oh no,' he said, 'You would be a guest artist.'

I was puzzled, as it was surely cheaper to have someone on a low salary singing almost every night of the week than a guest who was paid per performance. But I let him continue.

'There is Frasquita in *Carmen*.'

'No,' I said.

'Inez in *Trovatore*.'

'No.'

'Mother in *Hansel*?'

'No.'

'Marcellina in *Figaro*?'

'No.' (The more roles he offered the lower down they were in the soprano register.)

'Berta in *Barber*?'

'No.'

Then he said, 'Well, the other one is Auntie in *Peter Grimes*.'

I didn't know anything about *Peter Grimes*, so I was in no position to say yes or no. I told him I would ring him back. I asked John when he came home from work, and he said, 'That one's lower than all the others, it's a contralto role, tell him to sod off.'

So I telephoned Mr Hargreaves and said, 'No, thank you.' He was silent, then he said, 'Well, there was one other role we had in mind . . .' I cut him short and said, 'What is it, Sarastro?' (This is the bass role in the *Magic Flute*.) He ignored my sarcasm and said, 'No, Electra in *Idomeneo*.'

My heart lifted. I had covered Rae Woodland in this role, but she had never been sick.

'Oh *yes*, please.'

He snorted. 'Oh, I see, only interested in the glamour roles, are we?'

I lost my patience. 'And why ever not? I'm the only one in your bloody company who can sing them.' And I slammed the phone down.

I'll say this for them, they did not hold my bad temper against me. They sent me a contract for the Electra, but Hunter's luck was out – they cancelled the revival.

*

In the summer of 1966 when I was pregnant we spent some happy times in our tent, and this time Mum came too, but she stayed in guest houses, eating her meals with us. One day we went to Land's End and when we returned for supper there was a violent storm. The rain began to run right through the tent; there was a flash of lightning and the top ripped away from the frame with a crack like thunder. We were drenched, and Mum said, 'You can't sleep here tonight, Rita, not in your condition. Come to my hotel, I have a double bed.'

'What about John?' I wailed.

'Dew dew Rit bach, I'll be OK.'

So I was reluctantly hauled off to the hotel. I didn't sleep a wink, and kept getting up to see if the tent and my beloved were still there. As dawn broke, I could see John in the field struggling to pull the soaking wet tent down on his own. Eventually he came to the hotel for breakfast and I went to the door to meet him, full of concern.

'Dew Rit, you do keep on. I had a great sleep without you snoring in there with me.'

The next year we took our six-month old daughter camping, and she too slept in the tent in her pram, and it was there in Dorset that she began to crawl and, like her mother before her, managed to find some cow dung.

CHAPTER ELEVEN

Little Buttercup's Baby

After my father's death I began to have dreadful nightmares, something I had never experienced before, and indeed they only began to dwindle about a couple of years ago. My poor husband has had to put up with a great deal on account of my career, and must surely have earned his little white cloud in those twelve months.

He lay beside me, one night, putting up with my moans and then cries and eventually screams. He was at first afraid to wake me, but after an hour and a half he was so disturbed that he began to tap me on the cheek, and was even more alarmed to find he could not wake me. In my nightmare I saw myself lying in a narrow bed in a white-walled room, with my parents at the end of my bed, and my mother crying, saying, 'Rita, please don't die.' My father said, 'Well, she will have a baby but they both might die.' I called out in protest and then the most awful pains wracked my body. I screamed and heard my mother say, 'Do something, Charlie, she's slipping from us.' My father said, 'Pull yourself together, Lucy . . .' and as I woke up I heard John saying, 'Pull yourself together, Rita.'

I was bathed in perspiration and yet I was freezing cold. I said, 'I'm dying, John.' He said, 'Don't be so bloody daft.' He was smiling.

'Don't laugh at me, I'm dying, please kiss me good-bye.'

'Sit up, Rit, and I'll go and make you a cup of tea.' I was shaking. 'Don't leave me alone, I can't breathe. I don't want to die alone.' The poor man got back into bed. 'Okay, cuddle up to me and you will soon fall asleep.' I wailed, 'I can't lie down, I'll die if I lie down.'

So we sat up in bed together and I leaned against his shoulder and eventually fell asleep.

The next day was Sunday. I was in the kitchen washing the dishes and John was over the road having his Sunday pint. All of a sudden my hands began to shake, and I began to sweat and found it hard to breathe. A cup slipped from my shaking hands. I did not want to be alone and fled downstairs, without waiting to dry my hands, and across the road to the pub. As soon as I saw John's face I was no longer afraid. I felt silly and made some excuse about being thirsty.

Afterwards, at home, John said, 'Okay, tell me the truth.' It all sounded feeble but I felt like a rock that was crumbling.

The next day after tea it began again. This time John was at home.

'It's a heart attack, I know it is.'

John didn't say anything but sat there beside me on the sofa and held me in his arms until the shaking and the sweating stopped. At midnight he said we should go to bed, but I couldn't face it. I was afraid that if I slept I would have another nightmare. So we stayed on the sofa, and at 3 a.m. I fell asleep.

I began to go for walks every time John went out of the flat, and then I dreaded meeting anyone from the theatre, so I started to wear large sunglasses in the hope that no one would recognize me or think that I hadn't seen them. It was well nigh impossible to avoid meeting members of the company since our flat was right opposite the stage door and there was always someone going in or out of the theatre. I even began to cross the road in order not to speak to my dear Tom Hammond. And that's when I knew there was something really wrong with me.

After about six weeks of this silly behaviour, John talked to his friend Dr Mattie Cranitch who called to see me, told me there was nothing wrong with my heart and gave me some pills and a pep talk. John went off with the company to Stratford-upon-Avon. I stuck it for a day and a half and then went up to Stratford without warning John. I must have been a pain in the butt, I was such a clinging vine that never let him out of my sight. I stood in the wings during every act and was reluctant to go to the canteen when he went to change his costume in the intervals. When we got home John went to see Dr Cranitch, who said, 'She needs something to concentrate on apart from herself. She was close to her father and he died and the Wells sacked her the same week.'

So John came home one evening and said right out of the blue, 'We'll have a baby!'

Though his words were a shock I was more than eager. We had often talked of a family over the six years of our marriage, but the time was never right as there would be another role lined up at the end of nine months. Then I began to think that, after avoiding pregnancy for so long, God would surely punish me and now I wouldn't be able to have a child.

In mid-January 1967 John suggested 'an early night', and next morning announced, 'That's it Rit, no need to try again.' I teased John about the way the Welsh boasted about their romantic reputations, but I had to eat my words.

When I began to feel sick in the mornings and could not bear the smell of tea I went to Dr Cranitch, and told him I thought I had gastric 'flu. 'Holy Mary,' he beamed with delight, 'sure as God made little apples, you're pregnant.'

I walked home on cloud nine, and when John opened the door he had that know-it-all look and a grin a mile wide. He just said, 'Told you to start knitting in January, didn't I?'

*

After about four months I thought the morning sickness would be dying down, but it didn't and it wasn't just mornings. John was distressed and insisted on coming with me to the clinic. The matron told him, 'Mr Thomas, by the look of your wife's size a few bouts of sickness aren't going to hurt her.'

They didn't believe I was keeping to my diet, and had me in hospital, saying they were worried about my blood pressure. But I knew they were going to check the diet. They brought me eggs for breakfast. I told them I never ate breakfast, and a glass of juice would do. 'Juice is full of sugar, Mrs Thomas, eat the eggs.' I did. I threw up. They brought me a lamb chop, potatoes and cabbage for lunch. I said the chop would make me sick and could I just eat the spuds and greens. 'No wonder you're fat, Mrs Thomas, living on potatoes. Be a good girl and eat the chop.' I did, and then threw up. At tea-time they made me drink tea. I said it would make me sick. 'Rubbish, Mrs Thomas, you have been spoiled by that husband of yours pampering you, drink the tea.' I did and threw up.

This went on for a week and on the Sunday they brought in the scales. I was 2 lb heavier than I was the week before. They began to search my locker after every visiting hour – clean as a whistle. The second week, when John was in London, unknown to me they were searching him before they let him in to me. They even thought he was passing sweets from his mouth to mine as he kissed me! Another week went by and they weighed me again, and I had put on another 1½ lb. They phoned my husband to come and fetch me – they said they needed the bed.

At the end of it all I had only put on 2½ lb more than the weight of the child.

Then I had an X-ray and they discovered the baby was breached. I was told they were going to turn the baby. This wasn't too painful just uncomfortable. The doctor had a number of students watching, and then to my consternation he suddenly dug his hands back into the mound of flesh and swivelled the child back into the breach position. This time it did hurt, and then he told the nearest student to turn it back again. The lad had no idea, and what he did made me cry out. The doctor said, 'You wouldn't have had all this trouble if you'd lost weight, Mrs Thomas.'

I felt that all this turning of the child had been done to punish me for not conforming to their expectations. I told Dr Cranitch and he looked after me for the next six weeks, and was satisfied that all was well inside. However when I went to the clinic at the start of the ninth month they said, 'We can't find the head at all'.

John found me crying my eyes out sitting on a seat outside the hospital, and when we told Dr Cranitch he said, 'Haven't I been feeling the head for a month at least, and did they not see the head on the X-ray. Then where has it got to?'

'Dropped off, I suppose,' I said. And we all laughed.

The baby was due in mid-November, and at the beginning of November they said I was overdue and they were going to induce the birth. John was in Glasgow and I sent him a telegram. He came all the way from Scotland and used up all his compassionate leave, only to have me sent home for another three weeks, with the information that the baby wasn't due till the end of November.

In the last week of November I was kept in again at the clinic and this time they did induce the birth, by several methods, none of which worked. They tried to break the waters, using two different lengths of cutters, or whatever they are, and couldn't reach the neck of the womb, let alone get inside. They had given me a local anaesthetic and I had not been allowed to drink anything that morning. I was trundled back to the ward and given tablets to put under my tongue, which they said would put me in labour. In the afternoon John and Mum came to see me. John said something that made me laugh, and the waters broke.

From then on the pains got steadily worse until 11 p.m. when my moans were 'disturbing the other ladies', and I was moved into a side ward. The night nurse examined me and said I would not give birth that night. She gave me something to make me

Prince Charming in *Snow White and the Seven Dwarfs*, produced by Dad who also made the props.

Aged thirteen: Little Buttercup in *H.M.S. Pinafore*. 'A plump and pleasing person.'

Hunter's Modern Minstrels. Apart from Dad, the troupe included Mum, Auntie Ruth and myself.

With John Darnley-Thomas on tour
with Sadlers Wells.

My first part out of the Wells
chorus: one of the two bridesmaids
in *Figaro*. I sang fortissimo.

My first part out of the Carl Rosa
chorus: Inez in *Il Trovatore*.

As Frasquita with Rosalind Elias
as Carmen. A film for BBC TV,
memorable for the wrong reasons.

Dressed as Musetta in *La Bohème*, for Sadlers Wells. The costume originated from *Carmen*, the fur stole and hat from *Tosca*, and the jewels from *Orpheus*.

Senta, a real soprano role, at last. With Alberto Remedios in the Sadlers Wells
production of *The Flying Dutchman*. We have been friends since we first took
lessons together, when Alberto was sixteen and I was eighteen.

Mum and Dad.

Our wedding day, December 9th 1961. The stage manager said, 'You could do the first act duet and then slip down the road to the town hall.' But I didn't . . .

At play. John and I took many holidays in the West Country.

At work.

With my daughter, Mairwyn, born November 30th, 1967.

My first Leonora in *Il Trovatore*. With the Basilica Opera Company, March 1968.

Brunnhilde in the Sadlers Wells *Valkyrie*.

Left, the '24 carat' Leonora in *Il Trovatore*.

Below, my first Donna Anna in *Don Giovanni*.

sleep, but in fact I didn't. I threw up all night. The next morning all I was bringing up was green bile. They sent for the consultant. I was completely dehydrated and a glucose drip was set up, then changed for a hormone drip to make me have contractions.

John stayed by my side all this time and by 1.30 p.m. I was having the most violent pains or none at all and they were not able to control the drip. At three o'clock I was in such pain that I asked John to ask them to give me a Caesarian. He went over to the other side of the room to speak to the doctor who said, 'No'. I called out to John, 'Make them help me for God's sake.' They sent him out of the room. I called for him constantly but they didn't bring him back. I have never felt so alone in all my life. He was, in fact, outside on the stairs, just as my father had been thirty-six years before.

At 10 p.m. they took me into the delivery room. My legs were slung up and they began doing things to my inside. The nurse was filling me up with gas and air, and I wasn't really aware of what they were doing. I wanted to push and was told not to, and guzzled more of the gas to kill the pain. They were in fact taking blood from the child's head. They sent it up to the lab and the message came back, 'Child dying from lack of oxygen.' I remember thinking, 'My God, all this for nothing.'

They rushed me back to the ward and shaved me again. They put a catheter in to drain my bladder and I was again taken to what I thought was the delivery room. They flew past John and he signed a consent form as I was whizzed past him. The surgeon had been out at a party and he operated on me in his dinner suit under his gown. The tab on the baby's arm said, 'Last second Caesarian, girl, 6 lb 15½ oz 11.50 p.m. 30 Nov 1967.'

John had grabbed the surgeon's arm as he passed on the way to the theatre and said to him, 'You make sure you sew her up right. She's going to sing again.'

My little daughter was put in an incubator and I was put under sedation, and did not see her for four days. I could not hold her properly as I still had a drip in my arm. The sister held her close to me, and I saw black curly hair and two large blue eyes. I said, 'Hello Mairwyn', and she blew a bubble at me and went back to sleep. I had wanted a girl, and I had got one. This was as well, as the doctor told John there was no way we should attempt to have another child. John didn't mind what we had; if we had a boy we would have called him Ieystyn Huw, but we had our super daughter and we called her Mairwyn Sarita.

*

When I was a few weeks pregnant I had received a letter from a company calling themselves the Basilica Opera Company, asking me to sing Leonora in *Trovatore* in March 1968. A few months earlier this offer would have been greeted with joy, but now I looked at it with disdain. I realised the child would be only about three and a half months old, and so I said, 'They can go chase themselves, I've had enough of this opera lark.' John opened his mouth to protest, but I stopped him, 'Don't you start now, I've tried opera long enough, now I'm going to be a mother and that's the end of the diva.'

He mentioned it again only when I was sitting up in bed with my daughter in my arms. Basilica had phoned and said there were just three months to the first night, did he think that Miss Hunter would sign the contract. My mother said 'No', and there in the ward we had the most heated of all our arguments. The sister threatened to throw John out. She also said that she would stop his extra visits. So we sat silent and sulking. During this time I had a good think. John was passionate about the human voice and I was certain that, after this awful pregnancy and even worse confinement, I would make the most appalling sounds when I did try to sing. So I snatched the contract out of his hands and signed it, and threw it across the bed at him. I lay down and shut my eyes, and as I peeped from under my eyelids I saw him creep away with it from the bed, and out of the ward. But I did not like the self-satisfied smile he had on his face. But then, I, too, had a little smile to myself, as I knew he would be the first to haul me off the stage when I began to sing in what I was certain would be a dreadful voice.

Six days after they took the stitches out they sent me home, and the next day my ever-loving husband brought a man round to play the piano, and I was told to: 'Go on, have a go at Leonora.' I put the baby down and with a smirk on my face began to sing . . . for the first time in two years. My heart sank after the first page, and I found myself thinking, 'Oh blimey, there's nothing wrong with the voice, it's just the support that's gone off a bit.'

I turned round to see John leaning against the door looking like the man who broke the Bank at Monte Carlo. I could have strangled him. I said, 'If you say anything like I told you so, I'll divorce you right now.' The pianist fled, and Mairwyn began to cry. 'There you are,' I said. 'How can I look after her if I'm going to be up in the North of England singing?'

'You learn that role, Rita, and leave the baby to me,' he said.

So there I was up to my eyes in 'that opera lark' again. I sang some of the best performances of my life and the critics raved.

CHAPTER TWELVE

'A Little Bit of Sunshine'

Soon after I had sung my first Leonora with the Basilica company, I was out walking Mairwyn in her pram and met Stephen Arlen. I proudly moved the covers back so that he could admire my offspring, but he ignored her.

'We are going to put on *The Valkyrie* and I have a role in it for you,' he said.

'Oh, really,' I said, smiling through clenched teeth. 'Swertleite I suppose?' (She is the lowest one.)

'No,' he said, 'Brünnhilde. Go and see Len Hancock tomorrow and get a score.'

'I'll go next week.'

'You'll go tomorrow, miss.'

When I got home my mother was making tea for John, and he asked me if I'd met anyone while I was out.

'Only that bloody Stephen Arlen, and he never even looked at Mairwyn.'

John laughed and said, 'What did he say to you?'

'Oh, some rubbish about doing Brünnhilde.'

As I was changing the baby's nappy I became aware of a strange silence. John was smiling and Mum said, 'That's great, Rita, that calls for another pot of tea.'

I carried on attending to the baby, and John said, 'Aren't you pleased?'

'Pleased?' I spat out, 'I'll believe that crew over there when I've stood on Brünnhilde's rock and when Wotan has put me to sleep. Anyway, I have quite enough to do being a mother without getting mixed up with that lot again.'

I thought no more about it until two days later when Len Hancock phoned me and said, 'I have a score here for you, come in and see me at 2.30.'

I took the baby, and left her to be spoiled by the stage door keeper.

Len said, 'This is a great day, isn't it?'

'Why?'

'Well, this is a great role for you.'

Still suspicious, I said, 'Which role is it?'

'Why, Brünnhilde of course. Didn't Stephen tell you?'

*

Before I knew where I was, I was up to my neck in coachings with Len and Tom Hammond. Then I began my work with Reginald Goodall, the conductor, four or five times a week. I enjoyed working with him immensely. It was never a case of 'This is how it should be', but always, 'What do you think?' or 'Should we do it like this?', and some days there would be more discussion than actual singing.

John was still working full time at the Wells, but fortunately Mother was still with us to look after the baby.

Then in August 1968 we were told that the opening night scheduled for mid January 1969 had been put back to August 1969 due to lack of funds. There was disappointment all round. Mother thought, as did we, that the visits to Reggie would be less frequent and she would be able to go home for a while. But the coaching continued, four or five times a week as usual.

One Friday in January 1969 I set off to the landlord's office to pay the rent, intending then to get a bus to Covent Garden. Half way there I was stopped in my tracks by a violent pain in my back; my right leg buckled under me, and I had to cling to the railing of a house to stop myself falling. In great pain and with many stops, I made it to the rent office and paid the rent, but by now the agony was excruciating and my right leg had gone numb. I stood a moment and considered what I should do. Even if I made it to the Garden, I would never be able to climb the stairs to Reggie's studio. As I reached our block of flats, John was just coming home for his lunch, and he had to half-carry me up the stairs. He sat me in the big chair and propped me with pillows, then handed me the phone.

I began by apologising to Reggie but I never got a chance to finish. His explosion of rage shocked me. 'If you go on like this you'll never learn it, you're just wasting my time.'

'But Reggie, I've hurt my back.'

'Excuses,' he bellowed, and put the phone down.

I sat and wept. Later in the afternoon, John Hargreaves, the company manager, rang. 'Mr Goodall says that you will never learn the role if you keep on cancelling calls.'

'What do you mean, keep on cancelling calls? This is the first call I've missed.'

I, in my turn, slammed the phone down.

This was the first of many rows with Reggie Goodall, during the years that I studied *The Ring* with him, and each time his tantrums seemed to me to be more unreasonable than the last. I once went to him with raging bronchitis to show him that I was really sick. It made no difference. He could not understand that people were sometimes ill, nor could he tolerate my being out of the country singing. I kept the news of my Metropolitan New York debut from him as long as I could to keep him sweet, but when the information finally leaked out he became sulky and belligerent and played the piano and lectured me at the same time. I asked him, 'But aren't you proud that I'm going to sing the role you've taught me?' 'When will you learn *Siegfried*?' 'But I know it now, and it doesn't go on till next year.'

In the late spring our rents went up drastically and we realised that it would be as cheap to buy a house. We found one in Northolt, and borrowed £400 from a friend for a deposit. Of course we assumed that by August we would have got *Valkyrie* on and with the performance fees our money problems would be over. But Hunter's luck was out again. No sooner had we signed the papers for the house than we were told that the August opening was now put back yet again to January 1970.

We moved into our house in July 1969, and in September John announced that we had no cash for my lesson with Reggie. I said, 'Oh dear God, if we were still in Islington I could have walked, but I can't walk from here.' There was, of course, the anticipated tantrum from Reggie.

John pointed out that I had been going to Reggie now for eighteen months and had not had a penny from the Wells in wages and that I had turned down concerts so as not to miss lessons with Reggie. I plucked up courage and phoned Edward Renton. After three weeks the Wells sent me a cheque for £100. That was the only payment that I had from them in the twenty-three months I was working on *Valkyrie* – the princely sum of £2 a week. It just about covered my bus fares.

My mother had to return home, as her social security was threatened because they maintained she was living with us. In fact, had it not been for her presence, Reggie would have missed me even more.

We now had serious baby-sitter problems. Our cash would

not run to a nanny or an au pair. John was always working mornings and had performances at night so I did my best to have my lessons with Reggie in the afternoons. This led to a complicated arrangement whereby I did the chores and baby-minding in the mornings; then just after noon Mairwyn and I would get the tube to Marble Arch and sit on the platform and wait for John to come along; then I would hand over Mairwyn and John would go back home, while I went on to the Garden to Reggie. Afterwards we would reverse the process: I would meet John at Marble Arch, he would go on and do the evening opera, and I would take the baby home and feed her and put her to bed and try to look at the music I had been working on in the afternoon.

We staggered on in this way for six months, but it was wearing us both out. Mairwayn loved it – she was on the 'choo-choos' all day long. Then the strain began to tell on John and he began to be ill with boils and abscesses. With one particularly difficult abscess, the doctor said John would have to go to hospital. I was frantic, as I had to be at Reggie's at 2.30. John was reassuring and said he would be home in time, but they decided to keep him in overnight. I was terrified of offending Reggie. I phoned the Garden to say I would be late, and left the message at the stage door.

We hadn't been in the new house long and I didn't know the neighbours, but I took my courage in my hands and gathered the baby's things together and went and knocked on the next door. I explained my plight to a very surprised woman, shoved my child into her arms and ran off down the road to the station. This lady next door could have been a drunk, a child-beater, anything, but in fact she turned out to be the best next-door neighbour any girl ever had. (Darling Auntie Symes, we still think of you.)

When I got to Reggie's 'lavatory' studio, he was sulking. I was six minutes late.

I tried to explain, but he cut me short. 'I've had enough of you, I am getting another Brünnhilde.' He went to the phone. I said, 'I wish you would, I'm fed up too.' He looked at me, then slammed the phone again. He said, 'No point in phoning them, they never take any notice of me anyway!' He returned to the piano and began to play my music, ignoring the tears that were slowly dripping down my cheeks, just playing on till I had stopped crying and was able to join in. As it happened I joined in on the words, 'Unworthy of you this foolish maid.' He snorted with disgust and closed the piano. I was dismissed.

These tales about Reggie and me may not meet with approval

among those who admire him so much. I too admire him, and always will, and this is what made his criticism so hard for me to cope with. It was the same with Eva Turner, whom I had idolised as a girl. Perhaps those who never understood why I broke with Eva or Reggie will now realise my point of view.

I was pleased to have a success with my first Isolde in Australia, even though this was done without the benefit of Reggie's advice. I wrote to him and sent him reviews about Alberto and me here in Sydney. I told him that 'his children did not disgrace him' – we were always 'his children'. I said I would go and see him when I came home for ENO's *Trovatore* in 1983. But to my hurt and disappointment, his reply was in the same old mould, 'I have always admired your voice but not always what you did with it.'

*

Eventually we got *Valkyrie* on stage, after a six-week period of production calls. The co-producers, John Blatchley and Glen Byam Shaw were a joy to work with. There was a costume fitting when we discovered that the wig was never going to be right. John Blatchley and the wardrobe master, Bill Strowbridge, asked me to say nothing to Reggie about it. (I realised I was not the only one who found him difficult.) The wigs were huge things made out of blue raffia, and mine was the same only red. I couldn't stop laughing when I put it on. Bill sat on the rock and played Wotan and I tried to put my head on his knee and one of the wires in the wig frame impaled Bill in a delicate spot and I heard him mutter in pain, 'Cor strike me!' Then when I raised my head to look in his eyes, as I was supposed to, the wretched wig fell off and rolled around on the floor, and I lay on my back and laughed till my sides ached. John Blatchley laughed too, but he begged me not to let Reggie know we'd found anything to laugh at in his *Valkyrie*.

One afternoon I turned up to do Act Two with Alberto, only to find doom and gloom everywhere. Alberto had been in one of his humorous moods that morning and when Reggie had told him he was singing a crotchet instead of a quaver, Alberto had laughed and said, 'Oh never mind, Reg, what's a crotchet between friends?' Reggie had stood up, shut his score with a bang and stormed out, vowing never to return. Of course, he did return, but he must have given the producers and management a sleepless night. Alberto told me he had thought it would ease the tension.

Six weeks of production was a long time to spend on one opera even if it was Wagner, and we were all glad to get to work on the stage, and even happier to get to the first night.

The first act with Ava June as Sieglinde, Cliff Grant as Hunding and Alberto as Siegmund brought the house to its feet, and I stood in my room listening to the cheers, my heart pounding. As they came off stage they were all grinning, and Alberto gave me a hug and whispered, 'Go on, Rit, it's your turn now,' so off I went to stand on the Valkyries' rock for the first time. As the curtain rose with me alone on the stage the audience burst into a round of applause. I was at first thrilled, then terrified, Wotan has to sing first. As it got nearer to his first words, I began to panic. I knew that Reggie would not stop and start again. I don't think he even heard the clapping. Fortunately they stopped just a second before Norman Bailey sang, 'Now bridle your horse, warrior maid', and there we were launched into the *Valkyrie* at last. I remember lying on the rock at the end after Wotan has put me to sleep, and I began to cry. When the tumult of applause greeted me as I took my curtain call the tears were running down my cheeks. Edward Renton turned to his wife and gave her the thumbs-up sign and said, 'This is it, now it has to happen for Rita.'

CHAPTER THIRTEEN

New Horizons

I was convinced that the success of the English *Valkyrie* would be a nine days wonder, and that soon my life would return to its humdrum pattern. John went off on a tour with 'T' company and I set myself to learn my first Donna Anna. This was the role that was to launch me into my three-year contract with Sadler's Wells. The first performance on April 20th 1970 was again greeted with approval from not only the audience and the press, but the management as well. Personally I am not fond of 'droopy ladies' and much prefer a role with some fireworks in it.

The £3,000-a-year contract was not six months' old before I realised that I had sold myself too cheaply. Considering the number of performances it meant, I was singing really big roles for about £45 a performance. They had been prepared to pay me £75 for the first *Valkyries* and now, under contract, I was singing the same for £45. So after discussions with Pat Bancroft, who was Mr Arlen's assistant, we were able to revise the contract so that I was paid extra for the Wagner performances.

We went on tour in the spring with *Don Giovanni*, and all this time John had not heard me sing Donna Anna, since he had been on tour himself. He told me afterwards that he had grave doubts about my ability in this role. However, near the end of my tour he heard me sing in Hull, and when I saw his face after the first aria I knew he was thinking, 'Oh yes, you are all right in the blood and guts roles'. After the second aria, 'Non mi dir', he was as white as a sheet. He said, 'Bloody hell, Rit bach, you're a bugger, you've got me beat.' I deduced from that remark that I had surpassed my Welshman's expectations.

*

Before the first night of *Valkyrie* I had remarked to John, 'Do you know, in all the years in the theatre, this is the first time I have sung the title role.'

'So what?'

'Well it's the first time that I'll get the final curtain.'

His eyes had gleamed.

Then, amid all the many splendours of the first night, I had been aware the the Wotan, Norman Bailey, had been given the final curtain.

'Rita,' John had asked, 'are you sure that *Walküre* isn't German for Wotan?'

I was disappointed, but put it down to my ignorance. But a couple of years later when I went to a *Walküre* at the Metropolitan sung by Birgit Nilsson I saw that *she* got the final curtain. Then I told myself that must be because *she* was Nilsson! However, two months later, when I sang my own *Walküre* at the Met, I went forward to take my call before the Wotan, Hans Sotin, and was hauled back by the stage manager, who said, 'Oh no you don't, miss, Brünnhilde's the star of this show.' I never mentioned it at the Coliseum but a few years later when Norman Bailey joined me at the Met in *Walküre*, he did little to hide his shock when he was sent on before me. I must say that the Coliseum was the only house in the world that did not give me the final curtain for *Valkyrie*. I certainly did not expect it for *Siegfried* – that honour belonged to Alberto, in fact any tenor who has the guts to embark on that role deserves danger money, never mind a final curtain. However, I did expect to go on just before him, as did Nilsson whenever I saw her. But at ENO I went on second after Erda, all the rest of the cast went on after me. I was told by ENO in no uncertain terms, 'After all you're only on for the last forty minutes!' I wonder what would have happened if they'd tried telling that to Birgit.

*

After our holiday in the West Country, I was back at work; more *Valkyries* and *Don Giovanni*s and also starting the monumental task of learning the *Götterdämmerung* Brünnhilde, working first with Tom Hammond and then with Leonard Hancock.

I already had a vague idea of the first act duet and some of the immolation, as I had worked on these with Reggie Goodall. However, learning the intervening music could be likened to the task of digging the Channel Tunnel. There was a wonderful day when, after turning over page after page of virgin music for months on end, I suddenly turned over a page and there were the words, 'Sturdy branches'. I exclaimed, 'Oh great, I know the next bit,' and Len slowly smiled and murmured, 'Nice feeling, isn't it!'

Then came months of trailing to Covent Garden to work with Reggie, who was his brilliant, dedicated, difficult self. We were to present the first *Götterdämmerung* on January 29th, and Reggie was none too pleased that we were given time off for Christmas. Not that we had much, we had a stage rehearsal the day after Boxing Day.

The day before the dress rehearsal I was cutting a joint of pork and managed almost to slice my left hand palm in half. We made valiant attempts to stem the blood but John decided I should be taken to the Harrow hospital. They fussed around, and I pleaded with them, 'Will you please sew it up and let me go home?' But they did not stitch it and the wound took ages to heal. The dress rehearsal photos show me with a large dressing on the left hand, and in fact the scar is still there.

The dress rehearsal stays in my memory for another reason, also. Alberto had had a wax mask made for the funeral pyre so that the movement group had only a dummy to carry on. These boys would carry on the bier and then carefully remove a pin from it so that at the end of the immolation, when the columns of the Gibichung hall fell on the bier, it would collapse. The chorus would have to place the 'sturdy branches' very daintily so that the bier would not disintegrate too soon.

I began to sing the immolation and after a page and a half I could hear faint murmurs from the chorus, shuffling feet, and then giggles. Someone from the prompt corner hoarsely whispered, 'Shift out of the way, Rita.' I did so, still singing, and turned around. There behind me, slowly sinking to the floor twenty minutes too soon, was the bier. The dummy Siegfried was slowly sliding off at a bizarre angle, his hand wearing the ring waving about making rude gestures. I stopped singing and buried my head in my hands, shaking with uncontrolled giggles. Reggie threw his baton in the air and screamed from the pit, 'It's disgusting, how can she sing with all that messing about going on, no wonder she's crying.' His last words made me laugh even more. Well, Reggie dear, your saintly and godlike Brünnhilde was not crying, she was laughing her head off.

Despite cut hands and collapsing funeral pyres, *Götterdämmerung* (*Twilight of the Gods* as it was known in English) opened on January 29th 1971 in an even greater blaze of glory than *The Valkyrie*. The audience went wild.

Reggie's conducting of the immolation went into the Guinness *Book of Records* as the longest ever. I know: it was I who sang it, and I have the scars on my lungs to prove it.)

However long the immolation was, the applause went on longer. It became usual for audiences to applaud sometimes for twenty to thirty minutes at the end of the performance, and it was clear from the papers that we had hit the jackpot and the English *Ring* was well on its way.

We took the *Valkyrie* on the 1971 spring tour. It had occurred to us that we were very much loved by our London fans and that perhaps we would not receive the same reception in the provinces. But this was certainly not the case. The Wagner-starved north greeted us with as much, if not more, enthusiasm as London. These were golden years for the English National Opera/Sadler's Wells Company.

*

It was becoming more and more difficult for John and me to cope with a child and hold down our jobs. At the end of the 1971 season the company were cutting back on chorus and some were being made redundant. John and I sat down and worked out our earnings for the coming year; it was clear that I was going to earn more but John did not want to leave the chorus, and said he would stick it out another season. Then we realised that if he left in June 1971 he would get the redundancy pay, whereas if he stayed another season he would get nothing. So he handed in his notice.

We took our usual tenting holiday in the West Country but unfortunately the weather was atrocious and I caught a really bad chest cold. John was worried that I would not be fit for the new *Cavalleria Rusticana* in the September, so with his redundancy pay, we bought a caravan. We had spent many happy summers in the tent but when we took our caravan for its maiden run, we were the happiest family in the world. We left in good time for a slow drive to Dorset but the low tow bar on the VW Beetle was a great hazard. The wheel of the van kept banging and jamming on the road – we did not know that you could remove it for towing. The gas pipe also made strange flapping sounds as it too hit the road. It was after dark when we got to Dorset but we were not unduly bothered as of course we had gas lights – but there were no mantles on them, and they could not be lit! Nor had we a torch, so I made up the bunks in the dark, and we fell over the dog and each other, and the baby fell off the bunk. John opened a locker to get cups to use up the tea in the thermos, and all the cups fell out onto his head, then into the recently used child's potty, so we had no tea. The next morning John lifted up the lid of the sink to wash the cups and there, all neatly wrapped, were the gas mantles, with a little note saying 'Always remove mantles when the van is in motion.'

Cavalleria opened on September 29th, in a very modern production (which I was not too sure about) with no set, just a sloped stage and a few tables and chairs. The costumes were 1940s. I longed for the traditional set with the church on one side and Mother Lucia's house on the other. But the audience loved it just the same.

In the midst of this I had my first overseas offer. Would I go to Berlin and sing the Liszt Missa Solemnis, two concerts – one to be broadcast, to be conducted by Lorin Maazel. I was overjoyed by the invitation, but not at the thought of going to Berlin alone. This problem appeared to be solved by Alan, the man who made my dress for this occasion and who offered to go with me while John stayed at home and looked after Mairwyn.

Alan was good company and had been overseas many times and knew what to do. We got to the hotel and unpacked and then went to the music rehearsal, then back to the hotel where Alan ordered me some supper in my room. He was going to meet some people he knew and would take care of my money. He wished me goodnight and said he would order a cab for 9.30 the next morning to take me to the orchestral rehearsal.

I slept badly, and had wild dreams about Hitler and being taken off to a concentration camp, and woke up sweating. Silly fool! Not so silly as it turned out. The next morning there was no sigh of Alan, no cab; I had just enough loose change for a taxi to the studios where I felt certain I would see Alan. He was not there and, as a result of worrying, all through the orchestral rehearsal I made mistakes which displeased the maestro. I had decided that if Alan did not turn up at the end of the rehearsal I would borrow a few marks off the mezzo, who was English. Just as the conductor put down his baton at 2 p.m. Alan showed up.

He said a brief, 'Sorry', and when I asked him where the hell he had been he simply said that he had met an old friend.

After the rehearsal we hired a taxi to drive us round Berlin, to show us the places of interest. The 'Wall' was the most chilling and forbidding sight I have ever seen. Later, in the hotel over dinner, we were interrupted by a policeman who wished to speak to Alan. They went into the foyer of the hotel, and as I peeped I could see there were three policemen with Alan. He came back to the table looking flustered and said, 'There is some problem with my passport.' Then one of the policemen came to ask me for my passport, which I gave to him. He said, 'You will both come with us.' I thought he meant to the foyer but found myself being pushed into a police car.

We were dragged up the steps of the police station, Alan still insisting it was on account of his passport not being in order. He was whisked away to another part of the building and I sat on a narrow hard bench, with policemen strutting up and down with guns in their belts. I made several attempts to go to the enquiry desk to try to ask, in poor operatic German, where Alan was, and each time I was dragged back to my seat by an armed police officer.

After about three hours I was told I could go. I ran out into the chill autumn night and then, to add to the nightmare, realised that I had not asked Alan for my money. I stood cursing myself on the steps of the jail, then reluctantly went back in and asked if they would take me back to the hotel. Not only did they refuse, but I was jackbooted out on to the steps. It was cold and I had no coat, nor any idea of the way to the hotel. I asked a woman, 'Dove Hotel Steinplatz?' She looked at me as if I was mad, then I realized that 'dove' is 'where' in Italian. I dug into my handbag and scribbled 'Hotel Steinplatz' on a bit of paper. A glimmer of light came into her eyes, and she pointed in the correct direction. I must have run all the way. I went straight up to my room and phoned John, in floods of tears and near to hysteria.

John said, 'Bloody hell, I knew I should have gone with you.' Then my agent in London rang me and gave me a number in Berlin to call, a friend at the Consulate. He sent a consulate car next day to take me to the lunchtime broadcast concert.

Later that day the consulate got Alan out of jail, with him still insisting it was his passport.

The next day, Sunday, we went to the Berlin Staatsoper to see *Don Carlos* and afterwards went backstage to meet Fiorenza Cossotto who had sung Eboli. On the Monday Alan wrote statements and went to the consulate and eventually he was given some sort of pass to get out of Germany. On Monday night there was another concert, and the next morning we went to the airport for our flight home. Alan still had no passport and there was interminable wrangling with the German immigration. As the time for take-off grew nearer I went through to the other side and left Alan calling after me, 'Don't go, I may need you.' I called, 'Sorry darling, I dare not miss this flight, I have to sing Santuzza to night in London.' They did in fact allow Alan on the flight. To this day I don't know what it was that he had done to upset the German police so much. But also to this day I have never gone away with any other man except my own bloody Welshman.

*

1972 brought revivals of *Twilight of the Gods* and *Cavalleria Rustica-na*, and in March there was the first performance of *The Rhinegold*. We took *Twilight* and *Cavalleria* on the 1972 spring tour.

Our caravan was kept in the showroom workyard in Maiden-head, where we used to go every Sunday after lunch, to give it a dust and make a cup of tea. Mairwyn thought it was great fun to have a 'little house' as well as the big one, indeed so did we, and before the winter set in we got the caravan people to put in an under-the-floor heater, so that if we had a bad summer we would not have to call off the holiday on account of the weather.

One Sunday we were there having our Sunday tea and soon had to take off our coats and jumpers as the heater was proving to be so good. I hit upon the idea that instead of a harassing spring tour with John forever driving me to Leeds or Bristol and always looked for baby-sitters, we would all go on tour with the caravan. Mairwyn had not yet begun school. We could always abandon the van if it should prove too cold, but in fact there were no such problems, and we basked in cosy warmth while the rest of the company froze in inhospitable hotels or wore themselves out travelling to and from London. It was like a ten-week holiday; we took our little Yorkshire terrier Senta with us and the goldfish Siegfried. I would sit in the back of the car holding on to the fish bowl, and putting my hand over the top whenever we hit a bump in the road.

There was a *Götterdämmerung* and a *Cavalleria* each week and the tour sped by. When we were playing Edinburgh we stayed at North Berwick, and between shows spent time touring round the Mary Queen of Scots castles, Linlithgow, Dunbar, Durlston, even the Nunraw Abbey and the Lammermoor Hills, the setting for Donizetti's opera, *Lucia di Lammermoor*. When we played Newcastle we stayed on a farm at Hexham high on the moors, not another soul for miles. We explored Hadrian's Wall, and had a great day at the Hexham races. John was amused to see me clad in my *Brünnhilde* armour one day and the next day in plastic mac and wellies. I think I enjoyed the wellies more than the armour.

In May 1972 in the middle of the tour, Lord Harewood took over as managing director of the company and during our two weeks in Leeds invited all those in the company who were in Leeds on Sunday to a buffet lunch. Alberto moaned, 'I'm not invited,' but of course he had been, but had chosen to go home for the weekend. At lunch Lady Harewood asked me where John and Mairwyn were, and I explained that they were doing a tour of Harewood House bird garden. They were sent for, to join us and eat. Lady Harewood took Mairwyn to the toilet and Mairwyn came back and announced to all that 'Lady Harewood's bed was ever so bouncy.'

I had acquired a cleaning lady with the glorious name of Carmen. A few weeks later Carmen was busy polishing when Lord Harewood appeared on the TV screen and Mairwyn said, 'Look Carmen, Lord Harewood.' Carmen replied in a bored voice, 'Oh yes?' Mairwyn insisted, 'Yes, yes, and I know him.' Carmen still displayed bored uninterest, so Mairwyn, stung, said, 'I have sat on his bed and seen his penguins.' At that Carmen stopped her polishing and said in a shocked voice, 'Madre de Dios, these Eenglish harrystocks, what hever will zey 'ave in ze beds next.'

In August 1972 we were to present a new production of *Il Trovatore* produced by John Copley and conducted by Charles Mackerras. Costumes were by Stefanos Lazaridis and, with the possible exception of my *Don Carlos* dresses I have never had better costumes. When it opened on August 23rd it was as big a success as *The Ring* – I was hailed as a 24-carat gold Leonora, the press reviews were glowing. I could hardly believe it. What I thought of as the peak of my career was still going on.

CHAPTER FOURTEEN

The Big Apple

In Cornwall, in the summer of 1972, we were experiencing one of many downfalls of heavy rain. We were out in the wilds on a farm near Boscastle and had run out of tea and sugar, so we all piled into the car to go to the shops. We hadn't gone more than a hundred yards or so when we were surrounded by a herd of cows. The car stopped and refused to budge further, so I got out to have a look and informed John that we were stuck deep in mud. I heard my mother mutter, 'What a crew, it's either mud or dung.' We sat Mum and Mairwyn in the barn out of the rain, while John and I tried to bounce the car out of the mud. Eventually the farmer came, extracted the plugs from the car, dried them over his stove, put them back in the car, and it spluttered to life. The farmer left us, with a cheerful farewell that we'd be all right now dearies, but alas, we were still stuck in the mud. While John revved up the engine I shoved from behind. The car suddenly shot forward and I fell flat on my face in the mud – only I then discovered that it was mostly dung. John drove a long way down the lane before he knew what had happened to me, and by that time I was sitting on a rock by the roadside oozing mud – and dung. He ran back down the lane and said, 'What the hell did you want to go and do a daft thing like that for?'

I began to laugh and he said, 'What's so funny?'

'Well,' I said. 'I'm thinking of all those people who stood and cheered after *The Valkyrie* – I wonder what they would say if they could see me now.'

Far from being just a bowl of cherries, life, as I have discovered, can be a combination of a terrified cat, a demented dog, a vomiting child, cow dung and an offer to sing at the New York Metropolitan Opera in the space of three minutes flat.

We were still on holiday in our caravan, now in Pucknowle in Dorset, and sick of two solid weeks of rain. John, myself, Mum, Mairwyn, dog and goldfish. We went every other day to the telephone box in the village to call my agent.

The rain was coming down in buckets so we went in the car, which John had parked as near to the phone box as he could. But he did not notice the large and deep pool of water, until he saw me leaping over it, and what I did not see until I jumped into it was the even larger heap of cow dung. My agent gave me the usual routine information but as the pips sounded said, 'Oh, by the way, you make your debut at the Met on December 19th this year.'

I staggered out of the phone box, stunned by these words and by the stink of the cowdung on my shoes. As I got back into the car my mother said, 'Any news, chuck?' I told them first about the cow dung, although this was self-explanatory as I had brought a large amount of it into the car with me. Then I told them about the Met.

'I knew it.' From my Mum.

'Never.' From John.

'I feel sick.' From my daughter.

A howl of rage. From Senta, who flew out of the car window after a farm cat.

John went to retrieve the dog, and he too found a pile of cow dung. Then my daughter threw up into my mother's lap.

*

After this vacation I went back to work in the new season at Sadler's Wells and also began to teach myself the role of the *Walküre* Brünnhilde in German. Fortunately we had done a fair bit of it in German while waiting for Andrew Porter to send us the English words. I went on the Russell Harty show to talk about my impending American debut. We were to send Mairwyn up to my mother's, so that she and Auntie Nellie could look after her while John came with me to the States.

One evening when we returned from a performance I went, as usual, to telephone my mother, who always wanted to know how the opera had gone, and I was surprised when Auntie Nellie answered the phone, as it seemed rather late for her to be in my mother's house. She said she had news for me, and my heart sank as I could tell from her tone that it was not good news. My mother had had a 'bit of a nasty turn' and was in the

Wallasey Hospital. I sank into a chair, while John talked to Nellie.

We drove up the next day. Although Mum did not look too bad, the doctor's report was not good. We stayed four days and then had to return for my final performance before leaving for New York. As I bade her goodbye I told her I would phone each Sunday from New York and arranged with the matron that she could be taken in a wheel chair to the matron's office to take the calls. But as I turned for a final wave, my heart was breaking. I knew she was very sick and could well die before I got home from America. Her last words to John had been, 'Don't let my illness stop you going, please,' and so instead of joy and anticipation the next four days were very sad ones indeed. And I would now have to make my trip alone as John would have to stay and look after Mairwyn.

The night before I left, Saturday, my agent phoned to say he would bring my ticket to the airport – in my misery I had not realised that I did not have it. He also casually said, 'Of course you've learned your *Siegfried* in German too, haven't you?' My heart turned to lead. I said, 'Why?' and he told me, 'Well you're covering that too.'

I screamed, 'For Christ's sake why didn't you tell me?'

He said it was the extra clause in the contract I had signed.

I was too fed up and sad to argue and asked when it would be. 'End of November.' Seven weeks – loads of time!

*

I phoned my dear mother before I left the house for the airport. My tears fell unashamedly as I said goodbye to John and my baby. I stayed too long with them in the departure lounge and had almost to run to the plane, and could hardly find the way for the tears which blinded me.

John said that he would sort something out and come over for the debut – a small bit of cheer on that bleak October morning – then I stepped onto a Jumbo jet for the first time in my life. 'This thing will never get off the ground,' I told myself. 'I'll be back in Northolt in time for tea'. I waited for the announcement 'Ladies and gentlemen, we are sorry but . . .' There was no such announcement of course and poor miserable Rita Nellie found herself up in the sky.

A man passed my seat and said, 'Well done, Rita.' A little later he sent me a glass of champagne and an invitation to go and sit with him. 'Can't come to much harm on a plane this size,' I thought, and as I was feeling very lonely I joined him. He said his name was Jack Luntzer and he knew the opera star Graziella Sciutti. Whoever he was and whether he knew her or not, he made that trip less painful for me, filled me with champagne and insisted that the hostess gave me a set of first class sleeping goggles. 'Every hotel in America is the same, no real curtains, just blinds so you need these things to have a good sleep to get over the jet lag.' If ever he reads this – thank you, Jack.

Before we landed in New York I had to go back to my own seat and in the chaos at immigration I lost my companion and I never saw him again. I stood in a queue for 1¼ hours to get through immigration and was hot and sweating as I struggled to get my two cases on to a trolley and stood in line for customs. I had to take my coat off because I was so hot, and I heard a little demon at the back of my mind say, 'You have a sore throat.' 'Rubbish,' Rita Nellie replied.

At last a customs man came and said, 'This your first time in the Big Apple, ma'am?' I resisted the temptation to say 'And the last' – he was kind and signed my cards and sent me through ahead of about 150 other passengers. I was thankful I had a trolley to carry my cases but to my consternation, when I got through the second gate, I had to heave my luggage off onto another moving belt and they disappeared up a tunnel. A man said, 'You can get them in the arrival lounge.' Then, as I got to the arrival lounge, my American agents, Marian and Gerard Siemen, met me and Gerard had the job of lifting them. I was taken to their home in Forest Hills, given tea and shown round the house. I phoned John and told him I was fine – but that little demon said, 'No you're not, Nellie, you've got a sore throat.' By now all I wanted was to get to bed and sleep. I told myself that my throat hurt because I had cried too much and it would be fine in the morning. I phoned my friend John Kander, and it was arranged that I should go to dinner at his place the next night.

In the hotel, I didn't sleep. I had a raging thirst, and as dawn came up over the Big Apple there was no sign of the sore throat diminishing. Next morning Gerard Siemen took me first to the Met to get my $1,000 refund for my fare and to introduce me to the Met bosses, then to the Chase Manhattan Bank to open an account. He insisted that we walked from 72nd Street to the Met. 'It's just a couple of blocks,' he said. I know now that a block in the US bears no resemblance to a block in the UK. Well, it just seemed like endless miles to me, though maybe it isn't all that far if your throat doesn't hurt and you're not in a daze.

When we got to the department in the Met that sorts out the

rehearsals, a man called Frank Paola told me that I had a call that afternoon at 5 p.m. – for a jet-lagged diva that was 11 p.m. My heart sank. But the worst was yet to come. Gerard could not find the bank. He walked me right up Amsterdam Avenue and back. Winnie on the switchboard at the stage door said, 'Oh honey, it's right opposite front of house,' so we went all round the front of the Met through the pass door and across Broadway and walked up and down, then Gerard walked me back to the Met and down past the City Opera and down the side street into Amsterdam Avenue again. He asked at the Box Office of the City Opera for the address of the missing bank. '1 Lincoln Plaza.' So off we went again across Broadway. I looked for the numbers of the buildings – we had passed it at least six times. I cashed the cheque and kept $100 for expenses and left the rest in the account.

When we left the bank he wanted to walk me back to the hotel. It was now 1.45 p.m. and I had been walking since 10 a.m. I said, 'No thanks, Gerard, I am going to take a taxi. I have a rehearsal at five and I must get some rest.'

When I got back to my hotel I stood in front of the bathroom mirror, and said, 'Nellie Hunter, you have a septic throat.'

I struggled through my call with Jan Baehr. He said, 'You seem out of sorts, when did you arrive?'

'Last night,' I said.

He slammed the piano shut, and said, 'Goddamn fools. Go home and sleep the clock round, don't let the rehearsal department con you into any more calls till you feel right.'

When I got back to the hotel I phoned John Kander and before I started to say 'I can't make it for dinner', he said, 'Jesus, you sound sick.' I crawled to bed and then realised I had not eaten a thing all day, and the only drink had been a coffee in the Met.

The next morning I knew I would have to see a doctor. I phoned Marian Siemen. 'Oh, you'll be just fine, drink lots of orange juice.' I sighed, said that I would, and then phoned the Met, to ask for the number of the theatre doctor. I was made to realise that you have to be dying before you can get a doctor to call on you in New York; they told me to get myself into a taxi, go over to the West Side. . . . I said, 'Look, I think I have a fever, and it's raining outside.'

Well, in the end, I had to go to the doctor. He told me what I already knew, that I had a 'severe septic throat', to go home, stay in bed, keep warm, lots of drinks, light diet. I sent the bell-boy for the prescription and then realised that I had no food or drinks. I got soaked to the skin going to the supermarket. In the evening, my agents phoned and said they would call on me in the morning and did I need anything. Yes, I told them, 'more orange juice'. I snuggled down in bed to ride out the storm. The Siemens could supply me with groceries.

John Kander phoned to ask how I was, as he was off to Hollywood. Next morning the Siemens arrived with just one carton of orange juice and the news that they were on their way to the airport to go to San Francisco.

After they had left, I took my temperature. 102 degrees. The antibiotics didn't seem to be doing much good. I looked at my watch. It was the middle of the night for John, but I risked his temper and phoned him.

'I bloody knew it, you looked rough on Sunday when you left.'

There was a silence.

'Is there room service in the hotel?'

I told him that there was not, and that I had been out in the rain to the supermarket, and that the Siemens had gone to California.

'Right, I'll be with you tomorrow night.'

I gasped, 'But what about Mairwyn?'

'I'll send her to my sister Betty.'

*

John phoned the airport and booked his flight, and then asked Betty on the phone to meet him at Paddington station. She came up from Wales and took Mairwyn back with her, adding a daughter to her three boys. She also took my Yorkie dog, Senta. Mairwyn went to school and was spoiled by everyone; she loved every moment of it. But the dog went broody, would not eat, and went missing. Betty had the whole street out half the night looking over the mountains for her – it turned out she had hidden in Betty's wardrobe. And when she went to bed thinking, 'Rita will kill me if I've lost her dog,' she was kept awake by the snores of the dog she'd been up half the night looking for.

Meanwhile at 9 p.m. my hero was knocking on my door. Before he took off his coat he went out and bought food and drink. Thus was Mafeking relieved.

He nursed me all the next day and fended off the rehearsal department at the Met. The day after that, he went with me to the doctor's. The fever was down but the throat was still painful. 'Don't sing for at least four days,' the doctor said. 'Rest all you can.'

That evening the tenor Helge Brillioth called round and said,

'Do please come tomorrow to the stage call of *Siegfried*. You can just sit in the stalls, no need to sing and you will at least get an idea of the production.'

I said, 'You mean *Walküre*, don't you?'

'No,' he said. '*Siegfried*.'

'But *Walküre* goes on first,' I said.

'Oh,' he said. 'That don't mean nothing to the Met.'

My heart fell. Where were my seven weeks to learn the damn thing?

I said to John, 'Helge said I don't have to sing, just watch.'

And so I was conned into the most embarrassing morning of my life.

I went in through the front of house, and John took a ciné film of me walking into the Met. I sat in the stalls with John. The house seemed huge compared with the Coliseum, and I wondered what it looked like from the stage. If I'd known how soon I should know the answer to that one, I'd have gone right back to bed.

They ran the final scene of *Siegfried*, then when the lights went up again, I heard Erich Leinsdorf tell Birgit Nilsson they would run the whole thing through again after the break. Then I saw Frank Paola heading for me. Yes, I was to sing the second run-through. It had been a put-up job between Helge and Birgit; she knew the Met always ran the acts twice, and thought that I, as her cover, should do the second run-through. Normally that was fine by me, but now I told Frank Paola frantically, 'The doctor said I was not to sing for four days.' It fell on deaf ears – I was there in the house, so I was fit to sing. But sing what – in *English*, I asked John?

They took me back stage and I took my score with me. They laid me out on the rock and I waited for my Siegfried to wake me up. I wanted to throw up. Never in all my career had I let myself go on to a stage rehearsal with a score in my hand. I had always made sure that I had done my homework. And here I was, about to make a complete fool of myself. I stood up, and of course I knew the first few lines, 'Heil dir Sonne . . .' but after that it would have to be head in the book and act as well as I could.

Then for the first time I saw the auditorium of the Metropolitan – it stretched way off into infinity. My heart pounded with fear.

Erich Leinsdorf was not overjoyed by a book-bound Brünnhilde. I was humiliated when he decided to cut the middle of the scene from 'Ewig war ich' and wanted to cry out that was the bit I knew. What was the use telling him my agent had not made it totally clear that I would have to cover *Siegfried* in German? I had heard that before from other unprepared singers and knew only too well that I had thought, 'Rubbish, you just haven't bothered to do your homework.' But I would never again be so uncharitable.

The next day I was called all day on *Walküre* and for a one-hour call on *Siegfried*. I really wasn't feeling at all well and, even though the antibiotics were clearing the throat up, I had no appetite and felt tired all the time. But the way they had planned the call sheet, I didn't need to have an appetite – there was no provision on it for me to have a lunch break. When I told John that I had a call from two to three o'clock on the diction, and then had to go to a production call from three to six he said, 'No way. You'll have some lunch. You've been rehearsing from 10 a.m., you need a break.'

This did not go down well with the rehearsal department. They threw up their hands in horror. And, as I was called to see Charles Riecker, the artistic director, almost right away, it was clear that my 'friend' Mr Frank Paola had complained to him. But Charles proved to be a kind and understanding man, and indeed was to become the best friend I had at the Met. (I never told him the reason for my not knowing the *Siegfried* in German.) Charlie hustled me off to the nurse's department to meet Mary, who was in charge, and arranged for a course of B12 injections. She and I became good pals (apart from anything else, she was acquainted with my backside!). She introduced me to her friend Norman, who worked in the Met bookstall. The next time we went to the Met, Mairwyn, Norman and Mary were together all the time. Mairwyn would spend hours in the nurse's department handing out pills and cups of water. Mary was a sort of baby-minder while mum rehearsed. When Mary was busy, Mairwyn would go round the front of house to find Norman and she would sit in the bookstall reading the books or Norman would tell her fairy stories to pass the time. In fact Mairwyn was so enthralled by Norman's telling of *Rapunzel*, that from then on his name was Rapunzel – and in the end Mary used it, too, saying 'Come on, honey, let's go and have lunch with Rapunzel.'

Within a couple of days I felt fine and Charlie came and sat in on a production call of *Walküre* and grinned for a solid hour. 'That's my girl,' he said when I had finished, and gave me a big hug.

However, for the rest of the two-month season, Erich Leinsdorf didn't bother to be pleasant to me. Of course, I understood his annoyance, but I hoped that once I had proved myself on the *Walküre* rehearsals he might at least try to thaw out. Sometimes he didn't even bother to say 'Good morning', and I felt less than the dust. These rehearsals were fraught with other problems, too, and I came to hope that Leinsdorf would be too busy with those to be nasty to me.

Theo Adam went back to Germany, sick. One afternoon I was doing a rather pointless stage rehearsal of Act Three without a Wotan, when Sotin offered to sing the Wotan Act Three. He pointed out that he had not really studied the role, but knew it a little, at least well enough to help me out. Theo Adam did not come back in time for my debut and my Wotan was Hans Sotin, and he was fantastic.

*

No matter what we were doing, and even if we had been out late at a party on a Saturday night, we would always set the alarm for 5 a.m. so that I could keep my promise to Mum and phone her at the hospital. She would listen eagerly to our news and was relieved to know that John was with me, and content that Mairwyn was with Betty.

One Sunday she told me there had been great excitement for her in the hospital, as the BBC had come with their recording equipment and asked her all sorts of questions about me. They were going to do a programme on me and would talk to me when I got back. 'Everyone was on it,' she said with pride, 'Eva Turner, Nellie, Martina Arroyo, Redvers Llewellyn.' As it turned out, the story she told them about the audience shouting to me in the Liverpool Clubs, 'Give us the Judy with the lovely voice,' gave the programme planners the title for the programme. But sadly it did not go on the air until after she had died, and I had to record my part of it just one month to the day of her death.

Myron Erlich, a good friend of Eva Turner, had organised a 'Welcome to the new English Diva' party a week or so before my debut at the Met. There we met Richard Foster, the pianist and coach, and also Herman Mallamood and his wife Anna. Herman was the leading tenor at the New York City Opera. As it was near Christmas, Myron had his apartment decorated with tinsel and holly and had laid out a great feast. During the course of the afternoon John came over and said, 'Good party, Rit, isn't it?' I said in a whisper, 'Yes, but don't eat the blackberry vol-au-vents, they're off.' John burst out laughing, 'You silly sod, that's caviare.' Nellie, the boilermarker's daughter, didn't know class when it was on her plate.

I spent my free time locked away in our bedroom studying *Siegfried*. Jan Baehr was pleased with me and eventually pronounced me fit to cover. But it did not escape my notice that another lady was brought in to do the same. Even though I was competent to cover, she actually went on for some performances. So Leinsdorf had his revenge. In a way I found it very hard I had to sit for another month after the first night, and wait around for my own first night. I wanted to get up there and show them.

Eventually the 19th December came round, and my dressing room was full of cards and telegrams from all over the world. Fans far and wide sent me good wishes – even a telegram from the Bristol Old Vic. Out front, along with my husband, were my London agents, and the New York ones, and Lord Harewood. John Kander was there and had invited us to a party afterwards, but I had to go to my official party given by the New York agents.

The actual performance went by without incident. In fact Erich conducted it so fast that I first remember singing 'Ho yo to ho' then suddenly I was singing 'Auf dein Gebot', and it seemed that the glory was over in the twinkling of an eye. We had to stay on afterwards as I still had a *Siegfried* to cover on the 21st December, and then with a sigh of relief we left New York on the evening of December 22nd, arriving in London on the morning of the 23rd.

*

Just before we left New York we were thrilled to find that Mum had been sent home from hospital. I was elated, certain that she must be well again. I did not know that they had sent her home to die in her own bed, as she had asked.

I shall forever regret that I did not go to Wallasey for Christmas. We were tired and it was a rush to get a Christmas together for Mairwyn. As soon as Boxing Day was over we were pushed into rehearsals for the recording of *The Valkyrie* that we did on the 30th and 31st of December. Reggie could not wait to get us back at the rehearsals, and indeed I think he would have rather we had forgone Christmas altogether. And so I did not get home for the New Year either.

I phoned my mother the moment I got home. I thought she sounded a bit vague, and Nellie said it was the medication, and I believed her. There is none so blind as them that don't want to see.

113

I wanted to go home to Wallasey the first weekend in January but we were kept rehearsing till 1.30 on the Saturday and I had a radio interview to do on the Sunday and back at the *Siegfried* rehearsals at 10.30 on the Monday. (*Siegfried* was to open on February 8th.) However, on Friday the 12th January we finished work at noon, and we drove up to Wallasey right away.

I first phoned Nellie to warn her we were coming, and to say that I was able to be with Mum on the 14th which was her wedding anniversary. Auntie Nellie said, 'I had better warn you she's had a kidney and bowel problem and there are times when she's not lucid.' I felt sick with fear. It was a miserable trip north and the leaden skies seemed to mirror our mood. We said little to each other. Mairwyn had been told that grandma wasn't well and was in bed, but of course she didn't really know how ill she was and bounced up and down in the back seat all the way with the prospect of seeing her beloved grandma. The nearer we got to Cheshire the lower my heart sank.

The first thing I noticed when we drew up to the house was that there was no face at the window to greet us. Mum always knew just how long it should take us to get up to Wallasey, and would even seem to know when to put the kettle on for our welcoming cup of tea, then she would sit herself in the window to see us the moment the car turned into Limekiln Lane.

I was the last to get out of the car, and walked slowly up the steps. I dreaded what I would find. I hesitated outside the sitting room where she was lying in bed. John put his hand on my shoulder and said, 'Go on, Rit, she'll be OK.'

My breath went out of my body with the shock. She looked dreadful, yellow and shrunken. It wasn't my mother at all. I stood a second and then she opened her eyes, and said, 'Ah, me girl . . . at last.' I gave the performance of my life, and never shed a tear. We would play the ciné film of me walking into the Met and then she would fall asleep, and when she woke would say, 'You won't let me being sick stop you from going, will you, chuck?' and we would say, 'I have been, and look here is a film of me in New York,' and she would smile and say, 'Oh good, I'm glad you went.'

It was heartbreaking. She was incontinent and I helped the district nurse to change her. 'Why won't they let me get out of bed to go to the toilet, Rita?' 'Well, darling, you fell the last time and they don't want you to hurt yourself.' She wasn't convinced and, as I held her in my arms while the nurse cleaned her, she whispered, 'Oh Rita, I'm so ashamed.'

She was a clean and fastidious person, and that was when I

found it hardest to keep back the tears. I covered her and told her to sleep while I made a cup of tea. In the kitchen I sobbed into John's shirt, 'John, if she's going to be like this I don't want her to live, she's so unhappy,' and of course immediately felt guilty and ashamed.

Mum cuddled her only granddaughter as best she could, and Mairwyn was wonderful with her, helped by the innocence of youth. She had no idea how ill her grandmother was, and nor, I think, did I, or I would never have gone back to London. Auntie Nellie was wonderful. She slept in my mother's room in a chair, and never left her for a moment. I can never thank her enough for what she did for Mum, the things I, as her daughter, should have been doing.

We stayed with Mum and Nellie until the Monday morning. I wasn't required for the *Siegfried* calls till the Tuesday but at 3 p.m. on the Monday I had to go and do 'Desert Island Discs'. I hoped that it would be 'live' so that Mum could hear it but I was told it might be a month before it went out. I could not see how Mum could live that long.

I worked at the Coliseum on the Tuesday, Wednesday and Thursday, and at lunch time on the Friday was summoned to take a phone call at the stage door. Birgit Nilsson's father had died, and she had to go home to Sweden, and would I fly to Munich that evening to sing a *Walküre* for her on the Sunday?

We phoned John's sister Betty in Wales, and asked her to get the next train up to London. Grudgingly, Reggie let me off the last half of the afternoon rehearsal.

We drove home to Northolt and packed a few things, and then left Mairwyn with Auntie Symes next door, till Betty could get there, and off we went to Heathrow. We left a message with Betty to phone Nellie and tell her where we had gone, and to say we would be back in London Monday morning.

It was snowing when we got to Munich and I was tired and wanted to get to bed, but at 8 p.m. had to go first to a music call – my Wotan was to be Donald McIntyre. After the music call I had a long and tiring costume fitting. When we finally got to bed at midnight I was too tired even to wash.

Next morning at ten I went to a production call. The producer was Wolfgang Windgassen's son. I recalled singing a Norn at Covent Garden when his father and Birgit were singing Siegfried and Brünnhilde. At coffee-break time, I was disappointed not to find John waiting for me in the canteen. Don McIntyre bought me coffee. When John did turn up he didn't sit at my table but took his coffee and went to look at posters on the wall. Somebody came up to Donald and asked for a private word and off he went, too, and joined John to look at posters. We went back to the rehearsal and John went off 'shopping', he said. Donald was rather quiet. But I got down to working out the moves for the next day's performance, and there were more costume fittings. On the Sunday yet another fitting, and then I went back to the hotel to rest. Again John went 'shopping'. On his return I commented that he'd done a lot of shopping and seemed to have bought nothing. His reply was that the shops were shut on a Sunday. During the course of the afternoon I found the usual Gideon Bible and was surprised to see it was all in German. I read out my favourite family psalm, the 91st . . . I thought it was good practice for my German diction. In the middle of it, John got up and abruptly went for a walk. I got busy, dressing to go to the theatre.

The performance went like a dream, and I didn't put a foot wrong. I thought I had never heard the Wotan farewell sung so movingly. Donald McIntyre had tears in his eyes. When the performance was over the audience went wild, and we took over thirty curtain calls. When the curtain fell for the last time, I saw John walk across the stage towards me.

It was something he had never done before. He always went to the dressing room or to the nearest pub for a pint. As he got nearer, I could see his face more clearly, and I had this totally empty feeling and, even though John was coming towards me, I felt entirely alone, and before he could get to me, I knew Mum was dead. John started to say 'Rit, I've got to tell you something . . .' I stopped him. 'I know,' I said. We stood on the Munich Staatsoper stage and wept in each other's arms. Don McIntyre joined us and the three of us stood there alone in the centre of the stage while the rest of the company looked on. They all thought we were weeping at the success we had just had. No one knew, except John, Donald and the director of the opera who had taken the frantic phone call on the Saturday morning. Auntie Nellie had begged them not to tell me until the curtain came down – and, dear God, there had been thirty of them, more than I have ever had before or since.

Mum had died early on the Saturday morning. I had gone to deputise for Birgit, on account of her father's death, and, while doing so, my own mother had died. A year later, when I told Birgit, she was much moved and said that she and I were joined by a strange bond indeed.

It took me ages to get off my make-up and dress. The company

manager had hired a car to take us back to the hotel; she wanted
to bring it round to the side door, as there were so many fans
waiting for me, and she felt I was too distressed to meet them. I
declined her offer and went out the stage door. There were a lot
of fans, and they were cold and wet and the snow was falling
thick and heavy. One of them brushed a tear from my cheek and
said, 'You are happy with the success, yes?' Some of them found
out later about my mother and some of them still send me a card
on the 21st of January each year.

*

We got to London the next day at 11 a.m. and Betty told us
Reggie was wanting me to go to a rehearsal that afternoon.
     I began to cry and laugh at the same time. I can't even write
what I called him. John went to Mairwyn's school and picked her
up. 'Don't tell her,' I begged him. 'I couldn't bear to have her in
tears too.' And so we drove to Aberdare in Wales and got there
about 5 p.m. We intended to drive to Cheshire after a meal but I
was in a state of utter exhaustion, so Betty persuaded us to stay
the night and leave early next morning. By the time we got
home, Nellie had already organised the funeral for the next day,
and before I had the chance of a cup of tea she shoved a pile of
papers and forms under my nose for me to sign. She also wanted
me to go up to the local auction rooms and get someone to come
and give us a price for all Mum's furniture. I signed the forms but
refused to be rushed on the subject of getting rid of the furniture
or closing the house up. I wanted time to think. The theatre were
on the phone and Reggie Goodall was playing hell about his
missing Brünnhilde.
     Late on the Tuesday afternoon the management called and
said, 'When is the funeral?' 'Tomorrow afternoon,' I told them.
Long silence, then, 'Yes, but what time?'
     'Two o'clock.'
     'Oh dear, well, could you please alter it? Reggie needs you for
a stage call at 6 p.m.?'
     I was shocked to the core. 'You tell Mr Bloody Goodall I'm
burying my mother, not planting some of his bloody asparagus
(Reggie's favourite crop).'
     Half an hour later they phoned again. 'Mr Goodall's very
upset.'
     'Hard luck, so am I.'
     'Well, could you be at the stage call Thursday evening?'
     'Yes,' I said, and slammed the phone down.
     I had hoped to stay for another two days at least, to arrange for

the sale of some of the furniture and to put the bits I wanted to keep in store. Mum had often said to John, 'When I go I don't care what you do with all this but please look after my best dresser, the china cabinet and my vases.' They were all antique and valuable, and so I had planned to have those put in store until such time as we had a house large enough to house them.

However, to keep Reggie quiet, I went to the rent office, and paid rent on Mum's house until April, and left the stuff there until we went to Liverpool for the spring tour.

I went to the rehearsal with a heavy heart. Alberto was sad too. He had known Mum and Dad well. He had been working on stage all day and had yet another call at 10 a.m. the next morning. At 8 p.m. he was allowed to go home. We had not, however, finished the duet and John Blatchley suggested that I be sent home, too, as I couldn't sing the duet alone.

'Get someone to stand in for Alberto,' called Reggie from the pit. 'We might as well use her now we've got her, she's done nothing for a week.'

I burst into tears. I tried to carry on singing. It wasn't easy and eventually I found myself being held in John Blatchley's comforting arms and taken off stage.

The next day Reggie began to harrass me again. As soon as we had done the duet we went to the stalls for notes. 'First you go gallivanting all over Europe and then you disappear to Liverpool.' I did my best to keep cool.

'Reggie, I went to Munich to deputise for Birgit Nilsson. I would have thought you'd be pleased that the Staatsoper thought your Brünnhilde good enough to replace her.' Still he sulked. 'And I went to Liverpool for my mother's funeral.' He turned away without a reply, and began to talk to Anne Collins, the Erda.

Reggie Goodall never forgave me for that week off, and I never forgave him. And when I sat and worked it out, looking at the call sheets of those seven days, one was a Sunday and on three others I wasn't called, so I had only missed three days anyway – not a great lot considering there were six weeks rehearsals and, as everyone tells Brünnhilde, 'You're only on in the last forty minutes.'

For the rest of my time with the company and whenever I worked with Maestro Goodall, he dragged up 'your dreadful behaviour in *Siegfried*!'

*

Siegfried opened on the 8th February and received the by now usual enthusiastic acclaim. Alberto had a great personal success and we were greeted at the curtain calls by thunderous applause.

'Desert Island Discs' was broadcast on 10th February – but the one I had most wanted to hear it was not with us any more.

'The Judy with the Lovely Voice' went on the air on the 21st, and I was able to sit through it bravely until it came to my mother's interview, when I was overcome. The next day it was the Russell Harty show again. We tried to repeat the success of the one which was done before I went to the States, but it was a disaster, which must have been my fault as I was in no mood for comedy.

Seven *Siegfrieds*, then on to *Trovatore*, and in between all this I made a visit to my throat specialist, Norman Punt. He was becoming concerned at my more and more frequent septic throats. On one of these visits I took Mairwyn along, and she pleaded with Norman to look at her throat 'just like Mummy'. Norman in his kindly way looked at her throat, then went quite pale and left Mairwyn to play with her books, and came and examined me. He said, 'I hate to tell you this, my dear, but that's where all your infections are coming from', and he nodded in Mairwyn's direction. I couldn't believe it at first, but he went on to ask if she was a poor eater, did she snore at night, did she have the TV turned up louder than you think is necessary. I had to say yes to all of this, and he said her tonsils were huge and messy and would have to come out.

And so it was arranged that at the end of February 1973 she would go into the London Clinic and have the offending organs removed. After my own experience as a child I wasn't going to have anyone but Norman Punt operate on her throat. We invited Betty, Windsor and the three cousins up for the weekend before, as a treat and to jolly Mairwyn along. On the Friday night the boys and Mairwyn were upstairs playing trampolines on the beds, Betty and I were watching TV, and John and Windsor were in the pub. There was much screaming and giggling, then one loud bang was followed by an ominous silence. Then Anthony, Betty's eldest son, shouted, 'Rit, Mairwyn says she's broke her arm and can't move.'

I laughed and said, 'No peace for the wicked' and dragged myself upstairs. Mairwyn was lying flat on her back on the bedroom floor, her face white as a sheet and her eyes closed. I thought it was a joke until I saw the way her right arm was spread on the floor – obviously broken. I shouted to Betty to go

119

and get John and Windsor from the pub. Mairwyn opened her eyes, and I tried to move her, but she screamed in pain.

I stood helpless until John arrived a few moments later. Then I phoned the doctor who lived just a few doors up the road, but he didn't want to come out. He told me to take her to the hospital. I explained that we could not move her and she needed pain-killers or something. 'Give her an aspirin,' he said. That was when John took the phone from me, and I won't repeat what he said, but that doctor was there soon after. He assured us that nothing was broken, and said we were fussing, and asked for a scarf to tie up the arm.

Betty took a hand, saying, 'Get out of the way, you're hope-less, I'll lift the child myself.' Then to me she said, 'Don't worry, Rit, she'll only scream once, plug your ears.' With one sweep she lifted Mairwyn off the floor and onto the bed, then turned to the doctor who was still mumbling, 'It's not broken.'

'Bugger off back to your TV,' she said. And we shoved him out of the room and down the stairs.

We all had a sleepless night and next morning knew we would have to take her to the hospital. The doctor came again and still said it was not broken and to give her some aspirins in water. We did this in the hope that it would make the trip in the car a bit less painful for her.

We had the usual wait in the hospital for treatment and then to my amazement John announced that he would have to go. I was livid and assumed that he wanted a pint. Worry and fear made me vitriolic, as I turned on him. He took Betty to one side, then she said, 'Let him go, Rit bach, he's not going to the pub.' I was not convinced and he left the Out Patients with my tongue still lashing him. They had to set her arm without anaesthetic because of all the water and aspirins the local doctor had made us give her. Then we had to go with her in an ambulance to another hospital for admission. There was no sign of John and we left a message for him to follow us. By this time I was mad as hell.

About three o'clock I could barely contain my rage and Betty went off (to the toilet she said, but I know now that she went to phone John). Soon after that he arrived, and I flew at him with utter fury. We did not speak much that weekend even though most of the Sunday we spent together by Mairwyn's bed. That evening I suddenly remembered she was supposed to go into the London Clinic on the Tuesday. I phoned Norman Punt and he came right away to the hospital and arranged that she would be taken from there on the Monday straight to the Clinic and he would still do the operation, and I would remain in the Clinic with her.

On the Monday Mairwyn was taken in a wheelchair to see the specialist and to my horror they had to reset the arm. Again John was missing.

And so on the Monday off we went to the London Clinic and John stayed to see that we were settled in – and I seemed to notice that he left us with a sigh of relief.

I swore I would have it out with him after Mairwyn's operation. I smelt a rat – another woman?

Just before Mairwyn's operation I had a strange phone call from Lord Harewood. Would I take part in a short documentary about how singers learn their roles? It was to be on Wednesday 7th March. I groaned and pointed out that was the night after a performance of *Siegfried* – I never could sing the day after unless he wanted me to do an imitation of Dame Clara Butt. 'You won't have to sing much,' he said.

He had already asked John to get me to do it, but John had told him, 'She won't do it for me, Lord Harewood, you're the only one who could win her round.' You will have realised by now that a lot of people were manipulating behind my back. Lord Harewood even phoned my agents to get them to ask me, but they had no luck either. Eventually he phoned me again, and with a sigh I said yes, then asked him what I should wear. 'Why, whatever you look your grandest in my dear.' I went back to the lounge and said to John, 'Silly fool, how can I wear a grand dress? Everyone seeing the film will laugh. No one wears grand dresses to rehearse in.' John sighed and said, 'Wear whatever you feel right in.' Then there was a phone call from Betty, who said she was coming up for a few days as she wanted to see *Siegfried*.

The night before the filming John Barker came into my dressing room to discuss what we would do for the documentary. By now I was sick of the whole thing and wasn't looking forward to getting up early the next morning to go to the hairdressers. I said to John Barker, 'Are you getting paid for this rat-bag film we are doing, or is it another of Lord Harewood's charity efforts?' John Barker coughed in an embarrassed manner, but I thought, 'Oh hell, I've said it now, if the dressing-room is bugged, hard luck'.

I repeated '*Are* you getting paid?' Poor John Barker said, 'No,' and slid out of the room, leaving me to prepare for the *Siegfried* Brünnhilde, cursing all charity efforts.

The next afternoon about four o'clock I was standing in our

front room looking for the car that was to take us to the theatre. When it pulled up outside the door I said, 'Come and look at this, isn't this typical of Thames TV. If it had been the BBC they would have sent a Rolls.' There was a hoot of laughter from Betty, and John, very much on edge, said sharply, 'Don't be such a bloody snob.'

We got into the car and off we went, and after a while I said to the driver, 'If you're going to the London Coliseum you're going in the wrong direction.' John said, 'Don't interfere, Rita, he knows what he's doing.'

I was not to be shushed. 'Are we going to the studios, perhaps?' The driver said, 'No, madam, the theatre.'

'Well, as I told you, this is the wrong way, it'll take ages this way.'

The driver said, 'We are a bit early for your appointment and so I thought you would like to see a bit of the countryside.'

'Not really,' I said sarcastically.

When we got to the theatre I said, 'Hello,' to the stage doorkeeper as we went in. He ignored me and seemed to have his head half-way into a telephone. Charles Kraus met me and said he would show me up to the ballet rehearsal room where we were to do the film. 'No need,' I said. 'I know where it is, I spend half my working life up there.'

Nevertheless Charles did climb up the stairs with us – there were a lot of them, the opera company could never afford to get a lift installed. Half way up, just outside Lord Harewood's office, I stopped to get my breath and said to Charles, 'You know why George has his office way up here? The bugger knows that by the time you get up here you have no breath left to ask for a pay rise.' Charles blushed purple and began to cough. Little did I know that George was right behind his door waiting for me to pass.

There were quite a few people in the room – Helen from the press office, Bill Strowbridge from wardrobe – and though I didn't mind them being there I thought it strange as they were never at a music rehearsal.

I shrugged and thought, 'Let's get it over with and get back to Coronation Street.' The camera began to roll and John Barker began to play and I began to sing. I was sharply interrupted and as everyone now knows it was: 'Rita Hunter – This Is Your Life'. The look I gave poor Mr Andrews could have killed a cobra. All I could think of was the lies I had been taking for weeks from John.

When he had left me in the hospital with Mairwyn he had

gone to see the research people from Thames TV. When he had been late visiting the Clinic he had not been having a problem parking, he had been down the road at Thames TV. The reason my filing cabinet was in chaos was not my interfering child but my Kojak of a husband. The shoes that were missing were taken and hidden for me to change into before I went on to the TV set. He had even taken my evening dress into the theatre the night before and got the wardrobe to iron it. Oh, he was the crafty one.

Betty was there for a reason, too. She had quickly got Mairwyn ready the moment John and I left the house. She had to rip the sleeve out of a dress to get it to go over her broken arm. Another car was waiting round the corner to take her and Mairwyn right to the studio. Everyone asked me if I had known. No, I had not. I always prided myself that nothing ever got past me. 'This Is Your Life' certainly did. I did not suspect a thing. Of course, looking back, it all seems so obvious – but I often wonder if the people responsible for the programme realise the strain they put on a relationship!

*

This next part is hard to tell and hard to write and I know that only a small number of my readers will believe it. But this is my life and everything I have recorded from page one of this book is the truth and nothing but. I tell it the way it was.

Mairwyn began to be a real pest about sleeping alone. We thought it was the result of the accident and the operation; perhaps she didn't like her bedroom after she had broken her arm in it. I didn't know, as the facts were kept from me by John for months, so this first part of the story is his. Mairwyn would not sleep in her bed and she would keep on coming to his bed and snuggling in with him. There wasn't much room in the single bed, and some nights, tired and cross, he would drag her back to her room and push her fairly roughly into bed and tell her, 'If you don't stay there I'll smack your bottom.' Then, as the nights were cold, he would relent and go along later to see if she was okay and to tuck her up. But she would be lying there, pillow tidy, sheets tucked in with real hospital corners, not a crease in sight. He would wander back to bed, thinking, 'Did I tuck her in like that?' After several such episodes, he knew that he had not tucked her in. But who then did? He asked me if I had been up to see Mairwyn in the night; I said no, and thought no more of it. One night, however, he took her back three times and each time she wailed and woke me. I had a performance next night and, in desperation, he went and slept with her in her room. Well, he tried to sleep but was aware there was someone patting the covers and rearranging the sheets. He told Mairwyn to lie still – she was asleep. He told me to go away – I was not there. Now, John is a tough guy and would scoff at tales of haunted houses, but he got up and carried the sleeping child back into our room and said there was no way he would sleep there again.

From then on he let Mairwyn sleep in our room without protest – and still he did not tell me.

We had for some time been contemplating getting a bigger house. Betty said she spent so much time trotting up to London to baby-sit she'd be better off living there; she also felt the schools would be better for her sons, and perhaps there might even be a better job for her husband Windsor. She knew I needed a housekeeper to relieve the strain on me. So we looked for a house big enough for all of us.

One weekend she and her family came up to look at a house in Hatch End that we thought would be suitable. Windsor, John Junior and Philip slept in the room that had been my mother's when she came to stay; Betty slept in Mairwyn's room; her eldest son slept on the lounge sofa; and Mairwyn slept with John.

Not long after she had got into bed Betty turned over and said 'No, Windsor, bugger off.' She put out her hands to push her husband away, and told him to stop patting her head and messing about with the bedclothes. She put on the light and the room was empty. She could hear Windsor snoring in the next room. The next morning she said to my husband, 'Jack, there's something wrong with that bedroom.' (John's family always called him Jack.) John hung his head, and she looked at him closely. 'Oh hell, you know about it, don't you?' He didn't answer and she went on. 'It's happened to you, hasn't it, Jack?'

He groaned, and said, 'Aye, it has. But for God's sake don't tell Rita, she'll have us out of this house before we can dress.' Betty said, 'You've got to tell her, it's her mother, you know that, don't you?'

John scoffed, but Betty said, 'If you won't tell her I will.'

She came upstairs and brought me a cup of tea and sat on my bed. 'You know Grandma is still with us, don't you, Rit bach?'

'Yes,' I said, as I sipped the tea. I thought she meant that we all still missed my mother and that she was keeping an eye on us from heaven, and that it was kind of Betty to say she knew how much I missed Mum.

'Well, as long as you know,' she said briskly and got up off my bed and went downstairs.

The next night the eldest son slept on a mattress on the floor, the middle one on the sofa and Betty slept in with her husband. I still didn't know anything was amiss. Two days later I had prepared lunch and saw there was still half an hour before John would be home, so I sat on a chair and put my feet up. I didn't lie down, and I didn't sleep. I heard something in the hall, and thought John had been quiet putting his key in the lock. Then I saw her. I froze with horror as my mother walked down the hall into the kitchen.

I sat bolt upright. She looked at me with a sad smile and shook her head and went into the kitchen. I remember thinking, 'That's funny, she's got no feet' – she had appeared to be floating. I have never moved so fast in all my life. I was out of that room, down the hall and out into the front garden before you could blink, and sat on the garden wall shivering in the hot sunlight. Remember that I knew *nothing* of what had happened to John and Betty. John was smiling as he came along the road from the station, but his face fell when he saw mine.

'What's wrong?'

And there on the wall I told him. He went pale and slowly sat beside me, and as I looked at him I said, 'My God, you knew all about this, how long has it been going on?'

He forced me reluctantly inside the house and made a cup of tea and told me just what I have told you. He tried everything to convince me that as she was my mother she would not harm us. 'If she doesn't want to harm me, why is she doing this to me?' And so it went on for days. I did not see her again but there was the smell of oranges when there were none in the house, and the smell of sweet geraniums when we only grew the unscented ones. It was the smell of the geraniums that made me realise I was not mad or seeing things. I recalled the day my father died. John, Mum and I had been walking down Oxford Street looking for black dresses for the funeral and Mum and I were stopped in our tracks by the smell of geraniums. Mum mentioned it to Nellie a few days later and Nellie went white as a sheet and said that she had been in Mum's house the day Dad died and about 11 o'clock she had been overwhelmed by the sickly sweet smell of the same flower. Dad died at exactly 11 a.m. So when I smelt them I was convinced it was my Mum trying to tell me something.

I would not stay in the house alone, and would wander round the shopping village, have a coffee, or sit in the back garden till John came back. One day, while in the garden, I looked up at Mairwyn's bedroom window and saw the curtains being pulled aside by an unseen hand. This time I knew where John was, and I fled down the street to the pub to fetch him. I made him go and check that there wasn't a window open, although I knew there wasn't and in any case the curtains had not fluttered, they had been pulled aside. I timidly followed him up the stairs. We went into Mairwyn's room and although the house was hot and stuffy and the day was warm, inside the room there was a freezing draught of air. I heard John say 'Bloody hell,' and I fell to my knees screaming, 'Leave me alone, Mam, for God's sake leave me alone if you love me, stop it.' John hauled me sobbing from the room.

A house was up for sale in Thames Ditton and, even though it wasn't really large enough for Betty's family and mine and it meant moving house in the middle of the *Ring* rehearsals, I said, 'That's it, we move.' Things were better for a time but the night before we moved, I thought that Mairwyn was coming to our room to sleep again and I went out onto the landing to send her back. It was the middle of July and yet out there on the landing was a freezing wind. I fled back to bed, locking our bedroom door.

I have experienced nothing like this before or since, but will never again scoff at such tales – I am cold just writing about it.

*

On Friday 20th July 1973 I went to work, leaving Betty and her family to cope with the removal men, and I left that awful house with the greatest of joy. After work John and I drove to our new home in Thames Ditton. There were two *Rings* in August, and then we went on to do a revival of *Trovatore*. I did the first three and then went down with 'flu. I stayed in bed and cancelled the *Trovatore* on the 10th September, the 'flu turned to bronchitis and then to pneumonia. I was ill for six weeks, and missed five *Trovatores* – not too good for someone who had a house full of people to support.

The loss of fees began to unnerve Betty and Windsor: they both felt that it was too much for me to keep them all, and in any case the house I had fled to in such desperation had indeed proved too cramped for eight people and two dogs. At the beginning of December Betty and her little brood moved back to our still unsold house in Northolt and, after spending Christmas there, moved into a house in Kingston-on-Thames, where they still are. The schools proved good for the boys and Windsor now has a job at British Aerospace in Kingston-on-Thames.

Betty, as I write this, is looking after the letting of our house while we are in Australia, and for her help, past and present, I am ever grateful – Thanks, Bet bach.

CHAPTER FIFTEEN

To Deeds of Glory

I was ill with bronchitis over Christmas 1973 and New Year 1974 and had to cancel *Attila* in Barcelona and Paris. I was most disappointed, especially since it was so soon after the pneumonia in the summer. However, I recovered in time to fly to Atlanta, Georgia, to sing three orchestral concerts. This was an enjoyable trip, as for the first time in ages I had time to do some sightseeing. It was always frustrating to visit some interesting place if all I ever saw of it were the hotel and the theatre. It was here in Atlanta that we met Dottie and Wilkes Davis, who introduced us to the wicked, calorie-filled black-bottom pie.

On the day after the last Atlanta concert we flew early in the morning to New York, expecting to get a connecting flight to Paris. But my agents' idea of a connecting flight was one that left New York at 9 p.m., leaving us to kick our heels all day in the airport, then a night flight to France, arriving much later at our destination than we wanted to.

I was to fly on to Nice for my first *Aidas* and I wanted a day's rest before I began to rehearse. I was tired when we reached Nice at lunch time and, with feet like puddings, I went straight to bed until the first rehearsal that evening. However, no sooner had I laid my head on the pillow than the phone rang. Where was I? I was late for rehearsal. I made my apologies but the French 'were not understanding my English', so I tried Italian, with no better success. So I phoned my agent in London, who spoke French, and told him to ring the Nice opera and sort it out and tell them I would be there at 6 p.m. the next evening.

When I went to the rehearsal the conductor was a bit snooty with me, as I had missed the call, but he melted when I sang. His name was Gianfranco Massini, and the tenor was a tall and divine-looking man called Francisco Ortiz. I was delighted as many tenors tend to be on the short side. Amneris was Bianca Berrini, and what a wonderful sound she made. I do not remember the baritone's name, although he had an ego a mile wide. When we did the Nile scene and after I had sung 'O patria mia', he came on right away to begin the Aida/Amonasro duet. The conductor told him in Italian to wait before he came on as there would be applause. I heard the baritone say 'Non posso,' and the conductor insist. 'Si, there *will* be applause'. Would I please sing the aria again?'

At the first performance there was a lot of clapping after the 'O patria mia' and as it died down I indicated to the conductor that we would sing it again, but he sadly shook his head and pointed to the Nile where the big-headed baritone had already come on, certain that there would be no applause. He was sitting on the bank of the river looking bored. However, my ruffled feathers were smoothed somewhat when in the duet his large and gaudy earrings fell off and bounced and rolled into the footlights.

The management of the Nice opera were delighted by my performances, and asked me what roles I would like to return and sing the following season. I told them I had *Trovatore* and Santuzza and *Ballo* in my repertoire and they said, 'Yes, *Trovatore*.' I was thrilled to give this news to my agent when I returned to London. He said he would contact Nice and get a contract! We never heard another word from Nice. When I saw, in *Opera* magazine, that Caballé was to sing *Trovatore* the next season I began to think that maybe I should have pushed for a contract before I left Nice and negotiated myself. Coming home with a contract was not unheard of if one had done well and made a good impression, as I certainly had.

*

I arrived in New York on 10th February 1974 to cover Birgit in *Götterdämmerung* and to do some performances in my own right. John Kander and his friend met us at the airport and took us to their home for a meal before depositing us at the hotel. It was nice to be met by friendly faces. The next day Mairwyn woke with a bit of a cold. My New York agent, Gerard Siemen, phoned and said that he was sorry he had not met us at the airport but he was low on petrol.

The next few days were spent doing music calls, either with one of the music staff or with Kubelik the conductor. On the 14th I called in to the accounts office to get the $1000 transportation; this was to be our food, taxi and general expenses for the trip. I wrote in the diary, 'Accounts gave me the third degree. Wouldn't give me my fare, after three quarters of an hour said they had better send it to my agent in London.' I remember telling them they were wasting postage as the agent would have to send it right back to me as I needed it to live on in New York.

On the 16th I was doing the production calls of *Götterdämmerung* while Birgit sang the orchestral. We met at the coffee bar in the break. The diary says, 'Birgit told me she was going to the Bahamas tomorrow for a holiday. Charming! This means for her to have a break I had to cancel the Los Angeles *Siegfried*'. The rest is unprintable.

On Tuesday the 18th I recorded, 'I sang Act 1 three times, with three different Siegfrieds and two different Waltrautes. I am knackered.'

The call sheet for that day reads: 10.30 Acts 1 & 2 . . . 12.15 Act 3 . . . 2 p.m. Act 1 . . . 3.30 Acts 2 & 3 . . . 6.30 Stage with piano Act 2.

Looks like they were getting their money's worth.

The call sheet for the 22nd reads: 10 a.m. Diction call till 11.30 . . . 12 noon Sitzprobe . . . 1 p.m. Stage call till 1.30 . . . 2 p.m. to 3.30 Sitzprobe . . . Lunch 3.30 to 4 p.m. . . . 4 p.m. to 6 p.m. Room 203 with Kubelik . . . 6.30 to 7.30 Diction call.

The diary says, 'I asked them to cancel the last diction call of the day as I felt it was too much. They refused and so I said casually, "Well, don't worry if I'm dead next week, Birgit will be back." They cancelled the call.'

Things did not let up the following week, despite the fact that Birgit was back. There was, after all, the second and third cast to rehearse. On Monday, 4th March, I went in to watch the rehearsal from the stalls. At the end of Act One Birgit fell down some steps, banged her face and hurt herself. The theatre fell silent. I heard her cry out in pain as they tried to move her. I buried my face in my hands and wept. Winnie from the stage door came to me and said, 'They need you real bad back stage, sweetheart,' I felt sick. I phoned John. I was worried that Birgit might have smashed her hip. Apparently all I said to him was, 'She's fallen, come over to the theatre. Oh, John, she's fallen.'

In the dressing room area, people sat around silent and worried. No one said a word to me except Jess Thomas, the Siegfried. He whispered, 'Looks like you're next in line, honey.' Then some fool said, 'Well, Hunter, this is your big chance.' I blurted out, 'You moron, who the hell wants a big chance this way?'

Then Wigs and Wardrobe shoved me into a dressing room and

put the dress and wig on. John arrived and was able to tell me that they had taken Birgit to the Roosevelt Hospital and that it was not her hip – she had dislocated her shoulder. I finished the piano dress for Birgit. The next day her chances of going on for the premiere looked black, and I had to do the dress rehearsal for her.

I stayed indoors the next two days. At 3.30 on the 7th the Met phoned and said that Birgit was asking me if she could postpone the decision about the first night until the morning of the première. I told him to tell her that as far as I was concerned she could change her mind ten minutes before curtain if she wanted, that was what I was in New York for. I realised that having done the dress rehearsal I could have demanded that I was allowed to do the first night, but I had too much respect for a fellow artist to do this (even though her vacation *had* cost me my Los Angeles *Siegfrieds*). The following day, the day of the premiere, Charlie Riecker phoned me at 1.30 and said that Birgit was going on and would try to sing. I spent the afternoon answering the door to florists' deliveries, from Mr Chapin, Mr Riecker and from the great Nilsson herself. I sat fully clothed right down to my shoes until 11.45 p.m. when I was certain that she had finished the opera, then I had a brandy and went to bed.

On the 11th I went to the bank and found we had $420 left. I wrote in my diary, 'So with the $300 in travel cheques if we are careful we should be able to manage.'

*

I had recorded in the diary on 25th February that my London agent had phoned and said that I was advertised in Buenos Aires to open the season in *Aida*, not *Trovatore*. I said that I was thrilled. In the autumn of '73 I had told Lord Harewood that I would not be able to do the first run of performances of *Don Carlos* in 1974 on account of the Argentina *Trovatores*, and so Margaret Curphey was to do them.

On Thursday, the 14th March, I had a letter from London to say they were still doing *Trovatore* at the Colon but with another soprano and no mention of *Aida*. I was shocked and disappointed. I had given up the first run of *Don Carlos* for nothing.

On 16th March Charlie phoned and said that Birgit was in great pain and had not been able to sleep and that I would have to sing the performance on Monday the 18th March.

I felt sick all day and could not eat. Just before we left for the theatre, John made me two pieces of toast. Never was so much sung by one person on so little. My Siegfried was Helge Brillioth. He kicked me on my backside for luck. As I was being made up in my dressing room we could hear the orchestra tuning up and then a hush came over the audience as the curtains parted and some poor soul had to tell them that Birgit was not going to sing. I heard the start of a protest, and the make-up man dived over the room to turn the tannoy off, as he thought my feelings might be hurt. But I was no fool – they had paid good money to hear Birgit and all they were getting was little old Nellie Hunter. When I came up out of the 'cave' and before I had time to sing my first line 'Zu neuen Thaten' (To deeds of glory), I could feel the hostility of the audience, faint murmurings, Helge embraced me and whispered 'Sing, damn you, sing.' I told myself I did not like New York and didn't care if I was not asked back. But I sang all right, and well before the end of Act One I knew I had won them round. It's a strange feeling – there are no breaks for applause in Wagner – but I knew I had them in the palm of my hand. Act Two was a piece of cake. And by the Immolation I felt so good I could have sung it all over again.

After the opera was over Mr Chapin came in to see me – he was over the moon. Charlie Riecker had stayed only for the first act duet (he told me after that he knew I was okay by the end of my first page of music!) Mairwyn's only comment was, 'Oh bother it, Mummy, now they will ask you back and we'll have to come here again.'

The next four days I stayed indoors most of the time, and my diary records it was raining. One evening we went to dinner to Herman Mallamood's – he was the tenor at the New York City Opera. At 9.10 p.m. on the 22nd March Charlie Riecker phoned to warn me that Birgit might not sing the matinée next day – it was the Met coast-to-coast broadcast. Next morning as I sat in bed having coffee, Charlie phoned and said, 'Well, sweetheart, you're making your Met radio debut this afternoon.'

I did not finish the coffee. I got up and showered and sang the words 'Zu neuen Thaten', and shouted to John, 'That will do, the voice is fine.' I was in the theatre at 11 a.m. as the matinée started at 12.30.

John stayed home to record the broadcast. I rang him from my dressing room each interval. Every time I picked up the phone Winnie on the switchboard said, 'That's my girl, keep it up, honey, you're doing just fine.' After the show John Kander and Larry took John, Mairwyn and me, and Helge Brillioth, to Peter Lugers' in Brooklyn for dinner.

Charlie came in to see me. He was hopping with joy. 'What are you going to do tonight, honey?' 'I'm going home to have the breakfast your phone call ruined.'

*

Two days later I went to see another New York agent as I didn't feel that the Siemen agency was doing much for me. I saw Herbert Barratt, and wrote afterwards in my diary, 'Barratts seem very on the ball, I may sign with them.' As I was writing this a huge display of red roses were delivered. They were from yet another agent. On Friday the 29th March I phoned my London agents to ask what they thought about going over to Barratt's, and also told them about a meeting that was planned between Mr Chapin, Mr Riecker and myself, the following Wednesday at 5 p.m. The agents explained that the only reason the Met management wanted to see me was to ask me to lose weight.

On April 1st I told Herbert Barratt's that they could handle me from June 1st 1975. I went to the Met meeting on the 3rd very much on the defensive. John and I sat opposite Mr Chapin and Mr Rieker (Mairwyn was with Mary in the nurse's office). First of all Mr Chapin asked me if I would return to the Met in the November of that year and sing two Santuzzas – I didn't need my arm twisting to say yes to that one. All I said apart from yes was that I thought it was time that New York heard some of my Italian repertoire. Then Mr Chapin smiled and said, 'Well, as for that – this is the list of operas for next year – is there anything in it that would interest you?'

I glanced at the list, and the first opera that caught my eye was *Norma*. I thought, 'Don't push your luck, Nellie, they won't let you do that one.' Then I looked further down the list and saw *Aida* – and casually as I could I said, 'Well, there is *Aida*.' Charlie Rieker rubbed his hands together with what looked like glee, and Mr Chapin said, 'Right – fine, but isn't there anything else?' I took a deep breath, and said '*Norma*?'

Mr Chapin said, 'Oh, I so hoped that you would want that.'

I couldn't believe this was happening to me. I said, 'You know I've never sung *Norma*?'

Mr Chapin said, 'What better place to make your *Norma* debut than here at the Met where we all love you?'

And so it was settled. I have never won the pools, but I have to tell you that those few moments in Mr Chapin's office were worth more than a pools fortune to me – they gave me a confidence in myself that money never could.

And I couldn't wait to tell my agent that they had never once mentioned my weight.

*

I sang *Götterdämmerung* again in New York on the 2nd April and on the 6th. We all flew home to London on the 7th. My agent said, 'Well, how did the meeting go?' I told him, and he asked if I'd got a contract out of them. When I said no, he said, 'Then don't count your chickens before they're hatched.'

On Monday 8th April I rested at home, and on the Tuesday we drove down to Bristol where I sang *The Valkyrie* for the Wells. After the show Lord Harewood took us and some others in the cast out to supper at Harvey's restaurant, then we drove back to London. The next morning I rested, but in the afternoon I had a coaching session to work on the German of *Valkyrie* as I was to sing it in Strasbourg at the end of the month.

The next day we again drove down to Bristol and I sang the *Siegfried* Brünnhilde. After this performance the Hippodrome theatre manager insisted on taking us out to supper, then we drove back to London. When I was working on the German *Valkyrie* on the Friday, the coach asked me, 'How do you manage with jet lag?'

'I haven't got time for jet lag,' I said.

On the Saturday we drove again to Bristol and I sang the *Götterdämmerung* Brünnhilde. Half way through the scene with Waltraute, a little thing called jet lag said, 'Haven't got time for me, eh?' and there in front of the audience who had come to hear the English *Ring*, Nellie Hunter sang 'Mit blasser Wange, du bleiche Schwester, was willst du wilde von mir?' Well, if the Waltraute (Katherine Pring) wasn't a *bleiche Schwester* when she began the act, she certainly was now. She looked up into my face with panic. Her next words, sung just a beat or two after mine, were 'Upon your hand' and then she sang 'der' Ring instead of 'the' Ring. Her mouth began to twitch. My next lines are supposed to be said as I walk away from her scornfully. We turned our backs on each other, took deep breaths, and the panic was over – probably unnoticed by many of the audience. But I made a vow there and then that flying the Atlantic, switching languages, singing a whole *Ring* plus two *Götterdämmerungs* in twelve days was something I would not repeat.

*

On the 28th April I flew to France to begin rehearsals for *Walküre* in Strasbourg. I went alone as we had not been able to find a

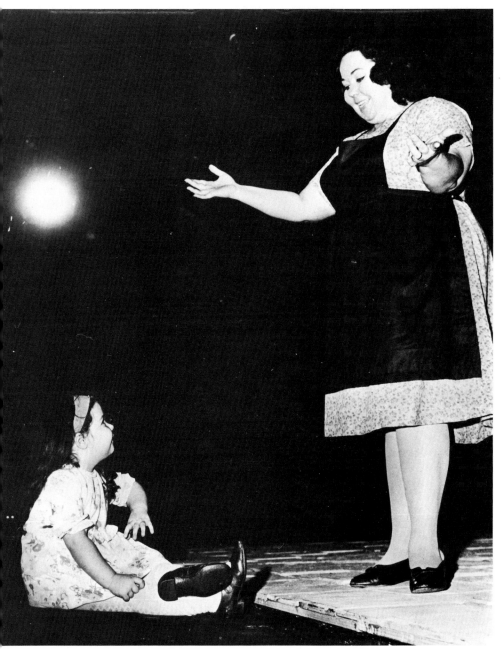

Santuzza in *Cavalleria Rusticana*. I had doubts about the '1940s' production at the Wells, but Mairwyn seems to like it.

At the Metropolitan Opera, New York:
my first *Walkure* Brunnhilde (above)
and my first *Gotterdammerung*
Brunnhilde (right).

Norma in San Francisco
(left). I loved this.

Norma in New York (right).
This was a nightmare.

Elisabeta in *Don Carlos* for
Sadlers Wells.

Abigaile in *Nabucco* for
New Orleans.

Turandot for Welsh National Opera.

Brunnhilde for the Pacific Northwest Festival, Seattle.

In recital, with Hazel Vivienne at the piano.

Macbeth, with Robert Allman, Australian Opera.

On the Michael Parkinson Show in Australia.

The sun shines on Rita Nellie Hunter. Diva and daughter, Australia, 1981.

baby-sitter. The hotel was dire, the room dark and damp. After I unpacked, a kind French Lady picked me up in her car. Thank God for the friends of the opera. No problems with the orchestral, and I went back to the hotel and called room service. But there was no room service, and no restaurant. So I had to wait till morning for the 'continental breakfast'. The next day the theatre management phoned to say it was a holiday in France and so I would not be required for two days.

So here I was in Strasbourg, no room service, a public holiday, so no shops open, and raining cats and dogs. I had left London on the 28th and had just the continental breakfast on the morning of the 29th. I didn't want to go out in the rain alone to a restaurant, so I went to bed. The next morning I was brought the continental breakfast again. By late afternoon I had been without proper food since my breakfast in London on the morning of the 28th. I was starving and so, despite the heavy rain, I went out and found a cheap café and had a steak and salad. I felt wet and wretched and alone, and after I had eaten went quickly back to the dreary hotel, took my clothes off and had a hot bath and went to bed. I was glad to get to work the next day, and it was at least warm in the theatre.

After the rehearsal the next day, 1st May, in the break between the morning and the evening call, I went into a big department store near the hotel, called Magmod. I bought myself an electric coffee pot, so that I could at least have hot drinks, then I bought cheese, yogurt, ham, fruit, butter, Ryvita, lettuce and tomatoes. I scurried back to the hotel with my treasures. To my disappointment the coffee pot plug would not fit into any of the points in the room, so I went back to the store and tried to exchange it, or get my money back. It isn't very difficult buying something when you don't speak the language – you just shove what you want under the assistant's nose, along with the money. But you try getting them to understand that you can't use it and that you want your money back! They got pretty mad with me, and as I did not want a repetition of the Berlin episode I went back to the hotel with the useless coffee pot, and hoped that John would be able to get it to work in London.

We rehearsed for another two days and then were told we were not required all day Saturday or Sunday and not until Monday evening. I had now been in Strasbourg six days and in that time had rehearsed for a total of fifteen hours and I was getting pretty fed up. I would not have minded if all my time had been occupied but now – faced with another three days of sitting in that cold and dismal room, the only TV in the lounge, and not being able to understand a word on it anyhow – I packed up a few things, and got myself on the next plane to London via Paris.

John was surprised when I walked in, but fully understood when I told him the circumstances. He asked what stage we had got to in the production, and I told him we had not yet done anything with the Siegmund (who was to be Jon Andrew) as he had not yet come to France, he was busy elsewhere.

Then John showed me my date sheet. I had turned down an engagement in Genoa from April 15 to May 6, as Strasbourg had asked if I would arrive on April 28th instead of May 6th. I remembered offering to commute from Genoa to Strasbourg for the first week of rehearsals but I had been told that this would not be acceptable. Now of course, considering the small amount of rehearsing I had done in that first week, the proposed commuting would have been quite feasible.

I found myself thinking I had once again been conned into passing up an engagement which I could have fulfilled.

So I went back to France and we rehearsed Monday evening, Tuesday evening, all day Wednesday and Thursday and Friday evening. After the Friday evening call Jon Andrew and his wife Victoria drove me back to my hotel. I had told Victoria about it and she came with me to see my room. She took one look and said, 'Jesus darling, even the prisoner of Zenda had it better.' They were going right on to their home in Mannheim for the week-end. She said, 'Sod this lot, darling, where's your passport and your nightie? Come with us for the weekend.' So I threw a few things in a plastic bag and off I went with Jon and Victoria to Mannheim.

Saturday was spent mooching about the house and sitting on their balcony in the sunshine. We were to drive back to Strasbourg on the Sunday evening so that we would all be in time for the Monday morning call. We stopped on the way to visit some friends of theirs in Heidelberg.

As I was sitting chatting with the people in Heidelberg I knew that I had a sore throat. I also knew that it was the sort that usually preceded one of my savage chest colds. The next morning my suspicions were confirmed, and I took my temperature which was 102°. I phoned the agents in London and told them that I needed to stay in bed and get lots of hot drinks. They said, 'OK, do it then.' I pointed out that there was no such things as hot drinks in this hotel except the morning coffee. They answered, 'Then get yourself on a plane and go to a specialist in Paris.' Nearly in tears I said, 'I have a temperature of 102°, I am not fit to go anywhere. There are three days to the first night, I am going to need antibiotics.' They told me to get a doctor from Strasbourg.

I tried everything to get the theatre people and the hotel to understand that I wanted a doctor, but it was just hopeless, my French was non-existent.

At noon I phoned John and as soon as he heard my voice he said, 'Oh my God.'

He could not find a baby-sitter and so he reserved himself and Mairwyn places on the 2.30 flight to Strasbourg, and then he went round to the doctor in Thames Ditton and got a prescription, rushed to the chemist and bought all he needed, then rang the agent and told him what he was going to do but added that if he was to catch the plane there wasn't time to get a taxi in the backwoods of Surrey and he would be glad of a lift to the airport. It was suggested that he took his own car and left it in the long term car park for twenty-four hours. He was convinced, it seemed, that a couple of pills and a hot orange juice would put me right and that he would be home next day. He did, however, point out how much it was costing for Mairwyn's fare, but what else could we do? We had no one to leave her with. So off John went to Heathrow and by the time he had put the car in the long term car park and waited for the courtesy bus to take him to the terminal, the flight had boarded and they were calling his name over the tannoy. He went to the check-in desk and handed over the case and begged them not to take off without him. When he got to the gate, the plane had already left the departure gate, but they said if he could make it across the tarmac they would let him get on the plane. By this time, Mairwyn was crying as her little legs could not keep up the necessary pace, so John picked her up and ran with her in his arms. She was nearly seven, and John thought he would have a heart attack, she was so heavy. Anyway, they made it and he arrived in the hotel room, took one look at me lying there and thought to himself, 'If she makes the first night it will be a miracle.'

This was Monday the 13th May. He nursed me for two days. I had to miss the dress rehearsal, and he had quite a job explaining that to the management. I made the first night on the 16th but I remember nothing about it at all, except that the Strasburg Opera management insisted we all went to a café next to the theatre for a reception after the show. All I remember about that was feeling ill and having to leave after ten minutes to get back to the hotel to bed.

I stayed in bed for the 17th and 18th during which time the weather was very bad and John was not able to take Mairwyn to the little park near the theatre. There was a little roundabout there, which she loved, and John used to buy several tickets for her and go and sit under the trees until she had used up all her tickets.

With the three of us in one tiny room things got somewhat fraught. There were only two beds, and so John had to take the mattress off his bed and put it on the floor for Mairwyn to sleep on at night. Mairwyn used to go round the other rooms with the chamber maids to pass the time; they all loved her. But on this one day she became separated from her favourite one and went to look for her. She went into the lift alone, something she had never done before. The doors were the sort that are in two parts. She put her hand on the door and leaned against it, and when the lift got to our floor she did not remove her hand. One part of the door slid back and her fingers were trapped between the two parts of the doors. We only found out about this when we heard her bloodcurdling screams. John ran out of the room, and even I got out of bed and went to the door. She was on the landing screaming and blood was pouring from her hand. We were horrified and thought for one awful moment that she had lost a finger. Three fingers had been badly gashed, and she bears the scars to this day.

The next day she was on the mattress on the floor just before bedtime and again she began to scream. This time she had found a power point near the floor and had put a finger in to investigate.

Needless to say, our nerves were not in the best state so it was not much fun on the next day when John had the job of telling the Opera management that I was still too ill to sing and would have to cancel the second performance. They were not pleased and asked if he was taking me to England. He told them I was not able to travel, which was quite true, and he hoped they would realise from this how ill I was. I was also not able to sing the performance on the 22nd, and on the morning of the 24th I had a bad nose haemorrhage, which scared us all. It went on bleeding on and off all day, and it was now quite clear that I would not be able to sing the next night either, the 25th. So with the hotel bill mounting and with no prospect of any fees coming in, John booked us all on the flight the next afternoon to London.

The theatre were of course distraught and once again they were forced to put on a substitute. There was only one plane on that Saturday between Strasbourg and London, and we stood and waited for it to arrive from London – it then had to do a turn-around and go right back again. We watched the passen-

gers get off. I saw Brian MacMaster, the Wells company manager, get off it and then remembered that he had said he would
come out to France to hear me. He saw me, and started to say
'How are you?' The words died on his lips – he stood mute for a
second, then said, 'Oh dear God, you look awful.'

On the flight home I felt so ill I just wanted to die, and as the
plane started down I moaned in pain as the pressure in my ears
built up. As the plane touched the ground I realised I was deaf. I
tried the usual remedies for this but didn't dare blow my nose in
case it began to bleed again. By the time we got home I was stone
deaf and could not hear a thing. John had told the management
in Strasbourg that he hoped I would be able to return for the last
performance on the 28th. The doctor sent me to bed and gave me
an injection to make me sleep, and drops to put in my ears, and
more antibiotics.

The next day John told me what the bill for the long term car
park had come to. I can't put down what I said in reply – it would
scorch the paper.

*

I remained deaf for nearly three weeks, during which time I
studied the role of Eglantine in Weber's *Euryanthe* that I was to
record in Dresden during the first week of July. It was a case of
re-swotting, as I had sung the role with the Chelsea Opera in the
sixties. My Auntie Ruth said she would use her two weeks
holiday looking after Mairwyn for us.

EMI had said that they would give me £2,000 for recording
Eglantine, and that they would pay my fare and pay for the room
and board. We had come back empty-handed from Strasbourg
and we also had to pay for the extra fares for the family, the car
park and the hotel bill. So when the time came for the agents to
send us our tickets for Dresden they said they had no cash in
hand for me, and I would have to go up to the EMI office in
London and get them to give me enough for the two tickets and
some pocket money. The tickets I did not mind asking for, but it
was very embarrassing to ask for pocket money. Still it had to be
done. We went up to EMI the night before we flew. They were
very nice about it, so the next day we did as we did as we
had been told, and used the pocket money to buy German
marks.

We flew to Berlin and got a taxi from Tempelhof airport to
Checkpoint Charlie, where we were met by an East German
guide. As we walked from West to East I was filled with dread.
The Russians in the German sector were a grim-looking lot. We

had already been briefed by our guide on how to act – one piece of advice was, 'Try not to look relieved when they eventually let you through or they will think you are guilty of something.' The Russians inspected our passports and asked our guide a great many questions about me and my reason for going into East Germany. Then they began to interrogate the guide about John. I could see things were not going too well – and I was right. We clearly should have got a permit for him too. The guide explained that 'Herr Thomas was not going to work, it was just to keep his wife company.' The Russians were not impressed. I began to panic and, despite having been told not to say anything, I began to plead on John's behalf. I told my guide I was not going through the iron curtain without my husband, and if he couldn't go then I wasn't going either. I eventually persuaded the Russians to phone the EMI office in Berlin. We had to wait while this was done, and then they drew up a paper saying I was responsible for John, and asked him if he had any money of his own, in case, as they put it, 'something happened to Frau Thomas'. This was when we discovered we should have been in possession of some East German marks – we had no idea that the currency was different on the other side of the Wall. We told the Russians that the hotel and the food for us both was being paid for by EMI. Fortunately they didn't check on that one, for reasons I will explain later.

We drove from Berlin to Dresden and the further east we got the lower my spirits sank. It was strange not to pass any other traffic, except for a few old men on bicycles. Despite the fact that it was a sunny day, the chairs on the porches outside the little houses were deserted. We stopped once for petrol. A house opposite the garage looked empty until John and I got out of the car to stretch our legs, then the little lace curtains were furtively parted and an old lady peered out at us. I smiled at her. She swept the curtains closed and disappeared as quickly as she had appeared. John turned to me and whispered, 'Bloody hell, Rit, It's like "Arsenic and Old Lace".' I burst out laughing and the two men serving in the garage whirled round. I don't think they had heard anyone laugh for years.

We drove through the outskirts of Dresden. Despite some rebuilding, it still bore the scars of wartime air-raids. What a beautiful city it must have been. I said to John what fools the human race could be, and I wondered if all that destruction had brought anyone to their senses. From what I had observed that day I doubted it.

It took us about three hours to get to Dresden and when we

had unpacked it was about 7 p.m. so we went downstairs for dinner. On each table there was a tiny vase with a single red carnation in it; we had also noticed there was one in the bedroom too, on the dressing table. As the week progressed we became convinced that the red carnations held a bug – a microphone. They probably did not, but in the end it was a standing joke, whenever anything went wrong we would speak into the red carnation and tell some mythical Russian just what we thought of him.

When we had eaten the dinner they brought us the bill, and we told the waiter to add it to the room bill. He said it was not possible. We could not understand why. Nor would they accept the West German marks, they wanted East German marks. John said, 'Why is it whenever we go anywhere there is a cock-up?'

At this point David Motley, the EMI recording manager, came into the restaurant and asked us what was wrong. When we explained, he said calmly, 'Well, of course they won't let you charge it to the room, we are only paying for your bed not your food.'

I was stunned. I told him that it was part of my contract for them to pay for the food. He shook his head. And he said, 'You will have to pay them cash.' I told him the currency situation. David Motley paid the bill for our dinner and said he would contact London in the morning.

Jessye Norman, who was to sing Euryanthe, arrived later in the evening.

*

After our return from Dresden I began rehearsals for my first Elisabeta in *Don Carlos*. There were seven performances and the first was on the 18th September. Margaret Curphey had done the opening night; I had to decline the offer from George Harewood of the first performances as I was supposed to be going to Buenos Aires. I had kept the time free, but to this day I have still not sung in Buenos Aires. When the *Carlos* ended on 5th October I began rehearsals for more *Trovatores* at the Coliseum. They began on 24th October and ended on 16th November – there were seven of them also. Between these performances I was learning Santuzza in Italian for my debut in the role at the Met.

In the autumn Martina Arroyo was in town and she and I went to the Garden to see Sutherland in *Lucia*. During one of the intervals on the grand staircase I met a tall and good-looking young man who said how much he enjoyed both Martina and me and wasn't it fantastic that we were both at Joan's *Lucia*. His name was Roland Brown, and he and I were to become close friends, and he eventually became my secretary. That evening Joan Sutherland gained a new fan – me.

We had decided that I would go alone to New York and that John would follow, leaving Mairwyn in the care of our French au pair, but in the event Edwige would not look after her, so John brought her with him. I flew to the States on 18th November, and our friend Herman Mallamood and his wife met me at the airport, along with Glenn Pressler from the Herbert Barratt management. We had decided to try the Mayflower Hotel instead of the Ollcott. Indeed it seemed much better, and the kitchenette was bigger. The Barratt management had sent me flowers. I was awake early next morning and, with no news of rehearsals, I went shopping to Layne Bryants which Jessye Norman had recommended. The following day it rained so I stayed indoors, and still there was no sign of rehearsals, so I seemed to have been sent over prematurely.

On the 21st the Met phoned and asked me to go for a music call from 10 to 11 a.m. After the call I walked over to the Chase Manhattan bank and was upset to discover that the bank in the UK had not transferred the $1,000 they had agreed to. Nor had my Diners card arrived. I went to the Met to ask for my fare in cash and I was rather shaken when they would not give it to me. I phoned the bank in London and asked them to cable some money, fast.

On Friday, the 22nd, I went to the Met and worked from 11 a.m. till 2 p.m. on the production. John phoned to tell me that the bank still had not sent the $1,000, nor had the agent, so he changed his flight, and instead of coming on the 26th, the day before my Santuzza, he would be with me on the 23rd and bring some cash with him. I was now down to $50 in travellers' cheques.

I went to see the *Cav* on the Saturday matinée, and that evening John and Mairwyn arrived.

Most of Monday I spent at the Met costume fitting and my diary records that I thought the costume 'dire'. At noon I had another music call, this time with the conductor, then at 4 p.m. a production call with the rest of the cast. The first Santuzza was on the 27th, and I wrote in my dairy: 'Worried sick all day, not about the music or the words but about the difficult set and the costume is so unbecoming. Once I got to the theatre at 5 p.m. I was fine and was delighted with the reception from the audience. We stayed after the *Cav* had finished so that we could hear the Canio of Richard Tucker. My God what a voice. I have never heard anyone sing it so fine and what a nice man he was.

On the Friday and Saturday Mairwyn went to stay with a friend, Battyah Godfrey, and she spent her birthday with her. On the Sunday I woke with the start of a cold and stayed in all day. On the Monday I tried everything to shift it but with deep regret I had to cancel my second Santuzza on the 3rd, and on the 4th December we flew home.

When we got home we saw that the au pair had completely neglected the house and left the dog unfed and unwashed – it seems all she had done was read and eat and make love to her boyfriend whom she had invited to stay in our absence. So we gave her notice and found her another post with a family in East Molesey.

Part Two

CHAPTER SIXTEEN

California, Here I Come

In January 1975 I began to rehearse the Santuzza again, this time in English for the Sadler's Wells, and found it hard going to remember the new translation after the Italian at the Met. All I could think of was the old Carl Rosa translation. The first of the revived *Cavallerias* was on 23rd January, after which we flew to New York to cover the *Rings* and to do some *Walküres* of my own.

We had a nice apartment at the Mayflower Hotel overlooking the park, and on the 8th I learned that Birgit Nilsson was to sing Sieglinde to my Brünnhilde with Vickers as Siegmund. When John went to the Chase Manhattan bank on 11th February to draw from his account for our food, again the same old story. There was no cash there, but later in the day they let him draw from my account as there was a little residue there from the *Cav* visit the previous November.

The rehearsals became boring as it seemed all I was doing was sitting in the stalls watching Berit Lindholm. This went on for five days so I was glad when the weekend came. Barratt's called to see how I was and I told them I did not like spectator sports.

On the Monday I had a call for *Götterdämmerung* but it was cancelled at the last moment.

My friend and Mairwyn's godmother, Marianne, was house- and dog-sitting for us back home, and on the 26th February I got a dramatic phone call from my agents to say our central heating boiler had packed up and they would have to install a new one.

Then on 1st March they rang again to say that John's mother was in hospital with bronchitis and a cardiac condition. Again the call was dramatic, as if she was at death's door, so we rang Marianne at our home, and asked her to call the hospital and get more information. We eventually spoke to the hospital ourselves and they told us she was poorly but nowhere near

145

on the critical list. I felt for John as I knew what it was like to be thousands of miles from home when one's parents were ill.

On March 3rd we were still traipsing to the bank to see if the $500 had come as we understood it had been sent on the 18th of February. The bank manager said that if it *had* been sent on the 18th February then it would have been in my US account. Later that day we phoned to see how John's mother was, and Marianne told us that the agents had said, on the subject of the dollars, that 'they were sick to death of the whole business.' I said to John, 'Not half as sick as they would be if they were trying to live on the pittance we have left!' I wrote in my diary that night, 'I really don't want to come here again under these penny-pinching conditions. I feel so mad I am thinking of cancelling the November *Normas* here.'

I sang *Walküre* on the 8th March, and saw Nilsson go into the wings to hear my battle-cry. I must say it felt odd to stand and sing the Todesverkundigung with her lying beneath me on the stage level listening. I had a great ovation at the end and was surrounded by fans after the show and didn't get to John Kander's party till 1.30 a.m. He had gone to a lot of trouble and it was a great party. There was a rave notice in the New York *Post* on the Monday and something else that cheered us even more – we actually got the long-awaited $500.

Mairwyn at this time was becoming something of a handful. She would go down to the foyer and into the coffee shop of the hotel. This we did not mind, as they would call us from the coffee shop to say she was there and then to say she was on her way up in the lift. But one evening when we went to meet the lift there was no sign of her; eventually we found the doorman, who had seen her go off with one of the old ladies who lived in the hotel. She was in fact quite safe, and being spoiled rotten, but she kept on doing this as she was made a fuss of and given sweets. We did our best to stop her but she found ways of sneaking out. Came the day when we found her in an old gentleman's apartment, and it was then we began to think seriously about sending her to boarding school when we got back to England. Up until now we had always brought all her school books with us but she got more and more bad tempered and would not do her lessons with her father. So we left her alone and told her she would have to face her teacher with empty lesson books when she got back. This thought did not upset her in the least.

I wrote in my diary on 14th March: 'I have learnt my lesson, I won't bring Mairwyn again. I won't come here with so little cash, and I won't come to cover again.'

Clearly I did not like the idea of doing rehearsals for the second cast while the first diva was sitting at home. No one did *my* calls for me to keep *me* fresh for the performances.

March 16th the diary records: 'We spent a boring day watching TV. Roland phoned from London and that cheered us a bit but by evening I was sick of TV. John was sick of Mairwyn and sick of me, by 9.30 we were all at each other's throats – what a bastard of a place this is.'

*

We went to Barratt's on the 21st and I was told that my hotel bill had not been paid. Barratt's phoned the agents who said they had had no money from the Met yet. The Met accounts department had paid me for the *Cav* I did not sing in December, and said they would deduct $500 a week when I returned till I had paid it off. But for some reason they had deducted it all at once. My diary reads, 'It was a bitter blow and a dreadful shock to think that when I return home I will have no money.'

I realised that something would have to be done about fees, as with 30% tax and 20% commission my fees were halved right away. I spent two hours the next day writing to the agents to try to explain that if I was not going to be able to make some cash I would be better off on the dole.

I phoned home on 23rd March and Marianne told me that my agents had had some trouble with the plumber over the new central heating boiler. I surmised that the trouble was he had not been paid.

On the 24th Marianne phoned with news of John's mother and also to say that the agents had told her they could not understand why I wanted the other $500 as they had paid my hotel bill anyway.

On the 26th Barratt's phoned to say the Met had offered me *Trovatore* in New York for a month in 1978. Three weeks back in England to fulfil the ENO contract, then back to New York for the Met tour with *Trovatore*. But the *Trovatore* at the Met never came to fruition.

We flew home on Sunday April 6th; we had been in New York for fifty-eight days, and I had only sung three *Walküres*, for which I had had the full fee, and small cover fee for the other nine performances. So after paying for the hotel for the fifty-eight days and food and 30% tax and 20% commission and fares for John and Mairwyn and paying back the Santuzza fee, we worked out that my agents had actually got more cash at the end of it all than I had. It did not seem to me to be worthwhile to carry on my career in this way.

Two days later we flew to Rouen in France to do two more *Walküres*, then flew home on the 14th April. On the 15th I was singing *Ballo* in Birmingham with the ENO. There was another *Ballo* in Birmingham on the 18th.

On the 28th we drove to Leeds and I sang a *Ring* there on the 29th, May 1st and 3rd. We went back to Leeds the following week to do *Ballo*. That tour took us also to Oxford and Manchester with *Masked Ball* and *The Ring*.

Then we went down to our caravan in Dorset for a much-needed break. I see from my diary that I had the grand sum of £73.73 – not a lot to show for all that running around. And one paper had the nerve to say that I had deserted the ENO to go and earn vast sums in the United States. If the person who wrote that reads this, then I would be delighted to show him my bank statement.

At 11 a.m. on Saturday 28th June 1975 I went to John Matheson for my first coaching for *Norma*. He was a wonderful coach, but I began to get a bit edgy when after nine sessions we were still messing around with the 'Casta diva'. There is a lot more to *Norma* than that aria. Going all the way to London wasted time that could have been spent studying at home, so I began to have a session every week with John Barker to get him to check what I had taught myself. I found this was a quicker and more satisfactory way of working and, as we were paying John Matheson £15 an hour, we could really not afford it after the financial disaster in New York.

Early in July my agents told me that Sir Georg Solti was looking for a soprano to record as Senta *Flying Dutchman* and would I sing for him? I explained that I did not know the Senta in German but could soon learn it and would display my German to him by singing some of *The Ring* for him. Arrangements were made for him to come to our home in Surrey. John Matheson was to play.

Roland said, 'Darling, your china leaves a lot to be desired. It's almost your birthday, I will buy you a set of real china and a smart cake from Fortnum and Mason.'

And so on the appointed day, Roland arrived with the china and the cake. Sir Georg was most impressed by my voice and wanted to know what I had been doing all these years. I wondered if I should tell him he had heard me before as a third

Norn in *Götterdämmerung*, and that he had been unpleasant to me. But wiser counsels prevailed.

Sir Georg did not wish for a cup of tea nor any of Roland's 'smart cake' – but Mairwyn could not wait to get into the divine confection and, while the diva stood on the doorstep saying her farewells to Sir Georg, her daughter had fled to the kitchen and attempted to get the large cake from the fridge by herself. Needless to say it fell to the floor. I heard a wail of grief from the kitchen. Roland and I rushed to see what was wrong. The cake had fallen face down onto the kitchen floor, which luckily was clean, so before Sir Georg had got to the end of the drive we were all sitting on the kitchen floor scooping up the lovely cake, as Roland remarked, 'Sod him, I'm not wasting this.'

Anyway, the Sentas went to some other lady. But if it had not been for Sir Georg Solti's visit, I would not have had such a nice new set of china.

By August 2nd I was well on my way with the preparation for *Norma* at the Met. I used to sit in the garden and play Callas's recording on my tape-recorder. One day, however, the man next door drove me mad with his constant bonfires, and so I rose at midnight and tore all the ivy from our connecting fence and lit a bonfire, and then went indoors and played 'The Ride of the Valkyries' very loud. Mairwyn thought it was great fun, but John wasn't so sure. But they never lit another bonfire next door, so presumably they got the message.

On 7th August I went to the studios in Abbey Road and recorded 'Casta diva' with piano for the ENO disc. I recorded it all, recit as well, but unfortunately there wasn't time to include it all on the finished disc.

On 20th August I began to rehearse for a revival of *Don Carlos*, for performances on September 17th, 23rd and 27th. Then on the morning of 29th September came a momentous call. On the 28th I had a run-through of *Norma* and was satisfied that I had memorised it all and now had several weeks before going to New York to get the role into my voice and to pace it.

But on the morning of the 29th we were woken by a phone call asking me, 'How is your *Norma*?' I was not too pleased by being roused so early, and replied acidly, 'Fine, how's yours?'

I was told that Caballé was ill and would I fly to San Francisco the next day to replace her on the 11th and 14th October? I said that I was pleased to replace her but could not fly out there the next day as I had first to go and buy a new coat and other clothes for myself and Mairwyn.

I spent a hectic day packing, and phoned Roland who came

out to help me. We decided he would go direct to New York at a later date and take all our winter things as by November in New York we would need them, and we would just take our summer things to California. Several times we were interrupted by phone calls from Kurt H. Adler, who was naturally a worried man. I had practically to swear an oath to him that I would be with him by the evening of 1st October. He called again to offer not just a first class fare for me but a part share in John's fare also and a half share of whatever the hotel in San Francisco would cost. The fee went up during the day, too, to $4,000 a show. In the end I told him to stop all this tempting as it would not get me there any sooner. I had to make arrangements for Marianne to come over, and as she had no phone John had to drive up to London and wait outside her house till she came home, then wait for her to pack, and then drive her out to Surrey.

On the following day I had a serious row with my agent who had called John and Mairwyn 'excess baggage'. He was moaning about having to pay the travel agent £900 for all the fares. I know it seemed a lot, but when I sat down and did some arithmetic, with the Met and San Francisco sharing my fare and Mr Adler's offer to pay half John's fare, then all we really had to pay was £142. 'But,' said the agent, 'I won't be getting that cash. You'll be picking it up in person and that's the last I'll see of it once you get in those New York dress shops.'

I hurled a stream of abuse down the phone and later phoned both the Met and Mr Adler to ask them to phone the agent direct, and for God's sake tell him he would get all the fares direct. I also asked Mr Adler to have some of my fee ready as an advance for food.

After about an hour I had a contrite phone call from the agents saying they hadn't wanted all the fares, just some, and what would I do for expenses. Would I like a £100 in dollars? I told him in no uncertain terms where to put his £100.

Mairwyn had been troubled for several days with a verruca on the sole of her foot, and was having treatment for it from the doctor. This was another reason that I delayed my departure, as I hoped that it would be cured in the two days before we left. However, this was not to be, and the poor child was in great pain. The air hostess was very kind and gave her some first class slippers to put on, and also something on which to raise her foot. All went fairly well until we had to change planes in Chicago, where there was a long queue through the immigration, and she slid along on her bottom. Then we had to go to the other terminal in a bus and she cried every time her foot touched the ground.

When we got to the other terminal we were in danger of missing the flight and John just had to pick her up and try to carry her the rest of the way, while I struggled along with the hand baggage. We were worried that our cases would not be put on the right plane, and by the time we got to the other plane John said, 'I don't give a shit if I never see the bloody bags again.' I said, 'Then I would have to go to all those New York dress shops, wouldn't I?' And we both laughed.

*

Mr Adler had sent a big limousine to meet us in California but, best of all, among the crowds was a friendly face, Cliff Grant. He said, 'I know how you feel after a trip like that, thought the sight of me would cheer you up.' Darling Cliff, you certainly did cheer us up.

We had been told by Mr Adler that we were to stay at the Mark Hopkins and, when we gave the driver this instruction, Cliff said, 'Rita, how can you afford to stay there?' Of course I had no idea that the 'Hopkins' was *the* hotel and I said to Cliff, 'Mr Adler is paying half the bill.' I thought Cliff would burst. 'Christ, Rita you *are* well in!' 'No I'm not, you fool. Adler's in a jam, if he'd sent for you at the eleventh hour, he'd have done the same for you.' Cliff said, 'No one has ever wanted me that much.'

It turned out that every room in town was full and the Mark Hopkins was the only place Mr Adler could get and when we saw the suite of rooms I knew that not even the $4,000 fee could pay for that lot. However, Mr Adler's kindness went even further; he found that our suite had no view and when we got back after the first rehearsal he had had all our things moved up to a higher floor so that we could see the city.

I had never been in such a suite of rooms before – it seemed an awful lot of space for just the three of us. I had a bedroom and a bathroom and huge sitting room, then down a long pass-age there was another bedroom and another bathroom and another sitting room and a kitchen. I had never known such luxury.

My diary records little until the first night. I worked all hours. And since all I saw of the city was from my window, thank heaven for a room with a view.

Two very strange things happened in San Francisco, one on the first day of rehearsal. We took a cab to the hall where we were to work, and when we walked into the foyer of the hall Mairwyn asked to go to the toilet. The young producer was

151

waiting for us at the door, so I turned to Mairwyn and said, 'It's down the hall first door on the right.' The producer looked amazed, but I thought nothing of it. I was about to go with him into the hall but decided to wait there for Mairwyn in case she was unable to find me, and the producer went on ahead to announce my arrival. As he left John said, 'I must go too,' and I said, 'Oh, the men's loo is down the other side of the passage.' I saw that his face was white and this made me realise what I had just said. How the hell did I know where the toilets were? I had never set foot in California before. I stood stunned by this feeling of having been there before. When Mairwyn returned I asked her, 'Was the toilet where Mum said?' 'Yes,' she replied. When John returned I didn't have to ask him the question, I knew I was right. Then John made me go cold all over, saying, 'I wasn't going to ask you where it was Rita, I knew already.' At the coffee break we went into the foyer and scoured the walls for signs that said 'Toilet' but there was none.

All the time we were in the city we had the same feeling, not as strong as the first time, but there was one other occasion that was even more spooky. After the first performance my dressing room was filled with admirers and there was no room for John, who was outside most of the time. At one point over the heads of all the people I saw a tall beautiful red-head waving to me. She wore the most spectacular outfit and she was laughing and seemed to have been bowled over by the performance. As I signed autographs I shouted over the fans' heads, 'Won't keep you long, Jenny.' Then that chill feeling came over me. Why did I call her Jenny? I had never seen her before. She seemed not to have heard me say her name, only that I would not keep her long. Yes, it was her name, and when she finally got to me she threw her arms round me and said, 'Jesus, Rita, I've waited all my life to hear *Norma* sung like that,' and I saw that she was crying. She and her friend invited us to supper, and when I accepted I saw John's eyebrows raise to a question mark; it was not like me to go out to supper with a total stranger. I introduced her to John, saying 'This is Jenny.'

She looked at me and laughed, 'For Christ's sake, how did you know that?' I did not know, and I saw John's face go pale again. I mumbled something about having heard someone call her by her name, but it was not true – and when she reads this she too may wonder. She and I have remained life-long friends and we meet from time to time in some far-flung corner of the world where she has travelled to hear me sing. Sometimes I don't see her for maybe two or three years, but it is as if the years between have never been, for somehow I know that we have known each other long before 1975.

*

When I went into the first rehearsal I saw that the conductor was Carlo Felice Cillario. He had conducted an *Aida* concert performance in North Wales back in 1969/70, but I did not think he would remember me. He did though, and greeted me with open arms. The rehearsals were tiring and I was doing the production on a role that I had not yet had time to sing into my voice. Cillario said not a word the whole time, just sat in on all the production calls and listened to what I was doing. The producer was a wonderful man, Tito Coppabianco, who taught me some useful things about deportment for a large lady that I have never forgotten. He eased me into using dramatic and flamboyant gestures that I would not normally have dared to use with my size. He said, 'Never think of your size as a hindrance. It can and should be used as an asset. Stand there and command the stage, stand tall and above all proud of yourself and your stature.'

This was a revolutionary way of thinking for me. I had always tried to make myself as inconspicuous as I could and it was not easy to change the habits of a life time in just ten days, but with Tito's help I did. Sometimes even now, when I make some large gesture, like at the end of Act 2 of *Norma* when I order Pollione out of my dwelling with just a gesture, it is Tito and his voice that I hear. Tito and I did not meet again for nine years.

Sometimes at rehearsals we would have no 'children' to work with and Tito would ask Mairwyn to lie in the bed and he would tease her and say, 'I hope that you have been a real good girl as this is where your mother has to try to kill her babies,' and she would grin up at him from the bed and say, 'I fink that I have, Mr Tito.' On the fourth day jet lag took its toll and we had to finish at 4 p.m. The diva fell asleep in the cab going home to the hotel despite the bumps in the road.

At the Sitzprobe there were congratulations all round and I was content that, providing I did not get too many nerves, I would sing it quite well. They couldn't find a dagger at rehearsals for the attempted murder of the children and I had to use a cooking spatula with a flat rubber blade. The stage management had cleaned it up and had it inscribed for me, and presented it to me on the first night. I have it to this day in my china cabinet. No golden statuette could be kept with such loving care as my *Norma* spatula.

My father was, of course, Clifford Grant; Adalgisa was Tatiana

153

Troyanos; Pollione Robletta Merolla. At the dress rehearsal it took quite a bit of nerve for me to enter at the top of the high ramp; I have never like heights. After summoning up all my courage, I was most surprised to find that Mr Adler was on stage and he stopped the rehearsal to 'Welcome me to San Francisco!' It was of course a nice gesture, but it did mean poor Nellie had to go off and make that dreadful climb again.

While I rested on the day between the dress rehearsal and the first night John took Mairwyn on the sightseeing tour, on the cable cars, down to Fishermans Wharf and then on a boat around the island of Alcatraz. She thought it was great fun and told me that they played 'San Francisco Open Your Gold Gates' as they went under the Golden Gate bridge. I envied them the trip and vowed that I would come back to San Francisco one day just to see the sights.

On the first night I was scared but it seemed not to affect my voice, as when I had finished the first part of 'Casta diva' the audience went wild. I dropped my garland of flowers into the sacred fire as Tito had told me, and still they did not stop. Apart from anything else, the clapping served one good purpose. It gave me a chance to collect my wits before the second half of the aria – for a big voice the most difficult – all those runs. When they finally did stop, I went on with the rest of the aria and then turned to make my exit, passing Clifford Grant on the way. He winked at me and said, 'Keep that up, Hunter, and Adler will buy you the bloody Mark Hopkins.'

It was certainly a night to remember. I was bombarded with flowers at every curtain call. At the end of each act I would stagger off, laden, and at the end of the scene with the children I had to give them some of the flowers as the audience was still throwing them. Some of the bunches I was able to catch in mid-air and one of the reviewers mentioned it and said I ought to play for the Cincinnati Reds. Before the week was out someone had sent me a 'Reds' tee-shirt. That also is one of my proud possessions. When the reviews came out on the Monday, they were all raves. I could hardly believe it. To please an audience is one thing, but to please the critics, quite another.

*

I had been corresponding for several years with a man called Frank Bottom, who had once heard me sing in London. He lived in Los Angeles and had been on holiday when he learned of my impending debut in San Francisco. He had fled the holiday resort and, as he put it, 'high-tailed it to California'. One of my visitors after the first performance was Frank. He was very shy, mainly on account of his severe sunburn and blistered nose. Well, I didn't care how blistered he was, the main thing was he was there, and we had at last met after writing to each other for so long. He was thrilled by the way I had sung and the reception I had received. We have since become firm pals and when I can't get to the States for my underwear he goes to Layne Bryants and buys my bras and panties for me – now that's what I call love!

My agent from New York, Joe Lipman, was also at the first night – in the full opera rig-out, the cloak lined with red silk. Mairwyn kept pointing and saying 'Dracula, Mummy!' Mr Adler was a happy man that night, in and out of the dressing room like a fiddler's elbow. At one point he said, 'I'm going to bring a guy in to meet you, please be nice to him as he has offered to sponsor a new production of *Turandot* for you.' Well, it was not hard to be nice to him, he was a charmer, and I said one or two things which seemed greatly to amuse them. When Mr Adler took him away he kissed me and whispered, 'Thank you.' I hoped that I had made a good impression, I was longing to sing *Turandot* – even John had said he thought, if someone offered it now, I could do it.

After the second performance on the 14th, Jenny took us all to Trader Vic's for dinner. It had been another flower-bedecked night and we were all walking on air. As we entered the restaurant a lot of diners turned their heads and began to clap and stand up. I turned round to see what great celebrity had walked in, hoping it was a film star. I said, 'Who is it?' Jenny was grinning and Mairwyn said, 'Oh Mummy, don't be thick, it's for you.' Well, that was a night right out of a Hollywood movie – I had seen that scene in the cinema, and now it was happening to me. We sat down as they still clapped, and John whispered, 'This is a turn up for a boilermaker's daughter.' There were tears in my eyes. Of joy yes, but also for my loving and loyal parents who had sacrificed so much to make this all possible for me. How I wished they could have seen their 'mistake' on her night of glory, for that's what it was to me and, out of many nights of success, that night in San Francisco will always remain the greatest for me.

*

Before I left the theatre Carlo Felice Cillario had given me a note in Italian that he had written to the New York conductor, Massini. He would not tell me what he had put in it and I would not have dreamed of looking.

On the 15th we had breakfast at the airport with Jenny, Neil and Frank, and then flew to begin my season as Norma at the Met. When we got to the Mayflower, Roland met us in the foyer. He was full of beans. 'Wait till you see your apartment, darling.' My jaw dropped when I did. It was full of flowers and baskets of fruit. I read the cards, and they were all from Adler, apart from one. Before I had time to take off my coat, the phone was ringing. It was Mr Adler thanking me, and wishing me luck for the New York *Normas*.

The next day I went to work at the Met with the conductor, Gianfranco Massini, who had conducted in Nice for my first *Aidas*. I gave him Carlo's note and he read it and said, 'So?' My heart dropped. What on earth had Carlo said to him? (I had to wait till 1981 to find out – in Sydney, Carlo told me. He had said, 'I send you not a virgin Norma but one that has been tried and has conquered all.') Now I know that a conquest on the West Coast is quite a different thing from a conquest in New York.

At 3 p.m. after my rehearsal on the 17th, we had a frantic phone call from Mr Adler. He had no Norma for the Sunday matinee. I went to see Charlie Reicker at the Met and asked if I could go and help Mr Adler out. He really did not like the idea of my going to California again and tried to talk me out of it. I reasoned with him that the production calls were not to begin till the Tuesday and there was a limit to what I could do with the conductor on my own as we had no tenor (it was to be Franco Corelli). Charlie reluctantly let me go, and John and I flew to California together in first class style, courtesy of Mr Adler. Mairwyn stayed with Roland in New York, and this time we stayed not in the Mark Hopkins but in Jenny's apartment overlooking the island of Alcatraz.

Mr Adler asked me to visit him in his office after we arrived and he offered me roles every autumn season for the following three years. Santuzzas, Brünnhildes and – it seemed that I had been as nice as was needed to the backer – there would be a new production of *Turandot*. As usual there were flowers thrown during and after the performance, and fans chanting outside my dressing room window: 'Favorita, Favorita, La Favorita.' My cup of joy was full and running over.

We went to a party after the performance at the home of the man who did my make-up. Carlo Felice Cillario told me to get my London agents to speak with the Australian Opera, as that was where he was conducting most and he wanted me to sing Lady Macbeth and Abigaille there in 1978.

*

On the Tuesday I did a music call with Massini in the Met and for the first time met my New York Adalgisa, Frederica Von Stade. On the 22nd I did the first production call from 4–6 p.m.

I wrote in the diary, 'Hate the set, it's a death trap.' On the 23rd a production call and still no Corelli. The set took an hour to put up and so all I sang was 'Casta diva'.

On the 24th I wrote in my diary, 'Sets still not right, didn't begin work till 4.30. Producer and conductor fed up, still no Corelli.'

At last on the 27th Signor Franco Corelli turned up for a Sitzprobe. I hugged myself with glee, he was so tall and handsome, and so famous. Again there were congratulations when I sang, and even Corelli turned round and said, 'Mama mia qual voce!' I did not like the conductor's tempos, now that he had the orchestra, and found a lot of things far harder than with Carlo in the pit.

I had a costume fitting on the 28th, after which I contemplated suicide. My San Francisco costumes had been made in New York from measurements given by the Met wardrobe, and they had been flown out to California just in time for the dress rehearsal. Now, in the little cubicle hanging on the wall was a dark grey crimplene dress in a sort of princess line (how that dates me!). There was a label, and I was surprised to see that it was not new but had belonged to a chorister. No harm in that, except that I really did not think it would fit. I mentioned this to the lady-fitter and her reply was to rip it up the seam at the back and lace it over with tape so that a panel could be put in to make it fit. She went out to get more pins. I turned to John and asked him what he thought, and he was pale with rage. 'Bloody disgusting if you ask me.'

The fitter came back with her arms full of grey stiff net and preceeded to drape the dress and me in this. The more she put on the larger I looked, and my heart was sinking rapidly. She assured me that once she had cut it all to shape it would look 'just fine, honey'.

I tried not to brood on this but could not help feeling that I ought at least to have had a dress that was new for my New York debut as Norma. Mr Adler had been able to provide one at short notice, and the Met had had a year or so to get organised.

I put the dress from my mind for the next three days and got on with the rehearsals despite the fact that, after a half-hour production call where all he had said was, 'There is a draught in this room going in my ear,' Corelli had disappeared again. No one seemed to know where he was; I did not know it then but my moment of glory singing with him had been and gone: the three-hour Sitzprobe.

On the 31st the piano dress was awful. I went to my dressing room and wept. I begged the Wardrobe to remove all the dreadful grey net – I looked like a monster ballet dancer in tutu. Roland spent the weekend at the Met in the Wardrobe showing them pictures of my Sadlers Wells *Trovatore* costumes to indicate the sort of line that would suit me. The problem was still the main dress itself. Roland had devised several panels to fit down the front of the dress, but the Wardrobe made them so heavy that they made the wretched crimplene stretch, and with every performance the damn dress got longer and longer, and I had to have the hem pinned up, sometimes in the middle of the opera so that I would not fall over.

However, they did not want me to wear Roland's panels in the 'Mira O Norma' scene, which created a problem. The panels were kept in place by two rows of the largest press studs I have ever seen; without the panels, from a distance they looked like two rows of teats.

On 1st November I wrote in my diary, 'I am so unhappy I know that it won't go as well here as in 'Frisco, the conductor isn't a bit like Cillario, and the production is dreadful.' On the morning of the dress rehearsal Charlie Riecker phoned me to apologise that there would be no Corelli for the dress rehearsal or for the first night and that my Pollione would be John Alexander from the City Opera. He sang the first few performances, and then my tenor was Bob Nagey, the Met's house tenor.

I enjoyed working with both of them. John Alexander was a quiet gentleman, but Bob Nagy was, I have to admit, more on my wavelength, that is a bit mad. After his first scene he would threaten to leave his Roman helmet on the Druids' altar for me to fall over. Of course he didn't, but he knew I was always in the wings watching and waiting for my cue, and some nights he would tease me by leaving the picking up of the helmet until the last second.

After the full dress rehearsal on the 3rd I wrote, 'It was a fiasco, I am dreading Thursday.'

The first night on November 6th was hard work, with Massini in the pit; he was either too fast or too slow for me, and paid no attention to what I had asked him for. The 'Casta diva' was a nightmare. I knew, of course, that nothing was nearly as good as San Francisco – but the audience liked it. The papers were divided. The *Post* and the *Times* hated me (I never knew the lady in the *Post* to like anyone). The evening paper came out with the opposite. But by the next day I was sick of hearing people who rang to commiserate with me about my reviews; I knew they were being kind, but it was like being at my own funeral.

The second Met *Norma* on the 13th was better. John Tooley from Covent Garden was there and was charming. Charlie Riecker was pleased with the performance and could not understand why the reviews had been so nasty. I wrote in my diary that night, 'If I have the chance I will never work with Massini again.' I haven't.

*

It was the unhappiest two months of my career, and I could not wait to get the rest of the performances over and get out of town. I knew that the conductor and I would never see eye to eye and the costumes would only get worse.

It was nearly Thanksgiving and Charlie Riecker had invited us to spend it with him and his wife.

On the 14th November we went to my agent's office to talk about fees and to sort out the offers from Mr Adler. Joe Lipman shook me by saying out of the blue, 'If Adler won't give you $3,500 for the Santuzzas next year, we will accept $3,000.'

I said, 'Don't you dare lower my fee.' I knew that the $4,000 was a special fee on account of my helping Adler out, and I did not expect to get as much as that, but I did expect at least my Met fee, not less.

On the 18th I recorded in my diary that I thought the performance was the worst that I had ever been involved in. I had even made my entrance from a different level in an attempt to cope with Massini's tempos which I found so erratic.

So many things had gone wrong that night and the one which the audience must have noticed involved me – of course. At the end of the scene where Norma goes to bang the gong, I was supposed to go upstage and stand motionless as the chorus piled on for the 'Guerra' chorus and, when they had done so, the whole set would turn round and we would all be discovered on a new set. Well, on this night, the machinery didn't work. We were being shouted at by Stanley the stage director to go back downstage into positions that would be almost the same as if the set *had* turned, except that the set and the steps would all be the wrong way round. I am a large lady and trying to get through all those beefy Met choristers all in a panic was no picnic – and this was no time to be polite, so I flexed my muscles and shoved with the best of them and in the end had to stun them into immobility with the words, 'Piss off out of the way.' It worked. Thirty of them stood stock still with shock and by the skin of my teeth I got there in time to sing. John Macurdy, who was singing Oroveso that night, waited till I got the sacred sword from him and then whispered, 'Piss off indeed – virgins don't swear.'

As I took the sword I smiled at him and said through clenched teeth, 'This one does!'

On the 20th I was asked to give an interview with one of the papers. On the 22nd John went downstairs to get the Sundays. To my horror the one to which I had given the interview printed the most insulting article about me. I could not understand why the journalist could write such filth when we had seemed to talk in a pleasant chatty way about my career, and I had made him coffee, and he had seemed so nice. I was upset and unsettled all day, and in the end I phoned Charlie Riecker and told him to go and buy the *Sunday News*. He was then most distressed when I told him I did not want to return to New York ever. A little later he rang back; he had read the article and he was near to tears.

I wrote in my diary, 'I am sick of being humiliated. Joe Lipman refuses to ask for more money so why come here to get hurt and end up broke?'

I sang my last *Norma* at the Met on the 28th November. I was sick and depressed and had not had a period for two months. I had put on two stone.

*

While we were flying towards London it was announced that there was fog over London and we would be diverted to Manchester. My heart sank. We landed at Ringway and they opened the doors of the Jumbo, and there we remained for two solid hours, doors open, frozen stiff. It seemed that every plane in the world had been sent there and Ringway could just not cope. The crew discovered that one of our fellow passengers was Dora Bryan. Now I have always loved her, but two hours of 'Hello, Dolly' on the intercom was a little excessive.

When they finally let us off the plane we made our way to an arrival lounge which was sheer chaos and not a porter in sight. We had nine cases and, as there were no trolleys, John had to drag them one by one past the customs counter. He got them all on to the counter and said to the customs officer, 'Don't ask me to open them, mate. If you want them you can have them, I am sick to death of them.' The officer sent us through with a sympathetic smile.

We had been told we would be put up in hotels in Manchester, but we were now informed that instead we were being sent by bus through to Crewe station where we would have to sit and wait for the first available train.

I exploded. 'If I sit there half the night I'll have bronchitis, I am sleeping in my own bed tonight. Go and hire a car, John.' Poor John, being asked to drive where trains had feared to go. But for once Bossie Nellie was out of luck, as every hire car in the north of England had already been spoken for and driven away. But, not to be outdone, I ran outside to the taxi rank and asked the first driver, 'Will you drive me and my family to London?' The surprised driver said, 'Yes, madam.' 'How much?' 'Fifty quid, madam.' 'You're on,' I said, 'don't you dare go with anyone else till I get back.'

By now John was sick to death with everything and Mairwyn in particular. As I got within earshot I heard her wailing, 'But I want my presents, it's my birthday now.' And, poor love, it was now November 30th. I helped John get all the bags into the cab and we piled in and began a long and cold trip down the M1 to London. I wrapped Mairwyn inside my large cape, and we did sleep at home at last. Home had never looked so good. I almost knelt to kiss the good ground.

I thanked God that at least the trip had begun in a blaze of glory even if it had ended in a fog of despair.

My doctor diagnosed severe depression and extreme stress. After a week on mild tranquillisers, weight started to fall off. I had been asked by Thames TV to appear on 'This is Your Life' for Alberto, but I was not able to leave the house, and the film unit had to come to me. I was sad and disappointed, for although I was on the show, it wasn't quite the same as being on the spot, and I hoped Alberto would understand.

On 15th December 1975 we began rehearsals for the *Valkyrie* that we recorded. Of course we did the whole *Ring* in the January but it was the *Valkyrie* that was recorded for posterity. I was in my bedroom getting ready on the 24th when the phone rang, and to my surprise it was Mr Adler. He invited me to dinner with him, but I had to decline as I was singing Brünnhilde that night. He apologised for disturbing me and asked if I could meet him for dinner on the Monday. I said I would be delighted, then he said goodbye, and told me, 'Be wonderful tonight, and looking forward to Monday.'

On the Sunday evening my agents phoned. They had been to lunch with Mr Adler and had bad news for me. Was I sitting down? It seemed that Mr Adler didn't want me at all now for the next three autumns on account of the bad notices in New York.

I was stunned. I had no illusions about Mr Adler, and knew he was a tough cookie. But I could not believe that he would call and invite me out and be charming to me one day, and then drop me like a hot potato the next. Mr Adler was quite capable of doing his own dirty work and I felt sure if he had not wanted me he would have told me so himself. I fought for weeks with my agents over this.

*

Despite my desire not to return to the Met I knew that they had already asked me to sing *Aida* there in the fall of 1976, and the contract for this was not long in coming. My agent phoned on 26th January to say it was ready to sign but there were some new clauses that had not been there before. For a start they had dropped my fee by $500.

Once again I told myself I would go there just once more, as I would have no other work in the fall in England.

On February 1st I began rehearsals for Electra in *Idomeneo*, my most unfavourite role. Charles Mackerras was conducting. In the middle of these rehearsals we went up to Manchester to sing in a concert with the BBC Northern Orchestra. Charles Mackerras was again conducting, and he had the great idea of me singing the Immolation and the 'Casta diva' in the same programme. It seemed to work and indeed some years later I found that the 'Casta diva' had been used on a pirate recording. I was never quite satisfied with that performance of it but it seems to have sold well – but unfortunately pirates don't pay royalties.

In February Mairwyn sat an exam to get into a convent boarding school, which she passed, and so began her years in isolation. It is now 1984 and she still hasn't heard her mother sing Aida or Abigaille, but that will soon be put to rights.

Early in March the Met called my agents and asked if I would sing *Aida* on the tour in Atlanta. I said, 'No,' and slammed the phone down. I could not bear the thought of going back there so soon. I was still licking my wounds from the last visit.

Two weeks later there was another call from the Met, this time there was on offer two *Aidas* in Wolf Trap, as well as the one in Atlanta, and another three in New York in the fall. This time I relented and said yes. On the 29th a letter came from the New York agents – they had apparently known all about the new offer from the Met since January 15th, and were now worried in case we were not able to get accommodation.

Things began to hot up. On 2nd April the London agent phoned to say that the Met wanted me to sing *Aida* in Cleveland on May 4th. I would have to fly there on April 25th. This made things difficult, as it meant asking Lord Harewood to release me from the Birmingham *Ring* and to do the Glasgow *Ring* instead. Unfortunately, the way it was announced to the press made the Birmingham people cross and there was a long piece in a Birmingham paper saying I did not want to do the Birmingham *Ring*, and that I preferred to go to the States to earn large fees. Would I never get a square deal? I didn't want to go to Scotland, I loved Birmingham, it was so near London. Why on earth couldn't someone explain to the press that every opera house in the world always tries to help out the others if they are in trouble?

I sang a *Ring* in Leeds the week of April 13th–17th. We were to fly to Cleveland on the 25th April and Mairwyn was to begin her life at boarding school on the same day. She was to stay with a friend on the night of the 24th as we were leaving early the next day. It was a sad way for her to begin boarding school and as the day wore on we all got more and more depressed. My friend, Mrs Rollason, came to pick her up just before bedtime on the 24th and we all cried. I felt so guilty about sending her away; it was something I had sworn never to do and yet it was the only way as I could not keep on trailing her after me round the world.

We flew first to New York and had to wait four hours for the connection to Cleveland. We were both glad to get to the hotel and relax; then I found out I had no call until the Wednesday. In the evening the company phoned and said I ought to fly south to Atlanta on Saturday as it was warmer there and I wasn't needed in Cleveland. On the Tuesday they sent all my new costumes from New York to Cleveland; they had made them to my *Norma* measurements, so of course they were all too big. They even tried Caballé's costume on me – and to my joy that was too big!

That evening we went to the opera to watch *Aida*; we had been told there would be tickets waiting at the box office. There weren't. We were saved from humiliation by a figure from the past – Anthony Addison, the chorus master of the Carl Rosa, who suddenly appeared before us in the foyer. He produced two tickets. I met Bianca Berrini, my Amneris from Nice four years earlier; it seemed to be a night for faces from the past.

On the 28th April, I had a three-hour production call on the *Aida*, and on the Friday I was so bored that I asked for a music call to pass three hours away. We were both missing Mairwyn and I still felt guilty about sending her away to school.

We left Cleveland on the Saturday and flew on the same plane as Bianca. The hotel in Atlanta was fantastic. The lift was a space capsule – I longed for Mairwyn to see it. On the Sunday we went to lunch with Dottie and Wilkes Davis. The following day I was to have a call with James Levine who was to conduct my first Met *Aida*. As I got into the shower the Met phoned and cancelled the call. 'Mr Levine has been delayed in New York.' That meant I would have to go on 'cold', not knowing what he was going to do.

The next evening I had my first encounter with 'Texas dirt'. This was the stuff the make-up man used on me, and I looked at the box of dust with some apprehension. But in the end he made me up with his usual genius and I felt like a million dollars. The performance went well – I recall I sang one wrong word and made one wrong move. After the performance Francis Robertson told John he thought that Aida was my best role.

The next day Dottie picked us up and drove us to the airport, where we bought the two local papers. One said I was great, the other that I looked like Radames' grandmother. We put the latter in a waste bin and the other we took home to show Mairwyn.

We arrived back on the Thursday at 8 a.m. and phoned the school and asked them to tell Mairwyn we were home. On the Friday she came home for the weekend and we had a joyful reunion. Then eighteen days rest at home, and on the 24th May we went up to Glasgow to do *The Ring* there, on the 25th, 27th and 29th. On the 28th Alberto and I went on Scottish TV and were interviewed by a ravishing red-head. She asked about our comings and goings over the past few years, and I said that the conductor in San Francisco had said that he wanted me in Australia. She pricked up her ears and asked, 'And what about Australia?' I told her that I would just love to go to Australia but that I had been told that the singers there did not like overseas artists coming and pinching their jobs. Her eyes flashed, and she said, 'Who, for instance?' I fell into the trap like a ripe plum. 'Oh, Ronald Dowd and John Shaw.' I added that I did not blame them in the least for protecting their jobs. Alberto too fell into the trap. 'Well, they should not try to stop us, they worked for years over here.' The lovely red-head then changed the subject. It was several years before we discovered that her name was Isobel and she was courting John Shaw and eventually married him. When I worked with John Shaw in *Nabucco* I was puzzled why he was so off-hand with me, until he hastened to tell me what a faux pas I had made.

On the 30th May 1976 we again crossed the Atlantic, this time via Prestwick. The movie was the same as the last time –

'Dillinger'. When the hostess offered us the headsets, John said, 'No thanks, darling, I know the dialogue, I'll lip read.'

On June 1st the Met told me that they didn't require me till the Friday. I wrote in my diary: 'I think it's naughty to get me here too soon, if I get here too soon in September I will lose £1,000 by missing the last two Donna Annas. Barratt's told me that Larry Stayer from the Met thought that one rehearsal was enough but forgot to write and tell me not to fly over so soon.' At the bottom of the page I had written, 'Bought three dresses, $10 each, one dress $20 and some stockings.' I made a mental note to confess to my manager about the wild extravagance in those New York dress shops!

On the 4th June I worked from 11 till 12.30 with the conductor but the afternoon rehearsal was a wash-out as James McCracken didn't want to work and so we all went home at 3 p.m.

We flew to Washington on the 6th and on the 7th and 11th I sang *Aida* in Wolf Trap park – a wonderful place with an open-air theatre. I wasn't too sure about all the moths and mosquitoes flying round in the final scene. One moth came near to being swallowed by Aida and Radames said 'This singing in the open air is for the birds.' I tended to agree.

On the 12th we flew back to New York and watched the skies, hoping for fine weather for the *Aidas* in the parks. On the morning of the Central Park concert, June 15th, I looked through our apartment window and saw thousands of people making for Central Park West with baskets and blankets. I thought they were off to a baseball match. When we reached the park in the evening, John said, 'Er, Rit, I think you had better look at the crowd before you go on.' (He knew I didn't like concerts where you could see the faces of the audience.) He added, 'This is it, Rita, kill or cure.' I almost fainted with the shock – the sea of faces seemed to stretch off into infinity, over 110,000 of them. I took a deep breath, and off I went to be killed or cured.

As the conductor lifted his baton I heard a rough voice shout, 'Oh come on, let's get going, buddy.' I wanted to laugh. Backstage, Charlie Rieker, who also knew of my dislike of a visible audience, said to his wife, 'Rita will never forgive me for this.'

Well, it was a great experience. Never before or since have I had hot dogs and hamburgers sold and transported in front of me as I sang 'O patria mia'. A child who had been holding a bunch of balloons let go of them and wailed; then they got impaled on the branch of a tree and burst loudly after my high C. As it grew darker candelabras were lit, and I smiled inwardly when I saw an Italian family light up a camping lantern. Over to one side a crowd of youths sat around a smart silver candelabra. By the time we got to 'O terra addio', it was dark and the sides of the park were illuminated by the lights from the skyscrapers and somewhere in the heavens a jet plane flew by on its way to some far corner of the earth. I found later that the rough voice which had shouted 'Let's get going', at the beginning, belonged to a large parrot that sat on the handlebars of its owner's bike all through the performance. And I have a photo to prove it.

On the 18th June it was Prospect Park in Brooklyn, and on the 22nd Van Cartland Park in the Bronx. On the 25th it was Cunningham Park in Queen's, and on the 26th June 1976, we flew home.

Between June and the end of the year there were more performances with the English National and then in January 1977 I flew once more across the Atlantic to sing the *Walküre* Brünnhilde at the Metropolitan. When they were over, we flew direct to New Orleans to sing two performances of *Walküre* and then back home to English National Opera. Another summer holiday in the West Country and more performances at ENO in the autumn of 1977. In November I was phoned by a frantic young man who was putting on a concert at Wyndhams Theatre in London on Sunday, 27th November, with Lucia Popp. Miss Popp was sick. Would I? Could I? I asked the young man, Peter Freeman, what Miss Popp was going to sing, and then had to tell him that there was no way I could sing her songs. Mr Freeman said, 'Sing anything you like, but please . . .' Then he added, 'Oh by the way, the concert is going to be recorded and brought out on a disc.'

Apart from the English *Ring* recording and the EMI *Euryanthe*, recording companies have not loomed large in my life – well, not at all – and this mention of a recording was too good to miss. I contacted Hazel Vivienne and we got a programme together. The concert was a huge success, and the two-disc recording greeted by the fans with greedy delight. But sad to say, because of the company's lack of knowledge of how to distribute the recording, hundreds of those discs now lie in a Cambridgeshire garage, mouldering away.

All was not lost, however, as it brought Hazel and me together and we toured the length and breadth of the British Isles with our recitals. We rescued some of the records and sold on the tours. When I went out to Australia, Mr Freeman said he had a distributor in Melbourne – but we never did meet him – he must have got lost in the bush.

December 1977 we were once more USA-bound, this time for

Walküre in Philadelphia with the world famous Wotan, George London, as the producer. There I met for the first time Henry Holt who was the musical director and conductor of the Seattle *Ring*. I had not been looking forward to meeting him as I felt sure he did not like me. The Seattle *Ring* had been going for some time and my interpretation of Brünnhilde was quite successful. So why, I reasoned, had I not been invited to Seattle? Well, whatever the reason, it was certainly not that Henry Holt didn't like me or my work. I fell in love with him right away; he was not only a charming man but also a conductor that I longed to work more with. I could tell by the quality of his *Walküre* conducting that the rest of his *Ring* would be great. Time was to prove me right – and, Henry darling, I would fly to the moon to sing with you, if you asked me.

January 1978 brought word of a D Litt coming my way from Warwick University and in the early summer a RAM from the Royal Academy in London.

The same month also brought a young lady into our lives, Miss Geraldine Unsworth. She had worked with Edwin Francis, and had written from Liverpool to ask if I would teach her and help her. I pointed out that the teacher in the family was John, but in the end, in return for help in the house, she came to have lessons from John and to be able to see operas in London. As it turned out, we were to take her further afield than London.

There was a phone call in early spring 1978 from Munich Staatsoper; Birgit was sick, would I fly out and sing *Götterdämmerung*? We were sitting having a late coffee in the breakfast room when the call came, and we had to get a flight around 2 p.m. I sent Geraldine flying in one direction to pack for herself and me and John in another. In the middle of this confusion our little dog, Senta, wanted to be let into the garden, and nobody took any notice, with the result that she left whoopsies all over the house. As I was dressing I heard a string of curses from Geraldine. I thought she had laddered her nylons and took no further notice and rushed into the bathroom to gather my toilet things and was horrified to find I had trodden on one of Senta's little offerings. 'Oh God, now I'll have to take off my stockings and wash my foot.'

John said, 'No, no, don't wash it off, it's good luck.'

I asked, 'What's so lucky about flying to Munich with dog shit on your foot?'

But John insisted I did not wash it off, so I sprayed my legs and feet with 'Jolie Madame', and hoped for the best.

While we were waiting in the boarding lounge Geraldine said,

'That bloody Senta, I trod in one of her turds and had to change my nylons and wash my feet.' I said with a wry smile, 'I've got news for you, Gerry. I did the same thing and John said not to wash it off as it would be lucky.'

I thought Geraldine would explode with mirth, and in her wonderful Liverpool accent she said, 'After the way them buggers bombed us in the war it serves them right.'

All through that weekend John watched me like a hawk and every time I went to shower he would stand there and insist that I kept the polluted foot out of the water, and so with the help of a great deal of 'Jolie Madame' perfume, I was able to bring a little of the lucky muck back to Blighty.

Despite the fact that I had not sung *Götterdämmerung* in German for two years, in Munich I made but two word mistakes and no musical ones. So maybe all divas should carry dog-dung around.

CHAPTER SEVENTEEN

Down Under

Whatever I did by way of performances in the early part of 1978 seems to have been blotted from my memory by the discovery that all was not well with my innards.

For about seventeen years I had been suffering with strange attacks of tummy pains and vomiting. No good reason was ever given, and once I was hauled into Bart's Hospital in the mid-sixties with suspected appendicitis. But I was sent home next day and told I was constipated! A spectacular array of doctors had visited me, mostly in the middle of the night, over the years. Some would prod my already tender tummy, look at my size, sniff and say I had had too much to eat for supper. One doctor diagnosed 'nerves', another 'hypertension' – but the attacks continued.

In the pub in Thames Ditton John had met a local doctor who was an opera buff and a great fan of mine. This was Dr Alan Miller, and he told John if I ever needed anything John was to call him. One night John came home to find me lying on the bedroom floor, semi-conscious. Our own doctor could not come. John then sent for Alan, and they got me to bed. Alan said, 'Sorry, John, but it's gallstones.' John shook his head in disbelief. Alan gave me an injection and said he would call next morning.

He then questioned me about the attacks, and John said, 'She gets very uptight when she has a lot of performances.' Alan insisted it was gallstones and, 'We shall have to do something when she's feeling stronger.'

The next night I was ill again. I had an attack every night for a week, and on the third night Alan said to John, 'You have to give in now, John, she's even jaundiced now and that's a classic sign.'

John hung his head and said, 'OK, where do we go from here?'

'X-rays, old man.'

I went up to Teddington hospital and was examined and given some very large tablets, told to eat nothing that night except the tablets and come back next morning after a really fatty and greasy breakfast, to be X-rayed.

I did as I was told, and in fact spent most of that night in the toilet. Next morning, after a fatty meal that made me feel quite ill, off we went to Teddington hospital. The doctor asked me if I had taken the tablets and I said I had but that I had been up all night with the trots. The doctor said, 'Oh dear,' and went on to explain that the tablets had been a dye that would have shown up what was wrong on the X-rays. He was afraid that I had 'lost the dye'. They took the photos, and off I went home to throw up that hateful breakfast.

Dr Miller came later and said that the X-rays had been a washout and, since I could not retain the dye when taken orally, I would have to have it intravenously and, since they could not cope with that method in Teddington, Alan made arrangements for me to go to Harley Street.

John waited outside and Mairwyn sat in the room with me. They tried for half an hour to get the needle in a vein, right wrist, left wrist, right arm, left arm, back of left hand. Then a nurse remembered that they had an extra fine baby needle, so they inserted this miniscule needle in the back of my right hand, and attached the phial of dye – there seemed to be a gallon of the stuff. They left me on the chair while it went round my body. I began to feel very sick, the room began to swim around. 'Get a nurse quick,' I said to Mairwyn, and she ran into the next room. By this time I was half fainting and they had to prop me up in the chair. The doctor gave me an injection and slowly the sickness and fainting passed and they dragged me off for my 'photo session'.

That afternoon Alan Miller came to see me and confirmed gallstones, and said that an operation was needed, and soon.

A few days later I went to Harley Street again to see the surgeon that Alan had recommended. He showed me the X-rays – the bottom of the gall bladder was one solid block and the rest of it was full of round stones.

Mr Maynard said, 'Well, miss, when can I have the pleasure of removing this for you?' I said that I had to go to New Orleans in October, but I could have it done when I came home? He looked shocked. 'Not till then? You must be mad.' I said, 'Well, I've had

it so long, another six months isn't going to make much difference.'

'You singers! This show-must-go-on bit will kill you all.' Then
he showed me some very large stones on the X-ray and explained that should they move I would be in dire trouble as they
were much larger than the tubes they had to pass through, and I
was running the risk of a blockage and a burst gall bladder. This
quietened me for a while, then I said, 'Okay, when can you do
it?'

'In three weeks, but you'll have to forget about New Orleans.'

'I can't. I have a signed contract to fulfil.'

Mr Maynard said, 'You will not be fit to sing in six months.'

I said, 'Why ever not?'

He then explained what was involved in the operation. I
listened quietly until he said, 'We have to cut through your
diaphragm.'

I stood up. 'No way,' I said. 'That's my boiler room. A singer is
no singer without that.'

Mr Maynard sighed and said, 'Go home and talk it over with
your doctor and your husband. Then phone me.'

We talked it over at great length. I agreed to the operation but
not until I had returned from New Orleans. We then realised
that just three months after returning from the USA I had
Trovatores with the English National. And while we were mulling this one over, the Welsh National asked me to sing my first
Turandots with them during the spring and early summer of
1979.

I had waited for years to sing this. It had been offered by many
companies but John would not let me do it so early in my career.
Now he said that I could do it. I told him it was just like him to
wait till I was half dead before he consented to my singing
Turandot.

Mr Maynard was very cross that I would not have the operation instead of going to New Orleans. He called John in and
begged him to get me to see sense. Eventually, after both of them
pouring over the date sheet, Mr Maynard said, 'Cancel those
Trovatores – she's done enough of those in her career to satisfy
her ego – then we can get her fit for those *Turandots*.'

I went home to think again. I reasoned that six or seven
Trovatores were not going to make or break me at this point. But
the *Nabuccos* in the States and the *Turandots* were important and I
wanted to do them desperately. I decided to call George Harewood and risk the wrath of God and cancel the *Trovatores*. Before
I could do this, fate, in the shape of the Australian Opera,

171

stepped in. I did not phone George Harewood – I phoned my surgeon and said, 'See you on August 28th, 1979.'

I crossed my fingers and hoped that for the next twelve months, the sun would shine on Rita Nellie.

*

In the midst of all the gallstone problems I still found time to learn and sing my first Lady Macbeth at the BBC Promenade Concerts. I had glowing reviews from all the papers. One said that my interpretation ought to be allowed to blossom in a full stage performance. The concerts were broadcast and therefore it wasn't long before a pirate recording was on sale from the USA. This record really is very good. But the recording companies have never been very interested in me. I can understand powers-that-be saying, 'Oh, we can't give you that role, you wouldn't look right'. But who's going to see on a record? I could not *appear* as Mimi or Butterfly – but I could sure as hell sing both of them.

I was busy preparing Abigaille in Verdi's *Nabucco* to sing in New Orleans. The offer from the Australian Opera was also for Abigaille in *Nabucco*, in Adelaide and Melbourne, and I was beside myself with glee. I had long wanted to sing in Australia, even before Carlo Felice Cillario had suggested it to me in San Francisco in 1975. I discovered that Richard Bonynge was to conduct – my cup of joy was full.

There was a problem about the date. I had to tell the Australians I could not travel there until after the last *Nabucco* in New Orleans. I was worried sick about having to tell them this and waited hourly for the dreaded phone call that would tell me that unless I was there on the day they wanted me they would have to find someone else. This had been the case so many times in my career that I even began to contemplate telling New Orleans I had changed my mind. However, the Australian Opera cabled to say they understood and just get there as soon as I could.

My friends at British Airways and Qantas came up with several routes. New Orleans via New York, London, Bahrain and Singapore, and New Orleans via San Francisco, Honolulu and Sydney – this latter one appeared to get us there a day sooner, but it was still only going to give me four days from the day we arrived to the first night, and it would leave me short on rehearsal time. But there was no alternative.

But before this much longed-for trip could begin, I had a contract to fulfil in New Orleans. Roland had gone ahead of us, and had spent a week in New York and was to arrive in New

Orleans the same evening as we did. John and I left Heathrow in the afternoon and changed planes in Washington. We were delayed two hours leaving London. We made up a half hour in the course of the flight but were still extremely late getting to Washington, and ran the risk of missing the last flight of the day from there to New Orleans. I made a note in my diary: 'Next time leave London earlier in the day.'

Since we were going straight on to Australia, we had quite a lot of luggage and, as we stood in the baggage hall in Washington airport, we became anxious waiting for it to arrive. As the vital moments slipped by, I was so agitated I could feel my wretched gall bladder beginning to play up. One of the British Airways staff was doing all in her power to hurry things along. She told us our flight had been called and that she had asked them to hold it. Eventually the bags came, except for one case containing John's clothes. The staff could not hold the flight for us any longer. The girl from British Airways swore that she would make sure the case, when it arrived, was sent on to New Orleans and delivered to our hotel. I was certain that we had seen the last of it, as we raced up the stairs to the departure lobby. They had already closed the door of the shuttle bus and reluctantly opened it for us, and I flopped into a seat panting and sweating. My gall bladder was aching and I felt sick. I took a pain-killing tablet but by the time Roland arrived in the hotel I was on the floor of the bathroom with my head down the toilet. John was pacing the room saying, 'We should have listened to the specialist. This is only the first leg of the trip, what the hell is she going to be like after 12,000 miles?'

I refused to think about it, but I made it quite clear to both of them that I was going to Australia even if I dropped dead at Sydney airport.

Next day, although queasy, I was able to get to the rehearsals, which were swift, efficient and hysterical. The producer, Jim Lucas, hurled instructions at the chorus in three or four different languages. I asked him why the multi-lingual production? 'Oh Jesus, sweetheart, can't you tell there isn't one true American here except me, they are all immigrants, and we all know they never bother to learn English.' Not true, I'm sure, but he did make me laugh. The chorus were divided into groups and they went on stage whenever their group number was called. I began to think Jim was right about them not knowing English. Even during the performances you could still hear Jim in the wings shouting, 'Move Group Two – move! Oh for Christ's sake, move, God damn you!'

173

The costumes, which had been hired from a firm in New York, arrived. When I went in for my fitting I looked at them hanging on the wall in my dressing room and came straight out again. I told John, 'They're men's costumes, mine must be in another room.' But they weren't – the ones hanging in my dressing room were for me.

One was a thick white wool and on the label inside was a man's name and the words 'Sarastro, Magic Flute'. Whoever had played him, he must have been at least six foot. There was also a limp and drab cloak. They assured me that 'Renata Scotto had loved it.' I replied that Madame Scotto wouldn't be seen dead in it.

Then they brought the costume for the last act, thin black wool, no ornaments and, when I held it up, I knew it had been made for Twiggy. I sighed with despair. I said to John, 'No wonder people like Caballé and Sutherland always took their own costumes every place they went.' Roland went to fetch Arthur Cozzenza, the artistic director. He had no solution for the first costume but for the last act he said, 'You know you are to be carried on for the last scene – you just lie there, sing, die and then they carry you off?' 'Yes, Arthur.' Well then, just slit the dress up the back. So long as you don't move, no one out front will know that it doesn't fit.'

I exploded. 'Arthur! I am not about to make my American debut as Abigaille with my underwear flapping in the breeze.' He had nothing further to suggest. It was clear I had to wear the costumes provided or go naked.

John, Roland and I sat in the dressing room, stunned. Jim Lucas was real mad and told us, 'And what's more, that dress hire firm is charging Arthur $500 for the week's hire.'

We went back to the hotel and wracked our brains. We went through all the evening gowns that I had with me for the trip thinking we might be able to convert a couple. But they all looked just what they were – evening gowns.

The next evening was the dress rehearsal with an audience made up of members of the Opera Guild. I said, 'If only I had my Met *Aida* costumes –' Roland was alive at once. 'If they'll lend them to you I'll fly to New York in the morning and get them for you.'

I phoned Charlie Riecker at once. 'No problem.' I had to pay for the hire but at least I knew I would look decent. We got Roland on the first available flight the next morning. He kept the taxi waiting at the stage door of the Met and did the quickest turn-around ever. Despite this speed, back in New Orleans I was made up and ready to go and still no costumes. I did the first part of Act One in Sarastro's dressing gown, wearing the cloak beloved (?) of Scotto. Roland's return wasn't as late as it might have been: we were having other problems. Jim Lucas had decided that Nabucco was to make his first entrance on horseback. The horse was a beautiful black mare called Sunny. Her handler looked after her in the wings and she seemed calm enough. Nabucco (Kostas Pascallis) hoisted himself on to her back; still she was calm. I went on and sang the next bit and, along with everyone else, awaited the arrival of Sunny and Nabucco.

As soon as the audience saw the two of them they applauded. I saw Sunny flinch, and then the sound of her breaking wind drowned out the applause. I heard a chorister say, 'Oh Jesus, a horse with gas.' I stifled my giggles. I was standing upstage on a flight of steps, the production plan being that, when the horse and baritone had got to their place downstage centre, I was to march down the steps and join them. As I was mulling this move over in my mind, Nabucco still on the side of the stage sang his first lines.

You could almost tell what Sunny was thinking – bareback riders are one thing, singing baritones another – and right away she had an attack of diarrhoea. Nabucco, unaware of this, moved her forward downstage centre – the further she moved, the more he sang, the more she deposited on the stage. The chorus could no longer sing for giggling. I managed to control myself and went to move downstage to join Sunny and Nabucco. Jim Lucas's voice rent the air, 'For Christ's sake, Hunter, don't move, remember the train on your cloak!' I remember thinking, 'A dollop of that is all this cloak deserves.'

By now the orchestra had begun one by one to stop playing and stand up to see what all the fuss was about. I sat down on the steps and laughed till tears ran down my face. Jim was hopping round in the stalls in a right old state. I heard him shout, 'Get a shovel. A local stage hand popped his head round the prompt curtain and called to Jim, 'Sorry Boss, we aint got no shovel.' Jim yelled back, 'Oh my dear Lord, don't you know you never hire a horse without a shovel?' By now most of the chorus had gone off stage and Nabucco had realised what was wrong and had guided Sunny off stage. She deposited another load on her way.

By now the genteel members of the Opera Guild had begun to leave the stalls and the curtain was brought down. I saw Roland in the wings hopping up and down, and I picked my way through the manure to join him. He said dramatically, 'Get that

175

crap off your back' – meaning the famous cloak. A stage hand said 'If I were you, boy, I wouldn't mention that word around here any more tonight.'

I didn't bother to go back to my dressing room, and let Roland dress me there in the wings. I put on the beautiful green dress that I wore for the Nile scene in *Aida*. Arthur Cozzenza stood close by. Roland turned to him and said, 'Now that's the sort of costume for a prima donna.' Arthur agreed that it was magnificent, that they were all magnificent. Nevertheless he refused to pay for the hire. He would not even pay Roland's air fare to New York.

For the rest of the evening a great argument ensued between Arthur and John and Roland. I left them to it. I was busy elsewhere. Nevertheless I was determined never to be without a costume of my own ever again.

I knew that there were only four days between my arrival and the opening in Adelaide. What if the Australian Opera's costume department was like Arthur's? I phoned the Met again and, after promising to bring the costumes with me whenever I was called to sing *Aida* at the Met in the future, I arranged to send the $2,000 they asked for me to purchase them and the four costumes were mine to take to Australia with me. John thought that $2,000 was rather a lot but the dresses had matching cloaks, and everything was made in beautiful fabric. I further reasoned with him that they were of such a classic style they could also be used for *Norma*, *Macbeth*, *Trovatore*, as well as *Aida* and *Nabucco*. So I considered they were a good buy.

The first night was a triumph. Even Sunny behaved. (Jim Lucas said, 'When in doubt, darling, keep a cork handy.') I adored singing Abigaille, such a wicked lady. Not difficult to portray; all I had to do was think of all the agents and managements who had done me down over the years, and the venom just flowed out. Arthur Cozzenza was over the moon. So he should have been. I had paid out $2,000 to enhance his production.

He began to talk of *Turandot* in 1981. John said, 'When she gets to Australia they will be talking of future seasons there, too, so you had best get your dates sorted out before we leave.' Arthur replied, 'We can't have a meeting till next month.' John told him that might be too late, but offered to delay talks with the Australian Opera for a month. Arthur was to phone us to tell us what his committee meeting had decided.

Indeed John was right. We had been in Australia less than a week when offers were made for my return in January 1980 and

August 1981. Arthur did not phone us in Australia in that year; he wrote several months later but regretfully we had to say no. We have not returned to New Orleans since, which makes us both sad; we loved the city and its people and despite the hassle with the costumes we loved working with its opera company. Arthur phoned in March 1980, by which time I was booked solid with the Australian Opera, so our answer had to be no again. (Arthur if you read this try again – you never know, 'third time lucky'.)

*

After the second and last performance in New Orleans, we departed the next day for Australia. Our flight left at 12.30 and we had to check out of the hotel at 9.30. We felt a little put out by this, but we were all eager to begin our adventure. John was pleasantly tipsy by the time we landed in San Francisco. We then had to wait till 9 p.m. for the Qantas flight – six hours – and after this length of time in the first class departure lounge, my Welshman was reeling.

During the flight to Honolulu I went upstairs to the lounge with Roland and we tried to get John to drink some coffee. By now he took anyone who went past us for a steward. When the new crew came on board a dapper little Scotsman asked my bleary-eyed husband if he wanted anything. 'Gin and tonic, sweetheart.' I groaned inwardly realising that he could not now distinguish between trousers and a skirt. I closed my eyes and feigned sleep. All the crews had been informed of my 'gallstones diet' and every time any meal was served I was given plain grilled steak and salad with no dressing. We had to change in Sydney from the international terminal to the domestic one and waited for the courtesy bus to transport us to the Ansett building. When the bus came Roland and I got in first. John was still smiling and said he didn't need help. But he fell up the steps of the bus. He was wearing the giant cowboy hat he had bought in New Orleans to keep the Australian sun off his bald head. He said loudly, 'Bloody funny grass you've got here, mate.' A couple of true-blue Aussies sniffed with disgust. Roland and I pretended he wasn't with us.

After we had got ourselves settled in the Ansett plane the hostess said she was sorry they were not able to produce any steak for breakfast. I told her, 'Thank God for that.'

John went off to spend a penny, and we noticed a man in front of Roland and me ask for a drink, and saw that he had to pay for it. We looked at each other and giggled and sat back to wait. 'Gin

177

and tonic, dear!' She brought it, and asked him for the money. John's jaw dropped. The ensuing encounter between calm Ansett hostess and my befuddled Welshman was just what we needed to shake off the cobwebs of the long flight. It ended with her giving him a complaint form to fill in – he passed it to me. 'I'm not filling it in, it's your complaint.' I left him to it, and he gave it to the hostess. She gave me a sneak preview when I went to the toilet. It was just about unreadable. I laughed and said 'Tear it up, sweetheart'. She did and we both laughed.

We were met at Adelaide airport by Moffatt Oxenbould, the artistic director, Peter Bloor, the company manager, and Glen Lehman, from the press office. I knew that I had met Moffatt before but could not think where. I heard John ask him, 'What are you doing here?' Moffatt replied that he was one of the directors, and I made a mental note to ask John where we had met before. It was about noon, and by the time we were ready to leave the airport it was 12.20. Peter Bloor said, 'You have a production call at 2.30.' My heart fell to my boots. I knew that we were pushed for time but I had thought that I would be able to have a rest till next morning. I sighed, 'OK, lead me to a hot shower and a pot of black coffee, and I'll be there.'

I rehearsed for three hours, then when I thought that it was time for home I was marched off to a costume fitting. In the middle of this the door of the dressing room opened and in came John Lauder of the wig department. Through the open door I saw Richard Bonynge walking past. I excused myself and went out into the corridor to introduce myself. He was very charming, and begged me not to sing for the first few days. He asked if I had ever done a flight of that length before, and I said no. He assured me that jet lag would hit me sometime, and if it hit me around the first night if I had sung too much beforehand I would be in trouble. I said, 'But this is my first time with your company, I ought to sing.' He replied, 'Not for me, my dear. I know what you can do. Don't go trying to prove anything to me – personally I don't care if you don't sing a note till the first night.' I went back to the fitting; the costumes were going to be all right. I need not have brought mine.

After the fitting they tried the wig on and then Glen Lehman appeared. My back was aching and my legs felt as if they would drop off. 'The press are in the foyer waiting for you.' I groaned. 'Oh my God, after thirty-six hours travelling, my hair's a mess.' Roland raced back to the hotel and brought my Carmen wig and John Lauder helped me to put it on. He was about six foot and so good looking. I thought to myself, 'No wonder everyone wants to go and live in Australia, the fellas are so divine.' After the press interviews we eventually got back to the hotel at 9 p.m. Then the inevitable salad, and I fell into bed at 9.45. Never has a bed felt so good – I had not slept in one for about fifty hours.

It seemed I had hardly closed my eyes before it was morning. After a cup of black coffee and an apple, it was off to the theatre for the rehearsal with the orchestra.

Mr Bonynge's smile assured me again that I did not have to sing. But I just could not help myself. I felt fine, and so I flung Abigaille's first few phrases across the orchestra. Mr Bonynge had his back to me. I saw his shoulders flinch, and then as I was still singing he turned round, still conducting. I grinned at him. He all but laughed out loud. I sang all the rehearsal full voice, and I know that I sang it well. Abigaille's fiendish and difficult aria was a piece of cake with Maestro Bonynge at the helm. The morning flew by. In the coffee break Richard said to me, 'Well, my dear, I had heard what you were like, but I had no idea that your voice was so spectacular. Why on earth don't you sing regularly at Covent Garden?' I laughed. 'I have no idea. If you don't know, then I'm sure I don't.' I added, 'Who cares anyway? I'm happy here.' Richard grinned and said, 'Well, my dear, their loss is our gain.'

We rehearsed for two more days and then it was the opening night. We were playing at the Palais Theatre at St Kilda; it was a huge place, and I was delighted to see a banner outside the theatre proclaiming 'Rita Hunter in *Nabucco*' in enormous letters. Backstage was pretty tatty, but no more tatty than some of the old music hall theatres in the north of England. I went in to see Richard Bonynge, and as soon as I got back to my own room the stage manager came in to see me.

'Miss Hunter, I do hope you don't mind that Mr Bonynge has more posters on the wall of his room than you have. But, you see, his walls have more holes in them than yours.' I fell about laughing. But when I investigated, sure enough under each of the posters on my wall was a large hole. I could see the sea through one of them.

All the management were delighted with my performance. I was so keyed up with Richard's admiration of me and his bubbling enthusiasm that I never did feel the jet lag.

I did, however, spend the night before the première in the hotel toilet having a gallstone attack. I took painkillers all day and then pills to wake me for the performance. But I suffered it all gladly, I was so blissfully happy working with the Australian Opera.

I discovered that Moffatt Oxenbould had been stage manager with the Sadler's Wells during the two years I had been out of the company, having Mairwyn. This was why John knew him better than I did.

I had found a new freedom, a freedom to express myself on stage, and I gave much more relaxed performances. Off stage I was more relaxed too, and John said that despite the gallstones I was easier to live with. There was far less apprehension before a performance, less pacing the floor waiting for the reviews in the papers. It was as if I was working with a family who loved me, cared about me, and supported me.

My fellow artists were great to work with. The tenor, Lamberto Furlan, kept speaking to me off stage in Italian, and I had to tell him that I did not speak fluent Italian. He replied that my singing Italian was so good he was sure that I did speak it, which gave a big boost to my confidence. I had an old friend as Fenena, Margreta Elkins. My Nabucco, Robert Allman, was someone that I had heard a great deal about but not met. I soon discovered what a great person he was, funny, naughty, a tease and, more to the point, a great Nabucco. On top of all this I had the ultimate luxury, Maestro Bonynge in the pit. I mused how lucky Joan Sutherland had been to have him behind her during her career.

The reviews were great, and I was walking on air. After four performances in Adelaide we flew to Melbourne where I sang three more. I seemed to spend all the time between operas being interviewed by press or radio. Glen Lehman did his job as press officer well, and we became good friends.

One day I was taken to the spectacular Victorian Museum of Art in St Kilda Road, and shown a display of the great Nellie Melba's costumes and jewelry; the press were in attendance again, and took photos of me in her beautiful necklace and the fantastic cloak that she had worn in St Petersburg. Roland had the job of robing me, and we both experienced a spooky feeling. He said in my ear as he fastened the necklace, 'Don't like this.' I knew just what he meant. It was as if Melba was there looking on with disapproval. Unknown to us, there was also in the exhibition a little button on the wall, and when one pressed it the sound of Melba singing 'No Place Like Home' filled the foyer of the museum. Roland had just got the words 'Don't like this' out when someone pressed the button. I thought I would die of fright. I was glad to take the cloak and jewels off. I had a strong feeling that Dame Nellie didn't think too much of Rita Nellie mucking around with her costumes.

During the three performances in Melbourne I was aware of a blond young man hovering in the wings. He came over and introduced himself as Geoffrey Arnold. He told me that Richard Bonynge was going to have to leave Australia a few days sooner than expected, and that he, Geoffrey, was going to conduct the final performance. He said he was from Port Talbot in South Wales. The last performance went with a swing and I knew that he had great talent. When we returned in 1981 Geoffrey was conducting all the *Nabuccos* in Sydney and we became good friends. I took his advice on many things. He lent us kitchen equipment to start us off in our new home.

The Palais Theatre in St Kilda is just over the road from the fairground called Luna Park. We had not noticed it during the week as it was closed, but on the Saturday it was going with a swing when we got to the theatre for the evening performance. We were all on stage at the moment when Nabucco has to sing something about being greater than God himself (at this point all the lights go out and there is a roll of thunder and God strikes Nabucco for this blasphemy. Then total silence while Nabucco and his court gather themselves.) It was in this silence that we and all the audience heard shrieks of delight from the thrill-seeking ladies of Melbourne who were on the big dipper. Bob Allman as Nabucco stunned by God was heard to whisper, 'Geez, just listen to all those sheilas.' I thought I would burst.

During our short stay in Melbourne it was Gold Cup week. This meant little to me but John informed me it was the event of the year in Australia in the racing world. Mary Jane Corderoy, who was singing Anna in *Nabucco*, said that the city would be 'quiet on Gold Cup day'. She asked us if we would care to go on a car trip to Mount Dandenong, and I was delighted by this chance to see something of Australia apart from its theatres and hotels and airports.

It was a glorious hot day. Mary Jane had understated the quietness of the city. It was worse than a Welsh village on a Sunday. However, as we made our way to the mountains we could see that we seemed to be the only ones going *out* of Melbourne – there were hundreds of cars going into the city. We stopped our car on a deserted mountain road and got out, amazed at the noise of millions of crickets – a sound I have come to detest. We did not see any lyre birds, or bell birds as the Australians call them, but we could hear their tinkling bell-like notes.

We drove to a restaurant called The Cuckoo, which looked something like a Swiss chalet. There was a dazzling array of food – everyone paid the same price and you could go on eating till you burst. Roland, who had a tremendous appetite, had a whale of a time, but I was stuck with the usual salad. As we drove back down the mountain I made a vow that I would bring Mairwyn here when she left school. Little did I know that she would see Mount Dandenong long before she left school.

All too soon it was over and time to think of going home to England. Glen Lehman presented me with a toy koala that had a music box in its tummy and played *Waltzin' Matilda*. I had sent John and Roland looking for Australian gifts for Mairwyn and had insisted on them buying me a didgerydoo. Of course it would not fit in any of the cases and we took it on the plane as hand baggage, along with my koala. I put both in the overhead locker. The flight was pleasant, and I had two first class seats to myself. The steward took out the middle arm rest and I was able to lie down. We were somewhere over Burma when I heard the sound of *Waltzin' Matilda*. The steward stopped it and we resumed our sleep. Half an hour later it began again. The steward came along and said, 'Miss Hunter, your Matilda is waltzing again.' We were both giggling and he said, 'I think she had better do the rest of the trip with the pilot,' and off went Matilda to help Qantas to fly us home.

It doesn't matter if it's Sydney or London, but if you fly the Australian run then you always land at your destination at around 6 a.m. You feel exhausted, dirty and dishevelled, and by the time you have got all your luggage you are in quite a vile mood in the customs hall. I had my handbag and Matilda on one arm and under the other my giant didgerydoo, the latter wrapped in brown paper. John and Roland had already got through customs with our nine cases with no problems, but now, as they saw me with my didgerydoo, the eyes of the customs' men lit up with anticipation of a kill.

'Excuse me, madam, what is that you have there?'

I smiled sweetly. 'It's a didgerydoo.'

Their eyes narrowed. Through clenched teeth I said, 'A didgerydoo!'

'Never heard of it, madam.'

I drew myself up to my full five feet six inches and said, 'It's an aboriginal musical instrument' (there was that smirk again) '– and what's more I can play it.'

I heard Roland say to John, 'Oh my God she's off.'

I sure was. Nellie's blood was up. I tore the brown paper off, took a deep breath, and the international customs hall at Heathrow was brought to a standstill by the sound of Nellie and her didgerydoo.

The customs' man grabbed it from me, and hastily wrapped it again, and shoved it under my arm. He hissed in my ear, 'Get lost!'

I swept out of the customs hall. John and Roland were almost on the floor laughing. I said very grandly, 'Now you know why I never do things by halves. I didn't just buy it, I learned to play it too.'

CHAPTER EIGHTEEN

Operation Gallstones

Despite my bravado at the airport with my didgerydoo I was nevertheless a sick lady, and spent a good part of December in bed with several gallstone attacks. The travelling had taken its toll, my diet became more limited. In the mornings I would drink a cup of black coffee or tea with lemon, but the tea upset me, so had to be dropped. Lunch would be a small portion of boiled rice and lean boiled ham. The ham was stopped because we couldn't be sure it contained no fat. In the evening I would have un-dressed lettuce and a jelly made with cordial and gelatine, but had to cut out the jelly, so by the time I was starting the rehearsals for the *Trovatores* at the Coliseum at the end of January 1979 my daily intake was just the cup of coffee, a portion of boiled rice and some lettuce in the evening. Any normal person would have lost a stone a week on such fare but not me. It's true I didn't put *on* any weight, but I didn't take any off either.

Half way through the run of *Trovatores* I had a very bad attack, and during one performance I remember actually being sick on stage in the middle of the Act 4 arias. I managed to swallow some of it and the rest I spat into a handkerchief with my back to the audience.

My doctor discovered that the Thames Ditton water was too chalky, so then my rice had to be boiled in Perrier water – and this water also had to be used for my coffee. They begged me to have the operation but I stuck to my guns, as there were still the Welsh National *Turandots* to do.

In the midst of the attacks and the *Trovatores* I had been busy studying the role of *Turandot* and was not going to be robbed of her at this late hour. My agents told me that the Welsh had me heavily covered in case I fell out. Well, whoever was standing by was disappointed. I sang all fourteen of them, and they were bloody good performances, despite a cold on the first night and the last night.

I loved every moment of working with Sally Day, the producer, and Richard Armstrong, the conductor. My costumes were superb; the Welsh had done me proud. They were made of pure silk, one lime green and the other midnight blue. The first headdress was fantastic and 'Billy Wigs' had made me two of the most superb wigs.

The first rehearsal in the studios in John Street, Cardiff, was a momentous occasion for me. Being married to a Welshman I was a bit apprehensive of singing 'In questa reggia' in front of the critical Welsh National Choral. But at the end they erupted into thunderous applause. I was so elated I did not realise that I had sung the wrong words in the riddle that followed!

I stood there with my 'ice face' on and waited for the Calaf (Ken Collins) to answer me, but he did not. Big-head Nellie thought that he was wrong, but then he brought me down to earth with a bump by saying, 'I can't reply, she's asked me the wrong question!' This broke the ice quicker than the Choral's applause and we all fell about laughing, and they gave us a coffee break so that law and order could be restored. However, there is a sequel to this story.

Some weeks later when the tour was well under way, Ken Collins had been working hard, and the night before the *Turandot* had sung in some other opera or concert, and was tired. All went well until we got to the riddles, and when I asked him the first one he seemed reluctant to come to the end of his 'answer' and after a long pause quickly said, 'Turandot?' with not much conviction. I warned myself not even to think of laughing. I asked him the second riddle – same answer, 'Turandot?' By now I could hear a few smothered giggles from the chorus behind me. All I could think of was, 'When the answer *is* Turandot whatever will he say then?' I heard some wag in the chorus say, 'Chop his head off, Rita.' Then I heard Ken mutter, 'Oh, shit.' I then heard Richard Armstrong hiss, 'Not shit – *il sangue*.' I don't know how I managed to keep from laughing. When I swept past Ken after the riddles to go and plead with my father, the old king, Ken said to me, 'Sorry, Rit, I didn't half cock that up.' My downstage face remained an icy stare – by my upstage face gave him a broad wink.

As soon as the *Turandots* were over I was immediately rehearsing for the August *Rings* at the Coliseum. It all seemed rather restrained and serious after the relaxed atmosphere of the Welsh company. After the second *Valkyrie* I was presented in front of the curtain with a framed costume design by Lord Harewood for twenty-five years service with the Sadler's Wells/ENO. I smothered a smile when I saw the design. It was the hated *Götterdämmerung* costume – the one I swore I'd flush down the toilet. (I eventually reverted to my *Valkyrie* costume without the armour for *Götterdämmerung*.) However it was the thought that counted. A lot of the company thought that my tears in the dressing room were tears of emotion but in fact I had miscalculated the time of my painkillers and I was in agony.

I completed the two cycles of the 1979 ENO *Ring* – I did not know that it would be four years before I would be invited to sing for ENO again. That's life, I suppose.

*

On the morning of August 28th I awoke feeling very apprehensive. The idea of anaesthetics and not being in control of myself I have always found disturbing, and I was half convinced there was something else responsible for my pain. I was due at Harley Street at 4 p.m. and at 1.30 Mairwyn decided that she would not come with us to the clinic. She announced that she was going to stay with friends. I let her go, but then felt utterly desolate, though I knew she hated the thought of seeing me in a hospital bed.

After being checked into the clinic I was weighed, blood pressure and temperature taken, and blood sample. Then they brought me a cup of tea – with milk! I couldn't believe it, and assumed they thought it couldn't matter any more. And how good it tasted. After about half an hour John announced that he was going home, although I tried to persuade him to hang around a little longer.

A nurse came and shaved my lower regions and a physiotherapist came to 'teach me how to breathe'. Then she laughed and said, 'Considering who you are it must sound silly, but after they have cut through your diaphragm you will have to learn to breathe in a different way.' After a session of these strange breathing exercises she said something that threw me into a panic. 'When you wake up you will find you have a drain tube up your nose and down your throat.'

Down my throat! My throat! When she had gone I phoned John and begged him to come and fetch me. 'What if they damage my vocal cords?' I wailed. He was unsympathetic, and started to tell me what Mairwyn's gerbils were doing in their cage by the phone. 'Sod the bloody gerbils, you unfeeling swine.' I could not make him understand, so I said good night, and knew that I had to face it alone, whatever it was.

After an early morning bath the next day I was given the usual pre-med. I remember fearing that they would drop me, transferring me from the bed to the trolley. John assures me he was there, but I saw no one. I do remember telling someone that I wanted to keep my gallstones, then somebody saying, 'She's coming round, quick.'

'Oh God, what a pain – give me something please, it's awful,' I said. And then I was being sick and someone washed my face with a cool cloth, then a prick in my arm, then no more pain. I wanted to sleep for ever, never wake up. I was sick again, and again my face was washed. I tried to lick my lips to see where the dreaded tube was, and could not feel the tube. I heard someone sob and sigh heavily, and I opened my eyes, and there was the ever-faithful John standing by my bed with tears running down his face.

'Good girl, Rit bach, you've done it.' I gave him a faint grin and said, 'No tube is there?' He blew his nose and said, 'No tube, bach.'

A nurse came in and said, 'Phone for you, Miss Hunter.' I thought she must be mad – I was barely awake and she was shoving a phone into my fist. I croaked a breathy 'Hello' – and the person at the other end was mortified by the way I sounded. She was a fan of mine, Jill Harris, who had rung the clinic just to ask how I was and was most surprised to find she had been put right through to me. I realised what the physiotherapist had meant about learning to breathe again.

When John had gone my nurse came and gave me a lovely cool wash and the phone rang again. It was George Harewood and his wife Patricia. As the afternoon wore on the room began to fill with flowers, cards and telegrams. The pain came on again and I was quickly given an injection. I had a drip in my left arm and when the nurse came to change my dressing she told me that there was a drain tube in my right side. I thought they had perhaps heard my wails of panic on the phone the night before.

The physiotherapist appeared and tried to get me to cough and breathe, but I did not do at all well. I was dying of thirst.

The next morning I was visited by an ogre of a sister, full of life and Irish blarney. 'Well now, Miss Hunter, have you had your bowels moved today?'

'No, Sister,' I said sheepishly.

'Well, sure I'll soon shift *you*, me darlin'.'

I had no doubt at all that she would. When she had performed her unpleasant task, she brought in a tiny nurse and an even smaller bed pan. 'Oh no, sister,' I protested, 'There is no way you are going to get me on to that thing. I'm going to the toilet.' Sister threw up her hands in horror. 'Holy Mother of God, you will be in agony.' I replied, 'Maybe, but I am going to the proper toilet.'

It hurt like hell when I went to get out of bed, and it hurt even more when I tried to walk, but I persevered and the little nurse scuttled down the corridor after me pushing my drip trolley.

When John called later that day I boasted that I had 'been for a walk'. He could hardly believe it. 'Well, one thing's certain, Mr Thomas,' said the sister. 'Your wife's not going to malinger.' John said, 'At eighty quid a day for the room I should bloody well hope not!'

The following day I was in and out of bed like a yo-yo. On the Sunday evening I watched the Dick Emery Show on TV and nearly burst my remaining stitches laughing. On the Monday my surgeon came to see me, and said, 'You're a bore; nothing wrong with you, you can go home tomorrow.'

I asked, 'What about the diet?'

'My dear Miss Hunter, go home and eat whatever you fancy your, nightmare is over.'

The next morning my temperature was up so they kept me in another day and I took sister's advice and swilled down as much cold water as I could, and on the Wednesday John came to drive me home. The streets of London were quiet and deserted; it was Lord Mountbatten's funeral. It was not possible to associate my wonderful, bossy and good-natured sister with the people who had murdered him.

*

As we drove home John said, 'Whatever you fancy today I will buy you.' I think he thought I would ask for champagne and caviare, but instead I asked him to take me to the Alma Arms for one of Vivien's fantastic sausages and a fresh bread roll with the first butter for four years.

It was a feast fit for a king; I had a second helping. Ray and Viv were so thrilled that they said it was on the house. When I got home I sat quiet, looking out at the garden. John asked, 'What's wrong?' 'Nothing,' I replied. He wasn't convinced. 'You sure?'

I began to cry. 'I don't feel sick, I can't believe it.' After the butter and the roll I was certain that I would be. It was only then that I realised that what the surgeon had said was true. I could eat whatever I wanted. It was now 6 p.m. and I was very tired, so

John helped me to bed, put the phone by my hand and switched on the TV, then went off for a pint at the Alma. At 8.45 I wanted to spend a penny, and discovered that it was impossible to get out of my soft and squashy bed. The one in the clinic had had a lever to tilt you to an upright position. I kept trying but could not make it, and at 9 o'clock I phoned the Alma and asked John to come home and told him why. I felt a real pest, but he didn't seem to mind.

Mairwyn came home the next day and I tried to sing. Nothing wrong with the voice but oh, the diaphragm. No support at all. I had to sit bolt upright with my back supported by the chair, and my tummy supported with my two hands. Even then I could only string two notes together. 'Six months, he said. At this rate it will take six years.'

I was bitterly disappointed, and as usual wanted to run before I could walk. I would try to stand at the sink to wash the dishes, and after three or four cups I was shattered. It took two weeks of singing three or four notes an hour before I could sing standing up. I was irritated and impatient, and I wasn't easy to live with. I was worried that the first thing I would sing would be the Abigailles in Sydney in February 1980, and did I not feel this was fair to the Australian Opera or to myself. I telephoned my friend Arthur Martin, and he organised a recital in the Pump Rooms at Bath in mid-November. I had three months to prepare. While I was busy on this, I was asked to do a concert in the Royal Albert Hall in December. That would give me two try-outs before Sydney.

I worked hard every day and at times John worried that I was pushing myself too fast. I went up to town a couple of times to work with my pianist, Hazel Vivienne, and one glorious day I was actually able to sing all of the first half without falling apart.

The concert at Bath went fine. I felt very tired half-way through the second half of the programme, but I made it and all was well. We stayed the night with my friend, Allan Taylor of Harlech TV, and the next morning I went to Milsoms record shop to sign records, organised by Arthur Martin. Then a tired but contented diva was driven home.

The concert in December at the Royal Albert Hall also went off without a hitch. Then I sat back with my *Nabucco* score to prepare for my second trip down under.

*

We left London on Sunday, January 17th 1980 and arrived in Sydney in very hot weather on the 29th. Moffatt Oxenbould met us at the airport and took us to our hotel in Elizabeth Bay. In the afternoon we were resting on the bed and trying to keep cool, when the doorman brought in the largest display of red roses and carnations that I had ever seen. They were from the artists and management of the Australian Opera. We went early to bed, as we could not keep our eyes open any longer.

Next morning jet lag woke us at 3 a.m., and we made coffee and at 6 o'clock sent for breakfast. At ten I phoned Moffatt to thank him for the flowers and he asked me if I could stay on longer in 1981 and do some *Toscas* after the *Macbeths* and the Brünnhildes.

As it happened I had nothing planned after my return in November 1981 – just Christmas. So I said I would be delighted to stay on. At three o'clock that day we met Moffatt and went to see the Sydney Opera House for the first time. When I went into the Green Room I realised where the star singers of Sadler's Wells had gone in the fifties and sixties – they were here in Sydney. They had gone back home. What a joy it was to see them all again. I knew there was no way now I would miss the ENO company, as so many of my former colleagues were here in Australia.

The following day Glen Lehman took me to do a radio show, which was crazy but fun, and I ended up singing without a piano 'On Mother Kelly's Doorstep'.

On 1st February we moved from the hotel into a little flat in Berry's Bay, North Sydney. There was a violent storm in the afternoon and I saw what I thought was a snake, which turned out to be a lizard. I also saw my first Australian cockroach. I screamed blue murder, and John said firmly, 'You will have to get used to them here, Rita.' I regret to say I never have got used to them and never will. I can't stand insects, and spend a fortune on sprays and baits for them. It is the only thing I have against Australia.

On Sunday 3rd February I woke with a feeling of doom, and asked John if I could phone Mairwyn. I did so and she was okay, but at eight o'clock Clio rang from the Opera House to say there was a wire from John's sister; his mother had had two heart attacks.

Two days later Betty rang again to say Mam had died. We tried everything to get John a flight home but none of them would have got him there until after the funeral, so John reluctantly said he would not go. I said, 'Why on earth did my mother and yours have to die when we were out of the country?'

On the 9th February we went after the matinée on a sunset

cruise round the harbour with the company, and the next day on a company picnic. John was playing cricket and I found myself recruited to cook chops and sausages at a barbecue. Although it wasn't a sunny day I got a considerable tan and John won two bottles of whisky in a raffle.

On Sunday the 17th Moffatt invited us to lunch and afterwards we went for a drive. They were supposed to take us to North Head to see the surfing beaches below. We got out of the car only to discover we had taken the wrong road and we all reeled at the smell – we had gone to the North Head Sewage Farm. Moffatt was scornful – 'They come twelve thousand miles to see the sights and all you can show them is the sewage farm.' We staggered back, laughing, to the car.

On Monday, 18th February, I made my debut in Sydney and was delighted with the reception from the audience. We were both very pleased with what the papers had to say the next day.

We didn't do much more sightseeing as there were three *Nabuccos* a week, so it was a case of resting in between. Also the weather was very hot; one night it was 107 degrees when we came out of the theatre after the show.

On the 27th February I had a letter offering me *Forza del Destino* with the BBC Promenade Concerts. The money was the same as it had been two years before, and in fact the rise in the cost of living really made it less, so I replied and said no thank you; it would have meant spending a lot of time learning a role that I might never sing on stage.

On 29th February I recorded in my diary that it was just six months to the day since my operation. On March 1st I sang my sixth *Nabucco* in Sydney and then on the 2nd we flew home. The first thing we did was drive up to Mairwyn's boarding school and give her the few gifts we had for her, also some long hugs and kisses.

The next day I wrote to my surgeon and thanked him. I had a contract in my pocket for 1981 with the Australian Opera to sing two *Walküre*, two *Götterdämmerung* Brünnhildes, fourteen Lady Macbeths and six *Toscas*. I was well satisfied that the surgeon and I had both done a good job.

CHAPTER NINETEEN

Commander Hunter

On the morning of November 15th 1979 I was first up, and went to collect the mail from the hall. We had staying with us a pupil of John's who was to audition with the Welsh National Opera that afternoon. Instead of going to make the coffee as I usually did, I sat down and sifted through the mail, and a long envelope caught my eye, 'OHMS – From the Prime Minister'. At first I thought, 'Oh lord, it must be about income tax.' Then a wild fancy entered my mind. I tore open the envelope, read the first few lines, and didn't wait to read the rest.

I ran upstairs (the first time I had run anywhere for twenty years), and stood at the foot of John's bed gasping for breath and with tears in my eyes.

'What's wrong?' he asked.

'I've got one,' I gasped.

'One what?'

'One of these.'

He didn't sit up, just lay there smiling.

'What sort, Rit?'

'I don't know, I haven't read it yet.'

I sat on the side of his bed, and had to borrow his glasses, as my eyes were so misted over. I had been made a Commander of the British Empire.

'Have you made the coffee?'

'Oh you infuriating man, you're not even excited.'

'Yes I am, but you'll wake Pauline and you can't tell anyone yet, not even Mairwyn – go and make the coffee, there's a good girl.'

I swept out, but on the landing hesitated, then put my head round the door.

'Sod you and your coffee. I'm going to write to Mrs Thatcher.'

By the time John had the beans ground, I had answered the letter, 'If Her Majesty were to offer me the Honour – yes I would accept it,' and it was in the post box before the beans were in the pot and before Pauline woke.

Then I began to fret about what I should wear on *the day*. Who did I know who had been honoured? Ah yes, Anna Pollock, wonderful artist and dear friend, and very down to earth.

'Darling,' she said, 'don't buy gloves. I paid a pound for mine at Libertys and some wretched flunky took them off me and I never saw them again. And whatever you do, treat it all like you were going for a general anaesthetic and don't drink anything in the morning – there are no toilets in the Palace and you'll be in agony.'

Anna went on, 'There is nothing to worry about really, darling. They give you a sort of rehearsal and there is a pretty awful tea-shop band playing all the time.'

I remembered then that when Reggie Goodall got his CBE and we had asked him 'What was it like?' – meaning of course what did the Queen say and what did she wear – Reggie's only comment on the whole ceremony had been, 'The violins were flat.'

I was not supposed to tell anybody until it was announced on New Year's Eve, but keeping it from Mairwyn was the hardest part of this, and we eventually told her on Christmas Day. We knew that she would not be going anywhere between then and New Year, so there was no chance of her spilling the beans. We tied the letter to the Christmas tree and got her to open it. She burst into tears, she was so proud and excited at the prospect of going to the Palace.

We watched every TV news on the day before New Year's Eve; they mentioned Colin Davis's knighthood, and Cliff Richard's OBE. Mairwyn sat glued to the TV, and got crosser and crosser as the day wore on and no mention of 'Mum'. The last news of the day was an extended one and they seemed to mention just about everyone – but not me. Since you are not told anything, just *asked* if you would accept *if* offered, until it is mentioned on the news or in the press you are not one hundred per cent certain that you've got it. We went to bed feeling downcast.

We were up early next morning and John went to get the papers, but before he got back from the village the phone had begun to ring. The news was out. I was busy cooking for our New Year's Eve party, and was so bemused by all the phone calls that I don't know what I put into the tagliatelle sauce – but as it all got eaten it must have been all right.

One of my well-wishers was Stephen Barry, one of my de-voted fans, who was at that time the valet to the Prince of Wales. He had a flat at the top of Buckingham Palace at the back overlooking the gardens. We had been there a few times, mostly after one of my performances, and of course we went in through the servants' entrance. When Stephen phoned, his first words were, 'And who will be going in through the front gate next time?'

He went on to say that we ought to make it an even more special day by having drinks up in his flat after the ceremony, and he would invite all our mutual friends, Christopher Biggins, the actor, William Tallon, who was in charge of the Queen Mother's household at Clarence House, and (since only hus-bands and one child are admitted to the ceremony) he told me to invite some of my own close friends and instruct them to go to the side entrance by 11 a.m. and he would entertain them until I'd been 'done'.

I asked Stephen about gloves. 'Yes, you need them.'

'And what about a hat?'

'Oh yes, that's a *must*.'

My heart fell. I am not a hat-person. My Auntie Ruth used to say when she saw me ready for church on a Sunday, 'Oh God, you look a bugger in a hat,' and she was right.

Les Lansdown, who was going to make my dress, reassured me, 'You'll look lovely. I'll make the hat, and then we'll be sure you get what is best for you.'

Mairwyn said, 'Wear a head scarf, Mum, you've got that lovely blue one from Pucci.' Well, I also look a bugger in a head scarf. In fact, I am of the opinion that the only people who can add class to the humble head scarf are the royal ladies them-selves.

I was told I must be at the Palace between 10 and 10.30. The night before, Les Lansdown brought our outfits along for the final fitting. My heart sank. The hat was very small. I think he was hurt at my lack of enthusiasm. He offered to make a larger one and bring it out the next morning, but that meant he would have to get to Thames Ditton very early indeed. I asked him to put veiling around it in the hope that it would at least *look* bigger.

When he had gone I remembered that I had overlooked a visit to the hairdresser, and at 10 p.m. I was putting rollers in my hair. The hat stared at me from the chest of drawers, and seemed to shrink before my eyes. I never slept a wink – Anna had been right about the general anaesthetic. I felt that I was not going to meet my monarch, but to have my innards cut out.

With lack of sleep my eyes were bloodshot, and I might have been on a boozing spree. I woke Mairwyn and John at 6.30, resentful that they dared to sleep. I showered and dressed and made up my face, and then brushed out my hair – I had forgotten to use a conditioner and the more I tried to tame it the worse it was. Eventually I had to put the hat on, and my wails brought Mairwyn and John rushing in.

'I'll be the laughing stock of the Palace.'

John said, 'Oh bloody hell, here we go.'

'Don't cry, Mum,' said Mairwyn. 'Your mascara is running.'

And it was, all down my face and on to the dress.

I patched up my face and after a dramatic scene went downstairs to the kitchen, and there was my husband looking like a Welsh undertaker, courtesy of Moss Bros, making the coffee.

I shrieked, 'Don't you dare have anything to drink, remember what Anna Pollock said about there being no toilets in the Palace.'

He sighed, 'Oh, bloody hell Rit, bach. . . .'

'Will you please stop swearing, Daddy, you're going to see the Queen.'

We sat down to eat some toast which was as reluctant to go down as my hair had been. Then we saw it was pouring with rain; curses from John and wails from me.

'My hair is a disaster now, what will it be like when it gets wet?'

'Perhaps it'll look better, Mum?'

We scuttled to the car. The traffic was dreadful and it took us 1½ hours to do four miles, with all manner of pile-ups on the A3. 'Oh God, I'll be late, they won't let me in after 10.30.'

I know now that you can't really be late, as your name is ticked off a list by footmen and they don't start till you are there.

We got half way down the Mall by 10.15, and I was beside myself with anxiety. We overook a long line of cars that all seemed to be crawling in the left hand lane and were stopped at the Victoria monument by a policeman. John, still in his undertaker's outfit, wound down the window and asked, 'Are we okay here, mate?'

'Are you for the Palace, sir?'

I snorted impatiently. 'Well, we aren't dressed for picking blackberries, are we, dear?'

The policeman ignored me and said to John, 'Well, sir if you will just go round the monument and down the Mall and join that line of cars there . . .'

John began to obey the law but I said, 'Cut into the line of traffic.'

John said. 'Don't be daft, I can't, the policeman . . .'

'Sod the policeman,' I said. 'If you go back down the Mall I shall be late. If you don't cut into the line I shall get out and walk and then I shall divorce you.' (Yes, I know, he should have socked me!)

Well, after a shocking row, he did what I wanted, and we ended up facing the wrong way in the Mall and with our bonnet up a tree.

'Well now perhaps you're satisfied.'

'I wish my bloody bonnet was up a tree,' I replied.

By now Mairwyn was yelling, 'Please stop shouting, you two, this is supposed to be a happy day.'

As we drove through the Palace gates she continued to try to restore harmony and said, 'If the Queen speaks to you, what will you say, Mum?'

By now quite exhausted, I said, 'If you're thinking of making me a Dame, dear, do it now, I'm not going through all this lot again.'

This made us all laugh and peace was restored.

The first thing I noticed in the Palace was a large notice announcing 'Toilets'. John said, 'She must have won a few bob on the horses since Anna was here and had some bogs put in.'

I was so busy gaping at all the splendour that I fell up the grand staircase to the amusement of some toffee-nosed footmen and one of the Household Cavalry. We were ushered into a long picture gallery, and I was amused to see that the MBEs and the OBEs were separated from the CBEs. We were in a corral surrounded by a red rope. A tall lady beside me commented on the 'segregation' and I said, 'Well, they have to separate the steers from the long horns.' Giggles all round, and the atmosphere was a little more relaxed. We never did get to see the Knights, which rather disappointed me – I should have loved to see the sword-on-the-shoulder bit.

A rather dapper young man began to circulate and put pins on our chests – strange-looking things with hooks on them – and it was explained that this was so that the Queen could just hang our medals on without fiddling with a pin. A woman said in a peeved tone, 'The men aren't getting pins, which means they'll get a nice yard and a half of pink and silver ribbon.' (Actually, when I investigated my box containing the CBE, there was a length of pink and silver ribbon in it too – so the peeved lady had her money's worth.)

A door opened and it was then I heard 'Reggie's orchestra' – he was right about the violins, and so was Anna – they did sound like fugitives from a Lyons tea-room.

The door had been opened to admit a sergeant-major type who asked us to gather round him and we were told how to walk, and where and when, and how many paces forward and how many back. This was the rehearsal Anna had mentioned – if only all rehearsals could be so brief. We were then lined up and escorted in single file down a long corridor. As we neared the end of it I could see the Queen reflected in a mirror, and as we moved nearer I could see her without the mirror. I had a lump in my throat. I hoped I would not burst into tears, as I had all those years ago when her coach went past us at Hyde Park Corner after she had been crowned.

We had been told to walk forward only when we heard our name called, then when we were opposite the Queen we must curtsey, and walk to the dais as near as possible so that Her Majesty would not have to bend too far.

The Lord Chamberlain began, as I thought, to say 'Miss Rita H . . .' so I began to walk forward. The footman beside me shot his arm out and halted me, and hissed 'Wait!' The Lord Chamberlain went on, 'The Most Excellent Order of the British Empire, to be made a Commander of . . . Miss Rita Hunter.' With my heart pounding I walked forward, and curtsied, thought to myself, 'God, I'm sure I bent the wrong knee.' Then I was shaking hands with the Queen and she said something about congratulations. I found my mouth so dry I could only croak a very husky, 'Thank you, ma'am.' She then said something about the English National Opera and I again croaked something about the sunshine in Australia, don't ask me why. She smiled and nodded, and stepped back. My brief encounter was over. I stepped backwards, curtsied, realised to my horror that I had only stepped back two steps instead of four, and said to myself, 'Carry on, Nellie, you're making a right mess of this,' and to try to redeem myself stepped back another two paces and curtsied again. I bowed my head this time and remembered the hat. Over the years came Auntie Ruth's voice saying 'Oh God, you look a bugger in a hat.'

I was then marched round another corridor and ushered into the ceremony room again, but this time I was one of the spectators – oh the bliss of being able to sit down and be anonymous. Then I began to look around. The tea-house orchestra was still at it, now playing selections from *The Bartered Bride*. I saw the huge crystal chandeliers, the thrones, the soldiers and the beefeaters, and wished with all my heart that my parents could have lived to share it with me.

I became aware of a pain in my hand. Had I hurt it when I fell up the stairs? No, I had been clutching the box containing my medal so tightly that my fingers were white. They were now playing *God Save The Queen*. It was all over. I turned to walk out and saw Mairwyn and John, faces flushed, two pairs of suspiciously moist eyes, and pride plastered all over them. None of us said a word, we just linked arms and squeezed hands and walked out to meet the waiting press.

The rain had now stopped, and the photographers gathered round. Stephen appeared and said, 'I say, your hat's a knockout.' How I loved him for that! I asked if the gang had all arrived. 'Oh yes, and they're pretty well oiled by now.'

We could hear ribald laughter floating down the back stairs. I discovered I was shaking like a leaf and when we arrived in Stephen's flat I asked for a brandy. (The non-drinker who hadn't eaten her toast was now on large brandies. And the usual from my ever-loving husband, 'Bloody hell, here she goes.')

I had invited among my guests Allan Taylor of Harlech TV and he seemed to spend the whole day saying, 'I say, this is great,' or 'Gosh what a day.' When we dropped him off at Paddington station that night, the last we saw of him was walking *away* from the platform. My friend Jenny from San Francisco was there and we all know how the Americans feel about royalty. She was bubbling like champagne, high as a kite just being in the Palace. I heard Stephen saying how sorry he was that she had to come by the servants' entrance, and she flashed her eyes and said in her deep husky voice, 'Sweetheart, I'd have swum up the sewer pipe just to be here.' Then added, 'Wait till I get back to the States, I'll dine out on this lot for years.'

By now the diva was on her fourth brandy and someone suggested we had better go on to the restaurant where we had a table booked for lunch. We were going to the Inigo Jones, owned by some friends of mine who were not in town but had left several large bottles of champagne for us. We stayed there till about 4 p.m. and my friend William asked us to 'go to his place for coffee and brandy'. We all staggered into the cars and several taxis. I knew where William's place was, but Jenny didn't, and as we drove down the Mall then turned into Clarence House I heard her say, 'Jesus Christ, where are we going now?'

We used the servants' entrance and went up to William's flat. William had asked the Queen Mother for the day off as 'a friend of mine is receiving today'.

'Do I know her, William?' she enquired.

Well, I don't know if my favourite royal lady did know me, but she gave William the day off. His friend Reg was standing in for him and he was dressed in the traditional black coat and knee breeches, white stockings and silver buckles on his shoes. He looked very grand, and Jenny's eyes were popping. By 9 p.m. we had consumed all of William's brandy and just about everything else. The phone rang and I ignored William's outstretched hand and answered it. 'Yes, darling, what do you want?'

A posh voice said, 'May I speak to William, please?'

I handed over the phone and after a second I heard him say 'Yes, your Royal Highness.' I had called Prince Andrew 'darling'. I thought it was about time for the diva to go home and take her tipsy mates with her before we all ended up in the Tower of London. William escorted us to the Mall and as we drove away he bowed and saluted us.

On the way home we called in at my husband's local, the Alma Arms. We must have looked out of place in our Palace finery – Mairwyn and me in silk, John dressed as an undertaker – but we were given a great welcome by Ray and Viv, and my medal was proudly passed around.

As we turned into our drive, my body suddenly yelled out that it had not been to the loo since 6 a.m. It *had been* a special day, spent with some very special people.

CHAPTER TWENTY

The Missing Turandots

In the spring of 1980 I had a telephone call from Glynn Ross, the director of the Seattle Opera, asking if I would sing the English *Ring* there that summer. I didn't really want to go as I was busy preparing for the *Turandots* at the Metropolitan in the autumn of 1980.

When I had been in Sydney in February 1980 Joan Sutherland had been kind enough to offer us the use of her house in Brooklyn for our Metropolitan season. We told her how much we loathed being cooped up in a hotel room for two months at a time; I had not known then that she had a house there, but by the end of 1980 we were very glad she had.

Glynn Ross phoned again the next day and I told him that my fee was $4,000 for each of the three *Ring* operas. There was a long silence at the other end of the line, so I put him out of his misery by suggesting he thought about it, no hard feelings if his budget wouldn't run to it, but to ring me back if he could afford me. He was back within ten minutes – he could afford me.

Mairwyn was looking forward to going, as Mount St Helen's had erupted and she waited with bated breath to see if Seattle had been wiped out before we got there.

I sat down to reorganise our travel plans. Going to the West Coast was a good chance to visit Frank and Phil in Los Angeles. I also hoped to celebrate my birthday at the Grand Canyon, and planned to arrive in New York on the 18th, giving me two days before my contract began.

And so I swotted up *Turandot* and *The Ring* in English. I was happy that I would be working again with Henry Holt and Lincoln Clark, with whom I had collaborated on *Walküre* in Philadelphia. Les Lansdown had designed and made a whole case full of new day dresses for me to take and, after Seattle

Opera Wardrobe sent me a photo of the *Walküre* costume, Les and I sat down to design my own costume; it proved to be a huge success.

The day after our arrival in Seattle I had a call from my friend Charlie Riecker at the Metropolitan. 'Welcome back to America,' he said. 'When do we see you here?' I told him I would be in New York on August 18th. 'Gee, so soon?' I pointed out that my contract began on the 20th. He was silent, and then went on to talk about my family. I realised later he was toying with the idea of warning me of the Union problems they were having at the Met. I wish we could have stayed longer with Frank in Vegas.

At the end of the two weeks' rehearsal we had of course got to the end of *Götterdämmerung* and, as I began to immolate, Mount St Helen's decided to blow her top again. We rushed home from work and out on to our balcony and were able to see all its fury and splendour and took many photographs. Indeed the Seattle Opera gift shop even sold tiny phials of the ash and they were labelled 'Genuine Immolation Dust' – and needless to say I have a phial in my own china cabinet.

It was good to be working again with Alberto and we were both in fine voice. We did several radio interviews together and they also broadcast the English *Ring*, and Frank and Phil were able to pick it up in Los Angeles. Alberto and I knew we were in good form but I was totally unprepared for the tumult of applause that greeted me at the final curtain after *Götterdämmerung*. The whole house rose to its feet and the eruption of cheers rivalled the thunder of Mount St Helen's herself.

During the final week in Seattle, I was aware that many of the artists were going in to see Glynn Ross to make plans for the following season. I didn't bother to do so; for one thing I had been hired in place of a sick artist and I assumed that when she was fit and well the next year she would be hired again. However, Glynn Ross phoned me and asked what I would be doing on the Friday afternoon. I told him truthfully, 'With *Siegfried* on Thursday and *Götterdämmerung* on Saturday, I won't be doing anything.' He said he would call round for a chat and a cup of tea. So Mairwyn prepared tea and cakes for him, but it seemed that he did not want tea at all but to talk about re-engaging me for a return visit to Seattle. He asked me if I would sing *Trovatore* for them in September/October 1982, same fee. So with great pleasure I accepted.

The reviews for *The Ring* were glowing, raving even, and a great many of them. I remarked to John that once again the West Coast was being more hospitable than the East.

After the final performance we flew to Los Angeles where we were met by Frank and Phil. It seemed to me that Seattle airport was full of *Ring* pilgrims, many of them going back to California on our plane, and the pre-flight time and the flight itself were spent signing autographs.

It was wonderful to sit on Frank's patio and relax and be waited on. We were lazy for two days and then we tackled Disneyland. It was fearfully hot, and the diva's feet were like balloons, and I ended up walking round in my bedroom slippers. We had our photographs taken with Goofy and Mickey Mouse, and I was as wide-eyed as any of the kids there. We went into the Sleeping Beauty's Castle – lovely but uneventful, until we got to the exit. There was a turnstile to go through that had been made for the Munchkins in 'The Wizard of Oz' – well whoever the designer had in mind, he did not anticipate that it would be used by a Wagnerian soprano. I was well and truly stuck and the only way for me to get out was to remove the turnstile from the wall. All the family had gone ahead of me, as I had lingered so long at each exhibit. They had to send for a man to unhitch the turnstile. It was hot and I was sweating and there was no place to sit. Mairwyn brought me an ice cream. It seemed that half of California went through, but I was trapped. Mairwyn brought me another ice cream. The man who was waiting for the technician to shift the turnstile said to Mairwyn, 'Jesus, sweetheart, don't feed her any more or we'll never get her out.'

After my rescue we stood in line for *The Pirates of the Caribbean*, and every foot-killing hour of waiting was worth it. We ate candy and had silly hats embroidered with our names and rode on the horse-drawn tram. And as dusk fell, the diva, along with millions of others, sat on the roadway to watch the world-famous electric parade.

We were starry-eyed. After a day's rest we went round Hollywood and saw the Chinese Theatre, then on to Universal studios. And, if we were thrilled with Disneyland, we were wild about the studios.

We had a few shopping sprees to the Galleria in Glendale where Frank lived and ate far too much ice cream and popcorn – but, boy, it was good fun. Frank and I are both Leos so we had a joint birthday party. Frank and Phil run a record club. We arranged that our joint birthday party would be a record evening, and I was surprised and honoured that the only records and tapes they played that night were mine, so at the end I got up and sang 'live' for them.

We were looking forward to Las Vegas but were loath to leave

501 East Mountain Street, and there were many tears at the airport. We do love you so, darling Frank and Phil; you are more than good pals, you are family.

We had seen the TV programme 'Vegas' many times, but were unprepared for the real thing. It hits you at the airport – row after row of one-armed bandits; you could start gambling the minute you stepped off the plane.

We were booked into the Las Vegas Hilton. Mairwyn wasn't allowed in the Casino so she and I would sit on the balcony surrounding it and watch. I would go to the poker machine near where she was sitting, so that she felt part of the excitement, and almost right away I won $60. I thought Mairwyn would burst. John also seemed unable to put a foot wrong, and in the eighteen days we spent there he must have won agout $10,000. Whatever he won, he always spent some of it on jewellery for me; he said it would keep his luck flowing and it was an investment. I was not about to question his logic.

We flew on Scenic Airlines to the Grand Canyon, and I confess I was scared stiff when I saw the size of the plane. I think it only held about twelve persons. It was a boiling day and the hot winds coming up out of the Canyon made for a very bumpy flight. I began to feel nauseated, and tried to take my mind off it by showing Mairwyn the points of interest. 'Look darling, there is the Hoover Dam.' I turned to see that Mairwyn had her head in a bag. And that just about all the passengers were doing the same. Except John – he sat in the front seat next to the pilot and was busy with his cine-camera, giving an imitation of Cecil B. De Mille.

After we had rested in our Grand Canyon cabin we took the tourist bus to the rim of the Canyon. From a very early age I had always wanted to see the Seven Wonders of the World, and had planned a 600-mile cruise down the Nile so that we could visit the Pyramids and the temples, but that had to be cancelled so that I could go to the Metropolitan to sing *Aida*. I had comforted myself with the thought that at least I had given up my trip for an Egyptian opera. So here I was at last seeing one of the Seven Wonders. I got out of the bus and walked to the edge of the Canyon and found that I was crying. I don't know if it was the majesty and beauty that moved me or the fact that one of my childhood dreams was being fulfilled.

That night we had a special celebration dinner at the Hilton, and John won another $1,000.

*

On August 18th, we reluctantly left Las Vegas and flew to New York, the Metropolitan and *Turandot*. The house in Brooklyn where we were to stay was owned by Martin Waldron and Dame Joan Sutherland rented the two top floors from him. It was a huge place. The top floor had a large, sunny and airy lounge and a kitchen and bedroom, with three single beds in it. John was to sleep there. Mairwyn said 'I bags Richard's room,' so Nellie got to sleep in Dame Joan's bed. It was very hard, and then I remembered the problems she used to have with her back. Richard's room had its own TV so Mairwyn spent most of her time there, as John and I did not want to see re-runs of 'Sesame Street' and 'The Love Boat' every day.

Almost the first thing I did when I had unpacked was to phone Charlie Riecker at the Met and ask when my rehearsals were to begin. They knew I was staying at Joan's, and I had expected a call sheet to be waiting for me when I arrived. He said that I could come to see him the next day. All we did the next day was to have security photographs taken, and we were issued with passes. Security was tight, as during this time they had 'Murder at the Met'. I went round to see all my pals, Mary the nurse was ill in hospital, Nick the coffee machine man had died, but thank heaven Winnie was still on the stage door. She warned us of the problems that were to lead to a strike, but Charlie played it down and said it would all be settled in good time.

Two days later I was asked to go and have measurements taken for my costumes, although I was not shown any designs. Luciano Pavarotti was in the adjoining fitting room. He said hello and shook hands and off he went. I never set foot in the Met again.

The strike became a fact, and all we could do was sit in Joan's flat, buy the papers and watch TV to find out what was going on. A few singers phoned and we got the inside gossip.

So there we sat for six weeks, living on John's Las Vegas winnings. The time came for Mairwyn to go back to school in England. We had made arrangements for her to fly alone and she was to be met in London by one of John's pupils, Len Williams. I was distressed about her going all that way alone and we were in tears at Kennedy airport. Then, two or three days later, came the news on TV: the 1980 Metropolitan season was cancelled.

We were stunned. John said, 'Now what do we do?' I decided I would give the Met till noon the next day to tell me officially and then I would phone them. They did not call me, so at 1 p.m. I phoned Charlie Riecker.

'Charlie, is what I heard on the TV last night true?'

'Yes, ma'am.'

'Is there any reason for me to stay here in New York?'

'I guess not,' he answered.

'Will it be okay for me to fly back to London the day after tomorrow?'

'Yes, ma'am.'

There was no further conversation. Eventually John said, 'But what about your fees?'

I called the accounts office and asked what would be done. They told me to send John the next day for the cheque. We sighed with relief. But, as it happened, the relief was premature. When we saw the cheque we realized we were getting only some of the cash due, just to cover up to when I left New York. When I phoned and asked about the bulk of the money I would have earned on the tour after Christmas, they said they would contact me in the UK about that. Again we sighed with relief; the majority of performances would have been after Christmas and the sum involved was in excess of $30,000. We had bought Apex tickets and, since we were going home two months sooner than planned, we lost on that too. We were dejected and miserable on the flight home.

August 1980 to June 1981 constituted a whole season's work. There are not many who could survive a whole year without earning anything, and we certainly could not. I know many people thought we were rolling in it, but the truth was that I had never earned enough to save anything for a rainy day.

At Heathrow Mairwyn was waiting for us with Len Williams, and her right arm was in plaster – the same one as before.

As soon as we had recovered from the flight, I sent the bank what I had brought back, along with the remainder of John's winnings from Las Vegas. I began to ask fellow singers how they had fared in the strike. One had settled for $30,000 instead of the $40,000 she would have received had she gone to the Met in the New Year; another had been given a role in another opera (by Christmas the Met was open again). My *Turandots* were never reinstated. My solicitor advised that once it became a working company again they should pay up.

I received a cable to say that I was now free to find 'alternative work'. There was none. Contracts for singers are arranged years ahead; my own *Turandot* contract had been in effect for eighteen months and every singer in the same situation was looking for 'alternative work'. I wrote to British Actors Equity and asked them to enquire from the Met what they were going to do by way of compensation or alternative performances. The Met passed the letter on to AGMA.

They came out with a lot of legal jargon which in the end meant there would be no cash. It was nearly December, and the bank manager was getting restless. I wrote myself to Mr Bliss at the Met and hoped that by December I would have some good news. Most other people I had asked seemed to have received some compensation, and I had also asked many other opera directors what they would have done in similar circumstances. The general opinion was that, once the company was working again, I should have some compensation. I also told the bank manager that I had been advised by the US tax authorities that I could expect a $26,000 refund, and showed him the letter, which satisfied him, and he proceeded to extend credit for about £1,600 for the agents' commission on the few fees that I *had* received from the Met. He also agreed to pay mortgage and basic household bills and Mairwyn's school fees and granted us £30 a week to live on. Our Christmas was quiet and frugal, to say the least.

But on 6th January came the first nail in our coffin – the London agents phoned my accountant to say that the bank had bounced the cheque for the commission. I had parted company with the agents in 1979 but the commission was still due to them.

Some acrimonious correspondence flew between me and the bank manager – it seems they did not believe my story of the engagement in Australia and wanted to see the contract. Then they sent it back because 'there is no date on it to say when funds will come from there'. The Australian Opera sent it to their solicitor to have a date put on it legally. This was again sent to the bank. 'But what will happen if they have a strike like the Metropolitan?' The bank then insisted on written confirmation from the Australian Opera. I told them they had the confirmation – the contract. 'Not good enough.'

I phoned Australia, and they sent a cable to my bank.

'You could have got anyone to send a cable. We need it from the artistic director and on Australian Opera notepaper.' I told the manager he was not doing my reputation any good by questioning the Australian Opera's word in this way. I also reminded him of the impending arrival of the $26,000 U.S. tax refund.

On the 14th January I arranged to cash in some insurance policies. I did not want the cheque for the school fees to be bounced – it was one thing for John and me to be embarrassed, but I would not have this happen to Mairwyn.

I looked through my list of performance dates in Australia and saw there was a gap from mid-November to mid-January 1982. I could see no sense in coming home for three and a half weeks for Christmas in view of the cost of fares, and sent word to the Australian Opera that I would be staying in Sydney over Christmas. In a short time I was offered a concert in the January Festival of Sydney – the die was cast for our 'flight into Egypt'.

On the 24th January I had a belligerent letter from the VAT authorities – I was to pay £500 within seven days or else! I sold some of my Las Vegas jewellery.

On the 28th January John spoke to the bank manager, and told him that I had a concert in Reading the next day and we would need either to write a cheque for petrol to get there, or extra housekeeping money. The answer was a refusal, so I phoned the bank and said, 'If you insist that I need fees coming in, then surely you could at least find the ten quids' worth of petrol to get us to the concert?' He replied that he had seen no contract for this concert and for all the bank knew I could be going on a joy-ride.

I phoned my friend Arthur Martin who was promoting the concert and explained, and he sent a courier round to our home with £10 in an envelope to pay for the petrol.

Despite having deposited the Reading concert fee with the bank, they now said they would not pay fuel bills, so John drove down to Dorset, using our food money for petrol, and brought up to London the portable gas fire we used in the van. He also brought up a camping gas lantern. We closed up all of the house except our bedroom. We lived and slept in one room. We left the fridge on and John went down to cook the meals as it was so cold downstairs. When the insurance money came through, we paid the phone bill and the school fees.

On March 7th I deposited £449.27 royalties for the ENO *Ring* recordings. A week later I got a reply to my letter to Mr Bliss at the Metropolitan. He had passed it on to their lawyers, and their answer was no.

At this time I was working at home on Lady Macbeth, in spite of a chill on the kidneys and chest colds and general ill health, due to all the stress. Then I received a phone call from my mortage company and at first I feared the worst. But they were laughing, 'You have a very strange bank manager. He's sent us a cheque for £764 and as you know your mortgage is only £409.'

We had planned to go to Australia in July via Seattle as I was booked to sing a recital there. On April 15th I had word from Glynn Ross that they would have to cancel as the theatre was too busy with two *Rings* and *Tristan* to cope with clearing all the sets off the stage for a piano recital.

A few days later I wrote to Peter Freeman and said, 'I have never had any royalties from the Wyndhams recital record, so how about it? But his reply was to tell me that they hadn't sold well.

I was booked to do a recital in Street, in Somerset, on July 10th and on June 2nd received a cheque for the fee five weeks too soon. I suspected that Arthur Martin was responsible, but I did not dare to cash it, as I was terrified in case I was ill and then I would have had to find a way of refunding it.

On June 8th, I received a cheque from the US for $26,688.

On legal advice, we opened an account with another bank and when the cheque had been cleared, John had the great pleasure of going to our original bank and paying off the overdraft. 'Where did you get the cash from?' asked the manager.

'That tax refund that you did not believe in,' said John.

Silence. Then, 'Well, Mr Thomas, you said you were waiting for $26,000 and this is nowhere near that amount.'

John smiled sweetly. 'Ah, you see, the rest of it is in another bank. Good morning.'

On the 13th June ENO agreed to a higher fee for the 1983 *Trovatores*, and a few days later a letter from the US announcing that a further cheque was on its way for tax refunds of $8,700, plus interest from 1975, so my spirits began to soar. I was happy that I was at least not going to Australia with my tail between my legs – I would be going there solvent.

I sang in Llanelli in June, which was another boost to my spirits and my bank account, and with my confidence restored I took the plunge and deposited the Street fee also, and even had the temerity to go and book our seats for Australia.

I also sang in Plymouth on the 2nd July. All these concerts since my return from the Met had been arranged by Arthur Martin, who was wonderful and did everything he could to help out with our financial problems.

On 16th July I sang in a concert in Leeds conducted by David Lloyd Jones. The press next day said, 'Miss Hunter, goddess as she is, was cheered, not just applauded, on her entrance, and after her performance was brought back to even louder cheers, four times. One wondered if she would sing the whole thing again.' I thought that was a good farewell to my native land.

Saturday, the 18th, dawned bright and clear. We firmly slammed the door of our Thames Ditton home and, in true operatic fashion, flew off into the sunset.

CHAPTER TWENTY-ONE

Poms in Paradise

As the Transworld airline Jumbo lifted off and sped westwards to California, there were no sighs of regret, no heart-searchings. I never thought that I would be glad to leave the land of my birth, and was somewhat ashamed to be feeling this way, but the sense of relief and freedom were overwhelming. John and Mairwyn were playing a card game in the business class, so Nellie, with her prepaid first class ticket from the Australian Opera, snuggled down and was pampered by the stewards.

We arrived in Los Angeles and were met by Frank and Phil, and some fans, and our arms were soon filled with flowers and gifts. I caught John throwing back his head and laughing at one of Frank's jokes, and I realised sadly how little we had laughed in the last nine months.

Of course eventually we had to part, amid tears and hugs. Then on to Las Vegas. This time I said to hell with investments, and bought some superb new concert gowns, specially made at the 'Suzy Creamcheese Boutique' – one of which I kept for my first Isolde. We were content to sit by the pool and unwind, although one night we went to the Razzle-Dazzle show in the hotel. We had front row seats, and John was disappointed to see that some of the topless beauties had false rubber boobs, which looked perfect, even down to the nipples. John said, 'Fancy travelling 6,000 miles to see Dunlop steel radials with sequins on!'

One afternoon Mairwyn and I were sitting by the pool and I noticed the waitress carrying some large glasses to a crowd near us. It looked like strawberry milk-shake, so I said, 'Gosh, they look good, let's have some.' Well, they were good, and we had about six each. We were playing our game of making up limericks and began to get very giggly. One really loud burst of laughter from me brought John over to see what the fun was all about. He took a sip. 'Bloody hell, can't leave you alone for a second, they're full of rum, you clots.' They were strawberry coladas. We were as drunk as rats, the pair of us.

After nine days we flew on to San Francisco to see Neil and Jenny, and also for me to have that long-promised sight-seeing trip. We got up at four in the morning to see the wedding of Prince Charles and Lady Diana, and Mairwyn and I cried along with the rest of the world. John thought we were crazy, but I noticed he was sitting nearest to the TV. Word had gone round that I was there and that we were soon to leave for Australia, and we had a gathering of the fans in the hotel. It was a great send-off for us.

I was impatient to get to Sydney and to work; I had not sung a role for so long I was almost suffering withdrawal symptoms.

*

The Qantas stewards let Mairwyn sit next to me as we drew close to Sydney, as she was eager to see all the things and people I had told her about. As the plane flew over part of the harbour she saw in the distance the Opera House, and they played *Waltzin' Matilda* on the tannoy. Mairwyn had tears in her eyes, and I was not far off tears myself.

Almost as soon as we landed I was caught up in the bustle of work. After a quick shower and coffee we went to the Opera House. I was needed for a fitting of my *Norma* costumes which had been designed by Michael Stennett, who was due to leave Sydney that evening for the UK. So, though the *Normas* would not take place until November, it was essential to have the fittings while the designer was still available. They were divine; the first, a beautiful moss green velvet and silver lamé, and the other a black velvet. It was an extended fitting and I was tired after the flight, but it was worth it.

About seven o'clock that evening we went home to the little flat at Berry's Bay that John and I had stayed at in 1980 and fell into bed, worn out but happy.

The second half of 1981 sped by, and I was so busy I had no time to wonder if I was homesick for England. On the 8th August I visited Channel 10 for the Parkinson show.

We rehearsed *Macbeth* and *Walküre* at the same time, and I would stand at the stage door in the mornings and wonder, 'Now what's first today, Verdi or Wagner?' The *Walküre* cast were all to fly to Melbourne on the 19th. I wanted to drive. Everyone said I was mad. 'Nearly a thousand kilometres; take at least fourteen hours.' Geoffrey Arnold said, 'Do it in two days.' Bob Allman's remarks were typical of him: 'What do you want to drive for? The countryside is as bare as a dog's bum.'

But Nellie was adamant. We drove, took two days to do it, and I would not have missed it for the world. The landscape may have been bare, but it had a strange beauty. We saw so many sheep, I couldn't face a lamp chop for months.

On the 30th August I wrote in my diary, 'First time in my career I have spare cash in my account in London while I have been abroad.'

The *Walküres* in Melbourne were greeted by the Wagner-starved Australians with wild delight. They were only concert performances but the audience reaction made me think that a fully staged down under *Ring* might be a good idea.

We delayed Mairwyn's return to school in England so that she would be able to hear my first staged *Macbeth* on 7th September. I was once more working with the irrepressible Robert Allman and we both had a good press. Even the often sharp-tongued Maria Prerauer surprised me by filling nearly half a page with compliments like, 'No praise is too great, her soprano is huge, flexible and beautiful, beautiful. And the voice is as gorgeous in its lower register as it is in its miraculous stratosphere.' I thought this was great praise indeed from such a critical lady.

Mairwyn undertook her longest solo flight to date on the 10th of September, when she returned to England to school. I had never felt so awful. The moment she disappeared into immigration, I knew that sending her back would not work. Much as she could irritate us with her untidy bedroom and her teenage temperaments, I missed her so badly I thought I would die of misery in the airport car park. John felt the same way, but then men, so John says, are made of sterner stuff. After a few hours of my weeping, he firmly told me to shut up or I would cry myself into a cold.

In the ensuing weeks there were eleven *Macbeths*, and then the Sydney concert performances of *Götterdämmerung*. This time it was the Sydney Wagnerians who were hopping up and down with joy, and there were faint murmurings of a staged *Ring*.

We began the time-consuming problem of becoming Australian residents. The red tape dragged on for almost a year. On October 1st I met with Patrick Veitch and Moffatt Oxenbould to talk over a proposed three-year contract. The flat in Berry's Bay, nice as it was, would not be big enough to stay in for three to four years, so we began to look for a house to rent. After the *Götterdämmerung* on October 3rd Charles Berg, the chairman of the board of directors, said that he had heard the news of my proposed long-term contract and was delighted, and added, 'Please stay a long time.' When the long run of *Macbeths* were over I plunged right away into rehearsals for the *Normas* that the Australian Opera were to present in Melbourne in November.

It would appear that all this time it was all work and no play, but the truth is that John and I had never done so much socialising in the whole of our lives. One evening in Melbourne we went to Glen Lehman's house for a party, which was quite a wild night. I actually got up the nerve to speak with John Shaw's lovely red-haired wife, Isobel, and explained the reasons for my faux pas on her TV show all those years earlier. About 5 a.m. we left and offered Peter Bloor a lift home. John may be a good driver, but he knew nothing about the Melbourne tram lines in those days, and I commented on how bumpy the road was. Peter was chuckling, the 'road' got worse, and when John realised why he said, 'Oh, bloody hell.' We went over a particularly deep hole between the rails and I felt my head hit the roof of the car. Peter said, 'Don't want to worry you, Hunter, but your boobs are now on the back seat!' I said breathlessly, 'Wondered where they had gone.'

We used to phone Mairwyn every weekend, which she spent with our friend Tina in Esher. All was well until we encountered the 'red phones' in Melbourne. I did not know that you could not make an international call on them. On this particular Sunday night we spent a fruitless and nerve-wracking two hours trying to get through to our home in Thames Ditton where Tina would take Mairwyn for our weekly chats. The poor child was sitting alone in a freezing cold house that had been empty for months, waiting for the phone to ring. In the end John went out at 2 a.m. and phoned Thames Ditton from the local call box. Mairwyn was tearful and frantic. John quickly gave her the number of our Melbourne town house and by the time he got back from the phone box I was talking to her, and crying, and he arrived in time to hear me say, 'I will book you on the next possible flight to Australia.' We had had enough of the separation and were all unhappy. I kept my word and a few days later, in time for my first Australian *Normas*, I had my daughter in my arms once more.

I suffered considerably from nerves before those first Australian *Normas*; it was almost six years to the day since my New York *Norma*, and the wounds inflicted by the press were still not healed. However, once the 'Casta diva' was over, I enjoyed myself. Carlo Cillario was conducting, as he had done for San

Francisco *Norma*. The management and the audience were thrilled, so were the Australian press, and on the 26th and 28th November the audience applauded when I made my first entrance – before I sang even the 'Casta diva'.

On the 25th we at long last kept our promise to Mairwyn and took her on a trip up Mount Dandenong to The Cuckoo restaurant. I was beginning to feel sunny, and contented with life.

*

Christmas celebrations began early with the arrival of a letter from Patrick Veitch confirming the three-year contract. We read through the list of roles: 1983 Donna Anna, *Trovatore*, a new production of *Walküre*, then more Donna Annas. The 1984 repertoire was to be *Aida*, Senta, a new production of *Turandot*, and possibly Madame Lidoine in *The Carmelites*. Didn't seem to me that a girl could ask for more!

We spent Christmas Eve 1981 with Moffatt and Graeham Ewer and watched the candlelight service on TV from Melbourne, then all five of us went to midnight service.

Christmas Day 1981 was damp and humid. I ignored the advice of Geoffrey Arnold, 'Don't cook a hot dinner, darling, you're mad in this heat, give the buggers salad.' But it had not seemed like Christmas at all (it seemed so strange to see the silver balls on the little tree while we were anointing each other with suburb cream). So I cooked the traditional turkey – I stuffed it, and looked in the usual place for the giblets. But with all my poking and prodding I found none. Auntie Ruth would have been most disappointed. A couple of days later, when we were having the inevitable cold turkey I came upon a strange brown paper bag in the bird's gullet – it was the giblets.

'Well, Mummy,' said Mairwyn, 'you might know they would be in the other end down under.'

On New Year's Eve we went to a picnic at Kurraba Point with Geoffrey Arnold and his friends and sat under the stars waiting for 1982. At midnight all the little boats in the harbour blew their hooters and the fireworks display began. It was the strangest feeling, sitting there swatting the mosquitoes, thinking of all the cold and foggy New Years spent at home in Auntie Nellie's house.

In January 1982 I made my Australian recital debut in the Sydney town Hall as part of the Festival of Sydney, an event held each year in January, with Geoffrey Arnold at the piano. Lauris Elms sang some arias and together we did the Norma and Adalgisa duet and the Aida and Amneris duet, both of which

214

brought the house down. The press, too, was splendid. Head-lines like, 'Rita thunders in on a high note' and, 'When Rita Hunter and Lauris Elms became duettists the house went wild with bravos'. One review ended, 'Miss Hunter has now settled in the lucky country, which is just another slice of luck for us.' Another commented on the fact that 'Miss Hunter had the audacity to open her recital with a roof-lifting "In questa reggia".' Well, what did they expect – I was a chip off the Charlie Hunter block, wasn't I?

We were invited to be on the official launch for the annual Ferry Boat race; all the harbour ferries race up and down the harbour with hundreds of small boats following behind. Lauris Elms declined the Festival directors' offer, but Geoffrey Arnold and Nellie were the first on the quay. John and Mairwyn were there too. Pancakes on the Rocks were providing the food and the wine flowed like water. It was the greatest bit of fun I have ever had. It got pretty rough out there when we got up speed, and it was not easy to balance a plate of pancakes in one hand and wine in the other and prevent yourself from going over-board. We shrieked our heads off for our favourite boat. It didn't win.

*

1982 began to fly past at an alarming rate, and I remarked to John, 'Don't time fly when you're having fun?' Melbourne again for Santuzza, then more Lady Macbeths, this time with the Metropolitan star Sherrill Milnes. He was wonderful, of course, but I missed the naughty Bob Allman. Then it was time to start to learn Isolde for performances in Sydney and Melbourne in August 1982. My old partner-in-crime, Alberto Remedios, was to come out to sing Tristan.

I had never thought that my years of turmoil working with Reggie Goodall would have repercussions twelve thousand miles away in Australia. Here I was, in 1982, being rudely reminded of something that had happened in 1974/5.

Almost as soon as we had done the complete English *Ring* – ten years ago – there had been plans afoot for a production of *Tristan and Isolde*, the same production team and same leading tenor and soprano. Came the day of my first call to Reggie's little 'lavatory' studio – I was not happy, but John assured me that Reggie would behave himself. I was not at all sure, and so I stood, score in hand, before him. He began to play and I began to sight-read. Then he suddenly whizzed round on his seat and said, 'This is no good, you don't know the role.' My jaw

215

dropped. 'But that's what I'm here for Reg, to learn it.' He said, 'You know I still have not forgiven you for your shocking behaviour in *Siegfried*.'

This time I went cold with anger, and he then went on to rake up all my sins, how I had been missing for weeks on end (not strictly true). I sat silent and listened for a solid hour, then, as my time was up, there was a knock on the door and in walked the bass, Gwynne Howell. Reggie said, 'Would you go out, Mr Howell? We are not finished yet.' Gwynne smiled and said, 'OK, Reggie, no rush.'

Then, to my horror, Reggie began to repeat his diatribe about all my wrong-doings. I was aware that the passages outside were acoustically vibrant, that Gwynne Howell must have heard every word, and I boiled with rage at the further humiliation. I said nothing, and when he had exhausted all his ammunition and asked me for a date for the following week, I gave it to him, and then said, 'Good bye,' and left the room.

When I got to the car where John was waiting, I opened the door and threw the score of *Tristan and Isolde* into the back. I said, 'Stuff him, that's it, no more, bugger him and his bloody Irish potato-picking princess. I am not working with him ever again, and I shall never sing Isolde for anyone. English National, Welsh National, no one, sod them all.'

John was laughing his head off, but my blood was up, and the next day I told the English National I did not want to do Isolde. I do not remember what I told them exactly, as my rage was so great, but I kept repeating never, never, never. But never is a long time and fate is fickle.

When I had accepted the Australian Opera's invitation to return to them in 1981 to sing, among other roles, Lady Macbeth, Brünnhilde in *Walküre* and *Götterdämmerung*, and a new production of *Turandot*, there were also on the agenda concert performances of *Siegfried* in 1982, conducted by Sir Charles Mackerras. Working with Sir Charles in the past had never been a peaceful experience, and I knew it never would be; there was something about that dynamic over-energetic man that laid my nerves bare and vulnerable and, however well I had done my homework, it always seemed that he could find the weak link in my armour. However, I felt that I was on a safe wicket with the *Siegfried* Brünnhilde. Imagine my dismay when I was told by the Australian Opera that the concert performances of *Siegfried* were cancelled, but worse was to come when they added 'But we will be doing *Tristan* instead.' I remember saying, 'Oh good,' but thinking, 'Oh God!'

Calls were arranged, and I began to work with David Kram. I would come home and wail to John. 'I hate the role. She's a fool. The music is vile.' And finally, 'I can't work with David, they'll have to get me someone else.' They did. I worked with Torben Peterson. 'He's so energetic he's wearing me out.' I found every excuse known to man to miss a call, and finally they put me down to work with Tony Legge. There were only a matter of weeks left. The arrival of Sir Charles was imminent. I knew that I was going to sing Isolde and that I would have to learn it. Indeed I was progressing better with Tony than with David and Torben. I hated meeting them, I felt a traitor. Then one evening I realized something about Reggie and his attitude and his treatment of singers. It made me stop in my tracks. A glimmer of light began to penetrate my brain. I made some excuse about being tired, made Tony a cup of tea and then off he went home. I awoke in the middle of the night – the glimmer of light had become a blinding revelation.

I realised that there was nothing wrong with David Kram. Nothing wrong with Torben Peterson. Nothing wrong with the role of Isolde. It was Reggie – across the miles he was still haunting me. In all the years I had known Reggie Goodall, Isolde was the one role he wanted me to sing, the one he himself had said I was born to sing. And yet, as surely as if he had put cyanide in my tea, he had poisoned me against her. My combined fear and admiration of him were so strong that I sat there in bed in the dark and said out loud, 'I *will* sing Isolde and I *will* be great.' John, awakened by my vehement outburst said, What's up with you, swearing in your sleep.'

My final preparations for Isolde were now child's play. When I sang it through for Sir Charles, even his perfectionist spirit was satisfied. I learned Isolde in nine weeks. On the first night Torben had gone to Europe, but I still had a guilt complex about David Kram.

They called 'Beginners and Orchestra' and off I went to sit on the side of the concert hall stage in the Sydney Opera House. I was wearing my blue silk kaftan from the Suzy Creamcheese boutique in Las Vegas. I was the first one of the cast there. I heard David Kram's voice in the distance asking where I was, and guilt pulled at me again: he was coming to wish me luck. As he came round the corner and saw me there, he stopped dead in his tracks, and said, 'There she is, my Irish Princess.'

'Hello, David,' I said, as he came up to me and kissed me.

'You're going to be wonderful.'

My guilt faded and I squeezed his hand, and for a few

moments more I was alone before the rest of the cast joined me. I realised I was but moments away from the Irish woman I had avoided so long; only a prelude and a sailor's song that separated me from her.

I don't have to say it. The public said it all. The cheers were loud and long at the end, but best of all were David Kram's comments after the audience had long been silent, words that Mr Goodall in all my years with him had never uttered: 'Oh, Rita, I am so proud of you.'

A few days later the press confirmed the audience's reactions. 'A *Tristan* to remember for a life time'. 'It was Rita Hunter's first Isolde and she sang it with surprising tenderness and great beauty, she developed the role with a rare lyricism – and made her first Isolde a breathtaking portrayal.'

A week later, after the last Isolde on the 14th August, and the day before my forty-ninth Birthday, I sat in my dressing room surrounded by flowers and gifts. Tony Legge came in and gave me a box. When I opened it I saw that it contained a superb Parker pen with just one word engraved on it, 'Isolde'.

*

The following day, my birthday, we flew to Brisbane in Queensland, for five performances of *Il Trovatore*, with the Lyric Opera, and once again I found that the audience applauded before I sang my first note. Brisbane was having power problems while we were there, and each section of the city had a power cut around 8 p.m. Towards the end of the rehearsal period we were all becoming somewhat tired of the rehearsal rooms and wanted to get on to the stage, when we discovered that the Thursday night would be our night for the power cut. We were filled with glee, as the room we were in had no windows, and so come 8 p.m. we knew we would all be sent home. Well, we thought we knew. But we had reckoned without Anthony Besch, the producer. We were doing the convent scene with the nuns progressing to the chapel and the count's soldiers trying to hide. Suddenly, out went the lights. Some of us went for our coats, but we were stopped in our tracks. Anthony had produced a camping gas lantern; he also ordered Mairwyn to shine a torch on the conductor's hands so that we would keep in tempo. Most of the nuns, and me too, were giggling too much to sing, but we could see that Anthony intended Business as Usual.

Mr Besch had decided that I should die sitting up. I was not overjoyed by this – I have always thought that a collapse with a wallop on to the floor was a pretty good way of letting the public know you had snuffed it. I had tried to talk him out of it, saying that sitting up on a stool would look funny. 'Couldn't I have a little log that I could gently slide down on to and then perhaps just slide on to the floor at the last moment?'

'Yes,' Anthony said, 'You can have a log but you mustn't slide on to the floor.' A compromise. The supers who were to put the stool on stage in the scene-change in a blackout were told that the stool would be a log. And stage management were sent out into the bush to look for a suitable log.

The quick scene-change at the dress rehearsal took ages. I couldn't think what on earth was going on. Cursing and swearing from the supers, frantic scuttling of feet. Anthony Besch flew from stalls to stage to find out what was causing the hold up. I went on stage to tell Manrico I had come to save him, and I almost bust my corsets in an effort not to laugh. There, in the corner of the prison cell, in quite the wrong place, was a gigantic gum-tree trunk – as I died (on the floor as the tree had twigs that would have pierced my bum) I could hear Anthony's stage whisper, 'Yes, I know, but it's in the *wrong* place'. The poor supers had been unable to move it any further. Indeed the Lyric Opera were lucky they didn't have to pay damages to ruptured supers.

On 12th September we flew to Seattle for more *Trovatores*. Nothing so dramatic there. I was able to renew my friendship with dear Henry Holt and our friends Charlie and Marilyn Treanor. Marilyn and I discovered that her ancestors were from Cheshire so perhaps we were related. I would like to think so. I can think of no nicer folk to have in one's family tree. Four *Trovatores*, and then a quick stop-over in Los Angeles to see Frank and Phil and to do some shopping in Layne Bryants, then back to Sydney before October 20th 1982 when we flew to New Zealand, where I was to sing *Aida* in Christchurch and Wellington.

During the run of *Macbeths* in 1981 I had met a fan named Marcus Craig, from Adelaide, but working in New Zealand. He kept begging me to go there to sing, and now he organised a concert in Auckland and some TV and radio shows. On the programme 'Good Morning New Zealand', I sang 'This is my lovely day'. Then John and Mairwyn joined me and we drove down to Lake Taupo where we were to have ten days' holiday, staying at the Hooka Fishing Lodge. The speciality of the house was wild game. The venison wasn't too bad, neither was the trout, but I took one sniff of the wild boar and threw it down the toilet. John did the same. I said, 'That pig ain't wild, it's positively hysterical!' Mairwyn said, 'Well, I'm going to eat it, I said I would try all the game, and I will.'

We rose early the next morning. TV New Zealand had a charter flight waiting to fly us to Auckland so that I could appear on the 'Hudson and Halls show'. It was a cold, wet and windy morning. There was not another soul at the tiny Taupo air strip, and my heart sank when I saw the plane. There was room for the pilot and co-pilot and two passengers, three if John didn't mind sitting hunched up where they usually put the cases. We all had to breathe in so they could shut the door. We had no luggage, except my train case which contained some make-up for my face and my dress. I had put the dress in a plastic bag in case the powder spilt on it, and it was as well I did. We had only been airborne fifteen minutes when Mairwyn said, 'I feel sick.' She was green. The wild boar was having its revenge. I said to John, 'Get the bag that's holding my dress – hurry.' I shoved it under her nose in the nick of time.

On the return journey I could tell that the pilot was flying at a higher altitude and the flight was smooth. Mairwyn fell asleep. It was freezing in the little plane, and it began to snow; visibility was nil. When I looked out of the window I saw that the wings were fast becoming laden with ice. Before we had left Sydney our solicitor, Roland Gridiger, had been shocked that we had never made a will. I had protested that we had nothing to leave. Of course, I was wrong: the house in England and contents were worth a fair amount. So Roland had drawn up a will for John and one for me. The wings of the plane were alarmingly full of ice, and all I could think of was that John and I had never signed those damned wills. My stomach was in knots. As we stepped off onto the windswept and freezing tarmac at Taupo, Nellie made another vow. That was the family's second trip in a small plane – there would not be a third.

We had two beautiful days on Lake Taupo fishing; we hired a boat and even though John fancied himself as Captain Ahab, it was Mairwyn and I who caught the most fish. At the end of the holiday we flew to Auckland for more TV and radio shows and a concert in the town hall. After that, down to the South Island to Christchurch for *Aida* with the Choral Society. Another *Aida* in Wellington and then back to Australia on a direct flight to Melbourne for some more *Aidas* with the Victoria State Opera conducted by Richard Duval. I must say I was most impressed by this young man – jovial, enthusiastic and talented. My debut with the Victoria State Opera was therefore not only successful but enjoyable.

*

The lease on our house in Neutral Bay was almost up and we wanted to find something larger, detached if possible. I felt I had already pushed my luck by inflicting my fledging Isolde upon the neighbours. My hairdresser had told us of a friend's house in Mosman that he knew was up for rent; it also had a swimming pool. Of course it was a good deal more expensive, but we took the plunge and moved in on December 1st, 1982.

And so we come to New Year's Eve 1982. Marcus was staying with us, and one of the girls from his show in Auckland, Leoni and her two children, were also house guests. Marcus and I had prepared a buffet, and there was a constant stream of visitors all evening. After a drink and a bite they eventually went off to their respective parties. Then the seven of us sat down to watch the film 'The Ritz' and laughed ourselves silly. The funeral march from *Nabucco* will never be the same again for me. I still want to laugh when I hear it.

It was a beautiful night and we had all the pool lights on, and at midnight everyone jumped in. Even Nellie – for I was trying to learn to swim. It had taken me a month to get up the courage to stand up in the pool, and on this night I was content to sit, as usual, on the steps with the water up to my chin. Everyone else was swimming, squealing and laughing. Someone yelled, 'Look, a funnel-web spider,' and Mairwyn and Leoni fled to the other side of the patio. I sat there sipping Great Western champagne and thinking on what was past, and what was to come.

There was the trip home to ENO for the *Trovatores*. I had been away a long time – four years since I had sung in London. How would it be? Would the press be good, would the audiences be the same, indeed would any of them remember the prodigal soprano?

Mairwyn said, 'Look at Mum, she's tipsy already'. (I was not.) John added, 'What's up, Rit, bach, you look miles away?'

I was: miles away and years ago. I was back on the beach at New Brighton. It was a warm July day with just a slight sea breeze and, on account of that breeze, I had to stand there in a woolly jumper, long black stockings, coat, woolly hat and scarf. I was looking longingly at the kids from the dusty Liverpool streets, half-naked, splashing in the muddy waters of the Mersey estuary. I heard my mother ask Dad if she could at least take off my scarf. Her voice was hesitant, anxious, 'Perhaps just this once wouldn't hurt, Charlie?' But Charlie was adamant. 'I don't like the cut of that wind,' he said.

I wondered, as I sat there with the warm water lapping round my chin, what Charlie Hunter would say about his delicate little

221

flower on this New Year's Eve. I could hear his words, 'Well, I mean to say, Lucy, sat in a pool half naked in the middle of the night, if she doesn't get pneumonia or a spider bite she's asking for malaria with all those bloody mosquitoes to say nothing of getting bombarded by possum droppings.' I saw my mother's little worried face. 'Well, perhaps just this once, Charlie?'

Their voices faded away as John's voice interrupted my thoughts. 'Come on, Rit, bach, take the plunge, try to float – it's 1983'.

I looked at him. There he was, my bloody Welshman, with his arms reaching out to me, grinning, infuriating, aggravating and exasperating. But oh, so dependable . . .

I thought, 'Well, why ever not,' and I put down my champagne glass, and threw caution to the winds, and flopped on my back into his arms. In between yells of, 'Don't you dare let go of me, John,' I kicked my feet in a frantic effort to stay afloat. 'Relax, Rit, bach, I'm supporting you.' I thought to myself, 'You always have, boy.'

For a brief moment all the splashing and laughing faded away and there was a fleeting moment of silence. Whenever that had happened as a child, my mother would say 'Oh, it's just the angels passing overhead.'

I looked up into the star-filled southern sky and thought, 'Thank you, God, this will do for me.'

Rita Nellie Hunter had found her elusive sunshine at last.

INDEX